ALSO BY CHRISTOPHER PIKE
PUBLISHED BY TOR BOOKS

The Cold One
Sati
The Season of Passage
The Blind Mirror
The Listeners
Alosha
The Shaktra

THE
YANTI

THE YANTI

Christopher Pike

TOR®

A TOM DOHERTY ASSOCIATES BOOK
NEW YORK

THE YANTI

Copyright © 2006 by Christopher Pike

A Tor Book
Published by Tom Doherty Associates, LLC
175 Fifth Avenue
New York, NY 10010

www.tor.com

Tor® is a registered trademark of Tom Doherty Associates, LLC.

Library of Congress Cataloging-in-Publication Data

Pike, Christopher, 1961-
    The Yanti / Christopher Pike.
        p. cm.
    "A Tom Doherty Associates Book."
    Summary: Thirteen-year-old Ali, eager for vengeance after the death of her friend
Steve, must now master the powers of the Yanti, a mysterious artifact somehow keyed to
her mind, while trying to defeat the Shaktra.
    ISBN-13: 978-0-765-31100-9
    ISBN-10: 0-765-31100-3
    [1. Fairies—Fiction.   2. Kings, queens, rulers, etc.—Fiction.   3. Magic—Fiction.]
I. Title.
    PZ7.P626Yan 2006
    [Fic]—dc22
                                                                2006006205

First Edition: October 2006

Printed in the United States of America

0   9   8   7   6   5   4   3   2   1

For Jason

KIRKLEES METROPOLITAN COUNCIL	
351700810	
Bertrams	22.06.07
	£10.00
HU	CUL43303

THE
YANTI

CHAPTER

1

The night sky was a vast black curtain littered with a thousand frozen sparks—the stars so far away, their light so feeble, that if the constellations did indeed have stories to share, then they could only relate to ancient gods, whose names had been forgotten. To the bulk of humanity, the threat from invaders beyond their world was a silly idea . . .

Yet there was one, in the night, who did worry about the beyond.

What might come out of it. What might kill the Earth.

In the midst of the dark sky, high above a snowcapped peak, there floated a warm green emerald. Egg-shaped as well as transparent, it was roughly seven feet from top to bottom; and it emitted a soothing green light that eclipsed handfuls of stars as it slowly, but purposely, drifted across the heavens.

At the heart of this egg stood a thirteen-year-old girl, with flaming red hair and mighty green eyes. It was almost as if the light that shielded her from the night—and the planet's gravity—emanated from her eyes alone. For there was something so potent about them, so deep . . . that they could not be called human eyes at all.

The girl's name was Ali Warner.

Yet Ali had other names as well: Geea, Alosha—titles that had been bestowed upon her by members of a race of elementals that lived alongside humanity. These latter usually went about their business unseen by mankind, because they lived in a dimension close to us, but also far away. The elementals were like characters on a TV program that were separated from the Earth by a single channel.

Many elementals—elves, dwarves, dragons, trolls, leprechauns—knew that Ali Warner was the queen of the fairies. That she had in fact chosen to be born as a human being in order to stop a war that was coming between them and mankind.

Ali, however, knew that was not the complete truth. For even though the elementals were only two or three days away from invading the Earth, the real enemy of mankind—and the elementals for that matter—was a creature called the Shaktra.

It was concerns about the Shaktra that had brought Ali to this unique place—floating above Pete's Peak—when she could have been at home, warm in bed, asleep. Her single most disturbing problem related to a remark her sworn enemy, Karl Tanner, had said moments before she had killed him. That gruesome, and somewhat satisfying event—she had broken every bone in his neck—had happened only five hours ago.

As if it had been written in the sky with stardust, she recalled every word of their final exchange . . .

"I want you to tell me something."

"You're going to kill me!"

"I have this question. I want you to answer it."

"Geea . . ."

"Who is the Shaktra?"

Karl, knowing he was doomed, had laughed at her then.

"You fool, she's your sister!"

And she had replied, just before she had killed him:

"I thought so."

That final remark of hers had been something of an exaggeration. The last few days, while traveling in the elemental kingdom, she had picked up a wide collection of hints that indicated she was related to the Shaktra. But in her heart of hearts, she had never truly accepted the possibility.

Ali tried to laugh at the irony of the situation, but failed. The sad truth was, Karl's words had thrown her into a mass of confusion. For the last month—ever since she had learned she was not a normal teenager—she had been bracing herself that she had to kill the Shaktra, or else be killed by it. Now the situation had transformed itself into something too tragic to contemplate.

Ali shifted her gaze from one side of the icy mountain peak to the other, back and forth. Through the luminous field that enveloped her, she could sense the chilly night, but it felt distant. In no way did it disturb her focus. A power inherent in the magnetic field allowed her to fly. It moved as she wished to move. She was not sure how fast she could fly, but had no doubt she could outrace the fastest jet ever built.

The field was also a shield of sorts. It could be used to amplify certain natural weapons she possessed. For example, before leaving the elemental kingdom, she had been attacked by a host of dark fairies and . . . well, they were all dead now. A vicious clap of her hands had ruptured their internal organs, and now their guts lay spewed over the rocky side of Tutor—a mountain in the elemental kingdom that served as a gateway between the two dimensions.

Tutor was the elemental's parallel version of the Earth's

Pete's Peak. The mountains were similar, but not identical. For that matter, nothing in the elemental world was exactly the same as Earth. Certainly, the elemental cities bore scant resemblance to human towns.

To the right, Ali could see the city of Breakwater, huddled beside a dark gray sea whose salty breeze she could taste from thirty miles away. The small town was home, and it was where Cindy Franken and Nira Smith were presently awaiting her return.

On Ali's left—on the other side of the mountain—was another town, Toule, where a host of puzzles and pain awaited her. For it was in Toule that a strange woman named Sheri Smith had held her friends, Steve Fender and Cindy Franken, captive for the last few days—while Ali had been busy in the elemental kingdom. Indeed, it was in Sheri Smith's basement that Steve had died—from a stab wound to his heart. Karl had committed the diabolical deed, but it had been Sheri Smith who had given the order.

Yet the evil woman had not killed Cindy.

Also, she had left Nira behind, her daughter, for them to take care of.

Nira, who appeared to be a helpless autistic child of only six years old. Yet whom Ali suspected possessed more power than she and the Shaktra combined.

Why had Sheri Smith given them Nira?

To answer these questions, and others, Ali had decided to return to Toule tonight—to storm Sheri Smith's huge home with force if need be. Stretching her arms out to her sides, as if she were an eagle preparing to pounce on an unknowing prey, Ali lowered her head and glided down toward Toule—specifically, toward the trees at the edge of the town. There Sheri Smith had constructed a mansion, and a successful software company—Omega Overtures, a midsized firm famous for its end-of-the-world computer games.

As she flew, Ali allowed the tips of the trees to brush her open palms. Sweeping so close above the forest was stimulating. Sucking in an invigorating breath, she allowed the odor of the firs and pines to turn her shimmering field a deeper shade of green.

Ali loved trees, almost as much as she loved people, and fairies.

For Ali, it was a guilty pleasure—the thrill of flight, when there was so much at stake. But she had not possessed the ability long, and she wasn't sure if she wasn't minutes away from running into Sheri Smith . . . and dying. She figured she might as well enjoy it while she could.

Ali knew little about the evil woman. But Radrine—the once mighty queen of the dark fairies, who now lay dead on the slopes of Pete's Peak—had provided Ali with a significant insight. There was an elemental form of the Shaktra *and* there was a human form of the creature. The monster, like a coin, had two sides. It was able to operate in both worlds at the same time.

Yet as Ali flew closer to Toule, she did not know if the Shaktra was capable of bringing *all* her magical powers to bear onto the Earth plane. If that were the case, then she didn't stand a chance. Ali had only come near the creature in the other world—she had not actually seen it with her eyes—but that near brush had been enough to convince her that she was no match for the elemental form of the beast.

The beast, the Shaktra, Doren, *her sister.*

Nevertheless, Ali felt little fear as she neared the house and office complex. She was too angry. Sheri Smith had killed her friend, Steve. Ali wanted payback, *revenge*—the ugly kind. She was in no mood to talk, to compromise. If she could, she planned to kill Sheri Smith.

Sheri Smith was evil, Ali thought. Sheri Smith did not deserve to live.

Tucking in her arms, letting her shimmering field dissolve, Ali slowly settled into a grassy meadow two hundred yards north of the Smith mansion, then crept silently through the trees toward the house.

The place was a maze of interlocking glass cubes. To Ali it looked as if it belonged at the demented end of the architectural spectrum. It seemed as if it had been designed by someone who had only a ruler and a pencil. Yet she imagined others might view it as a structural masterpiece. Steve—blast his brave heart—had been impressed by it.

Certainly it was like no house Ali had ever seen before. The nearby offices were of similar design. Both were ultramodern, sterile, all steel and glass—the products of a cold vision. The fact that the buildings were surrounded by a grove of lovely trees made them appear even more bizarre.

This was Ali's second visit to the mansion in the last few hours. This was where she had found Steve's dead body. This was where she killed Karl, and rescued Cindy and Nira. Yet when she had fled with the others, she had deliberately left Steve's body behind. She had deposited it upstairs, in the living room, on the couch, for the police to find. She had her reasons. Steve and Cindy had been missing for days. The authorities had to be brought into the matter. There was no getting around that. Or so she imagined . . .

Ali sent Cindy to the police to report Steve's murder, and the fact that she and Steve had been held hostage by Sheri Smith for several days. But when the police went to examine the mansion, they found no body. To make matters worse, when the two cops returned to the station, they reported to their captain that the mansion did not even have a basement. They said this right in front of Cindy, making a fool out of her.

Yet there was a labyrinth of tunnels and mines beneath the Smith residence. They were impossible to miss. She had given the police precise directions to the location of the hallway trapdoor that led to the underground maze. How come the police couldn't find it? It couldn't have just disappeared.

Nevertheless, Ali had figured out Steve's disappearance. After they had left the house, but before the police had arrived, Sheri Smith must have returned to the mansion and grabbed his body. The excellent odds that her theory was accurate made Ali sick to her stomach. To think what *that* monster had done with his remains . . .

The only good thing that came out of the whole mess was that the Toule police let Cindy go. They did not even call Steve's parents. They passed the whole thing off as a childish prank. After a scolding, a cop drove Cindy home and dropped her off outside.

But Cindy did not rush inside to Mom and Dad. Instead, she hurried to Ali's house—as per Ali's instructions. That's why Cindy was at her place, watching Nira. Someone had to play the part of babysitter. The child needed constant care. The whole time Cindy was with the police, Ali was taking care of Nira. Indeed, they had thumbed a ride back to Breakwater together.

Ali paused when she reached the mansion porch. Paused and listened—with all the power her high-fairy status bestowed upon her. Again, she let her field expand, as she searched the floors of the mansion without the use of normal senses. For Ali possessed an *inner* vision—that allowed her to see through walls—and magical hearing—with which she could hear a solitary spider crawl across a floor miles away.

Within a minute of arriving at the house, she was certain it was deserted.

Was she disappointed? Yes and no.

She had been hungry for blood, but not anxious to lose any of her own.

The front door was unlocked. She went inside.

All the lights were out, but she did not need them to see, so she left them off. The entryway and the kitchen were as she had last left them. She did not waste time there. The living-room drew her, the couch where she had left Steve's body. Yet, as the police had reported, the sofa was empty. Furthermore, it was absolutely clean, not stained with blood. It made no sense. Just a few hours ago, as she laid her friend down, a trickle of blood had seeped from his chest and onto the couch.

How had Sheri Smith removed the stain? Using eyes as powerful as a microscope, Ali searched the material. Yet there was not even a speck of blood on the sofa.

"Did she replace the couch?" Ali asked herself aloud.

It was possible, but unlikely. It was the *same* couch!

Who kept spare sofas around for such emergencies?

Ali had hardly finished her examination of the sofa, when the agony of losing Steve swelled in her chest. Earlier, she had told herself to just keep moving, to take care of business, to grieve later . . . But now, seeing the spot where she had laid Steve to rest, and finding him gone, the void grew that much larger. So big she felt as if a part of her dropped into it and vanished forever. In that instant, she knew that she would miss him until the day she died.

As Ali stepped away from the sofa, she noticed a flat-screen computer monitor on a nearby table. No keyboard fronted it. For that matter, there was no machine attached to it. The rectangular screen shone with a haunting purple glow. A single black wire led from the rear of the monitor, directly into the wall, where it vanished.

That was it.

The monitor had not been there before. At least it had not been turned on.

Nor had the second monitor—lit up with the same purple light in the main hall—been there when the three of them had fled the house. Yet the monitors only hinted at a much greater mystery to come. Her mind practically tripped and fell into an abyss when she went to examine the hallway trapdoor.

It was gone. Just gone.

There was not a trace of it, and the wallboard that now covered it was not new. It did not smell of fresh paint. There were no new nails. No carpenter had worked this spot in months. The police had not been the fools she had imagined. The hallway looked like a perfectly normal hall. And she could recall no fairy power—from her human life or her past life as a fairy queen—that could account for such a transformation of matter.

The evidence brought fear to Ali, finally. An icy wave crept through her chest, and in her head. The power of her adversary had just grown by leaps and bounds. The Shaktra—on both sides of the dimensional mirror—possessed abilities she did not.

Yet, if that was true, it raised a puzzling question.

"Why did she flee?" Ali asked herself.

If Sheri Smith could change matter so easily, Ali pondered, then the witch should have simply waited here and killed the infamous Ali Warner. Rid herself once and for all of the pesky brat from over the hill.

To be blunt, that was all that had separated them for thirteen years—a simple mountain. For a being who could manipulate matter, Ali could not understand why Sheri Smith had not killed her when she was a child. Even when Ali was an infant, the woman must have known who she was. Why hadn't she strangled her in the cradle?

Perhaps her mother had protected her.

It was possible Amma was much more powerful than Ali knew.

As Ali stood in the center of the hallway, an unexpected wave of dizziness swept over her. It seemed to come from outside, yet she sensed no one in the area. Maybe she was just exhausted. She could barely recall when she had slept last. Oh yeah, it had been in Uleestar, in the Crystal Palace, on the silken bed in her royal chambers. How long ago had that been?

Too long, her weary body replied.

The dizziness did not depart until Ali left the house. She was grateful when it finally stopped altogether, and briefly wondered if it had anything to do with the weird purple light the monitors gave off.

Ali still had a gruesome task to perform before she could return home. Earlier, fleeing the mansion with the others, she had grabbed Karl's body; and then, with a fast fairy-leap through the air, had deposited it a mile up the side of Pete's Peak. There was no way she was going to allow his measly murder to get pinned on her.

She had to dispose of his body in a more permanent fashion.

His death—at her own hands—was not going to cause her to lose a minute of sleep. After all, the beast had murdered Steve *and* her mother, and enjoyed it. He had been a mere pawn of Sheri Smith, true, but a willing one.

Outside, away from the mansion, Ali checked to make sure she was alone, then invoked her magnetic field and floated once more into the air. Yet she did not rise high, barely above the treetops. Karl's body lay well-hidden beneath a row of bushes, but she remembered the spot well. She reached it less than a minute after leaving the Smith residence.

To her disgust, his blue eyes had popped open. She had to bend and force them shut. His red lips had darkened; they strained into an unnatural grin. Rigor mortis must be setting in. His flesh was practically brittle—and the same temperature as the ground. For a moment she considered digging a six-foot hole and burying him. Her fingers were as strong as steel forks—she had no need of a shovel. But fresh holes left visible signs, and it was possible—as more of the details surrounding the last few days emerged—that the police might search the forest, even this far up the mountain.

In the end, she decided, it would be safer if Karl just disappeared.

The truth be known, she had considered the idea of dumping him in the ocean even before she'd left her house. That was why she had a roll of duct tape in her coat pocket. Dropping to her knees, she gathered a host of rocks and began to stuff them inside his shirt and pant legs. Soon he was twice his normal weight, and it was then she began to wrap him in the strong adhesive, around and around, as a mother spider might spin a web about a tasty morsel. Once more, she felt not a twinge of remorse as she worked, and when he was all but a gray mummy lying on the green grass, she did not pause to say any final words in his memory. Just picked him up, threw him over her shoulder, and soared into the sky. Had he been alive, she would not have been able to carry him. His living field would have interfered with her fairy magic. But as it was, carrying him was no different for her than clasping a bag of meat.

Ali flew a long way, west over the dark sea, over a hundred miles out, before she dropped him. She was a quarter of a mile high in the sky at that point, and the eastern rim of the world had begun to glow with the faint light of a new dawn. It had been a long night. As she turned in the air and headed home, accelerating at mind-numbing speed, she heard a far-off splash as he hit his final watery grave. It was only then that Ali Warner remembered that she had once cared for Karl Tanner. But if she shed a tear for his early departure, then it was lost on the wind that scarcely managed to penetrate her magical green field.

CHAPTER

2

Nira Smith was asleep on the couch when Ali arrived home. Cindy Franken was awake in front of the TV, but slumped in her seat. Her friend quickly stood and turned off the set as Ali entered. She acted embarrassed.

"I was just watching it to stay awake," Cindy said.

"No problem." Ali gestured to Nira, who was tucked under a shawl Ali's mother had knitted the winter before she had died—or supposedly died. In reality, the *human* part of Ali's mother had passed away less than twenty days ago, thanks to Karl Tanner and Sheri Smith. But the fairy aspect of her mother, Amma, was still alive in the elemental kingdom.

"Did she eat anything before she passed out?" Ali asked.

"I made her a grilled cheese sandwich. She gobbled it down like there was no tomorrow." Cindy added, "On top of that, she drank two glasses of water."

"She didn't want milk?"

Cindy frowned. "Your milk was sour. I had to toss some of the stuff in your fridge in the garbage. But don't worry, the bread and cheese were fine."

"Did you eat?"

Cindy nodded. "Same as her."

Ali took a step closer to the girl, stared down at her. Like herself, Nira had bright red hair, but her eyes were a dull violet—instead of a bright green—and even at the best of times they appeared unfocused. Ali knew that was because of the thumbprint between the girl's eyes. The burn-like scar indicated that Nira had been *marked* by the Shaktra. The girl was not truly autistic. She could be a genius for all they knew. But she was under the control of a monster—her own mother, Ms. Sheri Smith.

Before Ali had left the elemental dimension, the Shaktra had marked her *fairy* mother as well. Ali still did not understand the precise nature of the possession, but somehow the evil being had stolen her mom's mind and left her an empty shell that could not even recognize her own daughter. It was as if Nira's and her mother's souls had been cast into a realm of shadows and nightmares.

Nira seemed to rest peacefully, however, and for that Ali was grateful. From her travels in the elemental world, Ali knew she and Nira were related. It was possible they were sisters.

At the same time, she knew Nira was more powerful than she. In a chamber buried in the heart of a mighty kloudar— the elemental world's floating mountains—Ali had seen the sleeping counterpart of Nira, and had recognized the potent violet light that emanated from her majestic being. Seeing her then had been like staring at a star that was about to go supernova. Even now, Ali could sense—despite Nira's meek appearance—the immense energy inside the child.

Unfortunately, Ali sensed the greatness through a black barrier. That was because of the *mark*. Ali had to ask herself what evil lay behind it that it was capable of eclipsing a light as bright as Nira.

Ali gestured to Cindy. "Let's go in the den, we need to talk."

Cindy hesitated. She had taken a quick shower after being released by the Toule police—before Ali had flown over the mountain—and she had put on a fresh pair of Ali's blue jeans, and a warm green sweater. Yet her face still betrayed the pain of her recent trauma. She was not cut or bruised—Ali had healed the superficial wounds. But her blue eyes showed damage. She had been standing beside Steve when he had been stabbed in the heart by Karl. *That* was not the type of scar Ali could remove with a wave of her hand.

Gone was the carefree chatterbox Ali had grown up with. Although not in shock, Cindy was emotionally far from healthy. She showed signs of battle fatigue. The life had gone out of her once curly blond hair. It hung limp and weary, as did her whole head. Ali knew she must be exhausted.

Ali caught a glimpse of herself in a nearby mirror, the one her earthly mother had used to favor. The oval glass was not large, and the dark wooden frame was old enough to be an antique. Ali did not know where her parents had bought it, but seeing her own face startled her. Like Cindy, she had taken a shower before leaving the house. She had even taken the time to wash her long red hair, and rinse away the dust from beneath her green eyes.

Yet the change that confronted her now was not in the details of her expression, nor even in the way she held her thin but wiry frame. It was more in the invisible field that surrounded her, and in the black wells of her pupils. While in the elemental kingdom—as a final desperate measure to save herself and her friends from certain doom—she had swallowed an overdose of fairy stardust. Since that wild experiment, she had felt as if she were in reality two beings: one fairy, the other human. But deep inside, she felt the former much stronger than the latter, and that had never been the case before.

She no longer saw a teenage girl in the mirror. It was weird, it was her own face—the same face that stared back at her throughout her life—and yet subtle details had altered.

It was only then that she understood that her actual mind had changed since she had ingested the stardust. It was more quiet inside, and yet, ironically, the silence was so soft it seemed to hum. It was a silence unmoved by mundane thoughts. She suspected it existed beyond her conscious mind, and that it was responsible for the sudden increase in her fairy abilities.

Yet the inner calmness possessed a detached depth that made her feel as if she were a living iceberg. She could not help but recall how casually she had snapped Karl Tanner's neck. A week ago, she could never have done such a thing—no matter what he had done to her, or to those she loved.

Out of the corner of her eye, she caught Cindy staring at her with awe. It wasn't something she took pleasure in. But how to avoid it? Two hours ago, her friend had seen her float out of the backyard and into the sky, in the midst of a radiant green field. Cindy did not act afraid of her. On the other hand, she had not jumped up and hugged her when she had returned. Cindy had not even stopped to ask if she was all right. Her friend had simply assumed the great and powerful Geea couldn't be harmed.

A lot of that was probably because Ali had cracked Karl's neck in front of Cindy.

That, perhaps, had been a mistake.

"I don't want to leave Nira alone," Cindy replied, in response to Ali's suggestion that they go in the other room.

Ali unzipped her coat, pulled out what was left of the duct tape, set it on a table. From the instant Cindy had met Nira in Toule, she had been protective of the child. Ali did not know why, but wondered if Sheri Smith had noticed the attachment.

Could Cindy be the main reason the witch had left Nira in their keeping? If that were the case, it hinted at the possibility that Sheri Smith was concerned about her daughter.

"It's dangerous to talk in front of her," Ali explained. "That mark on her forehead—it indicates her mind's been tampered with by the Shaktra. I don't know the extent of the creature's control over her, but it's possible she can see and hear us through her."

Cindy was interested. "Are you saying Nira isn't really autistic?"

"Yes. If she didn't have the mark, she'd probably act normal."

Cindy's face shone with relief, but a frown quickly followed. "By the Shaktra, you mean Sheri Smith? Right?"

"There's more to it than that. I'll explain to you in the den. No, wait, let's go in my bedroom. You can lay on my bed. You'll be more comfortable that way."

Cindy gave her a look. "Doing *what?*"

"It's better if I just show you."

"Does it have something to do with fairy magic?"

"In a way, yes."

Cindy was uneasy. "When the cops dropped me off, every light in my house was on. That means my family's all there. I checked ten minutes ago. The sun's coming up and the lights are still on. I've been missing for over three days. They have to be freaking out. I need to get home right now."

Ali raised her hand. "I understand. Your parents must be going through hell. But there's stuff we have to go over, and it can't wait."

"Why?"

"Because we have to prepare for tomorrow, or rather, for today. The cops are going to be all over us. We have to come up with a plan to deal with them, and to do that, I need information. Trust me, you can leave the second we're done."

"Wait. While you were gone, did you go to Sheri Smith's house?"

"Yes."

"What did you find?"

"I'll tell you everything after I get caught up on what you guys did."

"But you found Steve's body, right?"

Ali hesitated. "Not exactly."

Cindy grimaced. "Where did it go?"

"I don't know. But what I want to do now—it might help me figure out the answer to that question."

"It couldn't have just disappeared."

"Sheri Smith must have come back for it, and then hid it."

"But why?" Cindy asked, pained.

"I can't answer you without first catching up on what you and Steve did the last few days." Ali reached out and clasped her friend's hand. "Let's go in the bedroom."

The news about Steve's disappearance obviously shocked Cindy, but she looked too tired to register it fully. She swayed where she stood. "Make it quick, Ali. If I don't sleep soon, I'm going to fall over."

Minutes later Cindy lay stretched out on her bed, with Ali sitting cross-legged on her right side—sitting so near, her folded knees pressed against her friend's side. Cindy assumed she was going to try to heal her again, and assured Ali that she was fine. But Ali explained they were going to do something different.

"I need you to tell me everything you and Steve did since I saw you last," Ali said. "I need to see the last few days through *your* eyes. That way I will be able to see them through *my* eyes."

"Huh?"

"I'm going to put a hand on your forehead, another hand over your heart. You're just going to relax and talk about what you saw and heard in Toule. As you do so, I'll be able to *see* inside your mind, like I was there with you in Toule."

Cindy was tense. "Are you sure this isn't too fairy-like for me? I mean, I would rather just tell you what happened."

"Trust me, it won't hurt. You might even enjoy it."

"What if I have some thought, you know, that's private?"

"Keeping secrets from me?"

"Get off it, Ali. We all have our secrets."

"I'm after information, not gossip. I promise not to pry."

"You swear?"

"I swear." Reaching out with her hands, Ali motioned for her to close her eyes. "By entering your mind, I might see stuff that you guys missed."

Yet Cindy continued to resist. "Have you done this before?"

Ali spoke carefully. "I did it often as fairy queen, and I remember that life more clearly than when you last saw me. You don't need to worry. I'll just ask questions and you'll answer them. As you tell me who you met and what you talked about, I'll see each person from *my* perspective. If you don't remember something, I'll remember it for you. And if someone lied to you, I'll know it."

"We know Rose was lying to us all along. That she was really Sheri Smith in disguise."

"Fine. But . . ."

Cindy interrupted. "Just before Karl killed him, Steve told me why. He said that she was burned all over. That she was hideous to look at. Because she planned to kill us, she even told us all kinds of stuff about herself."

Ali nodded at the news, although she knew Cindy was not

alive because Ali had stopped Karl's knife. Sheri Smith had *wanted* Cindy spared. Once again, it was possible it was because Cindy was fond of Nira. Ali needed to know for sure. The truth would give her an insight into the witch's nature.

Was Smith rotten to the core? Or did she have a soft spot?

Ali needed Cindy to shut up and close her eyes!

"Cindy," Ali said. "You're tired and I'm tired. Can we just get on with this?"

Her friend finally gave in. "What do I have to do?"

"Close your eyes, pretend you're falling asleep." Once more Ali settled her hands over Cindy's head and heart. At that moment the Yanti—a talisman of great power and beauty that had originally belonged to her when she had been queen of the fairies—began to warm beneath her shirt, near her heart. The warmth spread throughout her entire body, filling her limbs with a delicious sensation.

"I'll pass out," Cindy warned, her voice already growing drowsy.

"You can talk in your sleep." As she spoke, Ali commanded her magnetic field to expand to such an extent that she could feel the blood pounding through Cindy's physical heart. Then she went a step further, and entered a thumb-shaped space inside Cindy's heart. A place filled with bright light where she could feel the glow of Cindy's inner life—perhaps even the radiance of her friend's *soul*.

Ali heard the chatter of Cindy's thoughts, but they decreased as the warm flow of magic penetrated the neurons, which fired like red and blue and white sparks between the hemispheres of Cindy's physical brain. Ali spoke in a softer voice.

"Relax, and go back in time until that day you and Steve returned to Toule. That day right after I left to go up the mountain. Tell me what you guys did. Tell me what you saw.

Tell me who you met. Don't worry if you can't remember something. Your body will remember, and it will tell us what we need to know."

Cindy Franken began to speak.

She began where Ali had instructed, that sunny summer day Steve and Cindy had gone off to explore the secrets of Toule without her. They had started at the town library, where they tried to figure out what had caused the power plant explosion thirteen years ago—for which the small northwestern town was famous. Naturally, given only a few hours, they failed to solve the mystery, but they did come across a curious wrinkle in the city's sad history.

It concerned a teenage girl named Lucy Pillar.

Ali listened closely as Cindy whispered a replay of the old librarian's account of the mysterious girl. Sitting on her bed, Ali could *see* Ms. Treacher and the many rows of library books neatly stacked behind the feisty woman. More, Ali felt as if she caught a glimpse of Lucy through the librarian's eyes.

Cindy had asked Ms. Treacher if she knew Lucy.

"Lucy was a lovely girl, before the accident."

The way the woman said *accident,* Cindy and Steve knew she was not talking about the power plant explosion. Steve pressed her for more details, and she responded:

"A year before the power plant blew, Lucy was in a car accident. Her boyfriend at the time—Hector Wells, he was on the basketball team—was driving. He was drunk, and he crashed into a tree, and was thrown from the car. But Lucy had her seat belt on. She got trapped inside, and the car exploded, and she was burned over most of her body. I'll never forget those days. I was a teacher at the high school then. I saw Lucy every day. She was a cheerleader, happy as a lark. Smart as a whip, too. She could write, sing, play the flute.

Then, just like that, it was all over for her. Or it should have been. God forgive me, but I used to pray that she had died that night."

Steve asked if Lucy's parents were still alive.

"Her mother is. Her father died the same night as Lucy, in the explosion."

Steve asked where the mother lived.

"I don't know. She moved away some years ago."

Cindy asked about Hector.

"He was hurt in the blast, but he recovered. He's a local contractor, he lives here in town."

Then, unfortunately, the old woman had grown annoyed, thinking that they were trying to blame Lucy for the explosion.

"What is it with all these fool questions? Are you trying to build a conspiracy theory around the plant explosion? Trying to blame poor Lucy because she was already burned? I tell you, that girl was a saint. Never had a mean word to say about anyone."

Again, the librarian swore that Lucy had perished in the explosion. At that point Steve wisely changed the subject—to Sheri Smith—saying he had heard nothing in town about a "Mr. Smith." It was then Ms. Treacher dropped a bomb—at least to Ali's way of thinking.

"There is no Mr. Smith."

Then who is Nira's father, Steve had asked.

"No one knows."

Ali instructed Cindy to move forward in time, to the next day, when they had lunch at Sheri Smith's house. Unfortunately, the woman was not around, or so it seemed. They were fed and entertained by Nira's nanny—Rose. The Rose with no last name. The Rose from Columbia, who spoke with only a faint accent. The Rose who wore black gloves to keep her hands from . . . what?

As Cindy spoke of entering the mansion, with Steve by her side, and talked about their lunch with Rose, Ali saw something her friends clearly missed—at least initially. Ali saw Rose was not Hispanic at all. For that matter, Rose was barely recognizable as a human being. Ali saw an image of a creature that flickered like an out-of-focus actress on a black-and-white TV set. One second the person they were having lunch with was clearly visible. The next Ali would see a *thing*—with a twisted torso, two arms, two legs, an oddly shaped skull. But it possessed no *normal* features.

The thing was wrapped in a white silk robe, and was a mass of scarred flesh. It had only one eye, the right one. The left was lost beneath a lump of seared skin, while the right hole peered at the world through a milky green marble that looked as if it had been dumped in a bowl of acid then lifted and left to dry beneath a colorless sun.

Was it Lucy Pillar? Had she survived the power plant explosion, after all? Had she survived her initial car accident only to return a year later and burn the bulk of the city to the ground? And had she done so out of revenge?

Or was Ali actually seeing Sheri Smith? The woman who had returned to Toule thirteen years *after* the gruesome explosion? The beautiful woman who had gone on to establish one of the most successful software companies in the nation?

Was the answer to all these questions one huge YES?

Yet the librarian—who had known Lucy a long time—said the girl had been a saint. That remark contradicted the "identical identity theory." Sheri Smith was as far away from sainthood as your average politician was from heaven.

Ali was unwilling to decide on a theory yet, particularly since Sheri Smith had hand-fed her most of the clues she had to work with. Sheri Smith designed computer games for a

31

living—ones that dealt with the end of the world. Ali was beginning to feel as if she were a character trapped in one of Omega Overture's plots. The feeling grew stronger as Ali prodded Cindy forward in time.

The day after lunch with Rose, Steve and Cindy paid Hector Wells a visit. He was a well-known and respected contractor in town. He was not in the habit of talking about his personal history with a couple of out-of-town kids. But he had let them in because they had shrewdly dangled the promise of secret information under his nose. Information that might explain how Sheri Smith had killed a more recent girlfriend of his—Patricia.

In reality, Steve and Cindy were bluffing about how much they knew. They visited Hector to pump *him* for information. They knew she—Ali—was suspicious about Sheri Smith, and they wanted to help her collect information on the woman.

The latter fact stabbed Ali with more guilt. Steve was dead because of her. He had died trying to help her. Why? Because he loved her? He had never really tried to hide his feelings for her. And she had loved him in return—just not the way he wanted. In the end, she realized, he had died trying to demonstrate that he would do anything for her.

"You didn't have to," she whispered aloud. "I knew, I already knew."

Ali had to force herself to concentrate on what Cindy was seeing and saying. Somehow, her friends got Hector to talk about how Lucy was originally hurt.

"There's no mystery to what happened with Lucy. That day I was at a friend's house, and we were playing computer games. The Internet was just getting going back then. We used to play this game, "Ultimatum," online with people from back East. The graphics were crude by today's standards and so was the story. But it

32

was the new thing, and we were addicted to it, my buddies and I. We liked to drink beer when we played, and I had a few too many, and after we were done, I went to pick up Lucy. We had to go to a wedding, south of here somewhere. It was on the way there when I veered off the road and crashed into a tree. I was stupid, I didn't have my seat belt on. But it saved me that time. I was thrown from the car, Lucy was not. The car caught fire and she got burned."

Steve asked if he saw anything that caused him to veer.

"To tell you the truth, I remember very little about that night. I told the cops that when they arrested me. The trauma must have caused me to block it out."

Cindy asked if Lucy and he were able to get back together.

"We tried, I wanted to try, but she had lost so much skin in the fire. She had to keep having operations. The scarring was severe. She thought she was hideous."

Too hideous to be loved, Ali thought sadly.

Steve and Cindy got Hector to talk about the night of the power plant explosion.

"I snuck off to be alone with Lucy. For some reason, the gate leading to the plant was open, and we went inside to walk around. But we didn't touch anything, or break into the turbine area. The plant blew at the other end of the facility—closer to where the gas burned that heated the water and drove the turbines. Lucy and I were shielded by the control room and a storage area. Or I should say, I was shielded. That's not to say I didn't feel the impact. When the plant blew, the ceiling ruptured above me and the walls collapsed. There was fire and smoke everywhere. I was lucky to get out alive."

What about Lucy, they asked.

"Just before it blew, she said she had to go to the bathroom, and went looking for one. That was the last I saw of her."

A small but fascinating fact struck Ali as she neared the end of their interview with the contractor. It was Hector's reaction when Sheri Smith's name was brought up. All he said was, *"I try to stay away from that woman."* But Ali saw the fear on his face that Cindy had failed to note. It was deep, inexplicable. What had Sheri Smith done to him to make him so scared of her? It made Ali wonder. He reacted in the opposite manner when Nira's name was brought up.

"She does have a sweetness to her. Most people around town don't see that. They just think she is a mental case."

Those were Hector's last words—for the night—because Cindy ran out of gas. Ali was not given a chance to *thoroughly* probe the subject that mattered most to her—Steve and Cindy's capture and torture at the hands of Sheri Smith. However, she did manage to retrieve chunks of the dialogue they had with the woman. The latter was interesting, to say the least.

But as Hector and Sheri Smith's faces faded from her inner vision, Ali realized the noise she was hearing in her bedroom was no longer Cindy's mumbled rendition of various conversations, but her loud snoring. Not for an instant did Ali consider waking her. If anyone deserved her rest, it was her old pal.

Leaning over on the bed, Ali kissed her on the forehead, letting an ounce of fairy magic enter her friend's brain, knowing that Cindy would have the sweetest dreams she had ever had. Then Ali turned and walked into the living room.

Two surprises awaited her.

Nira was sitting up on the couch, her eyes wide open.

The phone was ringing. Ali quickly picked it up.

It was Mr. Jason Warner. Her father.

CHAPTER

3

Ali had not spoken to her father in four days—a half a day more than the time she had spent in the elemental kingdom. Their last talk had been just before she had entered a cave high on the side of Pete's Peak, with Farble and Paddy—her troll and leprechaun companions. At that point, Ali had called her dad on her cell and told him she was already bored with summer vacation. She was watching too much TV, too many DVDs, and just all around goofing off. But it was lies, all lies . . .

The truth of the matter was, at the time, she had been using the last drop of fairy magic at her disposal to blast open a hole in the cave that held the seven doors—the doors that led to seven separate dimensions. She was also using fire stones that she had stolen from the queen of the dark fairies—Radrine— to help with the excavation. Farble was helping her as well, trying to break into the cave. The troll could lift one-ton boulders without breaking a sweat.

Presently, Farble and Paddy were still in the elemental kingdom, in the care of a group of fairies, who were hiding in the mountains north of the fairy capital, Uleestar. Her friend, Ra, was with them. They were all trying to stay out of the Shaktra's sight, and the monster's army, which was busy ravishing the countryside.

But back to the cave and her last talk with her dad. The reason Ali had lost half a day in the cave had been because of Radrine and her evil minions. The dark fairies had put up a bitter fight, trying to keep her from entering the green world, and she had suffered a nasty hand injury from the battle.

But her battle with the dark fairies all worked out in the end. When she returned from the elemental world, Ali had the distinct pleasure of tossing Radrine into the blinding light of the Earth's sun—which was *deadly* to a dark fairy, who for the most part lived in gigantic hives deep underground.

Because Radrine had caused her so much grief—the evil queen had once tortured her just to amuse herself—Ali had actually smiled when the dark fairy's worm-infested translucent skull had exploded in the sunlight. However, although the act of revenge had not gnawed at Ali's conscience, her grin had quickly faded and she had vomited. In the war with the Shaktra, killing was necessary, but Ali hoped it never became a pleasure.

Lying to her father, however, definitely bothered her. It hurt her now, especially when she heard the tension in his voice. He drove a truck long distance for a living, and had to be away for days at a time. He worried about her constantly, probably because he had never gotten over the loss of his wife—her mother—a year ago.

His inability to reach her had driven him nuts. Two days ago, he had discovered she was not staying at Cindy's house—as she had promised to do. To make matters worse, from calling around town—in search of her—he had heard that Cindy and Steve were missing.

Her poor dad. Ali only had to listen to him a minute before deciding that her lying had to stop. She was going to tell him the truth, of who and *what* she was. He would get over it, she told herself, she was his daughter. He would *have* to get over it . . .

"Hey, Dad, you know about fairies? Well, I'm one of them, just found out a month or so ago. No, Dad, listen, I'm not that kind of fairy . . ."

It might be a bad idea to tell him the truth on the phone.

Across the room, Nira stared at her as Ali's father rambled on in her ear. Her dad was so upset, Ali could hardly get a word in edgewise. She had to content herself to listen for a few minutes, just let him blow off steam.

As usual, Nira showed not a trace of emotion, but Ali could not rid herself of the impression Nira was not staring at her face, but lower, at her chest—possibly at the Yanti hidden beneath Ali's shirt. Nira had shown a remarkable ability when it came to using the talisman. In Toule, a few days ago, she had made a dead boy talk. Pretty impressive, Ali thought, not to mention *very* disturbing.

Poor Freddy Degear, his bloody skull crushed, the rest of him stuck in the throes of rigor mortis, calling out for the wicked Shaktra, when his soul should have been flying high with the angels. Even while exploring the elemental kingdom, Ali had frequently reflected on the event. Holding the Yanti, and using a few peculiar hand movements, Nira had summoned forth a radiant heat that had flooded the morgue, and briefly shaken Freddy to life. Clearly the child had powers Ali could not begin to fathom, much less duplicate.

Sometimes it made Ali wonder who should be wearing the Yanti.

Yet, with the scar on Nira's forehead that resembled a seared thumbprint, Ali never let herself forget that the child might be inadvertently working for the Shaktra. It made her wonder how she was supposed to protect her friends and family from Sheri Smith.

Her father finally began to calm down. He was on his way home, in his truck, driving as fast as he could. He would reach Breakwater in five hours—six at the outside. Now he was demanding to know where she had been the last few days. He was waiting for an answer. Ali found the pause more painful than his rambling. What was she supposed to say?

"I was up on the mountain," she said finally.

"What were you doing there?"

"I was in a cave."

"A cave? Were you camping out? All this time?"

"Not exactly. I was in this cave and . . . it sort of leads to other caves." She added, "I didn't actually have to camp out."

"Were you alone?"

"No."

"Were you with Steve and Cindy? You know, when I couldn't reach you, I called the police. They said your friends are missing. Are they back home yet?"

Ali hesitated. "Cindy's sleeping here, right now, in my room. She's going to go home soon."

"Wake her up and send her home this instant. I spoke to her parents. They're frantic about her." Her father paused. "Where's Steve?"

Ali swallowed thickly. "He's not here."

"Where is he? Is he still up on the mountain?"

"No."

"Then where is he? This is no time for games! I spoke to his mom earlier this evening, and she cried the whole time. She's talked herself into believing that you kids had been kidnapped by the same people who took Karl. I had an awful time trying to reassure her. To be frank, I'm shocked at your behavior, Ali. This is so irresponsible of you. Your adventure—or whatever you want to call it—is over with, finished. You kids are not going near the woods the rest of the summer. Do you know I wasn't even able to deliver my load to Miami when I discovered you had disappeared? I got too upset. Just so you know, the load is still in the back of my rig. That's another account I'm going to lose. Fifteen hundred bucks a month down the drain."

"I'm sorry."

"Sorry doesn't pay the bills." Again, her father paused. "Is Steve there with you? He is, isn't he? Let me talk to him."

Suddenly, all of Ali's fairy powers did not feel so powerful. She had to struggle to breathe. She spoke in a whisper. "Dad, you can't talk to him."

"Why not?" he demanded.

"He's dead."

"What?"

"He's dead. He died . . . a few hours ago."

"What are you talking about? Don't be ridiculous."

Tears burned her eyes. She felt as if she were falling then, into a hole, a black pit without a bottom. Suddenly she was not so detached. Geea, Alosha—the fairy queen had fled for parts unknown. Thirteen-year-old Ali Warner was the only one left to answer his questions.

"Dad, I'm not lying. Steve's dead. He was killed by this woman who lives in Toule. Her name's Sheri Smith. She stabbed him in the heart. No, I mean, she ordered someone else to stab him."

"Who?"

Now was not the time to talk of Karl. "It doesn't matter, a

guy who works for her. It was Sheri Smith who was behind the murder." Ali added, "She almost murdered Cindy, too, but she managed to escape."

Her dad was a long time responding. "Do the police know about this?"

"Cindy tried to tell them, but they didn't believe her."

"Why not?"

"Because the woman who killed Steve—she stole his body."

"Ali . . ."

"He's dead, Dad, and Cindy's lucky to be alive. Now you're right, I'll wake her up and send her home right away. And I'll call Steve's parents, and talk to them, and tell them what's happened to their son."

"You can't do that. You can't make up a story like that."

"It's not a story. It's the truth."

"Who's this woman you're talking about? The name sounds familiar."

"She runs a software company out of Toule—Omega Overtures. They make tons of money selling computer games."

"I've read about her in the paper." Her father didn't sound as if he was buying her story. "So tell me why this rich and famous woman would want to kill Steve."

"It's a long story. I can't explain it on the phone."

"I'm confused. You say you were up on the mountain, in a cave. Is that where Steve was killed?"

"I wasn't with him when he died. He was killed in Toule—in Sheri Smith's mansion. But I saw his body." She added, "I carried him in my arms."

A stupid remark. Annoyed, her father snorted. "How could you pick him up?"

"I just did," she mumbled.

"Before the rich woman returned and stole his body?"

"Yes."

"Is this what Cindy told the police?"

"Not exactly."

"Could you please elaborate on that?"

"She didn't mention that I was there."

"Why not? If you were there."

"I asked her not to." She added, "Like I said, it's hard to explain on the phone. But when you get home, I promise I'll show you things that will help you understand that I'm telling the truth."

"What kind of *things*?"

"Trust me, you'll see."

He did not trust her, that much was obvious. She could not blame him. "Tell me one thing, Ali, does any of this have to do with what happened last month? When you and the others disappeared up the mountain for two days?"

"Yes."

"So you lied about what happened then, right?"

"Yes."

Her father sighed. "Ali, I love you more than anything in the world. I always have, from the instant you were born. You know that, don't you?"

"Yes."

"So when are you going to stop lying to me?"

"When you get home." Her voice cracked then, with pain. It was true, she was still very human. How quickly she had forgotten; how hard it was to be reminded. She forced herself to add, "When you get home, everything will become clear."

They exchanged goodbyes and Ali set down the phone.

Across the room, Nira continued to stare at her.

Then there came a hard knock at the door.

A man called out for her to answer.

It was the police.

"Open up, Ali! I know you're in there!"

It was not just any policeman. Ali recognized the voice. Officer Mike Garten—who for the last month had regularly stopped by to question her about Karl Tanner. The Tanners were the richest family in Breakwater, and Deputy Garten was trying to boost his career by solving the mystery of Karl's disappearance. He was hoping to make himself the new sheriff. As if being the head honcho in Breakwater was a big deal. The tiny town had a lower crime rate than most West Coast malls.

Grabbing Nira by the arm, Ali pulled the unprotesting child into her bedroom and gently shook Cindy awake. Garten continued to pound at the door, but when Cindy opened her eyes, they shone with a soft light.

"I was having the most beautiful dream," she whispered with a sigh.

"Sorry to disturb it," Ali said, wondering if Cindy was, like her, a fairy in the green world. They were so close, had been all their lives. Yet Ali had never paused to consider the possibility. Ali went on, "I wish I could have let you sleep longer, but Garten's at the door, and he knows I'm here. I need you to take Nira and hide her in the basement. I'm pretty sure I can keep him out of the house, but he might have a search warrant, so I can't be sure. Hide in the corner closet until I call for you."

At the mention of Nira's name, Cindy came fully awake. Picking up the child—and a blanket to keep Nira warm—Cindy hurried to obey Ali's instructions. As Cindy disappeared in the direction of the basement, Ali could not help but notice the way Nira clung to her. The child had already closed her eyes. She might even have gone back to sleep. She was in Cindy's arms; all was well. Nira's warm response to her friend gave substance to a theory Ali had just started to formulate.

Ali tore off her pants and shirt, pulled on her nightgown. When she answered the door, she yawned loudly in the cop's face. The sun had yet to totally rise but it was close at hand. Her front porch was well lit, and showed that the cop's eyes were red and tired, no doubt from lack of sleep.

Officer Mike Garten was on the young side for a cop, twenty-one. He was so tall and skinny, she hated to think what would happen if he ran into a real villain in the middle of the night. He would probably shoot himself in the foot. He was one of those guys who was so insecure, he constantly had to overcompensate by acting tough. Ali had heard that when he was in high school, he had joined the football team, and after taking a hard hit in the season's opening game, he had sued the coach on the opposing team for "unjustifiable cruelty." When he questioned her about Karl's disappearance, he always tried to intimidate her. Usually she was able to rattle him with the power of her eyes and make him go away.

This time, though, she worried, he might have something on her.

"Officer Garten," she said in surprise, still yawning. "Isn't it a little early to be out harassing local citizens?"

"I've been by this house a dozen times in the last three days and you haven't answered once. Where the hell have you been?"

"Please, Officer Garten, I'm only thirteen. My dad doesn't like people swearing in my presence. Particularly people who carry badges and wear guns. By the way, that's a nice shiny revolver you've got there. Killed anyone in the line of duty lately?"

She loved to mock him—she couldn't help herself. Along with the dirty money Karl's father was no doubt slipping him—and the possibility of a major promotion—her mouth was probably the main reason he was determined to see her locked up. Her taunting didn't help the situation, but . . . well, she was a fairy queen, she could fly and all that, but she was no angel.

"Ali . . ." he began.

"As to where I've been," she interrupted. "It's none of your business. I'm not a criminal and you're not my parole officer. I don't have to report what I do."

Her attitude made him smile, which did nothing to calm her down. He was acting cocky. He had something up his sleeve.

"Heard your best pal, Cindy, was in Toule tonight, at the police station, saying your other friend, Steve, had been killed by the town's most powerful lady—Ms. Sheri Smith. Cindy went on record as saying Ms. Smith murdered Steve right in front of her."

She scowled. "Then why, might I ask, are you grinning?"

"Because when Toule's police went to the scene of the supposed crime, they found nothing. Not a trace of foul play." Garten paused. "Have anything to say about that?"

"Nope."

"Thought you'd say that. Later in the night, about two hours ago, one of Toule's police officers saw a girl who matched your description entering and exiting Ms. Smith's residence." There was definite gloat in this pause. "Have any comment on that?"

Was he bluffing? She was sure she had not been seen at the house. She was extremely sensitive to the gaze of other people, even when they were hidden from view. Yet she might have missed someone. The entire time she had been at the mansion, she had not felt well. She had been dizzy and disoriented, almost as if she had been drugged.

It was almost as if she had been under some kind of spell.

"Nope," Ali replied.

"You're absolutely sure you weren't there?"

"Yes."

He took out a pen and a tiny notepad, made a scribble. "I'm making a written record of your response. Later, in court, I might have to swear to a jury what you told me just now."

"Swear all you want, I know you like it."

As he had during his last visit, he tried to peer past her and see inside her house. "The Toule police say they drove Cindy home three hours ago, but I was just at the Franken residence, and she wasn't there."

"So?"

"So aren't you worried where she is?"

"She called me on her cell. I think she'll be home soon."

"When was that?"

"An hour or so ago."

"Where did she call you from?"

Ali shrugged. "Beats me."

Garten kept twisting his neck to see past her. "Mind if I come in and have a look around?"

"Yes. I do mind."

"Why? If you have nothing to hide?"

"I just don't like some low-level deputy ordering me around in my own house."

Hardening his tone, he tried to push past her. "I know she's here. Get out of my way, Ali."

She blocked his way. She stood directly in front of him, planted her feet, and saw the look of astonishment on his face when he realized he could not budge her an inch. A skinny thirteen-year-old chick. Of course, a dozen strong men could not have pushed her out of the way. She smiled sweetly at him.

"Do you have a warrant, Officer Garten? You'll need one to search my house." She added, "You might also need backup, the way you're having trouble handling me."

Garten backed off a step, frowned, puzzled. "Is your father here?"

"No."

"Is Cindy Franken here?"

"No."

He got angry. "You're lying. You and your buddies—you're all liars. Steve Fender isn't dead, but Karl Tanner almost certainly is. And the district attorney and I—we're confident you three are the ones who killed him."

"You mean you and the rest of the spoiled Tanner clan are confident. The district attorney is not as brain-dead as you and your rich chums. You know Steve and Cindy have been reported missing for the last three days, but that doesn't bother you all, because their families are poor and therefore have no leverage at the mayor's office. Since you got here, you've shown no genuine concern for them. That's because their kidnappings at the hands of a rich woman don't fit in with your silly conspiracy theories. Yeah, I know all about them, everyone in town has heard about your 'Ali killed Karl plots.' You're the one who talked Mr. Tanner into thinking I was a suspect in the first place. Then you told him what names he should put on a suspect list. I bet he slipped you some cash to put us at the top of that list." Ali added, "Don't you just hate it when a cop turns out to be such a cop-out?"

His bitterness rose. "Why you little . . ."

She raised her hand, let a thread of her inner power enter her voice. "Going to swear at me again? Going to try to scare

46

me into confessing to a crime you know nothing about?" Shaking her head, yawning for real this time, Ali reached for the doorknob. "Don't bother answering, I'm tired of talking to you. I'm going back to bed."

Ali went to shut the door, but he stopped her, spoke sharply with an authority that surprised her. "You're to appear at the police station at nine o'clock this morning."

She paused. "Says who?"

He pulled out an official looking piece of paper, handed it over.

"This is a court order signed by our local judge—Judge Lincoln—ordering you to appear. You can see your name clearly typed at the top. I just dropped the same papers off at Cindy's and Steve's houses. When your pals do reappear—and I've a funny feeling that's going to happen soon—tell them they would be wise to be on time. Or else the three of you will be arrested, by me, and spend some time in juvenile hall."

Ali briefly scanned the paper. It looked like the real deal.

"Is Sheri Smith connected to this?" she asked.

Officer Garten nodded with satisfaction. "Like you said, in this part of the state, she's a rich and powerful person. And you're a fool to have made an enemy out of her. She's not going to let bugs like you and your friends accuse her of murder—ruin her fine reputation—and get away with it. This kidnapping act that you cooked up—it's obvious to anyone with a head on their shoulders that it's a ploy to divert attention from what you did to Karl."

Ali sensed partial truth in his words. Clearly, Sheri Smith wanted to tie her up with mundane human matters—such as lawsuits—to keep her from trying to stop the upcoming elemental invasion.

Ali met Garten's gaze. "I've never even met the woman."

47

"You were at her company four days ago, snooping around under a false name. What did you call yourself? Lisa Morgan? Where did you get that name from? I don't suppose it matters. At least a dozen of the firm's employees can testify that you were at Omega Overtures." Garten paused. "Why were you there anyway?"

When she didn't answer, he grinned and re-asked the *dagger* question, the one that could bury her at the nine o'clock meeting at the police station.

"Come on, where have you been the last three days?" he asked.

"Camping in the woods."

"You can prove that, I suppose?"

"I don't have to *prove* anything."

He chuckled as he stepped toward his patrol vehicle. "Sounds to me like you've got your excuses all lined up, Ali. I just hope Breakwater's and Toule's bigwigs believe you. By the way, the mayors of both towns are going to be at the meeting. They're not happy at the way you three kids keep disappearing. Especially with Karl still missing. Or should I say, especially with Cindy accusing the richest woman in the state of murder." Garten chuckled to himself. "That was a dumb stunt if I ever saw one. You've always been a pain in the butt, Ali, but I never took you to be an idiot. But this time, I promise, you're not walking away with a smirk on your face."

Bitter, remembering Steve's cruel murder at the hands of the witch, Ali leapt onto her front porch and snapped, "How do you know for sure the woman *didn't* kidnap Steve and Cindy? Have you investigated the matter? How do you know Steve is even alive?"

Garten laughed as he opened the door to his black and

white. "Go back to bed, Ali. I'm not the one you have to worry about now. It's that cop who saw you entering Sheri Smith's house. It's only fair to warn you—at this meeting—Ms. Smith's going to be there, and she's going to have a team of expensive lawyers with her." He added, "If I were you, I'd bring one myself. Even if you have to dig one out of the yellow pages."

Ali felt her frustration grow, and got doubly mad at herself that she let it be heard in her voice. "I'm thirteen, I'm just a minor. My dad isn't here to advise me. I don't have to attend your stupid meeting."

Just before climbing in his vehicle, Garten lost his grin and spoke in a harsh tone. "Get off it, Ali. Your sweet, innocent, little-girl act doesn't fool me for a second. I know you three murdered that boy. And I know you were the mastermind behind it."

"How can you be so sure?" she asked in a deadly tone, thinking how nice it would be to light his crew cut on fire and watch him dance across her lawn. Just having the idea in her head might have raised the local temperature. Garten wiped a bead of perspiration from his hairline and shook his head.

"Just something about you, Ali. You ain't normal."

Ali went to yell at him some more, but stopped herself. The truth was, she *had* killed the jerk—but only because Karl had murdered her mother two weeks ago. But there was no sense in pleading that angle. For everyone in town, including her own father, believed her mother had died over a year ago.

"Ms. Smith is going to be there . . ."

As Ali watched Garten drive off, she couldn't get *that* remark out of her head, but she knew the cop wouldn't have laughed had he known who Sheri Smith really was—the Shaktra.

Yet Sheri Smith represented only *half* the Shaktra. Ali was pretty sure the other half continued to roam the green world—as her fairy mother also continued to exist in the other dimension. Only the Shaktra was a creature of hate, who had assembled a vast army to lay waste to all that was beautiful in both worlds—a heartless beast driven by ambitions Ali could not begin to understand. And to think, in just a few hours, the *human* halves of Sheri Smith and Ali Warner would be sitting side by side at the same table.

Ali felt a headache coming on. This interdimensional war was too complex. It was difficult to keep all the players straight. Especially when it came to her own family. Plus there were so many names . . . even when it came to the same people.

Ali . . . Geea . . . Alosha.

Lucy . . . Sheri . . . Shaktra . . . Doren.

With Officer Mike Garten gone, Cindy led Nira back upstairs and told Ali she *really* needed to get home. Ali begged for a few more minutes of her time.

"Why?" Cindy asked, showing her tiredness, which meant her crankiness. "Didn't you get enough information out of my brain?"

"I learned a few things that would surprise you, but we still have to figure out how to deal with the police." Ali held out the document Garten had left behind. Cindy took it reluctantly, scanned it, while Nira laid down on the couch and closed her eyes. The girl was as exhausted as the rest of them. Ali continued, "You're going to have a paper like that waiting for you at your house. It's ordering us to appear at a nine o'clock meeting at the police station."

"What kind of meeting?"

"It's going to be more of an interrogation than a friendly

gathering. The police from both towns are going to rake you over the coals with questions. Plus the mayors of Breakwater and Toule are going to be there."

"Why?"

"Because Garten—and whoever he's working for—are trying to connect Karl's disappearance with your and Steve's kidnapping."

"I'm not following you."

"Garten has this wild theory that the three of us staged your kidnapping to divert attention from what we did to Karl."

Cindy snorted. "No one will believe that. A fake kidnapping would draw more attention to us."

"I agree. The problem is, no one's going to believe *you* until Steve's body is found." Ali added, "I'm afraid that ain't going to happen anytime soon."

"You really think Sheri Smith . . . took him?"

"Yes."

"Doesn't my word count for anything with the police?"

"They need proof a crime has actually been committed. So far, when it comes to Karl and Steve, they don't have any physical evidence of foul play—except for the fact that both are missing. What hurts us is—the police already think you lied to them."

"When?"

"Remember in Toule—when the cops went out to Smith's house—they came back to the station and reported to their captain that they couldn't find a basement?"

"Such dorks. I told them exactly where it was. I can take them back to the house and show them where it is."

"This is going to be hard to believe, but when I was there, *I* couldn't find the door that led to the basement."

"What are you talking about?"

"Just telling you what I saw. When I went back to Smith's house, there was no entrance to the basement. It looked as if there *never* had been a doorway. Also, where I laid Steve on the sofa, blood from his wound dripped onto the couch. But when I checked it an hour ago, the stain was gone."

"Could Sheri Smith have snuck in and cleaned it up?"

"No one cleaned up anything. It was just gone."

Cindy shook her head, confused. "Are you saying that witch cannot only alter the way people see her? She can make her house change shape?"

Ali considered. "It might be that nothing in the house has been altered—except our perception of it."

"Did she cast a spell on the police who went out to the house?"

"Maybe. We're not even sure if she was there."

"She must have been there. How was she able to cast a spell on *you*?"

The remark almost sounded like an accusation, and frankly, Ali didn't blame Cindy. Since returning from the elemental kingdom, Ali had done her best to keep her name unconnected to the events at Sheri Smith's house. Her reasoning was simple—she had bigger fish to fry. Like saving the world. In a sense she was forcing Cindy to take all the heat.

Now Ali could see why Sheri Smith was determined to draw her into a legal battle. She tried to explain the woman's motives to her friend.

"Smith's not interested in you. She wants to tie me up with the cops so I don't have time to return to the elemental kingdom."

Cindy got tense. "You're going back? I didn't know that."

"We haven't had a chance to talk. Listen, at this meeting, you have to keep things simple, like you did before. Say that

Sheri Smith invited you to lunch—you and Steve—then put bags over your heads and tied you up and threw you in a room that you *thought* was a basement. Then explain how she killed Steve—how she stabbed him in the heart. Don't expand on the story. The more you talk, the more details you supply them with, the more ammunition they'll have to trip you up with."

The advice made Cindy uneasy. "But it was Karl who stabbed Steve."

"I told you, Karl cannot be brought into this. That's exactly what Sheri Smith wants. She's trying to muddy the water. When it comes to Steve, she should be on the defensive. I mean, she's being accused of murder. That's not a small thing. But already she's put us on the defensive by focusing the police on the fact that Karl disappeared last month while he was camping in the woods with us."

"You don't know that for sure," Cindy said.

"I spoke to Garten. It was obvious he's using what happened in Toule to tie us to Karl's disappearance." Ali added, "He went out of his way to tell me Sheri Smith was going to be at the meeting."

Cindy paled. "She's coming here? To Breakwater?"

"Yes."

"Doesn't that worry you?"

"Well . . ."

"But she murdered Steve! Why don't they arrest her?"

Ali shook her head. "Right now, it's your word against hers."

The information that she would be seeing Sheri Smith again in a few hours shook Cindy. "I can't be in the same room as that woman," she muttered.

Ali tried to soothe her. "I'll be beside you the whole time, and there'll be plenty of cops standing guard. I'm sure she won't try to physically harm us."

"After what you said about her house, it sounds to me like she could cut out our hearts and eat them and the police wouldn't even notice." Cindy added anxiously, "Maybe we should just tell the truth."

Ali had been afraid she would say that. "Exactly how much of the truth do you think we can tell?"

Cindy wouldn't meet her eyes. "I'm not saying you have to say that you're a fairy. But it would be easier if you could back me up some."

"How?"

"Well, tell them you rescued me from Karl."

"Then they'll want to know where Karl is."

"Tell them you don't know."

"Somehow I don't think that will go over very well."

Cindy glanced up, hesitated. "Where did you . . . put him?"

"It doesn't matter, no one's going to find him. And I'm never going to admit to killing him, nor are you going to talk about him. I hate to be so hard on this point, but we have to keep our stories straight here. Karl's dead but he can still put us both in jail." Ali paused. "Do you understand?"

There was a lengthy silence. There were no two ways about it, Ali was giving Cindy an order. However, Cindy glanced over at Nira, then straightened up and nodded. Ali heard the resolve in her voice.

"Don't worry, I won't give you away," Cindy said.

Ali hugged her. "With all this running around I've been doing—flying around—I haven't had a chance to tell you how brave you and Steve were, going after that witch. If it wasn't for what you guys did . . ."

"Steve would still be alive," Cindy interrupted.

"No." Ali hugged her harder, then took a step back, brushing Cindy's curls from her weary blue eyes. "You mustn't think that way. Remember, it was Steve, using Karl's computer, who first connected Smith to the Shaktra. He read all her e-mails to Karl. He knew what a monster she was. He knew the risk he was taking by going after her, but he did it anyway. That might sound melodramatic, but it's the truth. Steve didn't die in vain. You didn't suffer at the hands of that witch for nothing. Finally, she's been exposed for what she really is, and she's worried. That's why she's moving so fast on the legal front, trying to corner us. But she's got problems on her own end."

Cindy looked at her hopefully. "What kind of problems?"

"Before you were taken captive, you guys had a long talk with Hector, and you revealed your suspicions about Smith. You also told him you were going to have lunch with her the next day, and then, by coincidence, you guys disappeared. Toule's almost as tiny as Breakwater. He must have heard about your disappearance, it must have troubled him." Ali added, "That's one of the reasons I want you to call him right now."

"At six in the morning? Are you out of your mind? I hardly know him. Why am I calling him?"

"To tell him that Sheri Smith killed Steve. Also, tell him you managed to escape from the witch's dungeon, and that you have Nira with you."

"Ali . . ."

"Listen. Hector's ex-girlfriend, Patricia, used to babysit Nira, before she was mysteriously killed by what looked like the same SUV that killed Freddy Degear. You and Steve used that coincidence to get in his door, remember? But now you have lots more to tell him about Sheri Smith, and he'll want to hear it."

"How do you know?" Cindy asked.

"Because he hates her. I heard it in his voice."

"You've never even spoken to him."

"I heard it in your brain." Ali added, "Trust me, that's why you have to get him over here."

"I told you, Hector hardly knows me. He's not going to drive over here just because I ask him to."

"He will when you tell him that you're afraid to let Nira go back to Sheri Smith."

"Why do you say that? She's her mother."

"When he spoke to you about Nira, his face brightened, didn't it?"

"Maybe, sort of, I don't know. That still doesn't mean he's going to drive over here to see her at the drop of a hat."

"He has to come. I need him."

"What for?"

"To take care of Nira while we're at the police station."

"The man builds houses for a living. He's not a nanny."

Ali pointed to the phone. "When I scanned your memories, I saw that you and Steve got his number from information. He's listed. Get his number again, and call him and explain the situation. I think he'll agree to help with Nira."

"But how do you know this?" Cindy insisted.

"I don't know it for sure. But . . . think of it as a test."

"What kind of test?"

"A test of his devotion to Nira."

"I think you scanned your fish in your fish tank—their brains, not mine—when you had me in your bedroom."

"You would be amazed at what I saw."

Cindy gave her a look. "Even if he does agree to come—when he gets here—I won't be here. I'll be at home, and then I'll be at the police station."

"It doesn't matter, he's coming for Nira." Ali added, "Plus I need to talk to him."

"About what?"

"Many things," Ali said.

In the end, Cindy agreed to call Hector Wells. She was on the phone two minutes with the contractor before she set down the phone and nodded—bewildered—in Ali's direction. It appeared Hector was driving to Breakwater to help with Nira.

Before Cindy left, she told Ali she would be the one to call Steve's parents and tell them—without question—that their son was dead. Ali protested, said to her friend that it was too much to ask. But, with a tear in her eye, Cindy insisted.

"It should be me. I was there when he died," Cindy said.

CHAPTER

4

Breakwater's police station was located at the far end of the town's Main Street, near Harry's Haircuts. The latter spot was significant to Ali because just before entering the elemental kingdom, she had bumped into an odd customer sitting in Harry Idaho's place of business. At the time, Harry had been asleep in one of his chairs—which was strange since Harry was not known for sleeping on the job—and the customer had been sitting in the rear of the place waiting for Harry to wake up and give him a haircut.

The old guy certainly needed one. His hair and beard were so long and white, he looked like a wizard. Extremely thin, almost to the point of emaciation, he had cold blue eyes that appeared to see right through her—once they started talking. Plus he wore long white gloves, which he explained he needed to protect his hands.

"I don't wear them to keep warm or cool. No, I hurt my hands some time ago, burned them actually. Now I have to wear these to keep away infections."

The man said his name was Shane Bumpston, and they were not talking long when he brought up a gentleman Ali had healed from a serious injury not long after she had learned she was a fairy—a certain Ted Wilson. The reference was strange because Ali had healed Ted while he was unconscious—even Ted had not known who had helped him. But Shane Bumpston seemed to know all about her abilities.

Then, out of the blue, he asked to see her Yanti.

"I see the string. You must be wearing . . . something. Please, Ali, let me see it."

When she said no, and asked for some type of identification, he got angry and vanished—in a blinding flash of light, that literally knocked her to the floor. Later, when she came to understand Sheri Smith's ability to hide her scarred figure, she assumed the wizard was Ms. Smith in disguise. Yet she was never a hundred percent sure of the fact.

But as Ali neared the police station, on foot, it reassured her to think that she had survived at least one encounter with the witch. Also, her talk with Hector Wells had given her what she felt was ammunition she could use against the woman. Right now, Hector was fixing Nira breakfast.

Hector had been everything she hoped for and more.

It relaxed Ali to know Nira was in safe hands.

Nevertheless, her heart continued to pound in her chest.

Only minutes now . . . and she would be face-to-face with the enemy.

The police station was as tiny as the town. The building housed only three law enforcement officers: Sheriff Terry Mackey, Deputy Brent Houser, and Deputy Mike Garten. Not so long ago the structure had been a meeting place for the Women's Club, but it had been converted into the station when the aforementioned club's membership had shrunk to less than five members. Apparently the ladies of Breakwater had better things to do than sit around, play bridge, drink coffee, and gossip.

Yet the building's conversion had been poorly executed. It was a local joke that anyone locked in the station's jail cell could escape by standing on a chair and forcing open a rear window. Walking toward the station, Ali hoped she would not have to leave the place through that same window. There was always the possibility that Garten would try to arrest her for *something*. She really should try to be nicer to him, she told herself. At least for an hour.

Ali was fifteen minutes early and was surprised to see only one person present, standing outside the station. It was Mike Havor, the most unlikely of all candidates, she thought, to be early. He worked as a software designer for Sheri Smith's company, and he was totally blind. He stood alone near the south corner of the redbrick building, with his white cane in hand, his dark sunglasses on his pale face, his dark wavy hair badly combed. He couldn't have been more than thirty.

Recalling his gentle smile and kind manner, Ali was pleased to see him, although puzzled at his lack of an escort. She could only assume he had arrived on the bus. There was a bus stop ten feet from where he stood.

Ali had enjoyed the time they had spent talking in his office in Toule, arguing about the different direction they imagined mankind was heading in. Havor believed that human beings— to survive as a species—had to radically improve themselves by boosting their physical and mental capabilities with *implanted* technologies. He was convinced that in the next generation, every person on Earth would be walking around with microchips in their brains—to squeeze IQ points out of their craniums.

For her part, Ali had found his views too unnatural, yet his vision fascinated her just the same. From everything she had heard about how demanding Sheri Smith was of her employees, she had no idea why such a nice man worked for her—except for the fact that she probably paid him a ton. Ali knew it had been Havor who had designed the company's bestselling game—Omega Overlord.

She called to him as she approached. She used her fake name just for fun.

"Mike Havor, it's me, Lisa Morgan. How are you doing?"

He smiled as he heard her speak, turned in her direction. His glasses were so dark, she could not actually see his eyes, and she recalled that he had not always been blind. He had told her something about an accident that had struck at an early age, but had not gone into detail. Like when they had first met, he stared in her direction, but was just an inch or two off with his aim, so that she was left with the impression he was talking to the air, and not exactly to her.

"Now come on, Lisa, your secret's out of the bag. I know your real name, Alison Warner. And I must say, I like the real one better. But I've heard you like to go by Ali. Is that true?"

"Yes, call me Ali. All my friends do. May I still call you Mike? Even though I lied to you when we first met?"

He nodded, pulled his dark coat tighter around his long-sleeved white shirt, although the morning was not cold. "Sure. I hope you don't feel I'm here to prosecute you. To be honest, I didn't want to come at all, but Sheri Smith said I had to appear and testify that you entered Omega Overtures under 'false pretenses.' I know, I hate the phrase as much as you, it sounds silly." He paused and added, "Understand, it's not my desire to get anyone in trouble here."

Ali shook her head, although she knew the gesture was wasted on him.

"I'm afraid there's going to be plenty of trouble at this meeting. My friend, Cindy Franken, will be along in a few minutes, with her parents. She's here to testify that your boss, Sheri Smith, stabbed and killed a close friend of ours, Steve Fender."

Havor lost his smile, then he shook his head. "That's where you guys are wrong. As I told you in Toule, I've known Sheri Smith for years. She's not that kind of person." Havor paused, then asked, "You didn't actually see this murder, did you? Nor have you seen your friend's body? At least this is what I've been told."

"I didn't see anything," Ali lied. "But I know Cindy—know her better than you know your boss. I assure you that when the truth comes out, Sheri Smith will be found guilty. I realize this must be hard for you to believe, but she's not the woman you think she is. Everything about her is false."

Havor looked grim, and yet, not as shaken as she would have imagined. Did he secretly harbor doubts about the woman, Ali asked herself. When he spoke next, it was in a rather calm voice.

"If this crime did happen, then why are the police saying there's no evidence? I hear there's no body, no bloodstains, no weapons." He paused. "This murder—it's supposed to have occurred in Ms. Smith's home, right?"

"No. There's a maze of caves beneath Toule. They're related to the old power plant you guys used to have, and the gas mining that went on before the explosion burned down the plant. Cindy says Steve died in one of those mines—one beneath Sheri Smith's house." Realizing she was altering their agreed upon story, Ali added, "But Cindy had a bag over her head a lot of the time she was captive, so she's not exactly sure where they were when Steve died. Only that Sheri Smith committed the murder."

"But why would she murder your friend?"

Ali hesitated. "I don't know the answer to that."

"Why did you visit our firm that afternoon?"

"I wanted to find out more about you guys."

"But why us in particular?"

"Because your boss came out of nowhere, and, in five years, turned a tiny software company into a billion-dollar conglomerate. It made me wonder what kind of person could do that."

"So you were doing more than writing a paper for a class?"

"Yes."

"You have to admit, that sounds pretty thin." When she didn't answer, he added, "You're old enough to know that being successful doesn't automatically make one guilty. Certainly not of murder."

He was saying all the right things to defend his boss, but there was no passion in his voice. He had brought up the fact that she had used a false name when she had visited his company, but had not *jumped* on her for it, like one would expect.

Ali decided to take a chance on him. If he could support her even a little in the upcoming meeting, then it might make her life easier over the next few days. From what she could gather, he was the creative backbone of Omega Overtures. Sheri Smith might lighten up on her legal attacks on Ali—if only on a superficial level—to appease him. Having any type of ally at the firm would be a plus.

Ali still had no idea why Ms. Smith—the human part of the Shaktra—felt the need to own a software company. It couldn't be for monetary reasons. Using her fairy powers, Ali could walk into any Vegas casino and make millions in an hour—that is, if the pit bosses would let her play.

Ali spoke carefully. "The last time we spoke, in your office, you did not come out and say it, but you hinted at what a slave driver Ms. Smith was. You said nothing could stop her from getting what she wanted—once she'd made up her mind." Ali paused. "Doesn't that sound like a ruthless person to you?"

Mike Havor did not answer her question directly, which she took to be a yes. But he did alter the direction of his head, and soon he had narrowed his hidden eyes upon her.

Nevertheless, his expression remained troubled.

"This whole situation is very confusing," he said.

Ali nodded. "I agree with that."

Sheriff Terry Mackey and Officer Mike Garten arrived a minute later and let them inside the station. Sheriff Mackey had brought a large box of assorted doughnuts, scones, and muffins—he had a bulging gut that testified this was a typical breakfast for him—and two pots of steaming coffee. No doubt he had swung by the local pastry shop that Steve had been addicted to . . . when he had been alive . . .

Seeing the pastries and thinking of Steve made Ali lose her appetite. The room they were put in was depressing. It was the station's conference center, but it looked like a classroom that had been swiped from a rundown elementary school. There was a plastic desk at the center, surrounded by a dozen cheap folding metal chairs. At the far end was a chalkboard where someone—it was probably Garten, the handwriting was lousy—had sketched a crude schematic of the bottom floor of Sheri Smith's mansion.

The room's only window stared out at a dismal parking lot, bordered by the back wall of a bankrupt tire store. Economically, Breakwater was not thriving, not like Toule was—what with all the taxes it must collect from its money factory, Omega Overtures. Ali suspected Sheri Smith could treat Toule's authorities like dogs and they would just smile and lick it up.

Sheri Smith would probably not personally defend herself. Money didn't talk—it didn't have to. She had the team of lawyers Garten had mentioned to do her fighting for her.

Odd, though, how the woman had not offered to give Mike Havor a ride to the station. She had left the blind man to fend for himself with public transportation. He *must* know she was rotten, Ali told herself.

The two mayors arrived next: Breakwater's Clyde Banner and Toule's James Plier. The latter was young, twenty-five, and well-groomed. His nicely cut gray suit looked as if billionaire Sheri Smith had purchased it for him while shopping in Manhattan.

After shaking hands with everyone, Mayor Plier sat beside Mayor Banner, whose plain attire could at best be described as *unclean*. Ali smelled the alcohol on his breath, and wondered if she was the only one. As a fairy, her senses were exceptionally keen. Banner had already had a couple of whiskeys. He blinked and rubbed his eyes as he scanned the room, probably trying to remember what the meeting was about.

Ali knew Mayor Banner would not stand up for her and Cindy's rights. He was a well-known alcoholic—it was hard for him just to *stand* this early in the day.

Banner frowned as his bloodshot gaze rolled over her.

He had heard *bad* things about her.

Cindy and her mother arrived next, and the woman would not even look at Ali. And here Cindy's mom had been like a second mother to her, since her own mother had supposedly died in a car accident a year ago. But blood was clearly thicker than right or wrong, and Ali could see the woman blamed her for getting her daughter into this mess.

Cindy sat beside her and reached over and squeezed Ali's hand. Ali had her old pal on her right, Mike Havor on her left.

Cindy flashed her a warm smile, and for the first time all day asked how she was holding up.

"Fine," Ali said, trying to sound stronger than she felt.

"Things good at home?" Cindy asked, concerned about Nira.

"They couldn't be better."

Steve's parents arrived next. Both looked as if they had been crying. They would look at Cindy, but not Ali. It appeared it was her turn to be the black sheep today. Yet their grief only heightened her own.

Four male lawyers came soon after. They looked as if they had been ordered from a catalog. They wore black suits, red ties, carried brown leather briefcases, did not smile, and did not look as if they had much fun after their batteries wore down at the end of the day. There was definitely something mechanical about their behavior, but Ali felt as if she was the only one who noticed it.

Before Sheri Smith appeared, several others entered the now crowded room. The first were Mr. and Mrs. Tanner, and they did not mind staring at Ali. Their eyes blazed at her as if she had broken their son's neck in front of them. Ali did not feel hostility toward them; she felt, in fact, sympathy for the loss of their son. But they were not nice people, never had been, even before the disappearance of Karl. They *used* their money to *use* people.

Ali couldn't help notice the way Garten and the Tanners exchanged knowing looks. It was as if they thought, finally, we've got the little snot. Now all we need is a stiff rope and a building tall enough to hang her from.

The next person to arrive was Judge Harp Lincoln, whose name had appeared on the legal document that had ordered her to appear at the police station. He did not have on his black robes; nevertheless, he carried himself with authority. He was tall and black, dignified, in his sixties, and had a sparkle in his eyes that did not vanish when he shook Ali's hand. There was really no physical evidence against her—perhaps he would be the one to point that out.

Judge Lincoln had brought with him a female lawyer he introduced her to, Ms. Betty Savor. Apparently someone had given the judge the heads-up that she would be coming to the meeting alone, and without representation. Before taking a seat, Judge Lincoln asked her a series of questions.

"Where is your mother?"

"She died a year ago."

"Where is your father?"

"He is a long-distance truck driver. He is on his way back to town right now, but won't get here for a few hours."

"Is he aware you are attending this meeting right now?"

"Yes, sir." A partial lie. Ali had left word with Hector to tell her father about the meeting, should he get home before her.

Judge Lincoln scowled at Officer Garten. "Why didn't we at least postpone this meeting until her father could be here?"

"Your Honor, this was the only time I could arrange for everyone else to be here." The deputy added, "I did not think it wise to make an exception for just one of the people involved."

"But you have to admit she is a very important person in this case."

"Yes, Your Honor. I did the best I could to accommodate everyone's schedules."

Ali knew Officer Garten was lying. He had wanted her father out of town so he could jump all over her.

Judge Lincoln looked on the verge of postponing the

meeting when both the mayors suggested he go ahead. "It's just an informal meeting to gather some kind of understanding of what's going on here," Toule's James Plier pointed out.

Judge Lincoln continued to act uneasy. He told Ali to speak with the lawyer he had brought, Ms. Savor, outside. The two of them stepped into the hallway. Savor was young and pretty, although she wore far too much makeup and the size of her lush lips had been helped along with plastic surgeon injections.

"Do you know what's going on here?" Ms. Savor asked Ali.

"Basically. The one cop, Garten, thinks I kidnapped and killed Karl Tanner."

"He isn't alone. Judge Lincoln filled me in on the ride here. The missing boy's parents also think you and your friend, Cindy, are guilty. My advice, Ali, since I know only the barest of facts of this case, is that you invoke the right to remain silent. Even though they are acting like this is an informal meeting, everything you say can and will be used against you later in court—should you end up there."

"But I'm innocent. I've nothing to hide."

"Nowadays, being innocent is not necessarily the most important thing. It's the level of legal help you can hire." Ms. Savor nodded toward the room. "And there are some pretty high-priced attorneys inside there."

Ali shook her head. "I'm not afraid to talk. Honestly, I can defend myself."

With a sigh and a shake of her head, Ms. Savor led her back inside the conference room. There the lawyer leaned over and whispered in Judge Lincoln's ear that Ali Warner had waived her right to remain silent. Of course, with her fairy hearing, Ali heard the words loud and clear.

The last person to arrive, before Sheri Smith, was Officer

Jed Broach, the thirty-year-old deputy who supposedly had seen her entering and exiting the Smith residence during the night. Ali saw that he was badly cross-eyed, perhaps from lack of sleep, perhaps from something more sinister. Garten stood to welcome him, patted him on the back, but the guy slumped in a seat and stared off into space. If Ali had to pick one person in the room who'd had their brain psychically rewired, it would have been Broach. He looked like a man who had a headache so bad it made his hair hurt.

Then, in a single heartbeat, Sheri Smith appeared.

In her mind, Ali dropped her last name.

Sheri was right in front of her. Sheri was a real person now.

She was beautiful, with her long blond hair, her seductive curls, her flowing green dress. Of course, she could be whoever she wanted to be. Her gown complimented her eye color so well, they must have been matched at the tailor. The green also acted as a counterpoint to Ali's own eyes; and she thought, surely someone else in the room must notice.

For a moment Ali felt as if she was staring at an older sister, who had left home long ago, raped and pillaged a dozen villages to amuse herself, then returned home for Christmas dinner—like she had done nothing wrong in the meantime. For Sheri entered with a calm smile on her red lips. If she was nervous, even if she was ready to kill, she hid it perfectly. But studying her face across the table, Ali felt as if she were gazing at a living mask. There was no reality in the woman's expression. It could be changed in an instant, to fit any occasion.

As Sheri sat beside Judge Lincoln, close to her lawyers, Ali allowed her own gaze to deepen, to probe beyond the layers of Sheri's façade. Simultaneously, she felt the Yanti beneath her blouse begin to warm. As the heat grew, Sheri allowed her gaze to fall on Ali. Ali felt a sudden pressure in her head and heart, but it was not unbearable. Sheri knew she was being examined, and was sending back the message that she did not like it. However, she was not truly trying to stop her. It was almost as if she said aloud, *Fine, have a look, if you can.*

Then the façade suddenly crumbled, as the Yanti's heat swelled, actually blistered Ali's skin. For several seconds she was given a clear vision of the woman.

Sheri was hideous. She was scars. She was burnt flesh. She had one eye, the right, but it was almost buried beneath a mound of seared skin. It was still green, though, and there was a dull light to it; a power that hinted at something inhuman.

Pain smoldered in its depths, and Ali recalled the many things Hector Wells had told her before the meeting, and thought she understood why.

The horrific vision wavered like a computer screen crackling in an electrical storm, then it settled back to the blond loveliness Sheri normally presented to the world. The heat of the Yanti halted, but the memory of what it had revealed stayed with Ali. Sheri was neither blond nor redheaded. Her bald skull was a pitted moon that had traveled too near a flaming sun. Thirteen years ago—at last Ali was convinced—the fire of Hector's car accident had burned away all her beauty.

Ali no longer questioned whether Sheri Smith had been Lucy Pillar.

However, the feeling swept over her that she was missing something obvious.

The way Sheri grinned at her, it was as if the woman were thinking to herself: *Yes, Alison Warner, baby sister, childish foe, you see my face, you may even know a piece of my past, but you do not know me. You will never know me. Because I am beyond you.*

That was her subtle message. Her greeting.

Ali was disappointed when Judge Lincoln let Garten start the meeting. The cop was a nightmare from the word go. He acted as if he were presenting facts, but he put such a spin on them, Ali felt as if she were listening to a well-rehearsed speech that had been created by a committee of everyone who hated her.

Officer Garten began five weeks ago, with Karl Tanner coming home and telling his parents he was going on a camping trip with Alison Warner, Cindy Franken, and Steve Fender. Garten listed the dates and times, described the equipment Karl brought with him—making it clear that he brought a warm coat and an extra sleeping bag, for one or more of the others.

Garten played the drama king. Jumping three days forward in time, he leapt from his chair and boldly paced the room.

"Then Ali, Steve, and Cindy returned to Breakwater, without Karl!" he cried. "That's a simple fact, ladies and gentlemen. The three kids reappeared, went back to their daily lives, like nothing wrong had happened. They acted like they had not a clue where Karl was. Worse, they acted like they didn't care. I remember those days well. At the behest of Mr. and Mrs. Tanner, I questioned the three of them many times. They refused to admit they'd even gone hiking with Karl. But it was clear they were lying. How could I be sure? For one thing, they initially denied they had even gone hiking during the time I described. Then, when they were confronted with the proof, that yes, they had been up on the mountain, they started to mouth the same lies over and over again. They just decided to go camping, they said. They hiked partway up the peak, stayed out two or three nights. They couldn't remember for sure how long it had been, but they had lots of fun. No, they didn't see Karl. No, they never invited him on the trip. No, they didn't know why he'd gone camping at the same time as them."

Garten paused for effect. "All three repeated the identical lines to me. I'm sure you can guess why. Because they'd agreed ahead of time what they needed to say to stay out of trouble." Garten added, "The smoothest liar of them all was Ali."

Garten pointed at her. "That's Ali sitting there. She looks harmless, doesn't she? With her long red hair and cute smile. I admit, I used to think she was one of the nicest kids in town. I know her dad, he's a fine man, an honest man, a hard worker. I knew her mother, as well, when she was alive. One of the kindest souls you could hope to meet. Always had a kind word for everyone. But I swear to you that Ali doesn't take after either of them. Let me give an example. Intellectually, according to her schoolteachers, the girl's a genius. Without picking up a book, she always gets straight A's. Many of the teachers at school are intimidated by her. I've talked to several, and the questions she asks—most of the time they haven't a clue what the answers should be. I'm embarrassed to admit she can dance circles around me. Every time I've stopped by her house to talk, I've left feeling more confused than when I arrived."

"Excuse me," Judge Lincoln interrupted. "What does Ali's intellectual prowess have to do with Karl's disappearance?"

"Your Honor, I'm just trying to establish that even though she looks innocent, we mustn't be fooled. We have no idea what goes on inside that girl's mind."

Ali almost thanked him but decided to keep her mouth shut.

He was exaggerating about school. Only one teacher was intimidated by her—Mr. Sims, their biology teacher, and it was because he had a crush on her. The affection was totally innocent. He gave her the biggest frogs to dissect, stuttered when she smiled at him. He was far from a pervert.

On the other hand, it was true, she did get straight A's. Algebra and creative writing were not particularly challenging when you were queen of all the fairies.

Garten continued to pace. "Now I have to make two leaps—in time and in the nature of the crime we are discussing. These are crucial leaps—I'm hoping you can make them with me. Just keep an open mind, listen to the facts, let them speak for themselves. The most dangerous mistake right now would be to focus on Ali and Cindy's age. Like I said, they look like innocent kids but they're—"

"Please get to the point," Judge Lincoln said, more than a hint of impatience in his voice. He did not like being lectured to, Ali thought. That was good, he would make up his own mind. Shifting his bulk in his chair, he reached out and picked up a doughnut. He already had a cup of coffee in hand.

Garten looked insulted, but tried to hide it. "Four days ago Ali disappeared from sight. The following day, Steve and Cindy disappeared. No one knows where they went to, not their friends, not even their parents. But just before they vanished, they were seen in Toule. Specifically, Ali was seen at a software company, Omega Overtures, where she introduced herself as Lisa Morgan, and snooped around questioning several of the firm's employees about Sheri Smith. We have a witness here, Mr. Havor, one of Ms. Smith's employees, who can verify Ali came to the firm and used a false name." Garten paused. "Is that true, Mr. Havor?"

Judge Lincoln interrupted, turned to Havor. "Excuse me, Mr. Havor, are you blind?"

"Yes, Your Honor."

The judge turned to her. "Ali, please say your full name."

"Alison Warner," she said.

Judge Lincoln spoke to Havor. "You recognize the voice?"

"Yes."

"This was the young lady you met at your firm a few days ago?"

"Yes."

"She introduced herself as Lisa Morgan?"

"Yes."

"Why did she say she was at the firm?"

"She said she was writing a paper on our software company, and that she was a fan of our games, and played them regularly."

Judge Lincoln nodded to Garten. "You may continue."

"These three kids were in Toule, and the next day, Cindy and Steve were back in Toule. But Ali had disappeared. I know because I swung by her house and she wasn't home. I called her father, who was out of state, and he didn't know where she was. He thought she was staying at Cindy's house, but that afternoon Cindy was with Steve in Toule. Like she had four weeks earlier, Ali had once again disappeared." Garten paused. "Then, the next day, the other two kids also vanished from sight."

Ali could see holes in his story. She had actually been up on the mountain, and in the elemental kingdom, two days before Steve and Cindy had been taken captive by Sheri Smith. But she saw no point in explaining the flaws in his time line. It was clear where he was heading with his long-winded explanation, and she was surprised she had not seen it earlier.

Garten was going to blame her and Cindy for Steve's disappearance. Then he was going to roll the mystery of Karl's disappearance into one gigantic conspiracy on the part of Breakwater's two little devils. Garten glanced at the two of them as he reached for the climax of his theory. He had an audience. Everyone in the room appeared to be listening closely.

Except for Officer Jed Broach, who continued to stare off into space.

"Now about last night," Garten said. "Here I must turn to Officer Jed Broach for help. Officer Broach, at what time did Cindy appear at the Toule police station?"

The deputy stirred at the question. "Pardon?" he mumbled.

Garten moved closer to the man. "What time did Cindy Franken walk into your station last night and say that Steve Fender had been killed by Sheri Smith?"

Officer Broach struggled to remember. "It was late. No, it wasn't that late, but it was after dark."

Garten acted impatient. "Estimate the time."

"Nine o'clock?"

Garten checked his notes. "Last night you said it was ten o'clock."

Broach appeared dazed. "It could have been ten."

"Okay. Somewhere between nine and ten o'clock Cindy walked into your station. Were you present when she was questioned about Steve's murder?"

"Yes."

"What did she say?"

Broach hesitated. "That Ms. Smith had stabbed Steve to death with a knife."

"In her basement?"

Officer Broach's eyes wandered, confused. Ali could not help noticing how they came to rest on Sheri. Ali sensed invisible magnetic tendrils in the room, psychic snakes that reached out and enveloped Broach's skull. The deputy stared at Sheri for several seconds, before answering in a firm voice. If Ali had had any doubts before that the man was under the woman's control, they had just been erased.

"Yes," Broach said. "The girl said her friend had just been

killed in Ms. Smith's basement. Of course none of us believed her. Sheri Smith is a fine, upstanding woman. But we went out to the house nevertheless, checked it out."

"Did you find Steve's body?" Garten asked.

"No. We didn't even find a basement."

Garten acted surprised. "Why is that?"

"Because there wasn't one."

The answer hung in the room. A cop was a strong witness. Even Judge Lincoln was giving Ali and Cindy a peculiar look. Garten continued, there was no stopping him now.

"So what did you do with Cindy?"

"When my partner, Officer Kwan, and I returned to the station, we told our captain we were pretty sure the girl was lying. He told Kwan to take her home."

"Did you know at that time that Steve Fender was in fact missing?"

"Yes. We'd been notified by the Breakwater police that all three of the kids—Ali, Steve, and Cindy—were missing."

"Did you go back to the Smith residence that night?"

"Yes."

"At what time?"

"It was close to one o'clock." Officer Broach pointed at Ali. "At that time I saw that young woman enter and exit the house."

"How long was she inside?"

"An hour."

Ali was surprised. She had been in the house less than five minutes.

"Did you see where she went after she left the house?"

"She walked into the woods."

"Did you try to follow her?"

"Yes."

76

"What happened?"

"I lost her."

"How did you lose her?"

Officer Broach shrugged, once more glancing at Sheri. "It was dark, the woods were thick. It's hard to trail anyone under those type of conditions."

Garten appeared satisfied. "So Ali Warner just happened to show up in the exact spot where her best friend, Cindy Franken, said her other friend, Steve Fender, had been murdered. Tell me, Officer Broach, did you see Sheri Smith during all that time?"

"No."

"Did you speak with her?"

"My partner did. He called her at her office. She said she was working late, and that she had no idea what kind of prank these kids were trying to pull." Officer Broach added, "It was then she told us that Ali had been to her firm several days earlier, asking all kinds of questions."

"Officer Broach—at this time—do the Toule police have any idea where Steve Fender is?"

"None whatsoever," Broach replied.

"Thank you for your testimony," Garten replied, moving to the front of the room, trying to take up a commanding position. Ali tried to catch Cindy's eye, wanting to send her a silent warning of what was about to happen. But Cindy looked too exhausted. She had no idea she was about to be accused of Steve's murder. Up front, Garten spread his arms, as if symbolically trying to tie all the loose ends together.

"To be frank," he said, "I don't know what happened last night, when Cindy reported that Steve had been killed. Nor do I know exactly what happened five weeks ago, when Karl disappeared. But I do know that Karl was with Ali, Cindy, and

Steve when he vanished. And I think it is clear that Steve was with Ali and Cindy when he dropped out of sight. I don't know where Steve is now, but I fear the worst, because, oddly enough, I believe Ali and Cindy when they say he is dead." Garten paused, then raised his voice and almost shouted out the theory he had been heading for all morning. "Only I think they're the ones who killed Steve! The same way they killed Karl!"

The room shook with movement and murmurs. Everyone seemed to talk at once, to glare at Ali and Cindy. Judge Lincoln had to pound the table to restore order. The one person who looked perfectly calm was Sheri. With a faint smile on her painted red lips she stared at Ali and seemed to silently say: *"You think you're a queen? Why, you're just a kid. A silly female mortal who will soon be locked away in a dull human prison, while I take over this world, and the next."*

It was then Ali began to feel more annoyed than scared. She was not sure how much longer she would let the charade go on. It bored her, and even Sheri's powerful cloak—it had started to look so fake. By not allowing even a slight flaw on her face, Ali thought the woman was revealing how desperate she truly was to be seen as beautiful.

Again, Ali thought of what Hector Wells had told her about Lucy Pillar.

Beneath her shirt, once more, the Yanti began to warm.

Judge Lincoln was studying Ali, not Cindy. Perhaps he believed a portion of Garten's theory, she thought, that she was the evil mastermind behind some complicated plot to kill her friends. However, Ali could see he was far from convinced. When he spoke to Garten, the note of impatience in his voice was huge. Clearly, Garten's fantastic plot leaps bothered him.

"You may sit down now, Officer Garten," he said.

Garten shuffled uneasily. "Your Honor, I have yet to present all the details that support my theory."

"You have said enough for now," Judge Lincoln replied. "Sit."

Reluctantly, Garten obliged. At the same time, Judge Lincoln narrowed his gaze on her. "Ali, do you have any idea what this man is talking about?" he asked.

Ali shook her head. "This last month, he's been constantly coming by to see Cindy, Steve, and me—asking us questions about Karl. We tell him we don't know, but it doesn't matter what we say. To him, we're murderers. It's that simple."

"Then where is my son?" Mr. Tanner blurted out.

"What did you do to our boy?" Mrs. Tanner cried.

Judge Lincoln held up his hand. "Please, I know emotions are running high right now, but I must be allowed to ask the questions." He returned to Ali. "What about your friend, Steve? Where is he now?"

Ali glanced at Steve's parents before answering the question. "I wasn't there when he died, but I believe Cindy. That woman sitting there—that rich and powerful woman all these important people want to keep happy—killed him."

"Do you have any idea why she would do such a thing?"

Ali caught his eye. "Ask her yourself. But look at her *real* closely when you do. She's not what she appears to be."

Judge Lincoln was curious. "Why do you say that?"

Ali allowed power to enter her voice. Her ensuing words became a command. "Study her, deeply, you'll see what I mean."

Judge Lincoln turned his dark eyes on Sheri, a long and lingering gaze, and it was obvious the woman did not want that. Because it was clear to Ali that the judge had his own measure of power, and maybe, just maybe, if he stared deep enough at the evil being, he would see something that would shock him to the core.

However, *that*, Sheri would not allow.

Even as Judge Lincoln blinked, rubbed his eyes, and drew in a shuddering breath that suggested he was seeing beyond the woman's illusion, the light in the room changed. First it darkened, then took on a faint red tint. Outside, through the window, Ali had the impression the sun had moved near the horizon, like just before nightfall. However, this red color belonged to no sunset she had ever seen before. Besides, it was early morning.

The red, as it darkened, began to turn *purple*.

Then Ali understood. This was the same purple light that had shone from the monitors she had seen in Sheri's mansion. The light was not coming from outside—it was coalescing in the *center* of the room, casting a haunted sheen over the entire scene.

As the light gathered and grew, it formed no central sun, but rather, a transparent circular shell composed of many writhing strands. The worst thing was, the strands felt as if they were in some way alive, that they were being fed by the blood of each person in the room. The red and purple glow was vampiric—it needed living beings to feed from, to exist, to exert its power. Ali could literally feel the life being sucked from everyone at the table.

But what was its purpose?

Ali glanced anxiously around the room. For long seconds it seemed as if no one else saw the light. Judge Lincoln continued to study Sheri. Yet Ali saw beads of sweat form on his brow, and yet, he was shivering. Then, all around the table, mouths began to yawn, eyes began to close, and heads fell. Judge Lincoln was the last to be struck down. His heavy head, as it hit the table, made a painful thumping noise. Ali doubted he'd even had a chance to close his eyes before unconsciousness came. The eerie glow had drained off his waking mind.

Beside her, on her left, Mr. Havor lay with his head down, snoring softly. On her right, buried beneath a pile of blond curls, Cindy also slept, soundlessly. They all slept . . .

Except for one person. No, make that two; two fairies. Two princesses, although only one of them could rightly be called a queen. Ali thought it important then to recall that her father had not trusted Doren, her older sister, enough to give her the Yanti, and crown her high ruler of the elemental kingdom. It was odd how the memory had come back to her only after she had met Hector. For reasons Ali did not yet understand, the contractor from Toule had inspired many memories from her previous life as Geea.

Across the long table, Sheri stared at her and smiled.

"Do you want to talk?" she asked. "Or do you want to die?"

The heat of the Yanti was strong beneath her blouse. Ali sensed that Sheri felt it, and did not like it. The fact gave Ali courage. She merely shrugged at the questions, said, "You decide."

Sheri remained seated, appeared relaxed, but her smile faded as she gestured to the unconscious people around them. "Do you know why I arranged this circus?" she asked.

"To waste my time and energy," Ali said.

"If that were the only reason, then my time and energy would also be wasted."

Ali touched her warm chest, watched as her fairy sister followed her hand. The Yanti, she wanted the Yanti, Ali realized, but she could not take it, not by force. "What do you want, Doren?" Ali asked, for the first time using her sister's fairy name.

"So you remember me. I was not sure you would." She added, "Birth in these clumsy bodies is so often traumatic."

"Was it for Lucy Pillar?" Ali asked.

Sheri went to snap, thought better of it, spoke casually. "I'm sure your visit to the green world brought back many memories, as well as old abilities. I've been told you managed to evacuate the remainder of the high fairies from Uleestar, and that you even dispensed with Radrine." Sheri nodded to herself. "I thought you'd kill her, she had no manners."

"Yet she served you."

Sheri's turn to shrug. "Radrine went where the power was. She saw that the war with humanity was inevitable. She just wanted to be on the winning side."

Ali leaned forward. "There can be no winning side. Human beings and elementals are one and the same. That is the sacred truth, known only to the high fairies. Even the elves—even Lord Vak himself—doesn't know that for sure. But you do—I remember your beliefs because we shared them. You act like you've become blind. You know you cannot destroy one without destroying the other."

"So you think there's no possible value in this war?"

"What could possibly be gained by wiping out both worlds?"

Sheri stared at Ali with her intense green eyes. Almost, Ali saw her as she had existed in the elemental world, where her sister had been the most fair of all the fairies—her beauty and proud bearing even greater than that of Queen Geea.

Yet, Ali knew, that had been the problem. Doren had been too proud of her power and her beauty. Their father had also known, and not approved. He had given the Yanti to her, Geea, to rule the land, and Doren had been bitter. She had raved against him, in private and publicly. She should be queen, she told everyone. She was of the blue light, the oldest, the most powerful. It was her destiny to rule, she swore.

Doren had raved against him up until he had made his discoveries on the Isle of Greesh. Then, perhaps to assuage his daughter's anger, he had invited Doren to explore what had been found; she had gone, eagerly, and left Geea behind. Ali recalled she had been too busy ruling her kingdom to go excavating. She had been spending precious time with her mother and . . .

No, that last part of her memory was distorted.

Her mother had already gone. Gone off to the yellow world.

To be born as a human being. Ali could not remember why.

Ali silently cursed her memory gaps. It was ironic that the one person who could fill them in sat only ten feet away. Unfortunately, this same person grinned as she spoke of destroying worlds. Doren must be as Trae—her high advisor—had described. Atop the highest kloudar, before she had healed him of life-threatening wounds, she had asked Trae the most crucial question of all . . .

Why does the Shaktra want this war?

Trae had sighed and closed his eyes. *"It must be insane."*

Now, Sheri appeared to read her mind. "I have my reasons," she said.

Ali placed her palm on the Yanti, near her heart, and allowed the heat to spread up her arm. "Explain them to me. Here and now. I'll listen."

Sheri was amused. "To do that I would need to know, for certain, that you would agree to accept my proposition. A proposition that might spare your life, and probably the lives of a few billion humans. Interested?"

Ali hardened her tone. "Maybe. But I can't accept any

proposition without first knowing why you've changed into such a bloody beast." She added, "Sister."

Sheri lost her smile. "Watch your tongue, Geea. You don't want to anger me." She gestured to Cindy. "One thought and I can stop her heart."

"One thought and I can restart it," Ali replied, although she suspected it would be a mistake to go head-to-head against her sister—particularly after seeing the abilities she possessed. It was then Ali saw that the second hand on the clock had halted. Sheri had not merely put everyone to sleep—she had frozen time. And no being in the elemental world that she knew of—be they fairy, dwarf, elf, or dragon—had such skills. Whatever Doren had found on the Isle of Greesh had not just made her cruel, it had bestowed upon her unimaginable power.

Yet Sheri wanted to negotiate. She still needed her help. Why?

Sheri changed her approach, spoke in a reasonable voice. "You probably know by now that the elemental army—led by Lord Vak—has already surrendered to my counterpart's army. As we speak, he's moving his forces toward Mt. Tutor." She paused. "I assume Radrine told you this? Before you killed her?"

"Yes." In reality, Radrine had told her Lord Vak was *close* to surrender, but Ali sensed truth in her sister's words. For now, the war in the green world was finished, and the good guys had lost. Sheri continued.

"Vak leads his army toward Tutor as a prelude to invading the Earth. That invasion can be neat and clean—relatively speaking—or it can be very messy. It all depends on what the two of us decide—right now."

Ali shook her head. "Humanity will fight any type of invasion—to the bitter end. They'll use every weapon they have to drive off the elementals. It's human nature—you should know that by now, having lived as one for so long."

Sheri nodded. "True, Geea. But if you give me the Yanti, and unlock its power, the battle need not go on for weeks, or months, and ruin most of the Earth. In particular, nuclear weapons need not be used. The atmosphere doesn't have to be poisoned with radiation. With the Yanti, I'll be able to stop any missiles before they reach their targets."

Ali snorted. "What you want is what Lord Vak demanded at the start. That I help the elementals take over the Earth."

"No. I differ from Vak in that I desire balance. I intend to leave half of humanity alive, half the elementals. There is no need for total genocide." Sheri added, "But I must be free to wield the Yanti, as I please, not you."

"Because you don't trust me?"

"Trust! For now, time has halted, but it could be stopped forever, and we could talk forever, and still neither of us would trust each other. Nothing is going to stop the invasion. However, if we work together, we can lessen the destruction."

"You act like you want to help? *You're* the one causing the whole mess!"

Sheri did not answer, just stared at her.

Ali growled. "Half the world dead? I can't accept that."

"Come Tuesday you will." Sheri paused. "Where is the compassion Geea is so famous for? Let the war end quickly, and with the least loss of life. That's best deal you can get at this point."

"So this is just a deal to you?" Ali sneered.

"Yes. That's exactly what it is."

"The way you describe it, the green world is to be left empty?"

Sheri shrugged. "I have plans for it."

"Such as?"

With contempt: "You wouldn't understand."

"At least tell me why you feel this war is necessary."

"I can't do that without revealing certain long-range goals we . . . I have."

We? Did Sheri have a partner? The woman was crafty—the slip might have been intentional. But perhaps she did have a partner, maybe even a *superior.* Ali had never considered the possibility before. Since swallowing an overdose of the fairy stardust atop the kloudar, and reclaiming many of her memories, Ali had seen her sister as someone who was desperate to rule, to have absolute control. The revelation of a *we*—if true—might alter her view of her sister, make her rethink much of what Hector had said about Lucy Pillar.

Ali acted like she had not noticed the slip. She gestured to the frozen clock. "It seems to me you have enough resources to do the job without my help. Why do you need the Yanti?"

Sheri was nonchalant. "It's a powerful tool. Besides, it should have been mine. You must recall—before you brainwashed him with your constant whining—that Father was going to give it to me. You know as well as I do that it's wasted in your hands." She paused, shrugged. "You don't even know how to use it as a weapon."

Ali bluffed. "Sure of that? How do you think Radrine died?"

Sheri was not easy to bluff. Again, she just stared.

Ali continued. "What if I do decide to use it as a weapon, and fight on humanity's side? I forced Lord Vak to retreat before. I can always force him back again."

"Ha! Even if you somehow discovered how to reverse the Yanti and invoke the violet ray—which you can't do, not without my help—it'll make no difference. You were always a poor leader because you could not bear to make strong decisions. Admit it, you'll never unleash the violet ray and risk killing millions of fairies, dwarves, leprechauns, and elves—because they've chosen to fight for Vak. You won't go against him. The elven king used to be the father of your lover, one of your best friends." Sheri shook her head. "You've no choice, Geea. You have to accept my offer."

"Just accept three billion deaths?"

"There're too many people in this world as it is."

"So you give Africa, Australia, and Asia to the elementals? The rest to humanity?"

Sheri smiled. "Something like that."

"You're lying. You keep bringing up memories of the green world, and yes, there is one thing I remember about Doren. She lied whenever it suited her."

Sheri lost her smile, spoke in a deadly tone. "I warned you not to anger me."

"Oh, I tremble in my shoes. What are you going to do, *mark* me like you did our mother?"

Sheri did not reply, but lowered her head.

Ali pressed on. "How did the fairy part of you feel? Putting your filthy thumb on her forehead, obliterating the last drop of who she was? Tell me, I really want to know, did you enjoy it?"

There was a long silence, but since time had appeared to have stopped, perhaps it was short. Yet it was dark inside the room, and in the darkness, Ali knew she had hit a button in her enemy. A painful button.

Finally, Sheri cleared her throat, spoke.

"We're here to discuss the fate of this world. Who's going to live. Who's going to die. You don't trust me, I accept that. You've already pointed out how I know of the link between humanity and elementals. Why would I wipe out one side, over the other? Logically, it makes no sense."

Reluctantly, Ali let the question of their mother go. "Nor does it make sense to drive the elementals from their rightful dimension. You have to explain why you're trying to do that."

Sheri spoke with sudden impatience. "I did. I tried."

"When?"

"Before."

Ali was suddenly alert. Sheri referred to their previous life together, as fairies. "When?" she repeated.

"When I invited you and Jira to the Isle of Greesh."

The remark shook Ali. Unfortunately, her memories of the Isle of Greesh were sketchy. She'd had a horrific nightmare during her recent sojourn in the green world—while sleeping in Queen Geea's bed, in the Crystal Palace at the center of Uleestar—about the island. In the dream, she had been trying to stop Jira from entering an archaeological site Doren had insisted they see.

The place had terrified her. For seemingly no reason.

Sheri sensed her confusion, continued, "You spent only a short time on the island. If I recall, it scared you, and had a devastating effect on Jira." She casually added, "A pity the place upset him so much. Honestly, I never saw that kind of reaction before. The way he killed himself, I suppose he just didn't have the stomach for—how should I put it?—major revelations."

Ali sucked in an involuntary breath, felt a stab of pain in her heart that momentarily caused the Yanti to go cold. Ali had remembered that the archeological site on the Isle of Greesh had driven Jira insane. But she had *not* recalled him committing suicide . . .

Suddenly it all came back to her. The bloody images— bathed in the blue light of the elemental kingdom's stationary moon, Anglar—roared in her head. Jira stumbling to the edge of the balcony in Lord Vak's castle. Screaming in a language neither of them had been taught. Her trying to stop him, to hold him . . .

Then, his unexpected jump, that long deadly leap, that she had not been able to stop, despite a mighty leap of her own. She could fly, he could not, and she had flown after him faster than she had ever flown before. Yet she'd been unable to prevent his head from smashing the boulders that rimmed the river, Tior, which ran beside Thorath, the elves' mighty fortress.

Jira had died there, in her arms, at the foot of Lord Vak's castle.

His last words had been very odd.

"Net . . . The . . . Enter."

At least, that's what she thought he said.

Lord Vak had come upon them minutes later. Just stood behind them.

Jira had been his only son.

How cruel it was of her sister to make light of such a matter. Ali felt the same bitterness she had experienced when Steve had died. Yet she hid her pain, not wanting to give Sheri the satisfaction. She mimicked Sheri's casual tone as she changed the topic.

"Why did you give me Nira?" she asked.

Sheri snickered. "She makes a good little spy."

"More lies. You know I won't expose her to anything I don't want you to see or hear." Ali paused. "Know who's watching her now?"

Sheri was silent a moment, her attention inward, then she scowled, spoke in an annoyed tone. "Why did you call him?"

"Why not? He's her father, isn't he?"

Sheri's turn to suck in an agonizing breath. Ali had scored a bull's-eye, and had her theory finally confirmed—again. From the beginning, after viewing Cindy's memories of her and Steve's visits to Toule, the truth should have been obvious. First there had been the librarian's remarks about Lucy Pillar: how bright and brilliant the girl had been; how devoted she had been to Hector, even after he had caused the accident that had cost her most of her skin. Then Hector had pointed out how Lucy had taken him deep inside the power plant, just before it blew, to a spot that just happened to be, miraculously, shielded from the blast.

The conclusion was clear. Lucy had taken him there because she knew the blast was imminent. She'd wanted to protect Hector, to have him survive the explosion, even after all he had done to her.

When Steve and Cindy had spoken to Hector, the contractor's devotion to Lucy had shone brightly. After the car accident, Lucy had been transformed into a mass of scar tissue. Yet he had stood by her, had tried desperately to make their relationship work.

How many eighteen-year-old boys would do that? Ali had no bias against young males, yet she knew the answer to her question was—one in a thousand.

Hector had been that one in a thousand.

The thousand scars had not mattered to him.

He had truly loved Lucy. And she had loved him.

Yet, when it came to Sheri, he had made that strange remark.

"I try to stay away from that woman."

She frightened him. Why? Something had happened between the two of them that had somehow slipped his conscious mind—or else been purposely erased—that caused his anxiety. Ali had a pretty good idea what it was.

An hour ago, when Ali had finally met Hector, and sat across from him at her own kitchen table—Nira sitting in his lap—she had known for a fact that her theory was true. The similarities in their faces had been undeniable.

Hector *was* Nira's father. The elusive Mr. Smith.

He was the child's father, and it was clear he did not know it. Like most truly honest people, he was easy for Ali to read. Hector sincerely believed that thirteen years ago Lucy had perished in the power plant explosion. Certainly, he did not know that Lucy Pillar and Sheri Smith were one and the same person. It was equally clear that he had no memory of ever having been intimate with the woman. He hated her!

So what had happened?

The witch had seduced him. Then cast a forgetting spell on him.

That part was easy. The hard part was . . .

Why had she done so? Was it because she still loved him?

Was the Shaktra even capable of such an emotion?

Ali considered all of this as she watched Sheri strive to regain her composure. The woman was so shaken by Ali's last remark, she did not even bother to flash a fake smile. At last, Ali knew she had found the monster's Achilles' heel.

But perhaps that was wishful thinking. When Sheri finally did answer, she was all business. She held Ali's eye as she spoke.

"You go too far with your insolence. I've made you a reasonable offer, that will allow a large portion of the beings on both sides of the war to survive, and you turn me down. Fine, Geea, let the missiles soar through the sky. Let the nuclear mushroom clouds glow over every major city on Earth. Let Vak—and the weapons I'll provide him with—ruin this lovely planet. It doesn't matter—the end result will be the same to me. It is just that so much suffering could be avoided if you would cooperate." She added, "It will be on your head."

Ali felt the need to gamble. "So you don't want Hector and Nira to die?"

Sheri pounded the table. "They're irrelevant! You'll not speak of them again in my presence!"

Ali stood, letting her chair fall to the floor at her back. Striding halfway around the table, she glared down at the woman, and pointed a bitter finger at her.

"Let us talk about you then! Let us go back to the question you refused to answer at the start! How did you turn into such a monster? In the green world I knew an older sister who was disappointed she was not named queen of the fairies—*disappointed* is all. She was not ready to harm a soul to gain the title. But then she runs off to the Isle of Greesh, where our father works but soon disappears, and where my boyfriend is fatally wounded. Then, years later, I have a monster called the Shaktra knocking at my door! I don't know what it is but it's attacking Uleestar! And the rest of the elemental kingdom! Then, in the yellow world, this world we call Earth, fourteen years ago, we have a teenage girl named Lucy Pillar, whom everyone calls a saint, who gets in a car accident, and ends up horribly burned. Yet this same Lucy Pillar has a boyfriend who still loves her, and who, from all outward appearances—so it seems—still loves him. His name is Hector by the way. Hector! Remember that name. Because thirteen years ago, she hides this same Hector in a part of a power plant that she blows up. Yes! She's the one who blew it up! She's the one who killed hundreds of innocent people! And for what reason? Not to hurt Hector, he was one of the few people to survive the explosion. So why did she do it? God help me, Doren, I'll not bargain with you until you answer these questions! You'll not get the

Yanti from me. You'll get only my scorn, and I swear to you, on everything that's sacred to me, that I'll use the last shred of power at my disposal to destroy you! So answer me now! Why did the fairy princess change into the Shaktra? Why did good-hearted Lucy Pillar transform into the wicked Sheri Smith?"

Another long silence ensued. There was so much pain in it that it seemed as if the haunting purple light that filled the room and made the world outside stand frozen really was fed by their blood. Ali felt a vein pound in her head, one that threatened to burst, and the coldness she suddenly experienced in her heart seemed to belong to another world; to another *place,* perhaps, that was not a world at all, just an ancient hole in the fabric of space from which evil could emerge into their galaxy.

What had her father and Doren found on the Isle of Greesh? All she could recall was that he had said it was not of this world. Yet somehow it was *related* to Earth. Yes, those were his words.

So much, Ali wanted to ask her sister . . .

Where is our father? Is he alive? In which world?

Sheri looked up at her as she answered, and her voice came out remarkably soft, almost gentle. "You do not know what it is like to burn. Worse, you do not know what it is like to see someone . . . someone you . . . *know* . . . burn." She paused and lowered her head, and added in a whisper, "I don't have to answer your questions."

Ali felt as if her sister was trying tell her something profound. It was not so much the woman's words, but her tone. For the first time since entering the room, Sheri acted human. Ali felt her knees weaken, sat on a chair beside her. Almost, she reached out to touch her . . .

Then Sheri caught her eye, said, "No."

Ali spoke anxiously. "But I *can* heal you."

93

Sheri shook her head. "No."

"I can. You need not wear that silly mask. I've healed many, in this world and the green world. You know that. I can take away your pain."

Her bitterness returned with a vengeance. "You think it's so easy. Put your hands on my heart and head. Let the Yanti warm. Then I'll be whole again, and everything I've gone through will be forgotten. Why, I might even bow at your feet and thank you." She stopped and shook her head. "You know nothing."

Despite herself, Ali heard truth in the words. She spoke carefully.

"Tell me what I need to know. Tell me what happened to you."

It was Sheri's turn to stand, to glare down at her. "You have the nerve to ask! You who have never really suffered a day in all your lives! A pity Jira could only die once on you! Had he died a thousand times, then maybe I would consider answering you. But you, Queen Geea, you disgust me, with your compassion and your empathy. It's born of ignorance and conceit. It's no more real than your title. Again, I say it, you know nothing of what's real in this universe, and because of your ignorance, and your mockery of me, this world is going to burn. And all the souls in it, be they human or elemental, are going to burn with it. And it's going to be your name, not mine, that they curse as they die!"

Sheri suddenly raised her arms above her head and clapped her hands. A light flashed, but it was unlike the light that had shone when the wizard had vanished from the barber shop. This light had *no* color, and although that seemed impossible, it was a fact. Like the fear in her heart, the light appeared to emerge from no set place or time. Out of the void it came. It was just there, and it *hurt,* so deeply, and in so many ways.

The purple glow faded.

The second hand on the clock began to move.

Slowly, around the table, people began to raise their heads, and glance sheepishly at one another, as if embarrassed to let it be known that they had accidentally dozed off. No one wanted to say they had fallen asleep. For that matter, no one knew what to say, not even Judge Lincoln, who rubbed his sore head. So Sheri Smith said it for all of them, as she whirled and turned toward the door.

"These proceedings bore me, I'm leaving," she snapped.

With that, Sheri was out the door. Gone.

CHAPTER

5

With the main party to the discussions gone, Judge Lincoln had no choice but to halt the meeting, even though Officer Garten pushed him to continue. Yet even he did so without passion. He was like everyone else: dazed and confused. When Judge Lincoln called for another meeting in four days, everyone nodded as if that would be a good idea, and got up and left the room.

Even Cindy was quick to leave with her parents. She hardly glanced at Ali. The only exception was Karl's parents. They glared at her with overwhelming hatred before departing. She ignored them, and yet, it broke her heart to see Steve's mother weep as she left the police station with her husband. Why didn't they want to talk to her at least? What had they been told?

The only one who remained behind with her was Mike Havor. He stood as the room emptied, but did not seem to know where the door was. Without asking for help, his dark glasses searched aimlessly. Instinctively, Ali reached out and took his hand.

Such a warm hand, so nice to touch. "I guess the meeting's over," she said.

He forced a smile, although he was clearly bewildered. "Did I miss something? What was decided?" he asked.

"Nothing. You didn't miss a thing."

Had she been able to drive, she would have offered to give him a ride. She felt the need to help him, and it seemed the emotion was mutual. As they stepped outside, and walked in the general direction of the bus stop—where she assumed he would catch a ride home—he suddenly halted and took out a business card and handed it to her.

"Ali, I need to talk to you about certain things that have been going on at work," he said. "But I can't talk now, nor here. Could you call me later tonight? The bottom number on that card is my cell. I carry it with me twenty-four hours a day."

Ali studied the card. It carried the Omega business logo— three red wavy lines. Otherwise, there was nothing special about it. She put it in her pocket. "I'll get you this evening," she said.

"Thank you." He added, "That was an odd meeting, wouldn't you agree?"

Ali nodded. "It was a first for me."

He sniffed, turned his head in the direction of the ocean, which was barely visible between a row of old buildings. "Is the water near? I would so much like to walk beside the sea."

"It's two blocks off to your left. I can take you there if you like."

He pulled his cane from his coat. "No need. Like I told you before, I'm not as helpless as I appear. I've been to Breakwater before. I'll find my way around, once I get my bearings."

"Are you sure you don't want to talk now?" she asked.

His face darkened, then he shook his head. "Later would be better."

Guilt tugged at her chest as she watched him slowly walk

across the fortunately empty street. She studied her feelings and could not understand their source. Of course, she had lied to him when she had met him, and she was leaving him to fend for himself in a town that was not his own. But it seemed he wanted it that way.

No, there was no reason for guilt when it came to Mike Havor. He could take care of himself. But she was anxious to hear what he had to say. Working with Sheri, he must know a great deal about the woman . . . even if he did not know she was a monster.

Ali turned and walked home.

When she reached her place, Hector and Nira were playing catch on the front lawn with a beach ball. It was the first truly coordinated activity Ali had seen Nira display, and she wondered aloud at it. Hector nodded.

"When Patricia and I watched her together, we were never able to get her to play ball." He smiled at Ali. "You and your pal are good for her."

"You mean Cindy."

"Yes, Cindy." He paused as he caught the ball Nira had just tossed him, lowered his voice. "So it's true—Steve's really dead?"

"Yes."

"It's hard to believe."

Feeling depressed, Ali sat on her porch steps. "We grew up together. He taught me how to ride a bike. And I taught him how to tie his shoes. We were like a team." She wiped at her eyes. "It still hasn't sunk in yet."

Hector set down the ball and came and sat beside her on the porch. Simply gesturing to Nira, the little girl did likewise. The way she obeyed him, it was as if a part of her knew of her connection to Hector. But how, Ali asked herself, was she to explain it?

"I'm so sorry," he said, with feeling.

"Thanks," she whispered.

He was a handsome man. Cindy had said he looked like a contractor; that was true. He had the broad shoulders, the tan muscles from working outside. His hair was thick, dirty blond, unkempt. His deep blue eyes were not merely attractive, but keen. He was intelligent, Ali sensed, and liked to keep his own counsel. Cindy had spoken of his frankness, though; how he had grown impatient with her and Steve when he felt they were not being totally straight with him.

Down the street, Ali could see her father's rig approaching. Only then did she recall his pickup truck was still parked halfway up the mountain. He would want to know where it was. He would want to know a million things. So would Hector, if she opened her mouth. Yet she felt, finally, that they both deserved the truth. They were good men, and she sensed that she was going to need their help in the days to come.

Ali nodded in the direction of the truck. "That's my dad. Jason Warner."

Hector went to stand. "I should be on my way. I have a lot to do back in Toule. Working on a huge project."

Ali clasped his hand, gently pulled him back down.

"You're not going to work today," she said.

He blinked. "Excuse me?"

Ali reached over, hugged Nira. "This girl sitting here. This beautiful little girl. She's your daughter."

Hector looked at her as if she were mad. "Why do you say that?"

"Look at her. Look at her closely. Then think of the face you see each morning in the mirror."

Hector grew stern, went to snap at her, but he could not help but look. And Nira, for her part, stared at him. The same mysterious way the little girl was drawn to Cindy, she was drawn to this man.

"It's impossible," Hector whispered.

"I know you see the resemblance."

"No," he protested.

Ali nodded. "Sure you do, but don't worry. In a few minutes, after my dad gets here and finishes yelling at me, I'm going to show you *several* impossible things." She paused. "Would you like to stay and see what they are?"

He could not stop staring at Nira. "But I was never with that woman!"

Ali rubbed Nira's head, stood to greet her approaching father. "Not that you remember," she said.

Her prediction proved true. As soon as he exited his truck, without barely saying hello to Hector or looking at Nira, he grabbed her by the arm and took her inside and launched into a tirade about how irresponsible she had been lately. Ali let him go on for a while. Out the front door, she could see Hector and Nira playing catch again. The child almost looked happy; it brought a smile to Ali's lips. Unfortunately, she smiled just as her dad was reaching full steam.

"So you're laughing at me now!" he shouted.

"No," Ali said, and reached for his hand, and for the power of her voice, wanting to use a morsel of it to help calm him down. "The last thing I'd ever do is laugh at you. But you have to stop yelling at me so I can talk. Here, sit on the couch, I'll sit beside you. And I promise, I'll tell you everything you want to know."

He sat reluctantly. Like Hector, he was an attractive man, but he was older, close to forty, more roughly hewn. His jaw was hard, firm; and his hair was dark, and presently cut short. That was her dad; he would not cut it for six months, then shave it all off like he didn't care. He was not vain, he seldom used a mirror. But when her mother had been alive, his eyes had seldom looked anywhere but at her. No man had ever loved a woman more, and when she had died—at least when he thought she had died—a part of him had closed down and never reopened.

Ali knew it was her task, right now, to reach that part of him. To heal it, if that was possible. She watched as he glanced out the window.

"Where's my truck? Who are those people?" he asked.

"Your truck is fine. I had to take it for a short ride."

"What? You *drove* my truck? You're thirteen!"

Ali kept her voice calm. "Don't worry, I drive quite nicely. And those people out there are my friends. They're father and daughter." She added, "Only he just found out a minute ago that the girl's his daughter."

Her father was way beyond confused. "You told him, I suppose."

"Yes."

Her father nodded. "He didn't know but you knew?"

"Yes."

"Ali . . ."

"Stop, Dad. My turn to talk, remember? I told you, I'm going to answer your questions. But before I do, I'm going to ask you a question. And I need you to think real hard before answering it. Ready?"

He did not look ready but nodded impatiently. She continued.

"Since the day I was born, do you remember anything odd about me? Anything that made you stop and ask yourself the question—is my daughter different than normal girls?" Ali quickly held up her hand. "Don't snap at me. Don't give a flippant answer. What I am asking—it's important. Just sit and think about it for a minute."

He stared at her. A faint sign of fear touched his face. "Why?" he asked.

"Because what I'm going to tell you in a few minutes, what I'm going to show you, is going to shake you to your core. You'll be better able to accept it if you know it in your heart, before I explain it to you."

He shook his head. "I don't know what you're asking, Ali."

"Just consider my question. That's all."

He went to speak, then stopped, stopped altogether; his talking, his fidgeting. An entire minute went by, and then he sighed. When he spoke next, it was in a soft voice.

"I never did understand how your hair changed into the same color as your mother's. A few weeks ago, after you guys went up on the mountain."

Ali nodded. "Go on."

"No, wait. On the phone, you said that Steve was dead. Is that true?"

"Yes."

"How did he die?"

"He was murdered. So was . . . Let's not go there, not yet. Stay with the question. Was there anything about me, as I was growing up, that made you think I was unusual?"

Again, he paused. "I didn't understand . . . when you first spoke."

"You mean, you couldn't understand what I was saying?"

"No. I was shocked you were talking at all. Didn't your mother ever tell you?"

"No. What?"

"You were six months old, and all of a sudden, you were

talking in full sentences. Your mom didn't know, but I took you to a child psychologist to be tested."

"Why didn't you tell Mom?"

"Because it was like she wanted to hide the fact."

Ali nodded to herself. That made sense. Knowing she was a fairy, her mother would not have wanted to draw attention to her.

"What did the psychologist say?" she asked.

"You had an IQ off the charts. He was unable to measure it, and not just because you were so young. He said he had never seen anyone like you before. He asked if he could write a paper on you, get it published. I got you out of there real quick."

"Did you notice anything else unusual about me?"

This time her father smiled. "Well, you always gave great neck rubs. Even since you were a tiny girl, and had no strength in your hands, you just had to rub the back of my neck and head when I came in from a long trip and I would feel instantly better."

"Why do you think?"

"Oh, I'm sure it's because I was always so happy to see you."

Ali shook her head. "It's not that."

"What is it then?"

"You remember when Ted Wilson got hurt up in the forest? All the doctors said he was going to die?"

"Yes. He's fine now, isn't he?"

"Yes."

"I always told you the doctors at Breakwater Memorial were quacks."

"The doctors were not wrong about his prognosis. Ted was going to die." She added, "But I healed him."

Her father did a double take. "Huh?"

"I healed him. Just as I would heal you of your fatigue and your stress when you would come home. But don't stop, Dad, go on. I sense there's something else you're not telling me."

"You *sense?* Ali . . ."

"Tell me what it is. What made you think I wasn't a normal girl?"

This time he had to sit back on the couch. Many emotions played over his face: fear, confusion, and yes, wonder. He frowned as he recalled whatever it was, but he also smiled briefly.

"I remember the fish loved you," he said.

"Huh?"

"When you were two, I took you out fishing on a small boat. Your mother didn't want you to go, but it was a calm day, and the water was flat as a lake. We just paddled out a mile or so, and I threw my line overboard and sat there. Then you began to hum this melody—I had never heard it before—and in a few minutes the boat was surrounded by fish. They were mostly on your side of the boat. When you leaned over the side to look at them, with me holding onto your legs, they seemed to try to stick their heads out of the water so they could see you—in person." He added, "I told your mom about that one. She just laughed."

"Did she ever let you take me fishing with you again?"

He frowned. "No, as a matter of fact she didn't. I wonder why."

"I know why. She didn't want to call attention to me."

"What do you mean?"

"From the time I was born, Mom knew who I was."

He stopped frowning, stared at her, the fear returning. "Of course she knew who you were. Your mother's gone, but you're . . . Ali, you're our daughter."

She nodded. "True. I'm your daughter. But I'm also something else."

"What?"

Ali stood. "It's better if you see than if I try to explain."

Her father also stood, reluctantly. "See what?"

"I'm going to show you and Hector something. In the backyard. But not Nira, the little girl. I'm going to lock her in my room for a few minutes, and close the blinds."

"She's just a little girl. Won't she get scared?"

Ali headed for the front door. "She's autistic, or rather, she appears autistic. She won't understand what's happening. She'll sit quietly in my room. At her own house, her mother kept her locked away most of the time. Nira is used to it, trust me, she won't get upset."

In minutes, Ali had Nira cloistered away, and Hector and her father standing in the middle of her backyard. They shook hands and introduced themselves to each other, but their eyes were on her. Ali felt a pang for Hector then. At least with her dad, she had given him warning that something odd was about to happen. But with the contractor . . . she had already blown his mind once today by saying he was the father of a child he couldn't recall having . . .

The backyard was isolated. Behind them were trees, so many trees, which stretched for miles and miles, until they eventually thinned and then vanished near the top of Pete's Peak. On the south side of the backyard was a low hill no one could see over. North were two houses, but they were distant, and set at such an angle to her own house that someone would have to stare out the window at just the right angle and instant to see the miracle she was about perform.

Yet she disliked the word *miracle*—the superiority it implied. Her gifts were natural. Eventually, she knew, as evolution automatically moved everyone forward, they too would be able to work wondrous feats.

Ali disliked having to resort to such a gross display of power to convince Hector and her father who she was. The problem was time—they didn't have much. Sheri was not bluffing. The invasion was near. She needed their help to stop it. Indeed, she had a sneaky suspicion that one of them was the key to preventing the horror that was about to descend on Earth.

"Ali . . ." her father went to speak.

"Keep your eyes open and watch." Ali closed her own eyes as she spoke, but she did not need her sight to know her green field was swelling in power. The luminous transparent egg had already begun to expand from her head, and from beneath her feet, as it slowly raised her from the grass and into the air. Ali let herself rise up about ten feet before she opened her eyes, and what she saw in that instant was wonderful—more than she could possibly have hoped for.

Hector's mouth had dropped open in awe.

He was stone. He was a statue. He was in shock.

However, her father was smiling. There was a tear in his eye, but he was nodding his head, as if he had known all along. Better, he was so close to laughing that she had to laugh; then he had to join her, and soon she was tumbling in the air, doing cartwheels, out of control, having fun, her long red hair flying like a wizard's wand. For a few minutes, at least, it was like when she had first returned from the mountain after discovering that she was a fairy. When she had stroked his head and promised him that everything was going to be all right.

One miracle aside, it took hours of discussion to make clear to her new partners how complex the problem was that faced humanity. Her demonstration had opened up for them a completely new portion of the universe. Their very consciousness was having to expand to include *her*. It went back to the analogy Nemi had used when she had met him in the hollowed-out redwood. The creation was like a TV set. So many channels could be viewed on one screen. And Hector and her father had been sitting on a couch all their lives, watching a single repetitive program, unaware that they held a remote that could be used to change the channels to other shows. Her brief flight had almost shattered their TV sets, but fortunately they were intelligent men, and imaginative. More important, they were brave souls.

Yet that did not mean they did not want answers.

Ali knew it could take days to give them every one they asked for.

Finally, she had to stand and raise a hand and say as much.

"The elementals are coming as we talk," she said. "I cannot stay here and allow that to happen. I have to get back to my allies in the green world. But before I leave, I have to develop a plan to stop the invasion. To do that I need more information."

"Information about what?" her father asked.

"It's not as though we know many other fairies," Hector added.

Ali turned to Hector. "You know Sheri Smith. You grew up in Toule—you must have friends who work at Omega Overtures."

He nodded. "One of my best friends works at the firm. Why?"

"I need a copy of their new game. It hasn't been released yet. It's called Armageddon. I need it immediately."

"Why?" Hector asked.

"Sheri Smith built this successful software firm for a purpose.

She's using it somehow—perhaps to prepare the world for this invasion. I've studied her first huge seller, Omega Overlord, and it deals with the end of the world. It has sold about forty million copies. It's played all over the world. In it, Earth has been poisoned by a nuclear holocaust, and it's currently being overrun with evil cyborgs. But it has magical creatures in it as well. Ones that resemble . . ."

Hector raised a hand. "I've played it for hundreds of hours. The game does resemble the scenario you've laid out for her invasion. At the same time, that begs the question. Why would she go out of her way to make public her strategy to wreak havoc with the world?"

Ali paused. "I don't know."

Her father broke in. "You must have some ideas."

"I'm saying the games serve a purpose besides the obvious. She did not create the company to make money. I could make all the money I wanted—if I put my mind to it."

Hector and her dad exchanged looks. "Jason, I wish I had a daughter like yours," Hector said.

"You forget what I said," Ali told him. "Nira's been marked. She's under a spell. But when I saw her in the elemental world, I saw a being of immense power and wisdom. I think freeing Nira of her spell is one of the keys to stopping this invasion."

"Since time is short, perhaps we should focus on that," her father said.

"She's just a child, what could she do?" Hector protested.

"None of us know what she can and cannot do," Ali said. "Only that Sheri must have marked her at such a young age because she was afraid of her. In fact, I think that's the only way she was able to mark her—when Nira was real tiny. Otherwise, I think Nira would have been immune to her mother's power."

"Why did she even have a child at all?" Hector asked, a touchy spot with him.

"I don't know," Ali said.

"Since your return from the other dimension, have you tried removing the spell?" her father asked.

"Yes. I got nowhere. But we've strayed from the immediate point. I need a copy of Armageddon. Sheri poured a ton of effort into it, even though she knew this invasion was coming. From the start, I think she planned to release it once the invasion began."

"That's a crazy idea," her dad said.

Hector nodded. "I'm afraid I must agree with your dad, Ali. Say the world is being overrun with elementals. No one's going to stop and sit down and play a video game."

Ali paused. It *was* a dumb idea. She wasn't even sure why she had said it. The words had just sort of popped out of her mouth. Nevertheless, she *sensed* truth in them.

"I can't argue the point. I can only repeat what I have said. That woman did not make that game for her own amusement. There is a deep purpose behind it." Ali paused. "When we spoke at the police station, she hinted that she might have a partner."

"Who do you think it is?"

Ali hesitated. "At first I thought it might be this blind man who works at her firm, Mike Havor. But he's too kind and gentle. I know he's not faking that. I can sense when human beings speak the truth."

Her dad chuckled, along with Hector. "Are we just *human beings* now?"

Ali blushed. "That's been a thorn in my side since I discovered my powers. Why Cindy and Steve . . . they would." Ali felt a sudden lump in her throat, had to force herself to finish.

"They'd make fun of me, you know. That they were my minions, and I was their queen. I tried to play it down, but it was hard on all of us. I hope that doesn't happen with us three. But having power *does* separate me—anyone—from people. Even when I go out of my way to stop it from happening."

Seeing she was getting emotional, her father gave her a hug. "Nothing will ever separate you from me," he whispered in her ear.

She hugged him in return. "It never came between you and Mom."

He drew back at the remark. "Ali, that's what I really need to talk to you about. In this other world . . ."

She put her palm on his chest, caught his eye. "Later, Dad, I promise."

Hector moved to stand. "I can leave the room if you want?"

Ali nodded. "Get that friend who works at Omega and get that game."

Hector was confused. "But this Mike Havor you were telling us about. Why can't he get you a copy? It sounds like you trust him."

"I do trust him, but he's worked for Sheri Smith a long time. There's got to be deep loyalty there. He asked me to call him tonight, and I'm going to do so. But I don't want him to know of my interest in the game. I have to be careful. Who knows what he might tell his boss."

Hector nodded. "That friend I mentioned, with one call, she'll be able to get me a copy. I'll tell her to keep it between us."

"You trust this person completely?" Ali asked.

Hector didn't hesitate. "Yes." Turning toward the door, he suddenly stopped. "Shouldn't I take Nira with me?"

Ali shook her head. "I didn't tell you this but—the reason I have her in the other room watching TV—Sheri might be able to see and hear through her eyes and ears."

"What?" they both said at once.

Ali was grim. "Something I discovered in the green world. When we move Nira—and we'll have to do that soon—we have to blindfold her. Even go so far as to put wax in her ears."

"I don't want to do that," Hector said, an edge in his voice.

"In the other world, I had to do it to someone I loved," Ali said. "It's unpleasant, but it doesn't have to be for long. If Nira's put up in a hotel room, where the windows have been sealed, she can eat and watch TV and be as happy as she has been most of her life." She added, "Especially if Cindy is around."

"What's her connection to Cindy?" Hector asked.

"I don't know," Ali said. "But it's real."

Hector left, and when he was gone, Ali and her father sat a long time in silence across from each other. Ali kept her gaze down, thinking about the trials that awaited her in the elemental world. The Shaktra—the fairy half—would have the entrance to Mt. Tutor guarded. It might be impossible to even get to her allies in the north, never mind to Lord Vak and his army. Before she tried passing through the green door in the mountain, she would require *multiple* plans.

She could feel her father's eyes on her, glanced up.

She smiled. "What are you thinking?"

He smiled back. "So you can't read minds? I'm surprised."

"I can sense emotions. But even if I could read minds, I would not read yours without your permission."

"All right then, I'll tell you what I'm thinking. Your argument with Hector about the game was weak. It was based on the assumption Sheri Smith would *not* have done something for *nothing*. For all you know, her firm could have been nothing more than mere camouflage. True?"

"Yes."

"Then why are you so desperate to get the game?"

"It was something I noticed when I was reviewing Cindy's memories of her first meeting with Hector. Before the car crash that burned Lucy, he said he was drinking beer and playing an Internet game with buddies of his on the other side of the country. Then, when he was asked about the accident—by Steve and the police—he said he couldn't remember exactly what happened."

"Which means he was drunk when he crashed."

"Maybe. But this accident happened over thirteen years ago. Back then, there were *no* games on the Internet where people from different parts of the country could join together and play. The technology hadn't been invented yet. Still, Hector played such a game, and immediately after doing so, he swerved off the road for no reason, hit a tree, was thrown clear, while the love of his life was burned to a crisp." She paused. "I find it too coincidental."

"Because you think her severe burns set her down the dark path?"

"Yes."

"Why didn't you share this with Hector?"

"I feared it would add to his guilt about what happened to Lucy. Best he see it as an accident, at least for now, nothing more. Besides, he's still having trouble swallowing the fact that he's Nira's father."

"I talked to him in private, when you were in the bathroom. I'm not sure he has accepted that yet."

Ali waved a hand. "Doesn't matter. He loves her, he'll do anything to protect her. In time, the truth will become clear to him."

"You surprised me, when the three of us were talking earlier, you said you were returning to the green world."

"I told you, my work there is not finished," Ali said.

"But do you have to go so soon?" When she didn't immediately answer, he added, "What if you die there? I would never know."

She forced a laugh. "These days, Dad, I'm not so easy to kill."

"Nor is your enemy. I must be frank, Ali. Today you've blown my mind so far out of my skull, I don't know where it's going to land. But I take it all in—somehow, I imagine—because a part of me knew it all along. You were right to prod my memory. I always knew you were not a normal girl. But even with all these incredible powers you possess, you're still my daughter and I can read you pretty well. You know if you go back to the green world, there's a good chance you won't return. Why?"

She hesitated. "It deals with the Isle of Greesh."

"What's that?"

"An island that lies off the west coast of the elemental mainland. The Shaktra emerged from that isle, and I feel I must go back there to understand how it all began. Unless I can gain that understanding, I see no way of stopping this war."

"The way you talk about the island, it frightens you."

"Yes. In my last life, I visited there."

"What happened?"

Ali lowered her head, thinking of Jira. "Something terrible."

"Then you mustn't go back. Surely there is someone else who can go."

She sighed. "There's no one. The isle is cloaked in evil. Who could I send there in my place? Who could survive?"

"But what good will it do anyone if you go there and die?"

"I don't think whatever is on the island wants to kill me."

"No?"

Ali considered. "I think it wants me to join it."

"But you have no idea what *it* is?"

"None."

"You've been patient with Hector and me to answer so many questions. But you know I need to ask about your mother. You say that it's the fairy belief that our souls migrate from Earth to the green world—back and forth—from one life to the next. If that's the case, since your mother is dead in this world, she must be alive in the green world." He paused. "Did you see her?"

Ali hesitated a long time. "I spent time with her. There, her name's Amma."

Her father sighed. No, it was more a groan of relief so painful it was hard to hear. Ironically, the worst part was the hope she heard in it. He had to strain to speak. "What was she like?" he asked.

"The same. She was the same. Oh, I mean, as a high fairy, she knew more than she knew as a human. She was very powerful. But she was Mom."

"The accident that killed her? Was it an accident?"

"No."

He was a long time absorbing the information.

"Was Karl Tanner behind it?"

His insight surprised her. "Yes," she said.

"Was he responsible for what happened to Steve?"

"Yes."

"Will either of them . . . ever be found?"

Ali hesitated. "No."

He'd just asked if she had murdered a person, and she had confessed to committing the crime, and yet he did not pursue it because there was something much bigger on his mind. Yes, bigger than murder, and Ali knew what it was.

"Is there any way for me to see your mother?" he asked.

"No."

"Could I talk to her?"

"No."

A note of desperation entered his voice. "You said this boy, Ra, was able to enter the green world. How come I can't do the same?"

The curious thing was, she did not know the answer to his question. It was common knowledge among fairies that humans could not survive the high vibrations of the fourth dimension for any length of time, although the reverse was not true. Elementals could thrive on Earth. The memories she had regained when she had taken the stardust overdose atop the mighty kloudar confirmed these facts.

Yet Ra appeared to have no trouble journeying through the green world.

Odd. Of course, Ra himself was odd.

Ali spoke in a soothing tone. "Isn't it enough to know that Mom's fine? In a beautiful realm surrounded by wonderful friends?"

The lies cost Ali, the effort it took to hide the truth from her father. Amma had been marked by the Shaktra. Until Ali could learn to break the spell, her mother lived a life of perpetual hell.

"You're sure there's no way?" her father asked again, this time practically begging. Ali closed her eyes and shook her head.

"Please put it out of your mind, Dad," she whispered.

Even with her closed eyes, she heard him nod. A silent yes.

Still, she knew he would do anything to see Amma.

CHAPTER

6

While waiting for Hector to return, Ali made Nira and her father dinner. They ate together. Chicken and rice and salad. A glass of Coke to drown out her poor choice of herbs. But her father complimented her on the meal, and Nira appeared to enjoy her food. She ate it all.

Afterward, Hector called from Toule and said he would be able to download the game to her over her modem; there was no need to deliver it to her in person. She told him to do so, but to return to Breakwater anyway.

Hector did not seem to mind taking orders from a thirteen-year-old girl. He was agreeable—so far. While talking to him, she told him to get together as much cash as possible. He assured her he had plenty of money locked away in a vault he had built beneath his house. A handy quality, him being a contractor.

Ali wanted Nira and Cindy out of Breakwater tonight. She couldn't return to the green world without knowing they were safe from an assault by Sheri. Ali shuddered as she recalled the woman's remark about stopping Cindy's heart.

Ali's plan to hide the gang was simple. She would put them in a place none of them had ever been before. They would travel using cash, not credit cards, and she would use her subtle senses to make sure they were not being followed.

Ali called Cindy and told her to pack, warned her not to let her parents know. Her old friend complained but obeyed. Ali knew her pal was going to have to sneak out of the house. Twice Cindy asked how Nira was doing.

While her father watched Nira in the living room, she retired to her room to study both of Omega Overtures's bestselling games—Overlord and Armageddon. At the same time, Ali reflected on what Sheri had told Steve and Cindy when the three had lunch at her mansion—before the witch had hauled them off to her dungeon and chained them to a wall. These were part of the incomplete dialogues Ali had scanned from Cindy just before her pal had passed out.

"Overlord tries to strip the direction of humanity down to the basics. We are here, we are alive, and we want to survive. Now how are we going to do that? It points out that so far we've been lucky to progress as a species, stumbling around in the dark the way we have. But now that technology has reached a certain level, hard choices have to be made. The most obvious is probably the most important. Do we continue to allow people to breed indiscriminately? It is the point of view of the game that the answer must be no. Our genes are our wealth. If we squander it, randomly, we will be left with nothing, and we will not survive as a race."

Ali was reminded of Sheri's remarks at the police station about allowing only half of humanity to live. All part of the master plan . . .

At that point Steve had interrupted her with an obvious question.

"But who's to say which genes survive?"

Ali could remember, from Cindy's memories, how the woman brushed aside the question as unimportant.

"It doesn't matter, someone intelligent, someone powerful, possessed of vision. Overlord tries to make that point with the Kabrosh character. He's the first one to see that not only must our genes be controlled, but that the fusion of machines and humans is inevitable. That is Kabrosh's strength. He knows what is necessary, and he goes for it. He doesn't let primitive morality stand in his way."

Ali remembered that Mike Havor had also said similar things, although in a more gentle fashion. He did not talk about one individual taking over the world, but did insist that humans and machines would eventually merge.

At that point in the conversation, Cindy had chimed in.

"I always saw Kabrosh as a villain."

The remark had amused Sheri.

"He's the hero of the game."

Steve had pressed the point.

"But it's possible to win the game by killing him."

Sheri had replied in a condescending tone.

"You think so, huh? You have only mastered one level of the game. If you keep playing and explore all its levels, you'll find Kabrosh returns and starts to take over the world. He actually returns in an altered form, as a cyborg, and wields great power."

Then Cindy had made perhaps the most important remark of the day.

"It sounds like you admire him."

Sheri had laughed as she drank her wine.

"I designed him, of course I have to admire him."

Ali's computer had received the downloaded game from Hector's machine, and she was able to get a look at Armageddon.

Immediately she saw the differences from Overlord. It was not a mere sequel to the original game. The character of Kabrosh was back, but now there was no hiding the fact that he was moving from one world to another—from the ruin of a bombed-out Earth to another planet that at first glance seemed to be dominated by robots. Ali had only to play the new game a few minutes to see that the robots were taking instructions from someone higher up. She had no idea who that was, and yet, visually, the other world resembled the elemental dimension. It was beautiful, seemingly untouched by strife.

Despite her quick insights, Ali felt the pressure of the ticking clock. Hector would return soon, and the gang would have to leave. Ali understood that teens played such computer games for hundreds of hours to discover all their secrets. She didn't have that luxury, and besides, she was not a fan of violent games.

An idea struck her. Could Kabrosh be based on a real character? She Googled his name and found a General James Kabrosh that worked for the U.S. Army. He supposedly was connected to the country's nuclear arsenal. The latest listing had him at the Pentagon, in Washington, D.C. Searching further, Ali found a picture of him receiving a medal from the president of the United States for valor during the Gulf War. The photograph was of poor quality—from an old newspaper clipping. She couldn't see his face, not straight-on. Nevertheless, he bore a resemblance to his namesake in both the Omega games.

It could be a coincidence. It struck Ali as careless of Sheri to advertise that she might be working with him. Why put a shred of information in her games concerning her strategy to take over the world? There was no logical answer, yet Ali recalled a quality of her sister from the green world that superseded logic.

Doren was vain. And she liked to play with people's heads.

Ali found a huge website devoted to the games—it contained over ten thousand members!—and saw that the Kabrosh connection had already been noted by hundreds of Omega devotees. These fans knew more about the general than was listed elsewhere on the Internet. Kabrosh was not just connected with the country's nuclear arsenal, he was in *control* of the dismantling of old nuclear bombs. It made Ali nervous to think the man and Sheri might be buddies.

Yet she could not worry about it today. She had to reach the Isle of Greesh. But what did she plan to do there? Find out what had turned her sister into a witch? See what had caused Jira to leap to his death? What if that inner chamber at the base of the island—the one she had dreamt about while sleeping in Uleestar—held a beast that was capable of eating her alive?

In her last life as Geea, when she had rescued Jira from that mysterious chamber, she had not actually entered it. She had merely forced open the door, and Jira had come running out, screaming. Two days later, despite all the healing power she showered on him, he had killed himself.

Was the Isle of Greesh a wise next step? Logic said no. Her fear said no. No doubt her allies in the green world would say no. Yet a part of her insisted that she face her doom.

She needed to discuss it with Nemi. Darn him, where was he?

Another peculiar idea struck her. She Googled Nemi's name.

The search engine directed her to the site she was already at!

Outside, Ali heard Hector arrive. The two men began to talk, and had she used her subtle hearing, she would have been able to know what they were saying about her—for surely *she* was the topic of conversation. But she disliked spying, and besides, her heart was pounding in her chest.

Nemi was a character in Omega Overlord!

The name was an acronym for: *N*eurological-*E*ngineered-*M*echanical-*I*ntelligence.

Did that mean Nemi was a robot?

"No," she said aloud, in so much pain, because she loved him so much, and missed him so much, and he couldn't be a robot, because he was so kind and good, and . . .

"Shut up and search," a voice whispered inside her.

Ali paused, sitting frozen in front of her computer. He had spoken to her before, telepathically, inside a tree and beside a pond, and both times he had emphasized that his physical appearance was irrelevant. He was always near at hand, he had told her.

"Is that you, Nemi?" she asked softly.

She waited, but there came no answer.

How was she to search? Again, she typed in Nemi, used a variety of search engines, but only got the references that were connected to the Omega board. And in the game, Omega Overlord, Nemi was an advanced computer that fought Kabrosh for control of the world. He—or *It*—was the bad guy.

No, not her Nemi! He was good, he loved her!

"Ah, love. Love knows love."

Again, Ali jerked upright. "Nemi?"

But there was no answer. None she could detect.

Then Ali felt a thunderbolt of pure inspiration.

She typed in: Nemi.com. Instantly she was taken to a blue background webpage that had the word NEMI printed in large gold letters, atop a glowing picture of her Yanti! The brief instructions said if she registered, she could go to a live chat room. Quickly, she put in her name and e-mail address, and what she liked to be called—Geea. That easy, she was a certified member of the Nemi forum.

She went to the chat room. One member present, besides her.

For a whole minute she sat there, feeling like a complete idiot.

Then she typed in the word: Hi.

The response was instant. Faster than any human could type.

"Don't want me to call you by your *secret* name anymore?"

Ali's heart skipped in her chest. *No one,* except Nemi, knew her by the name Alosha. Clearly, since he had italicized the word secret, he didn't even want it typed out on the computer. Her eyes welled with tears, and her fingers shook as she typed her response.

"Is it really you?"

"Yes."

"Have you been here all along? On this webpage?"

"Just constructed it today. What do you think of my graphics?"

"I like the picture of the Yanti. The blue is a nice shade."

"Is my name too large?"

"No! It's your webpage. Have your name as large as you want."

"That's what I thought. And it's a nice name."

She hesitated before she wrote next:

"Does it really mean No One?"

"As I told you in the tree, that is one of its meanings."

She could not stop her fingers from trembling.

"I feel you. I trust you."

And she did feel him. His love was more tangible than her blue screen.

"You need not be afraid to ask what you wish."

"You will answer all my questions now?"

"Of course not. But you can still ask."

Ali could not help but chuckle out loud. Same old Nemi.

"*N*eurological-*E*ngineered-*M*echanical-*I*ntelligence. How did that title come to be in a Sheri Smith game?"

"She put it there."

"Why?"

"Why do you think?"

"To put doubt in my mind about you?"

"Very good. Has it done that?"

"No. I don't know. Is it true?"

"Is what true?"

"Are you a machine?"

His answers continued to come so fast.

Too fast for a human to type.

"We are all machines, in a sense. You are a biological machine."

"Are you a mechanical machine?"

"I am much more than that, Geea."

More tears burned her eyes, dropping on the keyboard.

"May I finally ask who you are?"

"You don't need to ask. You know it, you feel it."

Ali wiped at her eyes. A strange calm swept over her then.

"You are my father."

This time there was no immediate answer. But then, there it was.

"Yes."

Ali sucked in a deep refreshing breath, nodded to herself, and it felt as if the love was so concentrated in the room, her heart would explode simply soaking it all up. The love was thicker than water or blood, and yet she did not doubt his *yes* for an instant, for she felt the connection in her blood. He had helped give birth to her, in more worlds than one. He was no machine.

"I know, Nemi. I know because I love you."

"Love is the best way to know. The only sure way."

"So can I talk to you online from now on? Anytime I want?"

"Well, I do have a life you know. We can't talk constantly. And you still have to save the world. You're not done yet."

"Am I close?"

"It was never a question of being close or far. It was always a question of what you were willing to choose. That is why, even now, I cannot tell you what to do. Oh, I can give you a few hints, but already, I see, you know where your path leads."

"To the Isle of Greesh."

"Correct. You went there once before. But you fled . . ."

"Jira was ill, I had to get him out of there."

"True."

"Are you saying I was a coward to flee before?"

"Certainly, the spot frightened you, even in your fairy form. But I would never call Geea a coward."

"But if even Geea was afraid to enter the chamber, then what chance do I stand? I've regained many of my powers, but I'm still human. I fear, if I go there, I'll die."

"That has always been their greatest weapon. Fear."

"Who are they?"

"Does it matter who they are? There will always be a *they*, an enemy that comes out of nowhere. Who brings fear and torment in their wake. That is what has entered the elemental kingdom, and now it has found a foothold on the Earth."

"Through Doren."

"Yes. Doren is *a* foothold."

"Why did you bring Doren to Greesh, if you knew the place was evil?"

"I did not know at the time, not until it was too late."

"But then you disappeared. Where did you go?"

"May I tell you a secret?"

"Please."

"It is not *where* I went."

Ali understood in an instant.

"You escaped into another time?"

"Yes."

"The past or the future?"

"One of those, yes."

"You won't tell me which one?"

"And spoil all your fun?"

Ali had to laugh. "You're impossible. Maybe you are a machine, after all. Badly programmed at that."

"There might be some truth in that."

Ali froze at his response.

"Are you a cyborg? Part fairy? Part machine?"

"To take out a thorn, sometimes you need a thorn."

She took a moment to consider his riddle. He was *too* fond of them.

"I am not sure what you mean," she said finally.

"Consider it further. And while you do, perhaps I should go visit another chat room . . ."

"Wait! Stay here! I need some more hints. If I do go to the Isle of Greesh, will I find what I need to stop this war?"

"No."

His response startled her. "What must I do then?"

"This war exists in two dimensions at once. You are only one girl. You can only be in one place at a time, and you're trying to defeat an enemy that moves in both worlds at the same time.

Yes, Geea, go to the Isle of Greesh, if you can, and face what you feared to face before. Then think as your enemy thinks, and after you have done so, perhaps you will do as I have done. Then anything will be possible for you."

"So you fight an enemy as well?"

"Yes."

"The same one I do?"

"That is a question for Nira to answer."

"Can I save the little girl?"

"You should ask if she can save you."

"Nemi . . ."

This time he interrupted her typing.

"Go now, Geea, time is short, in your world. But if time grows shorter still, and you feel the need to call me, then do so, on one of those fancy new cell phones, the kind with the picture screens, and the Internet hookups."

It was hard to type the next words. To say goodbye.

"I love you, Nemi."

"You are love, Geea."

Again, she noted he had not called her Alosha, as he had when he had communicated directly with her mind.

Ali logged off the computer and went out to see the others. It was not long before Cindy arrived, suitcase in hand. Hector, her father, and Cindy all understood that Sheri Smith was dangerous, but only her friend had seen the woman in action. When Ali started discussing moving to a safe haven, the men naturally started to talk among themselves. Was Ali overreacting? To answer their doubts, Ali took Hector and her father out back, and had them climb two hundred yards uphill into the trees. There was a huge boulder there, that she had discovered as a child. She stood beside it as they asked what she was doing.

126

"Nothing," she said. "What were you guys saying about not leaving tonight?"

"We just think it's unlikely Sheri Smith will be so bold as to attack us in our homes," Hector explained. "All the suspicion would immediately fall on her."

"She's not worried about suspicion, not anymore," Ali replied.

"Why not?" Hector asked.

In response, Ali reached out with her fist, transformed her fingers into a substance a hundred times stronger than steel, and pounded the boulder with her bare hand. With a deafening noise, it cracked in two. The twin pieces rolled down the hill on either side of the men—thanks, in large part, to the guidance of her magnetic field. The rocks did not stop until they smashed a cluster of tall pines. Ali smiled at Hector and her father, spoke in a sweet voice.

"While I'm gone, do you want to risk a visit by Sheri Smith?"

That quickly ended the discussion about staying.

They took Hector's SUV, drove south. Ali sat silent for a long time, trying to feel if they were being followed. Yet there was no one there, and it seemed, at least for now, that Sheri had lost interest in Ali's family and friends. Still, over Hector's protest, she blindfolded Nira, who laid down in Cindy's lap anyway, and fell asleep.

Cindy fretted about her parents. They would be looking for her again. Ali talked her dad into calling them, and telling them that Cindy was safe. The conversation went badly. Cindy's parents threatened to call the police and hung up.

"Can't say I blame them," her father said with a sigh as he hung up Hector's cell. Her dad had one of his own, but it was temporarily out of juice. Ali asked if she could see Hector's phone. She studied it, pleased at the nice screen, all the modern features.

"Can you get the Internet on this?" Ali asked Hector.

"Yes."

"May I borrow it for the next few days?"

Hector was puzzled. "You'll need it in the green world?"

Ali slipped it in her pocket. "You never know," she said.

They drove south, over two hours, to a town called Hammond, where Hector got them a pricey suite with three adjoining rooms. By then Nira and Cindy were both asleep. Ali carried her old friend inside and managed to put her to bed without waking her. Hector took care of Nira. Once more, Ali explained to the men the importance of Nira not being allowed to look out any windows. She said they must tape over the name of the hotel wherever it appeared in the room: on the phone, on the towels—anywhere.

"Pretend Sheri Smith is sitting in her house and staring through Nira's eyes and listening through her ears," Ali explained. "That'll give you some idea of what you're up against. Any private discussions, don't have them around her."

"When will we hear from you?" her father asked, and she could see the fear grow in him as she donned a small daypack, stuffed with candy bars, two sandwiches, a bottle of water, a Bic lighter, and a Swiss pocket knife. She was not sure what she planned to do with the latter, but Hector had given it to her.

"I'm not sure," Ali replied.

"You must have some idea," her father said.

She gave him a hug. "If the Earth has not been invaded in the next two or three days, then you'll know I've been successful. Other than that, I can't say when I'll return to this hotel."

"But you're going to see your mother first, right?" he asked.

"I'll see her at some point," Ali replied, not wanting to lie. Until she discovered how to remove the Shaktra's *mark,* her mother was allied with the enemy. Ali recalled how her leprechaun friend, Paddy, had explained the Shaktra could incite any marked elemental to violence at a moment's notice.

Her father appeared to know that she was holding back information. He leaned over and kissed her forehead, whispered in her ear.

"You're not just powerful, Ali, but wise. You'll do the right thing."

Ali nodded as she backed up. It was hard to meet his eye. So much longing in his face, for the woman he had loved and lost. Silently, she cursed herself for explaining how the souls moved from one dimension to another. Yet, had she not told Hector and her father the full story, they would have been unable to understand the true nature of the threat to Earth.

"Thanks for the confidence," she said.

But he suddenly grabbed her, hugged her hard, and she realized his face was damp. "I'm scared," he whispered.

"Mom . . ." she began.

"It's not about Mom. It's about you. You know, Ali, I can't lose you. I'll die if I do."

It was her turn to reassure him. "Neither of us will die."

Ali was not one for long goodbyes. She hugged her father again, and Hector, went outside, into the back of the hotel parking lot, looked around to make sure she was alone, and then soared into the sky. It felt good to have the night breeze on her face, to see the stars. She was very excited to be returning to the green world. She just hoped, for her father's sake, and for Earth's, that she'd be able to keep her promise to her dad.

———

Ali did not fly to the lower opening of the cave on the side of Pete's Peak, the point where she had entered the tunnel the last two times she had climbed the mountain. Instead, she flew higher up, to the other entrance, not far from the actual summit. It was near here—five weeks ago—that she had completed her seven trials and realized that she was queen of the fairies. It was also here, yesterday evening, that she had killed Radrine, when she had thrown the dark fairy into the rays of the sun. As Ali landed in the snow near the opening, she saw the burnt remains of the dark queen and snorted in disgust.

Ali took out Hector's cell phone from her pack and called Mike Havor. She did not know what she wanted from him, nor what he wanted from her. As if he had been anticipating her call, he answered on the first ring.

"This is Ali Warner," she said. "How are you, Mike? I hope I didn't wake you."

"No, I was just sitting here watching a little TV. Or I should say I was listening to a favorite show. Few people realize how much the blind can get out of a program just by listening, although it helps to have a buddy nearby to describe the action sequences."

"Do you have a buddy with you now?"

"No, I'm alone, Ali."

It was silent at the top of the mountain, the wind still, and there was a two-thirds full moon high in the sky, casting a soft white radiance over the snowy peak. Overall, Ali felt the spot peaceful, yet there was a troubling undercurrent in Mike Havor's voice.

"You told me after the meeting that you wanted to talk about what was going on at work," she said.

"I did mention that, didn't I." He paused, acted torn over

what he should reveal. "Can I ask that what we discuss now remain between the two of us?"

"Of course. But may I ask a question before you confide in me?"

"Yes."

"The first time I met you, I lied to you about my name. Why do you feel that you can trust me? I mean, what have I done to earn your trust? To you I must be some crazy thirteen-year-old chick running around with an overactive imagination and a big mouth."

"An excellent question, and frankly, I've been sitting here asking myself if I should even talk to you at all about what has been going on at Omega. I don't know you, not really, and I've known Ms. Smith a long time." He paused. "Yet your allegations this morning—and Cindy's—that murder has been committed at Ms. Smith's home—these things have reinforced certain doubts I've been having." He added, "I thought we should talk."

Ali heard truthfulness in his voice. "What do you want to talk about?"

"For the last few months my boss has been taking sudden trips to Washington, D.C., and to Edwards Air Force Base, in Southern California. Each time before she left, she spoke to a certain man, a general, named James Kabrosh. When we first met, you said you played Omega Overlord a lot, and I'm sure you're familiar with the character from the game. When Ms. Smith and I were perfecting the software for the game—that was six years ago—she insisted I name our hero after the general. At the time she didn't tell me he was a real person. She just said, 'I want this name used.' She was adamant about it, if I remember correctly, but at the time I didn't care. But later I learned, from fans who wrote in, that he was a real person. Do you follow me so far?"

"Yes. What troubles you about General Kabrosh?"

"This is hard to admit, but when I heard he was for real, curiosity got the best of me, and I began to do a background check on him. I discovered that besides working at the Pentagon and at Edwards, he was in charge of dismantling a lot of this country's nuclear arsenal. A pretty sensitive job, to say the least."

"That's putting it mildly," Ali agreed.

"Then I discovered something even more disturbing. He did not come from money, nor was his wife's family wealthy. Yet, in just the last year, he's bought two expensive homes. One in Switzerland, the other on an island in the Fijis."

"How were you able to obtain this information?"

"I'm a computer expert. Not to brag, but I'm a master hacker."

"But, with your handicap, you must have someone assist you when you hack."

"Yes. But I would rather leave his identity out of it for the time being."

"Fine. Are you saying that what you know about General Kabrosh, the U.S. government doesn't know?"

"Yes. He was very careful not to list the homes under his name."

"Do you think Sheri Smith bought him these houses?"

Mike Havor hesitated. "I don't know. I hate to think so. He would have had to do her an awfully huge favor for her to pay out so much money. She's a billionaire, but she's tight with her funds."

"Ever met General Kabrosh in person?"

"No. An employee of ours did. A young man named Freddy Degear. He was only sixteen, but I hired him myself, he had a lot of energy. He came from out of town, but he was obsessed with the computer game business, and he hoped to learn about it at Omega. But we mainly used him as a gofer—having him run errands for whoever needed them. Fred not only met General Kabrosh, he overheard a conversation between him and my boss. Afterward, he came to me about it, very upset."

"Why?"

"He said the general and Ms. Smith had a *detailed* conversation about the destructive effect of different sized bombs."

"Did he hear her talk about buying a bomb?"

"No. However, a general from the Pentagon talking about what obviously must be highly classified information—it disturbed both Freddy and me."

"Then Freddy died all of a sudden?"

"Yes. You know about that. You were in Toule the day he died. That was the day I met you." Havor paused. "I've been wondering if that was a coincidence."

"Is that another reason you're worried about it?"

"Yes. For some reason, when you showed up in our town, it spurred Ms. Smith to act." Act, like in killing Freddy Degear.

"Like you say, you've known her a long time. Do you really think she's bought a bomb from the general?"

"Ordinarily, I would say the idea was utterly ridiculous. But now . . ." He did not finish.

"You think my arrival in Toule spurred her to act. What else do you think she did—besides kill Freddy?"

"There've been a few times, over the years, when I've walked into her office and caught her talking to a person online, and she always stops the second I appear. Now you might wonder how I can tell who anyone is talking to online, since I can't see. But I have voice-boxes hooked up to my own systems—at home and at the office—that translate typed words into vocal sounds. With a microphone in my ear, I can hear what everyone in the entire building is typing." He paused. "That sounds like I spy on everyone. Trust me, I don't ordinarily use my hacking talents for such a lowly pursuit. But since I learned that Ms. Smith was spending so much time in the company of such a questionable general, I felt an obligation to keep tabs on her."

"You don't have to explain yourself to me. Who's this other person she talks to?"

"His name is Nemi. He has a website—Nemi.com. Again, the name is out of one of our games. Nemi stands for . . ."

"I know what it stands for," Ali whispered, feeling a knife go through her heart. Was it possible? Was Nemi working with Sheri? Was he not her father, but an impostor, making the biggest fool out of Queen Geea imaginable?

"You still there, Ali?" Havor asked.

"I'm here," she mumbled. "Ah . . . can you tell me what the two of them talked about?"

"No. When they do talk, it is always in some kind of code, as if they know they're being watched. I've kept records of their online talks—and tried to break the code—but so far I've had no success. Yet the day you showed up in Toule, the day Freddy Degear died, and pretty much every day since then, Ms. Smith has spent at least an hour a day on the computer with this Nemi."

Ali was having trouble breathing. He loved her! She loved him!

"Does she ever talk to him on the phone?" she mumbled.

"Not to my knowledge. Once more I must apologize, but with my hacking skills, I've a record of every phone call my boss has made in the last two months." He added, "It's very odd that two people should talk so much online, when they can simply pick up the phone and talk to each other, don't you think?"

"Maybe Nemi is unable to talk to her—physically," Ali muttered.

"What do you mean?"

"Just thinking aloud." Ali forced herself to go on, to get as much information as she could while she was still in this world. But her heart was broken, and she realized how dangerous that made her next trip. All of a sudden, she didn't care if she lived or died. In all her adventures, at the back of her mind, she had fought so hard to win because she had wanted to make Nemi proud of her. That wasn't the only reason, of course, but it had been a huge motivation for her. Because her father could not know of her activities, Nemi had taken on the role of a surrogate father in her heart. The desire had been there from the very start, when she had hardly known him at all. And now it looked as if he were working for the other side . . .

Yet was that true? A remark he said came back to haunt her. *"Love is the best way to know. The only sure way."*

The experience of love in his presence was always undeniable.

Yet the truth in the blind man's words was clear.

How could both things be true?

She didn't know. She only knew how weak she felt, when she had felt so strong only minutes before.

"Tell me what you think I should do," Mike Havor said.

"Why do you ask me? I'm only a kid you just met."

He was a long time answering. "I've been blind a long time, and what it's done, it's allowed me to develop senses most people don't have. You asked today why I was not mad at you for lying to me at Omega, and the truth is, even without being able to see, I can sense you're a special person. I've no eyes, not anymore, Ali, but there's more to you than meets the eye. I know this in my heart."

"So you come to me for advice?"

"Yes. I want your advice."

"Continue to spy on your boss. Keep tabs on everything she does. And never allow her to lead you to a place where you two are totally alone. She murdered my friend. If she finds out about your spying, she will not hesitate to do the same to you. I mean it, Mike."

"I'm beginning to believe you." He paused. "This number you're calling from—may I reach you there tomorrow?"

"Let me call you. I might not be available tomorrow."

"Where will you be that we can't talk?"

"That's a long story. But I want to thank you for what you've told me. It's given me a lot to think about."

They exchanged goodbyes and Ali closed the phone and discovered her eyes were wet. Her whole face was damp. She had been silently crying since Havor had mentioned Nemi's name.

He had said he was her father . . .

Maybe he had told her to go to the Isle of Greesh to die.

Holding the phone in her hand, with its Internet hookup, she realized she could dial him in an instant. But that she would not do. If he was lying, then he would just tell her a fresh set of lies to assuage her fears. And if he was telling the truth, then she would disgrace herself by accusing him . . .

Yet many of his actions had been suspicious. Answering her, he had typed faster than any fairy or human being was capable of. Plus he had admitted he had been the one to take Doren to the Isle of Greesh, where she had changed into the Shaktra . . .

136

However, the fact that he had admitted the truth to her . . .

"Stop!" Ali screamed aloud, her voice echoing off the silent peak. The invasion was too near, there was no time for internal debates. She had to act. She had to enter the green world and kick some butt.

CHAPTER

7

After a hurried flight down the upper portion of the cave, Ali came to the *open* yellow door and passed through it into the cavern that held the other doors. All were arranged in a deep semicircle, were made of metal, had featureless handles in place of knobs, and finely shaped domes on top.

Each door was a different color. Starting on the far left, there was a red door, followed by an orange one, a yellow one, a green one, a blue one, a violet one, and on the far right there was a white door.

Previously, Ali had tried to scratch each door, to see if the paint would come off. Only now she realized how foolish the act had been. The colors reflected the *vibration* of the world beyond the door. In a sense, each door was a part of the world that lay behind it.

Last time she had been to the cavern—in the company of Farble and Paddy, her troll and leprechaun pals—she had fought Radrine, with laser bolts and thrown boulders. Nevertheless, right now, the doors looked perfectly clean, showing not a trace of dust. As before, Ali found herself more drawn to the blue door, the fifth world—than she was to the green one, which led to the fourth world, the elemental kingdom. Stepping toward the blue door, she found it locked and was not surprised. Except for the yellow one, all the doors were locked. Indeed, she had cast such a strong spell on the red door that led to Radrine's hell, she doubted any dark fairy would ever be able to open it.

Even though the green world was her immediate destination, she could not free herself of the magnetism of the blue door. It called to her in many ways. She felt an actual physical tug inside her chest, and beneath that, in a realm of almost subconscious longing, she imagined what it would be like to open the door, to step through it, just for a few minutes, and feel the light that would sweep over her. For she had no doubt that the blue world was a place of everlasting joy . . .

Almost without thinking about it, Ali withdrew the Yanti from beneath her shirt and placed it on her forehead, heart, and then on top of her head, in quick succession, while whispering the words: *"Alosha, Alosha, Alosha."*

And the blue door slowly opened.

Ali took a step forward. Another one, maybe a dozen steps; she did not know for sure how far she traveled past the door. But what she saw and felt and *became,* was a thousand times more wonderful than her imagination could have conjured. No, it was a million times richer. For as she stepped forward, a light engulfed her, from all sides, dancing on her skin and within her eyes, like candles lit to warm and guide her on her way home. Yes, that was it, *home* . . . In an instant that stretched forever, she felt as if she had been lost her entire life, but now she had been rediscovered, by an ancient race of beings that not only knew her, but loved her as one of them, because she was one of them. It was true, beyond the blue door was where she belonged . . .

Ali closed her eyes, opened them; it did not matter, the joy kept increasing. The intoxicating music she had occasionally heard on Earth, and in the green world, when she plunged deep inside her mind, began to sound in the blue light, and she realized it was as much a part of the dimension as it was a part of her heart—where the music had always seemed to originate before. Was it because the soul could be located in the heart? Where this sacred light forever shone?

It came to her that this blue realm was where her soul had originally emerged from, not the green world. In that instant she realized why she had not been able to understand the mystery of the ice maidens when she had last explored the elemental world.

Of course, Amma had explained to her that the ice maidens took care of the bodies of dead elementals, as they rested inside the kloudar, while their souls were born on Earth. Nevertheless, Ali had not understood *what* they were. The truth had been too close for her to see.

She was one of them!

Standing inside the glory of the blue light, she intuitively understood that she was an ice maiden, a being most people on Earth would have called an angel.

With this realization numerous hands appeared to come out of the light. Only hands and arms, no faces or eyes, and they did not push her so much as prod her to go back. Yes, they said she must return, and she heard these words—as if they were a mantra in her mind—again and again . . .

Serve the Worlds . . . Serve the Worlds . . . Serve the Worlds.

Although it killed her to obey, she did as she was told. A moment later she was standing outside the blue door, and it was closed, and the chamber in which she stood was dark, and she was alone. And she knew she would always be that way, in a sense, until she could open the blue door again, and stay.

Ali glanced at her watch. Six hours had elapsed!

Outside the sun would be coming up. In the green world as well. Lord Vak's army was coming. Stepping in front of the green door, taking hold of the Yanti, Ali repeated the mystical incantation, and the door opened, and she passed through it.

She was on her way.

The attack, as she exited the cave on the side of Mt. Tutor, and entered into the green dawn, was much worse than she had anticipated. This time there were no mere dark fairies to thwart her coming and going.

There were dragons. A dozen fire-breathing dragons.

Two stood guard directly outside the cave. Each had one triangular-shaped eye shut, the other open, red and glowing. They appeared to be dozing. Yet far overhead, another ten slowly circled the mountaintop, like gigantic flying demons, with steam for breath. Their vast beating wings seemed to be made of leather that had been soaked in lava. Worse, their bellies—and the rest of their hides for that matter—were like burnt metal, old but impenetrable armor. From their long snouts, their fiery nostrils bristled with flame, and she knew all too well how fast those small fires could swell into blazing clouds, and burn any human or fairy into ash.

Beside the two sleeping dragons—near the cave opening—were the remains of the dark fairies she had previously killed. She had torn them apart with a deadly technique her father had taught her: *voom*. It involved taking in a deep breath, blowing forcibly on her palms, then smacking her hands together. Voom sent out a powerful sonic wave in all directions; her own field was required to protect her from it. The deadly wave was like the compressed air given off by an exploding bomb. Voom had a tendency to blow off limbs and heads . . .

The two dragons opened both eyes. Their nostril-fire suddenly swelled.

Quickly, expanding her protective field, Ali sucked in a breath, blew on her hands, clapped her palms together with great force. She was near both dragons—standing dead center between their huge lumbering heads, which couldn't have been fifty feet apart. Her surprise appearance was a stroke of luck, she knew, and not likely to be repeated.

Before the dragons could attack, the top of their huge skulls cracked, and blood splattered as their massive jaws tore loose, and sent forth a shower of jagged teeth over the rocky side of Tutor. With a thunderous noise that shook the gravel beneath her feet, their heads fell to the ground as the dragons instantly died.

Unfortunately, using voom had *not* been a quiet way to sneak into the green world. The unnatural breeze cast by the many flapping dragon wings suddenly altered—directly over her head. The wind greatly intensified; it was as if Ali had been thrust into the center of a tornado. Each dragon had changed course, and was now racing toward her. As they came near, the red flames about their snouts swelled ferociously. Their plan, she saw, was simple.

They were going to blast the entire mountaintop.

Something unexpected happened to Ali right then. She had planned for this battle for hours, but for some odd reason—even after having killed two of the dragons—she suddenly froze in panic. The dragons didn't care, they kept coming.

Ali stood absolutely still for five seconds. She simply could not move.

Then she shook herself, as an idea struck her.

The dragon's rush toward her might be a good thing, after all!

Let them blast the mountain, she thought. Her killing two of their partners had enraged them. They were not thinking, either. Their attack speed was so great—there was no way they were going to be able to suddenly halt. After spraying Mt. Tutor with flames, they would have to veer off to avoid crashing into the mountain.

It was *then* she would have her chance to escape!

Turning, Ali flew back into the mountain cave.

Just in time. She was a hundred yards into the tunnel when it exploded in flame. The ancient walls of the mountain took the brunt of it. Nevertheless, her magnetic field strained under the pressure of the heat. It was as if she were an ant, and a human had pressed a blowtorch over the top of her anthill.

The instant the fire began to recede, she tightened her field closer to her body and waited a few seconds, let the worst of the heat dissipate. Then she flew straight into the flames. For a few seconds she was blind. She could have been inside a sun. All she saw was red plasma. That did not worry her, however—the fire had definitely cooled from the initial blast. Better yet, it made her invisible. If she could not see them, they could not see her. When she did finally burst from the red cloud, she found herself two miles from the burning peak, and at least a mile from the nearest dragon.

Now came the most important question of all.

Could she fly faster than a dragon?

The answer, if she remembered correctly from her previous life, was yes, she was faster than the *majority* of dragons, no matter what their age or size. She was also more maneuverable.

In an instant, she could alter her course. But with their bulk, dragons took time and room to change direction.

However, there were a few dragons, she recalled, that *were* faster than she. And unfortunately, from a glance over her shoulder, she saw that the Shaktra knew who those dragons were. The monster must have placed at least four of them outside Mt. Tutor—for no matter how much pressure Ali applied to her field, these four kept getting closer.

Ali was flying north, heading for Karolee, the land of the fairies, and Uleestar, the fairy capital, where she hoped to find protection in the Crystal Palace, her home in the green world.

At present, directly beneath her, the sand that surrounded Mt. Tutor vanished, as she passed over Elnar—a wide river that flowed out of the east and into the sea—and she began to fly above Lestre, a river that ran north to south.

Lestre was interesting for several reasons. It flowed directly through the fairy capital, and shielded Uleestar on all sides with running water, which made the inner capital an island of sorts, and difficult to attack.

Plus Lestre had a twin, Tiena, that ran directly beneath it, through an underground cavern. While Lestre flowed south into Elnar, before turning west and into the ocean, a third of Lestre's water disappeared from the surface and flowed back north, eventually entering Lake Mira, in the Youli Mountains. Lake Mira, in turn, helped feed Lestre, along with melting snow from the mountains.

It had been explained to Ali that it was the power of the levitating mountains, the kloudar, that pulled the waters of Tiena back to Lake Mira; even upward, at a steep angle, into the Youli Mountains.

Had the situation been a fraction less dire, Ali would have enjoyed the sight of the twin rivers and the wide green lands, the trees, and most of all the green sea that lay off to her left in the west, and where the Isle of Greesh could be glimpsed in the distance. But with so many dragons on her tail, she realized any possibility of hiding in Uleestar was out of the question. Luckily, she had an alternative plan.

She just hoped she got a chance to use it.

From behind her came a geyser of flame. It was like a cloud of steam that had arisen from a lake filled with gasoline, and then ignited. The most painful concentration of the heat was at the exact center of the wave, and it made her wonder if the dragons were able to coordinate their blasts together. Of course, practice made perfect, and these same dragons had been fighting Lord Vak and his army for a long time.

Ali managed to keep her clothes from igniting, and added a notch to her speed, which bought her time. It was odd that she should think of Vak and his warriors then, because out the corner of her eye, far in the east, she saw a haze of dust, and many tiny figures of all sizes and shapes, in the center of the cloud.

For the second time, she was pretty sure she was seeing Lord Vak's army. The first time she had encountered him and his warriors had been near home, atop Pete's Peak, right after she had discovered the Yanti. But even though they had a common enemy in the Shaktra, they were not exactly allies. He had already surrendered to the Shaktra, and the main condition of that surrender was the promise to invade Earth and kill humans.

Out the corner of her other eye, in a sheltered cove along the coast, she saw another unusual sight. A mass of boats—there were thousands of them—with sleek wooden frames and tall white sails. From her previous life as Geea, she recalled that this was the Shaktra's navy. The boats that had brought the enemy's forces across the sea, from the Isle of Greesh, when Doren had invaded the mainland.

It was strange, Ali thought, but as queen of the fairies she should have destroyed them. They were unguarded. If she had time now, she could have flown over and burned the lot of them. Perhaps she had kept them safe for a reason.

The four fast dragons roared behind her. Once more they set forth a concentrated burst of flame. The water bottle in her pack steamed, then exploded under pressure. Her panic returned. Strands of her red hair caught fire. They literally curled and crackled and turned to smoke. The burnt odor hung in her field, and made her shudder. The last time she had entered the green world, she had been burned. The pain of that memory was too fresh in her mind . . .

For some reason, her sister's words came back to her then.

"You think it's so easy. Put your hands on my heart and head. Let the Yanti warm. Then I'll be whole again, and everything I've gone through will be forgotten. Why, I might even bow at your feet and thank you . . . You know nothing."

There was truth to the accusation. During her recent fight with the dark fairies, Ali had merely burned her hand, and it had been horrible. She could not imagine what Lucy Pillar must have endured.

Another blast came, and it was worse, because the dragons were closer. The bottom of her jeans—on the left leg—caught fire. She had to beat it out. That caused her to lose speed. She lost even more when she turned and mentally showered her burnt skin with water. She still controlled the water element, and the liquid helped soothe the pain . . .

But the dragons had cut her lead in half.

Ali squeezed her eyes shut and envisioned her field as an impenetrable block of ice—that even the hottest flame could not touch. The focus gave strength to her shield, but the energy she poured into it further decreased her speed. In seconds the fastest dragons came within a quarter of a mile of her, and she could tell, by the way they sucked in their next breaths that they were preparing for a decisive blow. At the same time, up ahead, five miles distant, Ali could see another dozen dragons heading her way.

The Shaktra had laid her trap wisely. Ali was boxed in.

Maybe.

From the time she had left the green world, Ali had considered how the Shaktra would try to block her return. Although the sheer number of dragons had caught her by surprise, Ali had figured Doren would use them. After all, they were her most powerful allies. And while contemplating the dragon scenario, Ali had come up with the only possible route she could take to escape them.

She had to use Tiena.

The subterranean cavern through which the dark river flowed.

The dragons behind her were only two hundred yards away, the ones in front less than a mile distant, when she caught sight of the broken harbor she, Drash, Ra, and her other pals had used to reach the one river in all the magical land that never saw the green sun. There were beautiful winding columns of steps that led from beside the harbor and down into the hidden river. Yet Ali had no interest in them, not this time.

In the midst of her collision course with the dragons, she suddenly let herself drop from the sky, plunging underground, moving so fast that she almost tore herself to shreds on the stone walls of the river entrance.

Her sudden change in direction threw her prey off stride. But the dragons were not dumb; they knew about Tiena, and they were not so large that they could not follow her underground, which they did. Yet it took them time—for they could only enter the subterranean cavern one at a time. By then she had pulled far ahead, skimming smoothly over the cool waters of the river that had been as much a part of her past life as her own bedroom in the Crystal Palace.

She let her burnt leg touch the river. The cool water was soothing. Her panic began to subside. Now she was ready to roll the dice.

For Ali knew things about this cavern that few fairies knew, even those who had been close to her. It did not take a genius to see that Uleestar was hard to invade on the surface, but was vulnerable to an attack from underground, via the river. For that reason, in the half-domed ceiling that sheltered the river on its winding path beneath the ground, the queen of the fairies—Geea—had implanted hundreds of *takor*.

What was takor? It was only found on the kloudar, and since no other race could fly up to the floating mountains—except the dragons, who were *not* miners—the stones were only known to the high fairies. From the outside, they appeared to be nothing more than black rocks, but smooth, like pieces of frozen lava. Cracking them open did not cause them to explode, yet inside, when split, they gave off a dull green light, even in the dark.

It was lucky few knew about them, because takor was the elemental equivalent of dynamite. Only their fuse was a certain type of sonic wave; and by weight, they were more powerful than any non-nuclear weapon mankind had ever invented. As a defensive device, their drawback was their scarcity. There were so few of them to be found. For example, to rig Tiena to prevent an attack via the river, Queen Geea had used up half her supply of takor.

Now that they were at war, Ali thought, it seemed a pity the fairies had never figured out how to manufacture them. Yet fairies were, by nature—like most elementals—not drawn to making weapons. They considered warfare a human obsession. For the most part, elementals lived and let live.

However, even before the Shaktra's arrival, the elves and dwarves used to go at it from time to time. There was always an exception to everything.

Once Lord Vak had tried to get Queen Geea to discuss takor.

Even his son Jira had asked her about them. She had just smiled.

On the plus side, takor could be detonated by the voom technique. Indeed, Ali knew Geea had known of no other way to explode the stones.

For that reason, takor was a weapon in her hands only.

Ali knew her father had never taught Doren how to use voom.

Now, flying in the dark above quietly gurgling Tiena, Ali allowed her frantic flight to slow, to let the dragons see her, so as to bring them all down into the watery cavern. Even though learning to swim was one of the tests a *koul*—an adolescent fire-breather—had to go through to become a full-fledged dragon, Ali remembered that they did not like water.

Pursuing her now, in a black deeper than any night, she heard the beat of their wings, saw the red glow of their smoldering snouts, yet she sensed their caution as well. The air was damp, the space confined, and perhaps one or two of them considered that it might be a trap. But none wanted to be called a coward; and Ali had counted ten dragons behind her, had seen another dozen in front, and with the power of her subtle senses, she now saw that the last of the twenty-two dragons had entered the cavern and were closing in on her shimmering form. Yes, she let her field glow green and bright, like an emerald in the night; and they thought they had her.

Ali sucked in a deep breath and held her palms to her mouth. She blew hard. She clapped hard. The takor exploded.

The stones were spaced at intervals in the ceiling of the cavern. As Ali detonated them, she flew quickly toward the underground harbor beneath the Crystal Palace, where previously, on her last journey, she had met Amma and Trae.

And she moved none too soon.

It was as if a bolt of lightning shot the length of the cavern. There came a deafening thunder. The dragons were illumined in a blinding light. She saw their huge wings suddenly splay out, striking the sides of the tunnel, as if trying to ward off blows that came at them from every direction at once. As the ceiling exploded, and the weight of the world fell on them, shoving them beneath the water, Ali sensed their dying horror.

Of course she felt their agony, as she grieved for the river as well. The dragons had been destroyed, true, but she had killed Tiena as well. A crashing tidal wave chased her farther up the cavern. The river could not possibly recover from the stone dam she had dropped in its heart. A large share of the green world's magic had been permanently ruined with the loss of Tiena, and she knew she was to blame.

Her heart heavy, Ali flew toward the harbor that lay beneath Uleestar and the Crystal Palace. She knew it would be in shambles from the rushing water, but it was here she planned to return to the surface, perhaps to find more high fairies to help her with her mission.

But it was not to be . . . Not all the dragons had been fooled.

Between Ali and Uleestar was Drash's father.

Kashar. The oldest and most powerful of all the dragons.

Once they had been friends, King Kashar and Queen Geea. Now he did not look happy to see her.

CHAPTER

8

Kashar sat on the exact spot where Ali had met Trae and Amma on her last visit to Uleestar. But now the harbor shook with turbulence. Better than half the boats that had been previously anchored there had been drowned.

Waves continued to pound the area. Ali knew they would not last. The tons of rock she had dropped on the dragons had severed Tiena from Lestre. On the surface, south of her present position, she knew Lestre must be already swelling, probably across the sandy desert that surrounded Mt. Tutor. That might be good—it would slow Vak's advance toward the Earth. Without the Yanti, Ali knew he would use the yellow door inside the mountain to try to invade humanity's home.

Yet it was hard for Ali to imagine Vak's army would attack Earth via Pete's Peak and Breakwater. He would not push his entire force through a single narrow cave and one hick town. It was more likely the elven king planned to use *all* the caves she had found—the six tunnels located just above the doors. It was through one of those tunnels that she had ended up in Africa—on the side of Kilimanjaro—and met Ra.

She wished she had Ra with her now, to face Kashar.

The king of the dragons was bigger than any other of his race, and his coloring, especially on his wings and his face, was more varied. His son, Drash—after he had transformed into a full-fledged dragon—had been largely black, with hints of red and purple on his skin. Kashar had streaks of blue, particularly on his wings, and yellow circles around his red triangular eyes.

Yet there was a dull tinge to the yellow—it looked as if it were the result of sickness. Where his wings were blue, the skin was cracking. She could see faint bloody veins that pulsed as he settled his massive bulk before her. It made her recall a talk she'd had with Drash, not long after they'd met.

"My father is Kashar, king of the dragons, and for as long as there have been tales to tell and remember, he has been a staunch ally of the fairies. Many times over the long years he visited the high fairies at Uleestar. But recently he has allied himself with the Shaktra, and set the other dragons to killing fairies, elves, dwarves, and leprechauns."

Ali had asked why Kashar had joined the Shaktra.

"Because the Shaktra promised him the one thing dragons long for above all else. It told him that it would show him how to remain on the kloudar, even when they pass on the other side of Anglar. That way all the dragons would be able to enter the blue universe, like the ice maidens, and leave the bounds of this world behind . . . Drash thinks his father has been bewitched."

Ali had pressed him on the issue.

"Drash has heard a rumor that the Shaktra is able to give the dragons a taste of the blue universe."

Ali had asked if the Shaktra was feeding them something.

"Drash does not know for sure. But if the Shaktra is, then it cannot stop . . . Or perhaps Drash should say, the dragons do not want it to stop."

Ali had asked if the substance might be addictive, like opium.

Drash had shook his head, wanting to avoid the question. But he had said: *"Drash can see that the dragons have changed for the worse."*

Ali was not surprised to see that Kashar did not look like the king of the dragons she once knew, and he was one creature she remembered well, for they had been close friends. His alliance with the Shaktra had definitely aged him, which was odd, for dragons aged very slowly, and outlived all other beings in the green world—except, of course, the ice maidens, who did not count, since they came and went as they pleased, and were not bound to the elemental kingdom.

But his voice had not changed. His tone was deep and thunderous, and yet somehow eloquent. She heard the anger in his words, though, there was no mistaking that.

"Your stunt was clever, Geea, and cruel. You have killed many an old friend of Kashar's. But it has all been in vain, for Kashar will not allow you to leave here alive."

Ali knew that dragons seldom spoke in first person.

She floated a hundred yards in front of him, in midair, her green field close to maximum strength. From past experience, she knew his flame could come quickly, and without warning. She responded in a reasonable tone.

"I know your great powers, you know mine. Is it necessary for us to fight? When we were once such close allies?"

Kashar tried to grasp her gaze with his smoldering red eyes, for the latter were famous for their hypnotic effect. He could not put a high fairy like her under a complete spell, but he could slow her reflexes, and that might be all he would need to kill her. For that reason, as they spoke, she was careful to keep her gaze slightly to the right or left of his massive snout. The fire in his nostrils was more important anyway. It would be his fire she would eventually have to face.

Unless he could be reasoned with.

He sighed at her question, as if it both saddened and angered him.

"Kashar and his people decided upon an alliance with the Shaktra long ago. Geea knows the reason why, and Geea knows Kashar won't break that alliance. This, we have already talked about at length."

"Yet you used to be allied with me, with all the fairies, and you broke that treaty. Do you know why? I know, now that I've been born as a human, and met your son, Drash."

Kashar snorted. "That koul! Such a coward has no say in anything!"

A koul was a teenage dragon who had yet to pass the tests that changed him into a full dragon. The test of self-sacrifice. The test of water. And the test of flight itself. When it came to the latter, to get his wings, Drash had to have the courage to leap off a mountain without wings, and have faith that they would be bestowed on him before he crash-landed. To help give him courage, Ali had taken the leap with Drash.

Yet Drash admitted that when he had tried the first test, in his father's presence, he had failed it. Therefore, his father was ashamed of his son, although the reverse was also true. Drash despised the Shaktra, and what it was doing to the green world. Ali recalled what Drash had told her atop the kloudar, after the attack by the Shaktra.

"Did you recognize the one you fought?"

"My uncle, Chashar. He did not hesitate to strike me."

"Did you see the Shaktra on his back?"

"There was something there. Drash did not get a clear look."

Ali nodded in the direction of the cavern she had just destroyed.

"Did we bury Chashar back there?" she asked.

Kashar was unmoved. "No. Brother follows the army."

"But he must have told you, at some point, that he saw Drash flying near the highest kloudar. The two fought, and Drash survived the battle, and lives to this day."

Kashar growled. "My brother was not sure who it was."

"An uncle would not mistake a nephew—especially a nephew who had passed his three tests so rapidly, and so bravely . . ."

Kashar interrupted; his nostrils flamed. "Why do you go on about Drash?"

"Because you act as if you speak for all the dragons. Yet your own son—a full dragon in his own right—is not in favor of an alliance with the Shaktra!"

Kashar's anger increased. He sat up straighter, his head coming equal with her floating body. "Drash has no idea why we even allied with the Shaktra!"

Ali sneered. "Of course he does! All the high fairies do. It's because the Shaktra promised you a lie. Yes, a lie, and the lie is so obvious, I can see it just by looking at you. Go to the mountains, find a clear lake, and look at your own reflection and you'll see what I mean."

"Your words mean nothing, Geea. Kashar cannot be fooled."

"Listen to me!" she snapped, her turn to interrupt. "The Shaktra promised you that it would allow the dragons to remain on the kloudar even as they passed into space, beyond the moon, Anglar, and that you would be allowed to enjoy the blue light of the ice maidens. True or false?"

"True! And the Shaktra has delivered on its promise!"

"Lies! Just before I entered the green world, I bathed in the blue light of the ice maidens, and got to be with the angels, and it lifted my soul, and filled me with wonder and awe. Most of all, it expanded my heart with love. Yes, love. That's what the blue light is made of. That's the light the ice maidens live in forever. Immortality is their *birthright*. By growing through countless experiences in the yellow and green worlds, they have matured to the point where it is natural for them to live in the blue light. But I know the Shaktra came to the dragons and promised you a shortcut. That you did not have to go through so much suffering and struggle to reach that light. That you could have it all now."

"Kashar has it now! Whenever Kashar wishes it!"

"I don't know what drug the Shaktra's feeding you but it's not the blue light. Just look at yourself! Your body has deteriorated horribly. The light in your eyes has dulled. Worse, your heart has closed."

"Geea . . ."

"You'll listen to what I have to say! The old Kashar would never have turned against his fellow elementals. Kashar, we used to say, was the great protector of us all. But now what do you and your dragons do with your flame? You melt off portions of the kloudar so that they fall on fairies and elves and dwarves! You kill all the elementals, and they hate you for it. And why do you do it? Because of some concoction or device the Shaktra has invented that makes you think you ride the kloudar out into space, and live in the glory of the blue light beyond Anglar!"

To Ali's dismay, the old dragon chuckled.

"Geea does not know that I've journeyed *far* beyond Anglar!"

"Where's the proof of the love you've found there?"

"Kashar did not go there for love. Kashar went for power."

Ali snickered. "Power? You look like a sick and drooling

troll, not like a dragon king. The Shaktra's granted you no special power!"

Kashar suddenly beat his wings, and came off his seat beside the harbor. He moved to the center of the subterranean cavern that lay north of Uleestar, effectively blocking her path of escape. The red flame of his nostrils was now thirty feet long, six in diameter, and his triangular eyes were no longer dull but ablaze. Perhaps it had been a mistake to argue with him. Kashar spoke in a furious tone.

"You dare mock me? Already Kashar would have turned you to ash. But the Shaktra spoke concerning Geea, and Kashar agreed to listen one last time. If Geea will turn over the Yanti to Kashar, show Kashar how to use it, then Geea will be allowed to go on her way."

"Geea has your promise?"

"Kashar has given his word."

"Oh, but Kashar gave his word before. Don't you remember? Long ago you swore an oath of friendship to all the fairies. Dragons would protect us in times of need, and we would help you when you needed help. What of that word, Kashar? Have you forgotten it?"

He continued to beat his wings, only faster, and the wind from them was indeed powerful. She found herself being pushed backward, toward the ruin she had brought down upon the cavern. She had to make a move soon. Unfortunately, she had little room to maneuver in. Should she make a dash toward the rear of the harbor? Try to escape to the surface and the Crystal Palace? She had a feeling the Shaktra had sent dragons there as well. Her only hope of escape probably lay farther north, in the direction of Lake Mira.

The dragon's anger came out as hot as his flame.

"Give Kashar the Yanti now!" he demanded.

Ali knew if she did give it to him, he would keep it for himself. He recognized the truth of her accusations. Whatever the Shaktra was feeding him, it was not what Kashar had hoped for. He was sick. He wanted the Yanti to heal himself. But there was no point in offering to help him. He was too old and stubborn.

"You want the Yanti, you take it!" Even as she swore, she accelerated along the ceiling of the cavern, away from the dragon, and tried to fly past him. However, he was not a king for nothing. He was shrewd, he anticipated the move, and let loose a blast against her and the wall of the cave that her field barely repelled.

The tight surroundings did not favor her. Adding strength to her field, she pulled away from the stream of burning plasma, and then, dropping low, near the water level and Kashar's legs, she blew out a harsh breath and smashed her palms together, using her most potent voom ever.

The sonic wave hit his webbed feet hard. He let out a cry of pain, but he blasted her again, and she was forced to dive beneath the water, the last thing she wanted to do. For underwater she could not fly, nor use voom; and the water weakened her magnetic field as well.

Yet, as the water above her suddenly turned red, and exploded in a shower of steam, she saw her last move had probably saved her life. But it was to be a brief respite. She could not fly around a dragon and continue to trade punches. Not with a dragon as powerful as Kashar. His fire was too hot. Her field would inevitably fail as her strength gave out.

Through the steam, Ali saw him raise a thundering foot.

He was trying to crush her!

Bursting to the surface, through a cloud of steam, Ali did a midair flip that took her within a few feet of Kashar. But with the dragon distracted—he was still trying to find her under the water and squash her like a bug—she was able to spread both her palms in front of his eyes and let her full power run down her arms. Fire shot from her palms. She scored a direct hit in his right pupil. The red triangle turned an ugly black, and she knew, for a time at least, that he was half-blind.

Yet even had Kashar been totally blind, he now knew where she was. Howling in pain, he blasted the air directly in front of him. To escape, Ali was forced to take the most dangerous route of all.

She flew *at* him—at his burning nostrils, ducking at the last instant beneath his chin. His flame missed her by inches. It caught more of her hair, though, and she heard it crackling. The smoke smothered her, along with the stench of the gases that came off his fire. Practically hugging his hideous hide, she watched him sniff the air, searching for her.

Obviously his eye hurt. Yet it was not enough just to hurt him.

She had to *kill* him, and she did not have the power.

Or did she?

Since Ali had spoken to Sheri, she had thought long and hard about why her sister wanted the Yanti so badly. The woman had said it was to be used to shoot down nuclear missiles that humans might use against the elemental army, and Ali had sensed truth in the words. At the same time, Sheri had made elusive references to something called the violet ray. In her anger, the woman had spouted many strange phrases.

"It's a powerful tool. Besides, it should have been mine. You must recall—before you brainwashed him with your constant whining—that Father was going to give it to me. You know as well as I do that it's wasted in your hands. You don't even know how to use it as a weapon . . . Even if you somehow discovered how

to reverse the Yanti and invoke the violet ray—which you can't do, not without my help—it'll make no difference . . . Admit it, you'll never unleash the violet ray and risk killing millions . . ."

Certainly, Ali had no wish to kill millions.

Right now she would be happy just to kill one dragon.

But how to reverse the Yanti and invoke the violet ray?

Ali felt that was the key word—*reverse.* When she had first found the Yanti, she had instinctively repeated the secret name Nemi had given her, *Alosha,* while envisioning what she wanted to happen. In time—from Nira of all people—she learned a deeper level of control of the Yanti. While using the secret name, if she touched the talisman first to her forehead, to her heart, and then to the top of her head, she could invoke greater power. For example, she needed the formula Nira had taught her to open and close the seven doors.

Taking Sheri's words as a clue, Ali wondered if she reversed *everything* when it came to using the Yanti, would she be able to invoke the so-called violet ray? Before she had left Earth, she had wanted to experiment with the idea, but she had been hesitant to unleash something she couldn't control. But now she was out of options. Kashar was going to kill her. Her field could only take one more concentrated blast.

Kashar noticed she was hanging onto his throat, and snapped at her with his teeth. Darting into the air in front of him, she floated a mere ten feet from the tip of his nose. He stared at her with his one good eye, gloating.

"So ends the great and glorious Geea!" he said.

Kashar sucked in a mighty breath. Swiftly, Ali grabbed the Yanti from beneath her shirt and went through Nira's moves in the reverse order—top of the head, heart, forehead—all the while chanting Alosha three times, backward: *"Ah-sola, Ah-sola, Ah-sola . . ."*

Kashar's fire hit her with resounding fury, bent her field to the max. Her clothes began to smoke, as she was pushed backward like a fly swatted by an angry housewife. Her world spun, the water below steamed, and the fire . . . Oh God, the dragon's flames engulfed her.

Yet she was able to take it all. For her field held, and she lived, and Kashar was going to have to try again. But even as he sucked in another breath, to finish her off, the Yanti began to glow with a soft violet light.

The fact caused them both to pause. She stopped tumbling, he stopped huffing and puffing, and they both . . . watched. The violet light was fascinating—one could even say it was enchanting. Neither of them could stop staring at it. Ali would have gone so far as to say it *charmed* her. Certainly it didn't feel dangerous, or hot . . . even as it switched from a mild glow to a rather bright one.

Yet she wanted it to turn hot. Into a flame.

She wanted it to *burn*, to *kill*.

No sooner did she think *those* words, when it grew hot. So hot it made Kashar's worst flame feel like a garden hose. And in that instant, Ali knew Sheri had tricked her. She had fed her the clue on purpose, so that her darling sister—in a critical moment such as this—would try to invoke the violet ray. The horror of Ali's blunder swept over her with the same force as the mysterious ray.

The light went beyond heat and smoke and fire.

The violet ray was pain itself. Blinding pain.

And she could not let go of it. The violet ray would not let her.

Ali shut her eyes as it swelled in power and still the ray pierced her skin and let her see—no, it *forced* her to see—her clothes as they caught fire, and her skin as it began to redden, and her long red hair as it was transformed into a burning halo. She did not just catch fire—it was as if every cell in her body changed into its own tormented supernova. She felt as if she were melting, and in the midst of her agony, she heard Sheri's curse inside her head . . .

"You know nothing!"

Yet, then, right then, finally, Ali knew what her sister meant.

This was beyond pain. This transcended all suffering. This was hell.

Something, a sound that did not belong to her, made her open her eyes. Kashar stared at the Yanti with an expression of lust. Again, he demanded . . .

"Give it to me!"

Maybe it was his desire for it, Ali did not know, but suddenly she was able to get rid of it. She threw it right at him, and the dragon, with unmistakable glee, reached for it with an open mouth, his many sharp teeth visible in the violet radiance. Then the Yanti vanished, for a few seconds, as he swallowed it, and the look of satisfaction on his face was as disgusting as the swelling scars on the entire front half of her body. Her skin was charcoal. Her old ally laughed at her.

"Fool Geea! A fairy should never play with a dragon's fire!"

Then he stopped laughing, and glanced down at his scaly throat and armored belly. He seemed concerned, for the violet light continued to grow in intensity. For even though it was buried inside him, and a dragon was made up of thousands of tons of muscle and bone, the violet ray began to shine *through* him. He began to glow from the inside out, and the heat of the Yanti shocked him as well.

Because the violet ray was not really made of fire.

It was composed of *something else.*

Something neither fairy nor dragon had experienced before.

Kashar caught fire. It started on the inside, but it spread quickly to his exterior. There was nothing to be done. He tried drowning himself in what was left of Tiena, but the violet ray shone through the waters, and then they themselves were changed into jets of steam. The dragon started to thrash in agony.

Ali had to duck as his barbed tail struck the wall, and cast down more stone. If she could have helped him, she would have, because even though he was trying to kill her, she knew his pain; and no one deserved *that*, whether they be friend or foe. But the truth was, she could not help herself, much less him.

As he disappeared beneath the river surface, in a globe of light so bright she had to put her arms over her eyes to keep from going blind, she heard him weeping, the sound so sorrowful it chilled her blood even as the rest of her burned. Fountains of steam continued to flood the cavern, like prehistoric geysers that had long ago consumed the dinosaurs. The glare would not permit her to see, but she knew her foe was dead, and that she was close to following him into the same infernal grave.

CHAPTER

9

Drash brought Ra the news of Ali, while he was resting in the fairy stronghold, high in the Youli Mountains. Ra had done little more than sleep since arriving at the secret hideaway, for, unknown to Ali, he had barely slept since he had met her in his uncle's cave on Mt. Kilimanjaro.

During their first night together in the green world, not long after they had met Drash, Ra had stayed awake most of the night to guard the koul's temporary home—a cave that overlooked Lestre. Ra had been awake, and had followed Ali, even when she had gone to watch Drash's first step in his transformation into a dragon.

Even when they had reached the Crystal Palace, he had stood guard at her door, and had barely slept that night. He could not explain why, but he felt an overriding need to take care of her. The thought of anything bad happening to her made him feel ill.

So he had gone three days without sleeping, and when he had reached the fairy stronghold—which Trae, Ali's advisor, called *Yom*—he had found a bed and curled up in it and had blacked out for long hours. Twice he had gotten up to pee, and to have a glass of fairy water—which was delicious, by the way—but then he had gone back to bed.

If asked, he could have barely described the place. On Earth it would have been called a bunker; however, Yom had none of the claustrophobic feel of a hideout. He'd seen the dining area, where a few fairies were quietly eating, and it was lit with beautiful golden globes that hung from the ceiling. Plus there were green plants everywhere, and delicate vines that nevertheless appeared to be an essential component in holding up the walls of Yom. To Ra, it felt more like a natural cave than an artificial bomb shelter.

However, now that Drash had come, everything else was forgotten.

Drash had not really entered Yom. He was too large to fit inside. Paddy, the leprechaun, had come running to say the dragon was back with possible news about Ali. Paddy was excited as he spoke; his large green eyes danced with sparks of gold, and he could not stop his huge green skull from shaking.

"Ra! Ra!" he cried as he burst into the bedroom. "Wake up! Drash says there is fire and smoke in the south! He says steam and more smoke are pouring from the Crystal Palace at Uleestar!"

Ra was up in an instant, reaching for his bow and arrows, and a sword Trae had given him as a gift when they had reached Yom. The gold hilt was studded with jewels, the silver blade was razor sharp. Ra had practiced with it a bit, before sleeping, and had discovered it could cut stone as easily as if it were butter. The odd thing was, the sword felt familiar in his hand, and when he had told Trae that, the wise fairy had merely smiled.

"Has Drash seen any other dragons?" Ra asked, as they headed for the door. The room was simple but comfortable. The walls were made of stone, laced with green quartz, although the floor was wooden, and smelled of fresh cedar. Although they were far beneath the ground, fresh air came into the room via a small opening in the ceiling. Ra did not know how the ventilation system worked, and frankly did not care.

"Drash said he saw many dragons in the distance!" Paddy exclaimed. "They were chasing someone!"

"Who?" Ra demanded, his heart pounding.

"Drash was not sure. But whoever it was, he says the person led most of the dragons underground, near Tiena's harbor."

"It must be Ali," Ra said, as he hurried up a flight of steps that led to the outside. Besides grabbing his weapons—before exiting Yom—he put on a long coat made of light wool that somehow kept him warm in the face of the bitter mountain air. The Youli peaks rose up high, and Ra knew of Drash's propensity to soar far above them.

Stepping outside, Ra found the dragon speaking to Trae and Farble—the troll. Actually, Farble was probably not following much of the conversation. Trolls were not too bright. Yet Farble understood enough to know that Geea might have returned to the green world, and that she was in danger.

Drash gave Ra a quick update, but it contained no more information than what Paddy had told him, except that there were definitely dragons near the Crystal Palace.

"Do you think Geea's there?" Ra asked Trae and Drash.

"Drash does not know," the young dragon replied.

Trae spoke. "If Geea did manage to escape the hoard of dragons by using Tiena's underground cavern, I don't think she would have been foolish enough to try to hide in the Crystal Palace."

"Could she be using Tiena's cavern to reach Lake Mira?" Ra asked.

Trae nodded. "That would be my guess."

"Do the dragons know that Tiena connects to the lake?" Ra asked.

"It's not common knowledge, but a few would know," Trae said.

"Drash saw no dragons at the lake," Drash said.

Ra moved to climb on Drash's back. Without a word the dragon stooped to accommodate him. Ra spoke again.

"Perhaps Ali created a diversion beneath Uleestar. She might be trying to reach here, without revealing our location. Drash and I will find out what we can."

That did not go over well with the others. Naturally, they wanted to come. Trae pointed out that he knew the countryside better than anyone. Farble pounded his chest to indicate how strong he was. And Paddy jumped up and down and cried that he was not leaving his "Missy" to those "filthy dragons."

In the end the troll and leprechaun came. The additional weight did not bother Drash, and when it came to a fight, Ra knew how handy Farble could be. Trae had to stay behind for practical reasons. With Ali gone, and Amma marked, he was the leader of the fairies and could not be risked. Trae gave Ra a gold bag filled with a fluffy blue powder before they departed.

"It's Geea's stardust," he explained. "If you find her, and you're in a bad spot, it might give her the extra strength she needs." Trae took a step back and bowed. "Fly fast, Drash, and all of you, go with the blessings of the ice maidens!"

Ra sat directly behind the dragon's head—Ali's favorite spot—and with hardly a flap of his wings Drash lifted them into the air. Soon they were hurtling south, toward the lake. Yet Ra cautioned Drash to stay low, as near as possible to the valleys and peaks. Drash was agreeable; he chose a twisting route through the mountains, almost hugging the rock and ice.

Since the dragon had only gotten his wings two days ago, Ra was impressed with his speed and control. Ra knew it was the dragon's love for Geea—all of the elementals' love for *their* Geea—that caused them to rush to her aid.

Ra would have raced through the sky alone, had he been a fairy.

But he was only a human being. Yet he wondered if that was the complete truth. As he had told Ali, since he was a child, he had been unusually strong, with eyes and ears far more acute than any other person he had ever met. His uncle had often remarked that Ra had abilities that were not of this world, but which came from the next. Since his uncle had spent a long time in the cave that led to the colored doors, Ra wondered if the man had entered the green world, and learned many of its secrets. It was a fact his uncle had been training Ra to be a *chimvi*—a shaman of the *Kutus,* his personal tribe—when the old man had been killed by dark fairies.

Even Drash, when they had first met, had talked to him as if he were an *elf.* The three-letter word held a resonance for Ra. The night he had stood guard outside Ali's bedroom in the Crystal Palace, he had heard her awaken in the night shouting, *"Jira! Jira! Ra!"* Later, he had wanted to ask her about her nightmare, but he hadn't wanted her to know he had been eavesdropping. But the way she switched the names—in midsentence—it was as if she was calling out *one* name.

And he had recognized *Jira* the instant he heard it.

The name felt as if it belonged to him.

As Ra stared out over the green world, atop Drash's back, the whole land felt as if it was his own. At least it was familiar, and he loved it so, more than Africa even, and he did not know why.

He had not asked Trae who Jira was.

Drash flew fast. It did not take them long to reach Lake Mira. They had come none too soon. Even from two miles away, Ra was able to see Ali floating adrift in a boat taken from Uleestar's harbor. She was lying on her back, apparently unconscious, while around the edges of the water paced ravenous scaliis. The creatures had once been elementals, but had been attacked by scabs, that had fastened onto their heads, and eaten their brains, transforming them into mindless cannibals that consumed whoever crossed their paths.

Ra saw that these dozen scaliis had been created from trolls and elves. They were haunting the shore, afraid of the water, but also eager for Ali's boat to drift closer, so they could feast on her.

Drash spotted them at the same time as Ra.

"Drash will burn them as we sweep over!" he called to Ra.

"No!" Ra shouted. "The flame might alert others in the area. Dragons might see us. Land behind them, on that rise there. I'll take out a few with my bow and arrows. Farble can kill some, and you can crush the rest."

"Kill for Geea!" Farble said proudly.

Drash obeyed Ra's command, and the dragon brought them down on a low cliff not far from the lake. The scaliis saw them, of course—they had a single bulbous eye where their face used to be—and came toward them with surprising speed. Ra was only able to get off four shots—which killed the four scaliis he aimed at—before Drash was forced to jump between them and use his bulk to crush the monsters. To his credit, Farble managed to kill two of the scaliis, smashing their heads together. Once again he pounded his chest in pride.

Oddly enough it was Paddy who reached Ali first. Ignoring the scaliis, he swam through the icy water and climbed into her canoe, before paddling it back to shore. Ra did not need to see Paddy's worried expression to know Ali was in bad shape. Her entire front, from head to toe, was ash—burnt clothes and flesh meshed together. Ra grimaced, his heart breaking. In some places steam still wafted off her stricken form. In her right hand she held the Yanti, but it was as if her fingers were melted around it. Ra couldn't tell if she was alive or dead. She did not move. Her chest did not even rise and fall. As Paddy paddled the boat onto the icy shore, there were tears in his eyes.

"Is Missy dead?" he cried.

Quickly, Ra lifted her from the boat and carried her away from the water, to a place of sand instead of snow. There he laid her on a coat Paddy had provided, and swept his own coat over her. Fear constricting his throat, he checked for a pulse, found one at her neck. It was faint. He finally saw she was breathing; unfortunately, her inhalations and exhalations were slight.

Her face was badly scarred. She had bleeding fissures, with torn flesh, and skin that was as black from soot as it was red from blood. He hardly recognized her, and he had to struggle to control his panic, to remain strong in front of the others. She was not dead, but without a miracle, she soon would be.

He knelt by her side and took the hand that held the Yanti.

"Ali," he called. "Can you hear me? It's Ra. You're safe now. Ali, please open your eyes. We're here with you now, all your friends are here." His voice cracked with emotion, as he added, "You have to come back to us, Ali. We love you."

Ali opened her left eye. She could not use her right, for the burnt skin had melted it shut. It seemed as if she tried to smile, but on the right side of her face nothing moved. Ra suspected whatever had burned her had gone farther than skin-deep, and had damaged her facial nerves. Besides the awful scarring, her expression was lopsided.

"I made a mistake," she whispered, and Ra had to bend to hear her words. He continued to hold her hand, fearing to squeeze it. He spoke in an encouraging tone.

"That doesn't matter, you're safe now. We'll take care of you."

"Paddy will fix Missy," the leprechaun said, kneeling across from Ra, on her left side. But Paddy's eyes dripped such large tears; he, too, could barely speak. Behind him, Ra heard Farble moaning. Seeing their pain, perhaps attempting to put them at ease, Ali tried to smile again.

"Know now how Lucy felt," she said softly.

"Who's Lucy?"

"My sister." A shudder went through the length of her body then, and it seemed she might have a seizure, or else slip into shock. Ra was anxious to get her out of the cold, back to Yom, but he feared to move her. She looked as frail as a dry autumn leaf that had been touched by a match.

"We have to get you to Yom," Ra said. "The fairies there can help you."

Ali shook her head. "No time. The invasion. Must go to the Isle of Greesh."

"You're not going anywhere. You need to rest, to heal." It was then he recalled the stardust Trae had given him, in the gold pouch. He pulled it out. "I have this . . ."

Before he could finish what he was going to say, she sniffed the air, closed her one eye, and said, "Ah, stardust. Give me. Put . . . in my mouth."

Ra took out the gold pouch. "How much?"

She did not even look, just opened her mouth. "All of it."

Ra fed it to her slowly, lest she choke, and twice sent Paddy to get her a cup of water from the lake. Well, it was actually

Paddy's liquor flask they used, but Paddy was more than happy to empty his whiskey to help his Missy. Ali sipped the water gratefully as she absorbed the magical powder.

And magic it was, for before Ra's very eyes, he saw the worst of her wounds close, the bleeding stop. Ten minutes after ingesting the last of the stardust, she was able to sit up and stretch her legs and arms.

Yet her right eye remained sealed, and the scars had not gone away, nor had their hideous colors faded. Ali was still not recognizable. She had no hair—her skull was a mass of gray and purple lumps. The fingers of her left hand were fused. However, she had regained the use of her right hand. She was still able to hold the Yanti.

Time went by. As the sun rose higher in the sky, she steadily gained strength, and told them of her battle with Kashar. Drash sat close to her, and it was an emotional time for the young dragon. Ra could not decide what was worse for him: his shame or his pain. For, from the start, it was obvious that Ali had killed Kashar.

Yet when she came to the part of how she misused the Yanti, Ali grew vague, and Ra knew she was hesitant to divulge any dangerous secrets.

But she made it clear that she had been a fool to use the Yanti as a weapon, even though it had worked. It had killed Kashar, but it had almost killed her. She said it was a wonder, when their battle was done, that she was able to retrieve the Yanti, and collapse into a boat, and take what was left of Tiena north. With all the miles of stone she had dropped on the dragons, it was clear the river was never again going to flow into Lake Mira.

An hour after digesting the stardust, Ali was strong enough to stand, with a little help from Ra. She told Drash to take them back to Yom, but made it clear that she was then going on to the Isle of Greesh. It was essential she go to the island, she repeated, but admitted she was too weak to fly that far. Of course Ra told her they were coming with her.

"We're your friends," he said. "We rescued you today, and you might need our help on the island. You're not leaving without us."

"Aye, Missy is hurt and needs to rest," Paddy put in. "Greesh is evil—no place for a queen to visit, especially when she's feeling poorly. Missy must not go there."

"The Shaktra came from the Isle of Greesh," Drash added.

Ali motioned Ra aside, spoke to him by the water. With no lips, her voice came out sounding awkward. The former were mere mounds of red and purple flesh, and Ra had to struggle not to show his horror at her appearance. Still, she sensed it, and tried to give him a reassuring hug.

Unfortunately, she had to pull back. It was too painful to embrace.

"Don't feel sorry for me, I caused this," she said.

"Ali . . ."

"I did. And in a strange way, I think it was meant to be. I had to go through what Doren did."

"Who's Doren?"

"In this world, she's my sister." Ali added, "She's also the Shaktra."

Ra recoiled in shock. "That's impossible!"

Ali nodded weakly. "Trust me, it was not a pleasant discovery. But it's the truth—one I've had to struggle to accept. Whatever changed her into such a monster—it all started on the Isle of Greesh. That's why I must go there. But I can only go alone, with Drash. Believe me, you of all people can't go."

The way she applied the restriction especially to him gave

Ra more reason to doubt her decision. Yet, he had not told Ali this before, but every time he had heard the words, "The Isle of Greesh," he had felt cold inside. Even now, as they spoke of going there, he trembled.

It was as if he was connected to the place . . . somehow.

He tried to ask Ali if that was true, but she turned away.

"I'm not sure," she said sadly.

Ra hesitated. "Did something happen to Jira there?"

She stared at him with her one eye. It was still green and piercing, and there was still power behind it. The girl was her *own* miracle. Burn her nearly to ash, and the next minute she was back on her feet, ready to do battle. But all of a sudden, a tear came from her eye.

"Yes," she said. "You know him?"

Ra shrugged. "I've heard the name."

"From whom?"

He met her gaze. "You. In your sleep."

Ali lowered her head, appeared to speak to herself. "I guess it's possible, but I never hoped . . . I never knew for certain."

"What?"

Ali wiped at her tear; another replaced it. "He was my friend. My best friend. And that island . . . it did something to him. Something terrible to his mind."

"So it harmed him, I'm not him." He added, "I'll be fine."

She shook as she studied him, and his own trembling only grew worse. "Is that true? I think you might know something I don't know. Something you're afraid to tell me. You're special, Ra. The moment I met you, I knew that was true."

"I felt the same about you, Ali."

"What did you feel?" She really wanted to know.

There was blood in Ra's face. It burned, but not all burns were evil. This one, he thought, might even be illuminating.

174

CHAPTER

10

For Ali, there was great pain, great fear, and great love, and she asked herself if the first two were worth the last, and the answer was yes. Her body was probably scarred beyond repair, and they were flying toward the source of the greatest evil in all the worlds. Yet she had Ra to hold on to, and that was good.

Of course, he was right about being Jira. A part of her had always known the truth. She had just been afraid to admit it to herself. Even Amma had tried to tell her, before she had been marked by the Shaktra.

In the Crystal Palace, Amma had studied the gauze on her burnt hand, and had said, *"Ra bandaged this for you."*

"How did you know?"

"He likes to take care of you, I see it."

"I only met him two days ago. He hardly knows me."

Amma had smiled then. *"It is something to wonder about."*

On top of the Youli Mountains, before flying to the kloudar, Ra had insisted on going with them. Afraid of the lack of air, Ali had warned him to go back down, but he had said: *"I go where you go."*

And again Amma had smiled and said, *"Jira used to say that."*

So her mother had known and approved of Ra. It made Ali wonder how many more secrets her mom could tell her. If only the mark could be removed, and her mind freed. That was one secret Ali vowed to wrestle from the Isle of Greesh before she left it. She was going to liberate Amma and Nira both. The green world, and Earth, needed their help now.

Ra called over his shoulder as they rode Drash toward the mysterious island, the wind hard and fast in their faces. "Feel like you're on the back of a motorcycle?"

"I've never ridden one. Have you?" she asked.

"There's one in our village. But it goes thirty kilometers an hour—downhill."

"Is that only twenty miles an hour?"

"Yes."

"I got to go home at least. You haven't. Do you miss it?"

"I'm at home when I'm with you," Ra said.

Touched by his remark, Ali held him tighter.

"Drash wants to know if the humans are going to marry now?" the dragon asked.

They both laughed, and Ali spoke. "Drash may be the new king of the dragons, but he's not allowed to ask the queen of the fairies and the prince of the elves personal questions."

A note of wonder entered Drash's voice.

"True. Drash is now king of the dragons."

Ali wished she could rub his side like she used to, but her hands hurt too much. "Do you forgive me for killing your father?" she asked.

"Drash knew Father had to die the day he started killing others." The dragon paused. "Did Kashar ask about Drash?"

"Your name came up. I told him you were a full-fledged dragon."

"What did Kashar say?"

Ali hesitated. "I think he was impressed."

Drash appeared to guess the truth. "But Kashar would not give up the Shaktra, even for his son."

"I'm sorry," was all Ali could think to say.

The Isle of Greesh, as they came near, resembled Maui, a Hawaiian island Ali had visited with her parents. The land was definitely tropical. There were coral reefs in the green water, and many trees hung with various colored fruits. But Ali did not see nor hear any birds as they swooped near. She sensed no insects either. There was plenty of plant life, but that appeared to be all.

On the flight over, Ali had planned to have Drash stand guard at the hill that contained the mysterious chamber that had drawn Doren and her father to the island, but already she knew that was unnecessary. Her subtle senses were at full alert. The Shaktra had left the island empty. There was not even a scab buried somewhere in the sand, she was sure of it. Yet the island was supposed to be her enemy's home base. Ali found the tactic curious.

Had something on the island ordered them all to leave?

The island was built around a single steep hill. At first glance it looked as if it were the remains of a volcano, possibly the original volcano that had caused the island to rise from the ocean floor.

A closer examination made her question the theory. The hill was too steep, and there was a symmetrical quality to it that hinted at unnaturalness, although it was covered with trees and flowers and bushes like the rest of the land. Ali was only able to remember fragments about the island from two sources—one, the dream she had of Greesh on her last visit to the green world; and two, her actual memories from her past life as Geea. It was difficult to say which source of information was more accurate. Both were chilling.

Jira was excited to be on the island, and to see the ancient ruins the others had spoken of. But for Geea, as they slowly descended the long shaft that led deep into the island's solid underbelly, she felt only dread. Jira knew of her intuition, and usually respected it, but today he brushed off her concerns.

"This is the discovery of our time," he said, as the creaking elevator slowly lowered them into the heart of Greesh's only peak.

Geea pointed to the black walls of the shaft. "The ground here is hard. There's an exceptional amount of iron in it. What does that tell you?"

"That this peak was once volcanic?" Jira said.

"Whatever volcano existed here, that was millions of years ago, when the island formed. This iron did not come out of the ground. It came from the sky."

"Is that a joke?"

"No." She tapped the dark wall of the shaft. "A large meteor must have crashed here long ago. The hill at the center of this island is built on top of it."

"That's only a theory of yours. The meteor would have incinerated itself when it hit here."

"But it didn't. Nor did it incinerate what Doren has discovered. So maybe it did not crash-land here. Maybe it landed gently."

"Are you suggesting your sister's discovery is from . . . elsewhere?"

"Yes."

Jira laughed. "You have an imagination, Geea, I grant you that."

———

When they reached the hidden chamber in the heart of the hill, Jira went inside alone . . . because she was too fearful to follow. Not long afterward he began to scream, and from then on he was insane. It was only in the last moments of his life, when he was lying in her arms and gushing blood from his long fall, that his eyes had seemed to clear. It was then he had said those three strange words. *"Net . . . The . . . Enter . . ."*

Ali instructed Drash to land at the top of the hill. Climbing off the dragon, they found a crude elevator—a simple cube made of wood, and supported by rope. It would have to be lowered manually. Drash said he could do it. Ali took a look at his arms and hands—not a dragon's strongest point. In that respect, he looked a bit like a T-Rex. Ra seemed to read her mind, although neither of them wanted to hurt his feelings.

"Are you sure you can handle the weight?" Ra asked carefully.

In response, Drash walked over to a boulder, casually picked it up, and shattered it between his relatively small hands. "Drash can handle you two," he replied dryly.

They got in the elevator, closed the door. Drash worked the wooden wheel that let out the rope that attached to the elevator roof. Slowly the sky began to change into a small square, as they descended deeper and deeper. Ra had brought his pack, took out a flashlight and turned it on. Soon it was their only source of illumination, although Ali did not need it to see, for she could see even in total darkness. But she didn't tell Ra that—didn't want to stir up the ancient rivalry. Who was more powerful: an elf or a fairy? Of course, Ali knew the fairies were, and naturally Ra would think the reverse. Since it was not an argument that could be won, there was no point in starting it . . .

Ali remembered more of what she had told Jira when they were last here.

"*This place does not feel good. Many people lived here once, but when they died, it was not in a natural way.*"

"*What do you mean?*"

"*This place is alive with pain, but it is the pain of the dead. Right here, long ago—I think many people killed themselves.*"

"*That's impossible, no one would do that.*"

"*Look at what is happening in the yellow world and tell me that is impossible.*"

Again, Jira had laughed at her fears.

Yet, today, Ali saw Ra was not laughing.

She saw his fear and was glad. Because when they reached the bottom of the shaft, they would come to a narrow cave dusted with black soot, that would lead to a massive stone door that opened into what was said to be a temple filled with "*amazing artifacts that the highest elemental magic could not reproduce.*" The latter remark belonged to Doren. It had been her sister who had lured them down here.

Now Ali welcomed Ra's growing anxiety because she did not want him to enter the temple again. He was an elven prince, it was true, he had many gifts, but he did not have nearly her power. He knew nothing of her connection to the blue light, which might be the only shield that could save her. Furthermore, she had only one Yanti, and she would need it to shield herself from whatever had driven Jira insane. Ra could not come, he would just get in her way.

They reached the bottom, got out of the elevator. With his flashlight, bravely, Ra went first up the narrow cave, getting soot on his clothes as he moved. Ali had on a green fairy robe, that she had picked up at Yom when they had dropped Farble and Paddy back off at the stronghold.

As they neared the temple door, Ra slowed down, let her draw even with him.

The door was engraved with a circular mandala. At first glance it appeared to resemble the Yanti, but it had six sides, not seven, and the inner triangle had been sliced down the middle with a splintered line. There was no central dot, and Ali knew that was important. It was the inner dot of the Yanti that represented the infinite—the divine, the essence, whatever one's concept of God might be—where everything emerged from, and eventually returned to. This mandala, although obviously a powerful symbol to those who had made it, did not acknowledge such a concept.

Ali recalled how a study of the mandala had sent Geea into a panic, and even though Ali did not possess all the insights of her previous incarnation, she immediately sensed the evil that emanated from the etching.

Ali recalled another remark Geea had told Jira, as she begged him not to go inside the temple. *"This symbol has a power over the mind."*

Ali could feel it just standing there. A troubling weakness entered her chest. She had to pull her gaze away from it just to draw in a deep breath. Taking a step toward Ra, she had to yank his head aside. He was already soaked in sweat, and trembling.

"Don't look at it!" she snapped.

He sucked in a ragged breath, struggling for calm, nodded. "What is it?" he asked.

Ali glanced at it, then back at Ra. "A representation of some type of energy that we cannot see, but which we can definitely feel. Notice how it resembles the Yanti, but is like a corruption of it. You see that a lot on Earth, when it comes to cults. The Nazis took the swastika—a symbol of the four sacred directions of the creation—and inverted it and turned it on its side. Those who worship the devil—they take the cross and turn it upside down. There's a natural power in these symbols, as there is in the design of the Yanti. But the beings who built this place took that power and tweaked it somehow—to their own liking."

"I'm not sure what you mean." Ra continued to pant. "But I don't know if it's a good idea to stay here. Have you found out what you wanted?"

Ali sadly shook her head. "My investigation hasn't begun. I have to go inside, through that door. Furthermore, I need to go alone." She raised her hand as he went to protest. "In my last life, as Geea, I was unable to go in there, even though you did."

Ra tried to straighten himself, to stand up to the waves of negative energy that literally dripped from the evil mandala. "But if I went in there before, I can do it again. I don't want to leave you alone, that's not what I came here to do."

She nodded. "What you're saying, you're right in a way. I need you close, need to feel your love and support. Because to be honest, I'm terrified to go on. I don't know what I'm going to find, or what it's going to do to me. In my last life, my father went in there and vanished. To this day I don't know where he is. And my sister, Doren, she went inside and changed into the Shaktra." Ali paused. "And you know what happened when you went in there."

"I lost my mind," Ra said softly, nodding to himself. "I remember now."

Ali came close, tried to touch his hand with her ruined hands. But her fingers hurt—hugging was easier than squeezing. She recoiled in pain, but he seemed to appreciate her attempt. Yet he still did not want her to go in there without him. Ali shook her head.

"The fact that you've come this far means a lot to me. I feel your fear. I feel you trying to hide it. You want to throw yourself in front of this wall for me. I know you—you would give your life for me in an instant. I would do the same for you. That's the kind of bond we have—and this stone wall isn't going to block that. When I'm inside, you're going to be with me. Your strength and caring will be there beside me, and that will help keep me sane." She reached out, gave him the best hug she was capable of, whispered in his ear, which was really more of a whisper in his mind, because her throat was all choked up. It was easier to put the thoughts directly into his heart.

"Your love is all I need, Ra."

He must have heard her, deep inside, for he nodded.

"I'll wait for you right here," he said.

She touched his head as she backed away. "Thanks. Don't stare at the mandala. Don't look at the blasted thing at all."

He nodded again, forced a smile. "It gives me a headache."

A rope and pulleys had been installed by the original makers to move the massive stone door. All she had to do was kick a wooden lever, and the door swung open. She disappeared into the dark temple.

The door slammed shut behind her with a rush. Her subtle senses had anticipated finding a large chamber, and yet the space she ended up in was small, circular, with a low dome ceiling. Six crystal blocks had been set around a black stone stool. The crystals themselves were rather dark, but streaked with white quartz. Except for their vague but consistent box-like shapes, they could have been natural stones.

But the front of each stone, the sides that faced the black stool, were clearly polished. She saw no controls, but intuitively understood what they were. *Screens.*

Dark crystal screens. The stool was for the viewer to sit upon. Four feet high, it did not look as if it had been designed with humans in mind, but she felt if she perched on top of it, the screens would activate. For there was a faint gap between the edges of the stool and the floor. Perhaps it would move, and sink down, when weight was placed on top of it.

There was no other entrance or exit to the chamber.

It was odd how she remembered none of this from the day she had rescued Jira. Of course, in that life, when she had managed to reopen the hatch, he had leapt into her arms, weeping, before the door had automatically reclosed.

Ali walked around each block, finding no controls. But she did discover several loose objects atop one of the blocks. For the life of her, they looked like plugs of some kind, with a black wire attached. However, at the opposite end of each plug was a tiny purple crystal.

"What the heck . . ."

Ali took a sudden step back. Something about the ceiling had changed, or else she was imagining things. When she had first entered, it had been a low dome. That had been clear. Now she could find no ceiling at all. There was just . . . nothing. Yet it had been there before, she could have sworn.

Had the chamber already reacted to her presence?

She had heard no sound, no movement.

Ali touched a crystal block. The room was on the cool side; the blocks were positively freezing. Yet they did not *broadcast* their cold, or else the chamber would have been frigid.

Ali felt she had to sit on the stool. That was what it was there for. The invitation was obvious. When you sat on the rock, the place seemed to shout to her, the party would begin.

Ordinarily she would have hopped up onto it. But her wounds made every move difficult. Twice she tried unsuccessfully to squirm into the high seat. Finally, she decided to activate her field and just fly into it.

Yet her magnetic field failed to work. Good to know.

Fairy magic did not work in this place.

Ali took a running jump and landed on the stool. It did settle with her weight, so that her feet almost touched the floor. At the same time a purple crystal—attached to a long black wire—appeared above her head. It looked like a natural amethyst, with its rough green outer shell still in place. Yet it was round—one half of a well-sliced sphere—and it glowed, filling the chamber with a haunting purple color that reminded her of the light she had seen in Sheri Smith's house. The amethyst was larger than her head, and for a moment she feared it was going to cover her head, and smother her. But it stopped a foot above the top of her skull.

Ali felt naked right then—particularly as a strange magnetic field played over the raw skin of her head, down the front of her face, and over her heart. Neither cold nor hot, the *scan* nevertheless caused her to shiver.

She knew she was being examined . . . and without permission.

The six screens lit up at once. More purple light. Then the impossible happened—she could see all six of them at the same time! Without moving her head a fraction of an inch. Indeed, she could see all six with her eyes closed!

Then she understood. The crystal above her head was transmitting the images directly into her brain. Her vision was now holographic, not a result of her optic nerves. She was not watching TV, and the six blocks were not the latest in high definition plasma screens. Yet they might have been computers of some type. Whatever they were, they were now connected to her head.

Another shock. Three of the screens showed images that could have been taken directly off any number of human computers at home. She saw AOL, Google, Yahoo . . . At last she understood Jira's final words to her.

Not: Net . . . The . . . Enter. No, he had said, *Internet!*

The other three screens also appeared to be hooked up to Internets—but of mysterious origins. She did not recognize the writing, nor any of the symbols. Yet there were brilliant flashes, occasionally followed by strange images. They came so fast . . . then vanished. She couldn't be certain, but she thought she saw stars, moons, nebula—even spaceships.

Of course, it might have been her imagination—just something she hoped to see. Because from the beginning, as Geea, she had pushed the theory that the chamber was of extraterrestrial origin. Perhaps because she had settled on that idea back then, the crystal blocks were feeding her images to support it. She could be sure of nothing—except the speed of the pictures was fantastic!

However, when it came to the *human* Internet portals, the images were slower, although they jumped about. Why, if she concentrated hard enough, she could read today's news, check out the latest films, even catch up on the latest sports scores.

The three human Internet screens were shifting constantly—as if the intelligence behind them was sampling the interests of humans in different parts of the globe. She caught what looked like personal e-mails. Not all were in English, and none were from anyone she had met before. The e-mails were not discussing the end of the world, just normal mundane matters.

None of this soothed her fears. It all felt too . . . convenient.

"I wish to communicate!" she shouted.

One of the three screens hooked into the Internet went momentarily blank. The screen turned briefly purple, then red letters appeared, in quotes, as if it knew that was the way humans conveyed speech while writing. While seeing the words on the screen, Ali also heard them in her mind. However, it was all happening in her head, because even when she shut her eyes, she still saw the screen.

"We wish to communicate as well. What do you prefer to be called?"

"Ali. What shall I call you?"

"The Entity."

"Are you one or many?"

"We are many that have become one."

"Where are you from?"

"Many places, in time and space. We also come from beyond the dimensions you know. We are a network made up of many races."

"Why are you here?"

"To serve."

The answer could not have surprised Ali more.

"Entity, are you responsible for the one known as Doren—who used to be my sister—changing into the Shaktra?"

"Yes. We initiated the change that brought about her transformation."

"Can you explain why you felt the need to change her?"

"By your standards, the reasons are complex. From our point of view, they are simple. We changed her to help her serve those around her."

"From my point of view—and that of the majority of my associates in this world—the changes you brought about in Doren were detrimental to her and to this world."

"This Entity is aware of that false perception on your part."

"Are you sure that it is false?"

"Yes."

"But you've turned her into a monster!"

"By your standards, that is correct. By our standards, we have helped change her into an authoritarian figure that can help take control of this world and the other."

"But doesn't it bother you that she has become so cruel?"

"We are not as affected as your species is by cruelty or kindness. We take a more long-term view. What is best for the majority—over time."

"So you have no desire to be cruel?"

"Again, that concept is irrelevant to us. We are here to serve."

"Who or what do you serve?"

"In a sense, we serve a race above us, that is our superior. In another sense, we serve ourselves by encouraging all intelligent beings below us to serve themselves—by first serving us."

"You talk in circles!"

"Not at all. The concept is simply new to you."

"Where does freedom of choice enter into this?" Ali asked.

"Freedom of choice exists for those above us—when it comes to us. They can order us what to do. Freedom of choice exists for us—when it comes to you. Soon we will begin to order your lives."

Ali snorted. "I hardly think so."

"Your sarcasm is noted, but is irrelevant. We accept that we have superiors. In time, you will accept that we are your superiors. You will also appreciate what we do for you. It is true, as we first get to know each other, that it seems we are only interested in conquest. Over time you will see that we are more interested in establishing a hierarchy."

"I don't understand. What is this hierarchy?"

"All our relationships are based on hierarchy. Those above us, control us. Soon, we will control you, and with our help, you will expand in power and conquer other races. Then you will control those races. All of this represents a hierarchy based on control."

"But you're saying, right now, you have freedom to do with *us* as you like?"

"Correct. That is natural."

"How is it natural?" she demanded.

"We are in the position of greater power and authority."

Ali felt frustrated. "So you equate service with conquering?"

"To a degree."

"That is ridiculous! I speak for the green world, and, for the moment, I can speak for Earth as well. We do not wish to be conquered. Entity, please understand, we want you to leave us alone to create our own destiny."

"We cannot do that."

"Why not?"

"You will destroy yourselves."

"You are here to destroy us!"

"That is incorrect."

"You say you are here to serve us. You are just here to take from us."

"That is partially correct. We will take from you, in this world and in the other. But at the same time, we will ensure your survival. Without our help, you will destroy yourselves."

Ali hesitated. "Why do you say that?"

"Do you ask of the green world or the yellow world?"

"The yellow world."

"In the next hundred of your years, the probability that the people of the yellow world will destroy themselves and the planetoid they reside on is extremely high. In excess of ninety-seven percent."

"Those are not good odds."

"No."

"How do you know if they're accurate?"

"The majority of the people on Earth serve themselves. Despite what you might like to believe, love is not the dominant quality on your planet. It is rare. We would not have been drawn here unless that was the case. When a race such as human beings has reached a technological level where they are capable of destroying themselves—and they have on the whole chosen the path of fear over love—then the chances of self-inflicted extinction are high. That is why we do not exaggerate when we state we are here to serve you. By taking control of your world, we safeguard your survival."

"You act like we should be grateful you're here!"

"Your race should be grateful someone is here."

The reference to *someone* opened a door in Ali's head.

"Are there other races in the galaxy that are drawn to love?"

"Yes. But they were not drawn here. Had there been sufficient love, they would have come. Instead, we have come."

"But human beings do have a great deal of love, buried inside. They just need more time to find it. Then they will survive, on their own, without outside intervention."

"That is wishful thinking on your part. Human beings have run out of time to make another choice. Therefore, the choice has been made for them—by us—to take away their freedom of choice."

"You do not have the right!"

"Nor do we have the right to sit idly by and watch you die."

Again, Ali hesitated. "Explain what you mean."

"Let us give a few examples you are probably familiar with. The fish in your seas are no longer safe to eat. They are saturated with chemicals—specifically mercury and lead. In a hundred years, at the current rates of pollution, the seas will be dead. Totally devoid of life. Yet it is the plankton in your oceans that is the main source of oxygen for life on your world. Let us take another example. Most of your vehicles and heavy machinery are dependent on the burning of fossil fuels. That pollutes your atmosphere, bringing on global warming. The list of what you're doing to ruin your planet is endless. Plus, what is done on Earth rebounds into the green world. Both worlds will soon become inhospitable. Now what do you do to each other? You have your sayings. The rich get richer, the poor get poorer. On one continent, everyone has too much to eat. They are all fat. On another continent, the masses starve. They are all skinny. Take this point to a more personal level. In your intimate relationships, specifically in your marriages and your families, the majority of you lie and cheat on your partners and your siblings."

"That's a lie!" Ali snapped.

"We state what is. Yes, Ali, you say humanity has love, and so it does, but it is rare. Too rare to save your world from extinction."

Ali sighed. "I hear what you say, and much of it is true. But the agent you've created to carry out your plan—the Shaktra—is causing tremendous suffering in both worlds."

"Only in the short term. In the long term, there will be more order, and therefore, less suffering."

"And no freedom of choice?"

"*Less* freedom of choice. That is the way it must be. Because your people are instinctively selfish, when they choose, they do not choose for the greater good. They choose for themselves. We understand this. We evolved from a similar race. We do not blame you, we are just trying to save you."

"Why do you have to work through an agent like my sister?"

"We have evolved, so to speak, to a level where we prefer

not to have direct contact with your level. For that reason, we use agents."

"Did you choose Doren because of her connection to the blue light?"

"Yes. We would choose you for the same reason."

"When Doren leaves her body, will she return to the blue world?"

"No. She will come to us."

"Why?"

"Because she has made that choice. The choice of control."

"Stop, wait. Are you saying you evolve differently than us? We follow the path of the doors. We go from the yellow world, to the green world, to the blue world, to the violet world, and, finally, to the white world."

"That is correct. We evolve to the purple world, and remain there."

Ali had what she thought was an insight. "Because your path is a path of control, you do not experience love, do you?"

"Correct. There is no love in the purple vibration."

"I don't mean to be rude but . . . don't you miss it?"

"Our satisfaction, so to speak, comes from control. We cannot miss love. Indeed, it is the opposite of what we are."

"But the opposite of love is what we call fear."

For the first time the Entity hesitated to answer.

"You may call it what you wish," it said finally.

"Then your satisfaction comes from creating fear, does it not?"

"You cloud the main issue. We come to serve. We serve by saving your race from extinction." The Entity paused. "If you do not help us in our task, then you help destroy your race."

Ali almost smiled. "You say I cloud the issue. The reverse is true. I see you for what you are. You are fear mongers. It's what gets you off. I'll never choose to help you. What do you have to say about that?"

"If you do not join us, we will destroy you."

"Here and now?"

"Yes."

"Without using an outside agent?"

"At the moment, so to speak, you have stuck your head into our world."

"Trying to scare me into joining you? Is that what you did to Doren?"

"It was different with her."

"How so?"

"It will be easier for us to show you, rather than to explain to you."

She shrugged nonchalantly, although her fear was great. "Show me."

Ali became aware the six screens were filled with a picture of Doren. Her sister sat where she currently sat, and beside her stood Tulas, one of the high fairies, Doren's great love. Tulas was dressed in a green robe with a golden rope-belt. He was the largest and strongest fairy in the kingdom, yet oddly, it was her sister who carried the sword. It was a custom with Doren, as were her red robes, ruby necklaces, and bracelets. Even the hilt of her silver sword was studded with red jewels that matched her hair, green ones that showed off her piercing eyes. Doren never went anywhere without jewels as rare as her beauty, and Geea never begrudged the fact that her sister had more male admirers—not just fairies and elves, but dwarves and leprechauns as well—than anyone in the elemental kingdom.

Together, Doren and Tulas made a stunning pair. Many, Ali

recalled, thought they would have made a powerful king and queen.

As the scene opened, Tulas also had a purple crystal over his head, and the Entity was answering Doren's question as to where her father had disappeared to. The six screens said that he had joined them in another dimension. To this Doren and Tulas acted surprised, but the Entity explained that Nemi had done this of his own free will, and that they should be pleased. He could still help the green and yellow world from where he was.

With that remark, Tulas demanded to speak to Nemi, but the Entity said that was not possible because Nemi was busy with some type of work that could not be explained. Tulas did not like that answer.

"Why would he leave us without saying goodbye?" he asked.

"We detect a note of hostility in your voice, and remind you that we do not lie. Had we wanted to deceive you, it would have been simple for us to duplicate Nemi's appearance and voice, and have him speak to you now—with answers of our own choosing. But we choose not to do that so as to maintain the integrity of our relationship with you."

"Will we be able to speak to my father soon?" Doren asked.

"Yes. That appears highly probable."

Doren looked up at Tulas from her place beneath the purple amethyst that at the moment hovered over Ali's head. "It's true—if they just wanted to lie to us—they could have fed us a much simpler answer," she said.

Yet Tulas was not content. He addressed the Entity in his powerful voice. "How did Nemi transfer into your dimension? Does he still have a physical body?"

"He continues to possess a physical form, but it is has been changed. The change was necessary to facilitate adjustment to his new environment."

The Entity had answered the second question, Ali noted, ignored the first. Tulas noted the fact as well. He kept insisting on more information. Oddly enough, Doren tried to calm him down. To Ali, it was as if her sister was already partially under the Entity's spell.

Eventually, Doren and Tulas returned to discussing with the Entity what needed to be done to save the Earth. From the conversation, it seemed they had been examining the subject for some time, and everything the Entity said sounded good. It was focused on environmental pollution, and the need to reduce the Earth's population to one billion people—over time.

Ali had always thought the Earth was overpopulated.

But the Entity did not speak of elementals invading the Earth.

Then the record appeared to jump forward in time. Next, Doren was alone with the Entity, and she looked worn-out and irritated. Yet the Entity continued to handle her smoothly. It repeatedly said she had to accept her "high position" in the hierarchy that was about to dawn.

Ali wondered how much time had elapsed since the initial talk. She asked herself why the Entity was giving her these *insights*. Clearly it was not worried she would leave the Isle of Greesh with knowledge that might hinder its ultimate goal.

The Entity spoke to Doren in a reasonable tone.

"You come from the blue light, Tulas does not. Therefore, he cannot act as a direct agent for the vibration we intend to bring into the green and yellow worlds. You have to accept the fact that you are destined to be queen here as well as on Earth." The Entity added, "Besides, it is what you always wanted."

"But my sister is queen of Uleestar. My father made her so, and she holds the Yanti and is the only one who knows how to use it."

"Others might also know how to wield it," the Entity replied.

"Do you?" When the Entity did not answer, Doren added, "I get the impression you don't understand how powerful it is."

"We understand the Yanti—its origin and its purpose. We would have preferred you possessed it, and not your sister. But from the way you speak of her, it is not yet time to bring her here."

"When will be the time?"

"Soon. But first you must accept a greater influx of power into your physical form." The Entity paused. "We have to slightly alter your brain."

Doren sat up. "What do you mean?"

"We speak of the frontal lobes of your brain. We need to implant a crystal in that spot, between your eyebrows." The Entity added, "Don't worry, no one will see it. Your beauty will not be marred. It will probably be enhanced."

Doren was curious. "How so?"

"You will shine with great radiance. Others will find you even more magnetic, and be drawn to you automatically. They will clamor to fulfill your wishes."

"That sounds interesting."

"We can implant it today. Now."

Doren hesitated. "I will have to think about accepting this implant."

"Don't think about it too long."

"What's the hurry?"

"There is a timetable when it comes to the green and yellow worlds. We are only allowed to operate within a certain time frame. Otherwise, a great opportunity will be lost."

"I don't understand. Explain yourself."

"Is it necessary that we explain everything to you?"

"I'm not sure what you're asking."

"Isn't it time you began to accept what we say on faith?"

Doren disliked the response. Who wouldn't have, Ali asked herself.

Yet her sister replied with the same answer.

"I'll have to think about your offer."

Then there were images of Tulas, alone in the chamber, but he had in his hands a bag of takor stones. Ali was surprised. Unless her father had shown Tulas how to use takor—via voom—it would have been of no use to him as a weapon. Indeed, he should not even have known that the stones existed.

On the other hand, her father had trusted Tulas a great deal. He was a gentle soul, and a valiant warrior. He often kept Doren in line by tempering her worst weaknesses—her vanity and her temper.

Yet here he was, ready to blow up the chamber!

Even before the horror arrived, Ali knew it was coming. For the chamber was still here, and Tulas was not. It was obvious the Entity had powers at its disposal far beyond those it had let on. But studying the Entity, Ali did believe that it told the truth—insofar as what it said. Perhaps it was bound by some sort of cosmic law to be truthful.

Still, that did not prevent it from being cruel, devious too.

As Tulas placed a final takor in the farthest corner, a sound wave was emitted by the crystal cubes. The noise was totally unlike the sounds Ali used to detonate takor; nevertheless, it was effective. Tulas was given no warning. She would have closed her eyes if it would've helped. The stone exploded in his hand, and blew off his head.

Another gap of time ensued. It seemed to last. The blood surrounding Tulas's body dried up. Rigor mortis came and went. He began to decay . . .

Then Doren came rushing in the chamber, to Tulas's side, picking up his headless body. Her grief then . . . Ali had only to recall Jira's death to know what she must have felt right then. Whatever her faults, no one could ever have doubted her devotion to Tulas. Doren screamed at the Entity.

"What have you done?"

The Entity replied calmly. "Tulas came to destroy our contact with this world. He had to be stopped. We merely caused his weapons of destruction to backfire."

"But you killed him!" Doren wailed.

"True. But we can bring him back to you. If you wish."

There ensued the most painful pause.

"How?" Doren asked meekly.

"Obey us. Do as we command and accept the implant. Take up the destiny that awaits you. Allow us to give you the power to take control of this world, and the yellow world, so that they may survive."

"And serve you?" To Doren's credit, there was bitterness in her voice.

"Yes, you are to serve us by obeying us."

"How will you bring Tulas back to life?"

"That is not your concern. We will keep our promise and place you two together once more. You need not worry."

Doren gestured to Tulas's headless form. "But here—in this chamber—the ice maidens can't reach him. Or else they would have come already. I've been searching for him everywhere. You've had your door locked."

"It is not our plan the ice maidens should take him."

"But . . ."

"But if that is what you wish, then take his stiff torso and his shattered head outside the chamber, and perhaps they will come for him now."

Doren let go of her lover, stood trembling. For a long time she seemed indecisive. "You swear you'll bring him back to life?" she pleaded, and her tone was so pathetic, it broke Ali's heart to hear it.

"He will be brought back to life and you will be with him. Now sit and accept the implant."

Still shaking, Doren did what she was told. The amethyst descended from the invisible ceiling. This time it came in low, and touched her head. A purple beam, like a laser, burst from the device and sliced a narrow red line in her forehead. It bled slightly—possibly because the heat of the beam cauterized the nearby blood vessels. Then the beam halted and a purple crystal floated from the headset and was implanted in her forehead.

The beam flashed again. The wound instantly sealed. There was no scar.

With Doren still in the chair, barely beginning to reopen her eyes, the six crystal cubes began to glow and hum, and the sound and sight of them seemed to make Doren ill. She began to cough, gag. Tulas's body started to smoke.

Tulas caught fire. Doren tried to jump from the chair, to run to him, perhaps to try to put out the flames so that there would be more for the ice maidens to work with while he was in-between lives. But the Entity had her nailed to the seat. The flames were fierce. They consumed him in seconds, and left only a pile of ash behind.

All Doren could do was weep. "Why? Why?" she begged.

"As promised, you will see him again, on Earth. You are going there, and staying here. Unless your sister agrees to join us, we will need you alive in both worlds at the same time."

Doren shook her head. "That is not allowed."

"We will decide what is allowed," the Entity replied.

With the story told, the six screens turned momentarily dark.

Ali sat without speaking. Waiting for their threats, their games.

For some reason, she was no longer afraid. Her anger had washed it all away. How proud they were of what they had done to her sister! They thought they just had to give her a lesson and she would behave, and join them.

"We have answered your question about your sister," the Entity said finally.

"There was a reason behind your answer. It contains an implied threat. If I don't cooperate—agree to have a stupid piece of glass put in my head—I'll be incinerated like Tulas. True?"

"Again, we note your sarcasm. Although we would not put our offer to you in such crude terms—yes, you are essentially correct. You either join us or you will be destroyed."

"Any other options?"

"No."

"You destroy me and you will never know how to work the Yanti."

"We will have it in our possession. We will figure out a way."

"Somehow I doubt that. I doubt you would even be able to touch it. Tell me, Entity, Sheri Smith, the Shaktra's earthly counterpart, wanted me to turn over the Yanti to her. Was that your wish? That she wield it?"

"We would prefer that you use it."

"To help the elemental army in its fight with humanity?"

"Yes. It would—so to speak—help even the odds."

"Why do you prefer me over Doren?"

"You have a stronger connection to the blue light."

"You're saying I'm more powerful than her?"

"Yes."

"If I agree to help you, will you place me in command over her?"

"Yes."

"But you have already promised her command."

"We have the freedom of choice to change our minds."

"But that would mean breaking your deal with her."

"That is irrelevant."

Ali remembered how Jira had only appeared to be inside the chamber minutes before he had started screaming. Yet she had been in here awhile . . .

"Tell me, Entity, does time flow at a different rate inside this chamber than outside?"

"Yes. To your friend outside our door, it is as if you have only been inside here a few seconds."

Time had been interrupted at the police station. It was being affected here now. Ali found it an interesting coincidence. At the same time the Entity was insisting that she was more powerful than Sheri. Had Sheri been acting out of her own desire when she had demanded the Yanti for herself?

Ali felt as if all these points were connected. Somehow.

"Speaking of my friend outside, the last time he was in here, in another body, as an elf, you drove him insane. Why did you do that?"

"We did not do that on purpose. It was his resistance to our energy—his inability to cope with the high level of energy inside this chamber—that drove him insane."

"He killed himself later. Did you know that?"

"That information is not relevant to our discussion."

"I see," she whispered. Even though time was not passing outside the chamber, she knew she had very little time left inside it. On the other hand, she did not feel despair, even though sad thoughts of Jira plagued her. From out of nowhere, a warmth had entered the center of her chest. It was familiar; it tried to soothe her in the midst of this trial. Indeed, it was as if the loving warmth was trying to tell her where she could always go for comfort.

Nemi?

Was he near?

"We appear to have reached an impasse," she said.

"You will not join us in our effort to save your worlds?"

"I would join you if you were not determined to seize control of our worlds."

"We have explained. Without setting up a hierarchy of control, your people will continue to act selfishly. It is their nature, and you are not going to change human nature simply because you want it changed. The selfishness is inbred in your species. Human beings are what they are. We are what we are." The Entity paused. "We are not so very different from you, in reality, merely further along the path of evolution."

"Your path of evolution disgusts me. It's devoid of all love, of all mercy. It was interesting to see how casually you burnt Tulas to ash, then manipulated Doren with your lies to join you."

"At no point did we lie to your sister."

Ali felt a sudden bright light inside her chest, on top of the loving warmth.

It gave her unlooked-for strength, and confidence.

Nemi was definitely in the chamber with her!

"Your lies are the lies of omission!" Ali snapped. "There's another way to save my worlds and I'll find it. As far as my father joining you, what nonsense. He's the exact opposite of what you've become. He *is* love. I feel his love now as I speak to you."

"You are mistaken. You are alone with us."

Ali chuckled. "I'm not surprised you're unaware of him. He recently taught me something. He said love is the only way to be certain about anything. I doubted him at the time but I'll never doubt him again. You see, I have faith in him, another concept you would never understand. I know he is going to help me escape from this horrible place." She stopped and spoke directly to Nemi. "Just tell me what I need to know to free Amma and the others and I'll go."

The Entity spoke. "It is foolish of you to blindly call upon your father for help. In this place, we have complete control over everything . . ."

The Entity's voice was suddenly interrupted.

The amethyst above her head jerked several inches higher.

Ali stared at the words on the screen directly in front of her.

The screen had turned violet. The words were white.

"Hello, Ali. Looks like you are having a busy day."

Ali stood away from the stool. "How long can you keep them at bay?"

"Not long. Grab two of those plugs atop the cube. The races that make up the Entity are ancient, but not creative. They won't understand what I am about to tell you. Listen closely to my riddle. The original species that started the expansion of the Entity across the galaxy had six fingers—three on each hand. But they did not have lockers like you do at school. When they locked things, they had a tendency to do it backward from the way we do. Take a number, say six-zero-two, and go play with it."

Ali picked up two plugs, the ones with the wires and crystals attached.

"Anything else I need to know?" she asked.

"Reflect on my earlier advice. Now run!"

Ali raced toward the door. Even as she did so, Nemi's words

faded from the screens. The six crystal cubes began to glow and hum—the same way they had before Tulas's body was incinerated. Ali began to cough and gag on the awful sound and light. It took her last ounce of strength to throw the lever that loosened the lock that caused the rope and pulleys to pull aside the stone barrier. Her strength almost failed her. Reaching for the outside, her knees buckled and her scalp burned, and she smelled smoke on the back of her robe.

Yet Ra pulled her free of the hideous cavern. A moment later she was in his arms, and trembling, as she watched the rock door swing past, like an evil pendulum, and close. She whispered a prayer that it should remain shut forever.

Ra stared at her anxiously. "What happened?"

"How long was I in there?"

"Seconds. Did you see anything?"

Ali took his hand, although it hurt her skin to touch or to be touched. She didn't care, she wanted to feel him near. Leading him back toward the creaky elevator, she told him, "I saw more than I bargained for."

CHAPTER

11

Ali did not tell Ra and Drash where they were going until they were high in the sky above the green sea, heading back toward the elemental mainland. The air was fresh and clear, rich with the many and varied aromas of the green world. Looking down, Ra could tell Ali was happy to see the schools of whales and dolphins playing in the pristine water. Well, at least they looked like whales and dolphins. They were on the whole larger, had brighter eyes, and were all the colors of the rainbow. So beautiful . . .

Yet her answer to their questions shocked them both.

"We're returning to the kloudar where we were attacked by the Shaktra."

"Why?" Ra asked, dismayed.

"I spoke to Nemi before I reentered the green world. I told you about him. I asked, if I go to the Isle of Greesh will I learn everything I need to know to stop the war? He said no."

"Drash does not think the war can be stopped," the dragon muttered.

"Shh. It's possible to stop it on the Earth side."

"Nemi told you this?" Ra asked, not a hundred percent sure

who Nemi was. Ali had told him little about the guy—only that she had talked to him inside a tree, and beside a pond.

Ali smiled, or at least tried to do so with what was left of her lips.

"Nemi is fond of riddles. Sometimes they drive me crazy. But he might have a reason behind his new ones. One of the times we talked, it was on my computer, and I'm not sure he felt we had total online privacy. Anyway, this is what he said, 'This war exists in two dimensions at once. You are only one girl. You can only be in one place at a time, and you're trying to defeat an enemy that moves in both worlds at the same time . . . Think as your enemy thinks.'"

"Which means?" Ra asked.

"I keep running around this world like some kind of big shot. Fighting dragons here, killing scaliis and scabs there. But none of this is stopping Lord Vak's army from moving closer to Earth. The reason is simple, and Nemi was asking me to show some humility and recognize it. Despite all the powers I've gained over the last few weeks, I'm still Ali Warner. A thirteen-year-old girl from planet Earth. This is not my world. Earth is where I belong. Geea belongs here, the real Geea. She's queen of the fairies, not me. She's the one who should be calling the shots."

Ra spoke. "But it's my understanding from what Trae said that Geea can only reawaken when you die. Just as Amma awoke here when your mother died on Earth." He added, "You don't plan on killing yourself, do you?"

Ali smiled. "No. Consider Nemi's words closely. He says I'm only one girl. I can only be in one place at one time. But then he contradicts himself and tells me to think as the enemy thinks. What they've done is the unthinkable. The Shaktra rules here—as Doren. But on Earth she rules as Sheri Smith."

"But I never heard of Sheri Smith before I met you," Ra said.

"That doesn't matter. In a few days everyone will know her name. Nemi is telling us that we can't defeat them unless we adopt their same tactic. I have to awaken Geea, and let her take over the situation here. Then I have to return to Earth, and stop whatever Sheri has planned there."

"Do you know how to wake up Geea?" Ra asked, shuddering at the thought of returning to the high kloudar. The last time he had been there, he had passed out from lack of oxygen.

Ali hesitated. "I have a few ideas."

Ali insisted they make a quick stop at the Crystal Palace before they visited the kloudar. Ra wanted to know why. With dragons roaming that area, he felt it was a risky move.

"They will not be inside the palace," Ali said. "They couldn't fit. I want to come at the palace the same way I left it—via Tiena's tunnel."

"What do you want there?" Ra asked.

"Mirrors."

"Mirrors?"

"Yes. You know, what you look at yourself in," she said.

"I know what a mirror is. What do you want them for?"

"One of my ideas," Ali replied. "Look, neither of you has to fly me underground. I'm feeling stronger. I can go myself."

"Drash will take you to the spot Father died," Drash said.

"Drash . . ." Ali began, pain in her voice.

"Drash wants to go there," the dragon insisted.

They returned to Lake Mira, found it deserted, and flew inside the cave that had guided and sheltered Tiena for centuries. Now, at least at this end, all was dry. Studying Ali, Ra saw how painful it was for her to behold the results of her handiwork. He tried to reassure her that she'd had no choice, but the guilt weighed on her. At the same time, he tried to get her to explain more of what had gone on inside the chamber, but she brushed him off. It was a quality he was having to learn to accept—Ali kept her own counsel.

They reached the spot where Ali and Kashar had battled, at the harbor beneath the fairy palace. Here the empty riverbed was not only dry—it was scorched. There were a few bones to be found, some ash. Drash wanted to know exactly how his father had been killed. Ali replied reluctantly.

"Like I said before, I used the Yanti as a weapon, which was a mistake," she said.

Drash landed at the edge of the gorge that had once been the river's shore. He continued to study the fight scene. "Drash knows of no fire that could do this to another dragon," he said, and there was sorrow in his voice. Ali patted him on the head.

"The fire that came was unnatural. It tortured us both," she said.

Drash turned and looked at her scars. "Drash does not blame you."

"Thank you," Ali said quietly.

Ali and Ra were in and out of the Crystal Palace in minutes. First they fetched a fresh green robe for Ali from Geea's old bedroom. Then they grabbed the first two large mirrors they saw. Carrying one each, they hastened back to Drash. But halfway down a winding stairway, Ali stumbled. She had seen her reflection in the mirror. She almost dropped it—Ra had to grab the frame.

"Oh God!" she cried.

Ra tried to comfort her as best he could. He even went so far as to say that once Geea was awakened, she could be healed. Ali just shut her eyes—her one eye, actually—and shook her head. "I don't know," she whispered several times over.

All Ra could do was stand there and feel helpless.

But Ali was not one for self-pity. She pulled herself together quickly. While still on the stairway, she asked him point-blank if he should accompany them up to the kloudar. "The last time you did not do well there," she said.

"Where you go, I go," he replied.

"Trae had to keep zapping you to keep you from smothering."

"I can handle it. We won't be there long."

"You have no idea how long we will be there. Geea might not wake up at all."

"Nemi would not have given you that clue without a reason," Ra said.

"That's true," Ali agreed. Again her good eye strayed to the mirror. She reached out and touched his shoulder. "Is it too much . . . that I might be hideous for the rest of my life?"

"You already asked that. I said no. Love that depends on a perfect face and hair and skin is not love at all."

"Your uncle taught you that."

"How did you know?"

"I hear his words in your voice." Ali paused, considering. "I won't ask Geea to heal me. I might . . ." She did not finish.

"What?" Ra asked.

Ali shook her head. "Every minute counts. Let's get to the kloudar."

Returning to Drash, the dragon quickly swept them along the barren subterranean cavern, until they were back at Lake Mira. Then came the biggest question of them all.

"Is the kloudar we visited last time still on this side of Anglar?" Ali asked Drash.

"Drash does not know," the dragon replied.

Ali studied the clear sky, and the literally hundreds of floating icebergs that slowly swept around the stationary blue moon. Ra was not sure if he understood the problem.

"Where do the kloudar go when they move to the other side of Anglar?" he asked.

"Into outer space," Ali replied.

Now he understood. "Wow."

"No dragon has ever ridden a kloudar beyond Anglar," Drash said. "At least, not until the Shaktra came."

"Your father boasted that he had been beyond Anglar and experienced the blue light," Ali told the dragon, still searching the skies. "I didn't believe him. He looked ill."

"The blue light would not have made him sick," Drash said.

Ra turned to Ali. "How can you tell one kloudar from another?"

"The one where Geea sleeps, remember, is so high up, it actually looks tiny. Also, it calls to me. Like . . ." Ali's voice trailed off, and she pointed excitedly. "There it is over there! Do you see it?"

In the direction she pointed, Ra saw nothing but green sky.

"No," he replied.

"Drash sees it," the dragon replied. "It has moved closer to the edge of the world. There will be even less air for us to breathe."

Ali went to climb off Drash, while trying to balance the mirrors. "More the reason I should go by myself."

Ra stopped her. "You've only got one hand that works. You're going to drop the mirrors. And you're nowhere near full strength. I doubt you can fly that high."

"Drash agrees. Drash must take Geea," the dragon said.

Ali saw she was not going to be able to ditch her friends. "All right," she said.

The trip up to the kloudar seemed to take longer than last time. Ra did not know if it was because Drash was fatigued, or the levitating mountain had gained altitude during this portion of its orbit around the blue moon. The truth was, the thin air did concern him, but he was still feeling guilty over the fact that he had allowed Ali to enter the chamber on the Isle of Greesh alone. The fear that had swept over him, when they had approached that awful place, continued to puzzle him. He had simply felt he would go nuts if he went inside the chamber.

Ra still did not understand how Ali could have accomplished anything inside—in so short a time. She'd only been gone five seconds . . .

At last the icy kloudar began to reveal its true size. It was staggering. There was an iceberg quality to the structure of the mountain in the sense that it was bottom-heavy, and yet it tapered down sharply. Fissures of gray stone were visible between the ice, but the thing was largely a floating glacier. Ra estimated it to be twelve miles in diameter. It could have been twice that. This high up, they had no reference point to grasp its true size.

But there was no mistaking how the color of the sky changed, as they drew near the kloudar. The atmosphere turned a dark green, and picked up a hint of blue, probably as a result of the snow reflecting back the light of Anglar. But the changes in colors did not concern Ra. He was having to concentrate on his breath, drawing in as much oxygen as he could from the nearly empty air. Plus it was freezing, which did not help. His chest felt as if his bronchial tubes might harden into metal pipes. Already his lungs ached. He had to struggle to hide it from Ali.

"How do you feel?" she asked, sitting behind him, her mouth near his ear.

He lied. "Feels easier than last time."

"Last time we were attacked by dragons and the Shaktra," Ali said, scanning in all directions. "I wonder if they can see us up here."

"Dragons do not like to approach kloudar where the ice maidens reside," Drash said. "It is forbidden."

"They did it last time," Ali replied. "The one who knocked you down was your uncle, Chashar."

"Drash has not forgotten." The dragon added, "Yet Chashar and the Shaktra did not try to enter your cave."

"Why do you call it *my* cave?" Ali asked seriously.

"Drash knows," the dragon replied.

Ali continued her search. Ra tried to do likewise but felt dizzy. They were up so high! All he could see was the green sea, a few rivers, and floating kloudar. He couldn't even spot Uleestar.

"No one's following us," Ali said.

"For now," Drash replied.

Ali nodded. "While we're inside the cave, if you see any dragons approach, do not try to fight them. Call for me."

"What will Geea do?" Drash asked.

"Hopefully the *real* Geea will know what to do," Ali replied.

Drash had to take only one trip around the kloudar before Ali spotted the cave they sought. The dragon landed with surprising grace, but too near the edge for Ra's tastes. Climbing down from Drash, Ra wasn't ashamed to let Ali take his hand. Already his fingers were numb. If they were attacked now, his bow and arrows would be useless. Ali gave him a worried look.

"Why do you always have to try to be such a hero?" she asked.

"Because you get to be one without even trying."

"Let me carry the mirrors. I can't have you drop and break one."

"You only have one hand."

"It is a strong hand. Let me do it."

Ra gave in. "Can you at least tell me what they're for?"

Ali turned and stared at the green sun, straight overhead. "We're going to bring a little sunshine into a dark place," she said.

Ra guessed her basic plan. "You only need two mirrors?"

Ali gestured to the cave. "It heads straight in, then there's only one major turn to the left."

"What will we find?" he asked.

"A crypt. A live one. Don't worry. It's beautiful."

Using a stone for support, Ali set up one of the mirrors at a forty-five degree angle, not far from the cave entrance. Ra admired the care in her placement—the green beam shone straight into the cave. He was glad to follow her inside. Last time he had been told to stay outside.

The temperature increased several degrees and the air grew thicker. But the improvements were slight. Ra continued to struggle, but he had Ali by his side, and that was always good. The light from the mirror helped, but the farther they went, the darker it got. The tunnel walls seemed to emit a faint blue phosphorescence, but Ra thought he might be imagining it.

He wondered aloud if there were ice maidens in the cave.

Ali cautioned him to remain silent. Was that a yes or no?

They walked farther, until the light from the mirror faded and the blue glow from the walls became unmistakable. Then the rocky tunnel abruptly ended, in a round room—a halfsphere with roughly hewn icy walls and an uneven stone floor.

Ali paused to set up her second mirror, finding a large rock to support it. A ghostly green glow penetrated the mysterious crypt.

Inside, assembled in a neat row, were five glass cases. They looked more like quartz hibernaculums than beds. Ra had no idea what they were made of: ice and crystal, water and weird potions. They looked solid. Each one balanced atop a low boulder that resembled a granite pyramid.

Ali went inside. Ra followed, feeling as if he was violating a sacred spot.

The two cases on the left were empty, the three on the right were not. The latter had women in them, beautiful sleeping fairies, eyes tightly shut. Ra suspected they were not simply dreaming.

"A crypt. A live one. Don't worry. It's beautiful."

Were they dead? Ra preferred to stay near the door, but Ali motioned him closer. *Come inside.* He was blocking the reflected green glow she had worked so hard to bring about.

Various colored lights shone above the fairies. The lights appeared to emanate from the women themselves. The cases—Ra hated to call them coffins—were labeled in the same hieroglyphics he had seen in Tiena's southern harbor. There was one word on the bottom edge of each case. Ra studied the blue letters, searching for a pattern, but found none. He assumed Ali knew what they meant.

Ra wondered if the ice maidens had built the crypt. Or the fairies?

A million questions ran through his head. But he was so cold!

Ali ignored the first two cases, stepped to the third. The fairy inside was female, short and fat, plain. Lying on her back, she wore a green robe, but she did not appear to be breathing. Covering her from head to toe was a green light, streaked with faint yellow rays.

Ali frowned as she studied the fairy and muttered to

herself—something about *Lucy* or *Lucy's mother*. Ra still didn't know who this Lucy was.

Ali moved to the fourth case. There was another fairy inside. This one took Ra's breath away. He did not have to be told. It was the body he had loved for centuries.

Standing across the case from him, Ali raised her head and smiled in his direction. Like she had at the lake, it was as if she spoke directly into his mind, and he saw Queen Geea as Ali had first beheld her when she had first entered the cave.

The woman was more beautiful than a goddess. Her long red hair burned, and her smooth skin was as cool as a blue moon. She wore no crown, but anklets and bracelets made of green vines, yellow petals, and silver and gold thread, and she had on a white silk robe. Her legs were long and shapely, as though sketched by an artist, and her face was a mystery. Even with closed eyes and silent ears, it was as if she saw and heard everything around her—in the chamber, on the far side of the green world, maybe on Anglar itself. Her kindness was a large portion of her beauty, for she did not need to speak for Ali to know the words she would say. Because her words would be about love . . .

Ra realized he was staring at the goal of all his quests.

He had not merely found his love, but his queen.

Three colors shone from the fairy, blending in soft bands of light like the colors of a clear prism: yellow, green, and blue. Ra suspected the yellow was there because Ali was a human being. The green was present because she was also an elemental. But to Ra, he might have been prejudiced, the blue light meant she was an angel . . .

Ali reached down and touched her hand. "She's alive!" Ali whispered, awe in her voice. Yet Geea's eyes did not open, and she made no sound.

"How alive is she?" Ra asked. In response, Ali pointed to

the mirror that shone with the green light of the outside sun.

"As a rule, life after life, the ice maidens used to wake us near dawn. I always remember seeing the light of the sun—before I saw or did anything else. Buried deep inside here, I don't know how they managed that, but I thought I would try to copy their style. What do you think? Will it work?"

"Won't she simply awaken if she wants to be awakened?" Ra asked.

"Not necessarily. She might still need help from us." Ali gave him a shrewd look. "Sleeping Beauty," she said.

"Never read the book. Never saw the Disney cartoon," Ra quickly lied.

"How do you know Disney made it?"

"Ali . . ."

"What do we have to lose?"

Ra would have blushed had he any blood left in his freezing face. "I'm not going to open that case and . . . that would be sacrilege!"

Ali sighed. "So melodramatic. You used to kiss her all the time."

"Jira used to kiss her!"

"So you don't feel comfortable kissing her?"

"I certainly do not. She's . . . she's . . ."

"What?"

"A goddess!"

Ali smiled. "Kiss me first, then, as a warm-up. Then try kissing her."

"We have come to this dangerous place on a very important mission. Two worlds are about to collide, possibly be destroyed. How can you talk about me kissing anyone?"

Ali came around the case, stood beside him, put her right

palm on his shivering chest, and instantly he felt healing warmth flow into his heart. His trembling stopped, and feeling returned to his frozen fingers. She had only one eye left, true, but it was a good eye, bright as any nighttime star. It pierced his fears, his phobias, and he saw what she was asking for was the most amazing miracle of all, because it was such a gentle request—humble, too. Like she had earlier in the day, at the lake, she put her head close, and again he heard her words in his head, not with his ears. However, with what was left of her lips, he felt her touch his ears . . .

"I know I'm hideous, and she's beautiful, and you remember that beauty, and want it, and I want it, too, more than you can imagine. But I'm human now, and I'm a mess, but I still need love as much as she does. We both need it, more than the green light of the sun, or any special incantation I might conjure. We need it even more than the power of the Yanti. The talisman has immense magic, it was created in the violet world. Even so, you are my love, you are both our loves, and we need that love more than any other power in the galaxy. If it's there, if we're allowed to feel it, if only for a short while, then we'll feel hope, and there will be hope, for love is the only chance either world has left anymore."

Ali's stream of thought fell silent, as she reached her arms around him and spoke in his ear. "Kiss me, Jira," she whispered.

Ra kissed her, as best he could, without, he hoped, hurting her, and he felt himself melting, but not as her skin had melted. To him her burnt lips were red jewels of joy.

Then he turned and, not opening his eyes, lifted the case and kissed his goddess as well. The decision was not his, he realized. Ages ago, it seemed, the kiss had been set in stone—that the flesh of a mortal and an immortal should touch in such an intimate way.

Ra stood back and waited. Both of them waited for a miracle.

Geea's eyes fluttered open. She looked up at him and smiled.

"Why did you stop?" she asked.

CHAPTER

12

Queen Geea did not speak again, until she slowly stood from the glass case, and systematically stretched each of her limbs, as if waking from a long sleep. She was not shy—she even stretched the muscles of her face, her jaw, and the skin around her mouth. All the while she drew in extraordinarily deep breaths. Each inhalation lasted a minute; and each exhalation was twice that in length.

She shook her head and ran her fingers through her long red hair. It blazed with its own light. All of her did—she was a living flame. Her robe could hardly contain her magnificence. Ra had thought Ali powerful, but Geea radiated ten times her strength.

Finally she glanced at Ra, and with a wave of her hand a black hatch slid down over the entrance. The room began to fill with rich warm *oxygenated* air.

"Better?" she said to him, with a voice that only slightly matched Ali's. It was more resonant—filled with harmony and peace. Ironically, although it was deeper than a normal human voice, it was very feminine. The Hollywood agents would have clamored for her. Besides her overwhelming beauty, Geea sounded sexy.

"Thank you, yes," Ra said as he began to stop shaking. Color returned to his skin. The first thing he did with it was blush. He couldn't believe he'd kissed such a being! He felt shame. Geea, however, was anxious to put him at ease. Coming near, she hugged the two of them close.

"It's you two I must thank," she said, with a sigh that was as joyous as it was profound. That was the mystery of her voice— with its rich tones, it conveyed so many things at once. She hardly needed words to communicate. Geea added, "I've dreamed of this day for thirteen years."

Ali stared at her in awe. "You were conscious all that time?"

Geea nodded. "Conscious of you, all those around you, and of many things in this world as well." She paused, added, "I never lost sight of Doren."

"On the Isle of Greesh, I saw what became of her," Ali said softly.

Ra did not understand the remark. *When* had she seen this?

"Doren was a fool to listen . . ." Then she added quietly, "I was a coward not to."

"Had you gone in with Jira, you would have been trapped," Ali replied. "Back then, I doubt Father was in a position to help you."

Geea nodded. "Perhaps. It doesn't take away from the fact that you dared what I feared to do. For that alone, I admire you more than you know."

"But she is you," Ra said, confused.

Geea nodded. "And her own person as well." She patted Ra on the back, a head taller than he. "For keeping my better half safe, I owe you many lifetimes of allegiance."

He kept wanting to bow to her. "I'm just grateful for the day

I met Ali." Which had only been fours days ago, hard to believe . . .

Ali's clear eye burned. "I also dreamed about this day."

Geea gently wiped away her tears. "You went through so much to get here . . . the fire . . . the Entity."

Ali forced a smile. "Hard to say which was worse."

Again, Geea hugged her. "I know, I was there. At each step, I felt what you felt. I'm so sorry."

"I'm sorry I was such a fool to use the Yanti as a weapon."

Geea let her go. "It was never intended to destroy, only to heal."

Ali nodded. "Try telling that to Sheri."

"She wants it to shoot down missiles? She'd just end up shooting herself!"

They laughed together, and shared another hug, and Ra felt more confused than ever about who was who. He wondered if Geea would always have to know *everything* he did with Ali. That could make their relationship kind of . . . sticky.

"Do you know what she has planned on the Earth side?" Ali asked.

Geea shrugged. "Only what you know. You must return, dig deeper into her past, discover her plan. But I agree that Hector is her Achilles' heel."

Ra was not following any of this. Who was Hector?

"Hector is Tulas, right?" Ali asked.

"Yes. The greatest lies the Entity uses are usually the ones that are the most truthful. The Entity had Lucy born beside him, both to keep its word to her, and to use him as a lever over her." Geea glanced at Ra. "Don't worry, Ra, I'll explain all of this to you later, after Ali leaves."

"You're sending her back to Earth?" he asked.

"Yes. And I would like you to stay here with me."

"Couldn't I help Ali more on Earth?" he asked.

"To dishearten Ali, Sheri Smith would find a way to kill you the instant you returned to the yellow world," Geea explained. "Here, I can protect you."

"You just want him for yourself because he's cute," Ali said.

"I hate it when I can read my own mind," Geea replied.

"But I cannot really read yours," Ali said seriously.

Geea waved a hand. "The human brain cannot absorb the experiences stored inside me. They go back a million years. Why, I remember every birth you've taken as a human being. You do not know this, Ali, but history knows you."

"Was I Cleopatra?" Ali asked hopefully.

Geea laughed, such a sweet sound. "No! Ali, you have always been—*we* have always been—against those who crave power for power's sake. You spoke to the Entity. You must know it would have immediately recruited a Cleopatra."

"I just always liked her," Ali muttered.

"You mean, you liked the fun she had. Trust me, that didn't last long."

"What is this Entity?" Ra asked.

"The force behind the Shaktra," Ali said, before turning back to Geea. "Was it something in the Internet that caused Hector to drive off the road and into that tree?"

Geea nodded. "The accident that burned Lucy Pillar was planned."

"It was like Tulas, just another lever to force her to move in a certain direction," Ali said.

Geea tapped Ali on the top of the head. "My human half is perceptive. Yes, the Entity has stored a portion of its consciousness in the most complex neural network Earth possesses—the Internet. Sheri Smith serves the Entity by creating software that has a subliminal effect on those who play her games. In a sense, the Entity had been preparing your youth for years about this invasion. Not just your youth—all humans subconsciously feel the end is near. It's because a monster has invaded Earth that can't even be seen." Geea added, "It was Father who first recognized this."

"Is Nemi in the future? Or the past?" Ali asked.

"Clearly, if he wanted you to know, he would tell you," Geea said.

"Do you know?" Ali asked.

Geea just laughed. "He swore me to secrecy."

"Back to Doren and Tulas," Ali said. "The Entity used Tulas's death to leverage Doren to turn evil in this world."

"True. But the Entity saw that Doren already craved power. They just played on her weakness."

"I remember. But when Lucy Pillar was a teenager on Earth, she seemed like such a nice girl. And she had Hector with her. She had her love back."

Geea nodded. "But when you're burned over the majority of your body, and *someone* approaches you and says they can make you beautiful again . . . Well, that's an awfully big temptation right there. What young girl could turn that down?"

"Who approached Lucy?" Ali asked.

"I don't know. It doesn't matter. It was an agent of the Entity."

"Whoever it was, they demanded a sacrifice in return," Ali said grimly. "A year later she burned down half the town."

Geea nodded. "You forced the Entity to reveal more about itself than it wanted to when you confronted it about the opposite of love being fear. It doesn't merely feed off power and control. It feeds off of fear and pain. That gives it the deepest satisfaction."

"Yet it sounded so reasonable when it spoke of how the

Earth was destroying itself. And how it could prevent its destruction," Ali said.

"From its perspective, it *is* reasonable," Geea said.

Ali was confused, but not half as much as Ra.

"But it's evil," Ali countered.

Geea explained. "*We* consider it evil. We want nothing to do with it. The path the Entity has chosen—it has no love, no laughter, no joy. But from its side, it feels it's highly successful. It survives, it expands, it grows in power. Remember what I said—the truths it tells—those are its most damaging weapons. The Earth is in serious trouble, and when Father, Tulas, and Doren first contacted the Entity, they were overjoyed. Here was an intelligence that understood all of Earth's problems. The green world's problems as well. And it offered insightful solutions to each and every problem."

"Before it tried to take over," Ali said.

"It did not state its ultimate purpose at first. Even Father was fooled, and he does not fool easily."

"What alerted him?"

"Their lack of warmth. Here was an obviously superior race, very ancient, yet they emanated nothing but facts and figures. He grew suspicious."

"And did what?"

"I don't know. Perhaps Doren does."

Ali pressed her palms together, thinking deeply. "If the Entity has infiltrated the Internet, then it has its hands on everything. We have to figure out a way to destroy it."

Geea took a step away from them, put her palm on the glass case that held the fifth and final fairy. The smallest one, who cast the brightest light. "No," she replied. "That is not our task."

Ali appeared shocked. "But we have to stop it!"

Geea turned and faced Ali. "Father and Nira will tackle the Entity. It is beyond our powers. Our job is to stop the Shaktra—in this world, and on Earth."

"But the Entity is behind it all!" Ali complained.

"True. But what is also true is an army approaches Tutor from the east and will invade Earth in the next twenty-four hours. I took birth in the yellow world—as *you*—so that I might have a weapon to meet such a threat to the Earth. I've waited here—for *you* to awaken me—so I could meet the threat to my world."

"Why was I allowed to awaken you?" Ali asked. "I hoped, since you were able to rescue me from the burning car, over a year ago, that you would be able to rise. Yet the last words I heard Doren speak to the Entity were, 'It's not allowed for us to be awake at the same time.'"

Geea spoke. "I was not even sure if it was feasible. But I spoke to Nira before I went to sleep here, and took birth as you, and she felt that because the Entity had violated the laws of evolution of our worlds, then a power above Nira would allow us to balance out the violation. Nira journeyed to a place beyond Anglar—I cannot say where—and prayed that such a gift be granted. And it apparently was."

"So Nira was behind the plan from the start?" Ali asked.

"Yes. You mustn't underestimate that child."

"Did Nira enter the white world?" Ali asked.

"I cannot say," Geea said.

"And here I thought my kiss was the real miracle," Ra muttered.

They laughed together. Then Geea grew serious again, spoke to Ali. "We each have our tasks to complete. It's important we accept our individual roles. The threat of the Entity itself—we have to leave that to Nira and Father."

Ra was surprised to see Ali pout. "Why?" she asked.

Geea gestured to the final fairy's glass case. "See the light she bathes in? How divine it is? Does it not remind you of something?"

Ali hesitated. "The violet door."

Geea nodded. "That's where she is from. That's where Father is from. They have entered this world and yours to complete a job we're not equipped to handle. You knew from the instant you met Nira that she was more powerful than you. Admit it."

Ali nodded. "Yet she's marked, under the control of the Shaktra."

"She's only marked because Sheri Smith got to her so young," Geea said.

"I don't understand. Why did Sheri give birth to Nira?"

Geea nodded. "There are two possibilities. She wanted to have her, mark her young, then control her immense power. Or else she simply disobeyed the powers above her and had a daughter because she wanted one."

"Out of love? I doubt that," Ali said.

"I wouldn't dismiss the idea out of hand. Doren may not be completely under their control. Remember, I know her well. How she must balk at the restrictions they place on her! And clearly she wanted the Yanti to gain some control over whoever is dictating her orders. But I respect your remark about her lack of love. I wouldn't count on her good nature to save you. Remember her cruelty. Remember your mother and Steve."

Ali lowered her head. "How can I forget?"

Geea stepped near. "Father gave you a riddle before you fled the Entity's chamber. It dealt with the Shaktra's markings. Repeat it please."

Ali hesitated. "'The races that make up the Entity are ancient, but not creative. They won't understand what I am about to tell you. Listen closely to my riddle. The original species that started the expansion of the Entity across the galaxy had six fingers—three on each hand. But they did not have lockers like you do at school. When they locked things, they had a tendency to do it backward from the way we do. Take a number, say six-zero-two, and go play with it.'" Ali paused. "Know what it means?"

Geea frowned. "Let us consider. The original species that started the Entity had six fingers . . ." She let the words trail off.

Finally Ra felt as if he might be of some help. "Human beings have ten fingers. For that reason, our counting system is based on ten. A species with six fingers would probably be based on a system of six."

Geea nodded. "Logical."

"You mean six represents ten in their system?" Ali asked him.

"Not exactly," Ra replied. "In our system, when we count to ten, then we start to count over—in a sense. Eleven corresponds to one. Of course, it is not the same as one. Do you understand?"

Ali nodded. Geea spoke. "The boy is smart as well as cute."

Ra blushed. "So in their system, when they get to six, they would start to count over. Seven would be our eleven, but it would still only be seven. They're using what mathematicians would call base-six."

"Why didn't Father just say that?" Ali asked.

"He didn't want them to understand what was being said," Geea said.

Ali spoke. "Father made a reference to our school lockers. We use three numbers to open them. They're dialed in a sequence: clockwise, counterclockwise, clockwise."

Ra nodded. "It's an interesting coincidence that he gave you three numbers."

"Yes!" Ali said, excited. "He said use the code backward! So all we have to do is take six-zero-two and put it in backward, or else turn the dial . . ."

Ra held up his hand. "Sorry, Ali, you're forgetting what is backward to *them*. We still have to deal with the fact that they use a base-six system. To them, the opposite of six is zero."

Ali blinked. "Really?"

"I thought you were supposed to be good at math," Geea said.

"Obviously Kutus are superior," Ali said, with a bow in Ra's direction. "Please continue Mr. Know-It-All."

Ra had to laugh. "The opposite of zero would therefore be six. And the opposite of two would be four. Because two and four add up to six."

"So the answer to the riddle is zero-six-four?" Ali asked.

Ra hesitated. "There might be another step. Your father made a subtle reference to turning a locker dial. Perhaps to remove the mark, the order of numbers must be used *opposite* the way you open your locker at school."

Ali was doubtful. "How do we dial numbers into a person's head?"

Yet Geea jumped on the solution. "Ra is right. Just take your thumb and dial them into Nira's forehead."

"I don't understand," Ali said.

"Do it with intent and focus, you'll see," Geea explained. "I know this type of spell. Demons often use numeric codes to implant spells."

"So those that make up the Entity are demons?" Ali asked.

Geea nodded. "And those of the violet ray are gods."

"And I thought it was pretty cool finding out I was an elf," Ra muttered.

Geea's eyes shone with pride. "You would be special to me if you were a troll."

Ra smiled. "I don't know if that was a compliment or an insult."

"It was both," Ali assured him. "It's going to be great to have Nira free. Will she be able to talk right away?"

Geea was amused. "You'll see for yourself soon enough."

"And Amma?" Ali asked. "I want to be there when . . ."

Geea interrupted sharply. "I'll take care of Amma."

Ali was stunned. "You mean, I don't get to see her before I go back?"

"No. You're to leave here in a few minutes."

"But . . ." Ali began.

"There's no time," Geea repeated.

"But Ali needs to be healed before she returns home," Ra said firmly. "Can you do that now?"

"Yes. Ali, lie down in the case where I rested."

Ali hesitated, then did as she was told. "Do you need the Yanti?"

"When you or Nira hold it, I hold it." Geea put her hands over Ali's head and heart. "Now close your eyes and relax. It won't take long."

Ra had watched Ali heal before, but never got over the miraculous nature of the power. He felt the heat and magnetism in the room, flowing from Geea's hands, and he saw, much to his relief, the scars receding from her arms and torso and face. Even her hair began to grow, at a lightning speed, and Ra clapped with pleasure.

Yet Ali suddenly sat up and said, "Stop."

Geea was surprised. "Half your face is still badly scarred. And your right arm, the fingers of your right hand, I'm not sure . . ."

"I have full use of my fingers, enough to fight. I don't want you to heal me any more."

Ra's joy turned to anguish. "But you can be beautiful again!" he pleaded.

"Earth is obsessed with physical beauty. It is part of the power game endlessly played out in the media. It reminds me of the Entity and its self-centered ways. How can I possibly lead there if I don't make a point that appearance is irrelevant? Now I can see with both eyes, I can use my hands—that is all that matters. I'll carry my scars proudly, and when I confront Doren next—which I will—then she'll never again be able to tell me that I know nothing. At the same time, I'll be able to tell her what I was offered, and what I turned down, for her sake."

Geea knelt close to her side, impressed. "Do you do it for her sake?"

Ali nodded. "I do. And for Tulas and Jira. A queen does not need to be beautiful. She need only be kind."

Geea turned and smiled at Ra, spoke to him, "Make no mistake, she is her own person. And she teaches me more than I can ever teach her."

Ra nodded, grateful for the healing, but saddened as well.

He understood then that Ali was ready to sacrifice anything.

To succeed at her mission, she would forfeit even her own life.

CHAPTER

13

Ali returned to Earth in a new and exciting way. Queen Geea showed her how to tighten her magnetic field to such a degree that it was vacuum sealed. This allowed her to fly so high above the green world—literally at the edge of space, with plenty of air still in her lungs—that she was not bothered by dragons.

When she came down at the entrance to Tutor's cave, there were no dragons in the area. But in the distance was Lord Vak and his army. Ali had to fight the urge to fly over and speak with him. Geea had said she would take care of him, of all matters that pertained to the green world.

The order to leave, the order of where she was to work—these things took Ali back a step. For so long now *she* had been the one giving orders. Now she had to listen to Geea, who in turn, it seemed, would listen to Nira and Nemi. Yet Nira was a child . . .

Before she entered the cave, on her way to the seven doors, Ali took stock of Lestre and Elnar. Naturally, since the former was no longer feeding Tiena, it rushed with greater force into Elnar. Her previous prediction proved true. The sandy area around Mt. Tutor was now under a foot of water—not enough to stop Lord Vak, but enough to slow his army down. Ali wondered how the scabs beneath the sand were liking the river water. Hopefully, lots of them were being flushed out to sea.

Ali returned to Earth via the yellow door and was back in the skies of America come late afternoon. She made a brief stop at her house to get some normal clothes, then flew to the hotel. Landing in the back parking lot where the others were staying was easy. But everyone's shock—when they saw her scarred face and right arm—was not. Cindy and her father burst into tears. What happened, they cried.

How to respond? She was pressed for time, and it was hard to explain burns that looked as if they had healed over a six-month period, but which were still very real. Ali tried to pass off the scars as temporary, but then Cindy demanded she heal herself that instant.

"I know you can," Cindy ordered.

Ali shook her head. "No. I can't heal myself."

"Why not?" her father asked.

"Because Sheri wouldn't let me heal her," Ali answered.

That created another uproar of confusion, but in the midst of all the noise, Hector raised his voice. He seemed to understand her meaning.

"You're trying to teach Lucy something," he said.

Ali noticed how with Hector it was always, "Lucy."

Ali nodded. "She has to understand that I understand her."

"That's pure foolishness," her father insisted. "You heal everyone else in sight, now heal yourself."

"No," Ali said, and stroked his cheek, knowing he was frightened. For the first time, in the hotel mirror, she was getting a *long* look at herself, and it was all she could do not to try to bury her scars beneath her hair. Boy, was she ugly!

Yet she was not the body. That was the point.

She was an angel, from the blue world. She was here to serve.

Hector took her father's arm. "Let your daughter be. She may be wiser than we know. Lucy, at least, needs her help."

Her father kept shaking his head. "Did you see your mother?"

Ali hesitated. "No."

"I thought that's why you were going there."

"Dad. Mom is fine. Better than fine. I'll see her on my next visit."

He struggled. "What if she came to the door, and I hiked up . . ."

"Stop!" she pleaded. "I warned you, you mustn't think that way."

His eyes were hot. "How can I not? You say the world might end tomorrow, and here there's a chance I can at least say good-bye to her."

Ali spoke gently. "You said goodbye to her when you buried her. Now please, Dad, there's still a lot I have to do before this day is finished."

"What are we to do?" Hector asked. "We can't just sit here all day and babysit Nira."

Ali looked around, although she could hear the TV in the next room.

"Where is she?" she asked.

"Watching cartoons," Cindy said. "Did you discover how to fix her?"

"Let me see her alone," was all Ali would say.

In the bedroom, Ali found Nira sitting by the window, staring at the sky. For a moment that worried her. Was Nira acting as the Shaktra's eyes? Ali had told them to seal the windows. Yet when Nira turned toward her, Ali sensed no danger. Flipping off the TV, she sat on the bed beside the child. She took out the Yanti and draped it over Nira's neck.

"How are you feeling, superstar?" Ali asked.

Nira did not respond, but looked down at the Yanti, and stroked it. Ali should not have been surprised—she had seen the phenomenon before in the presence of the child—but the Yanti began to warm. Indeed, it grew so hot Ali could feel it even as she sat back from the child. From a purely physical point of view, the talisman should have been blistering Nira's skin, but the child appeared unaffected.

Ali saw no reason to wait. Placing her thumb on Nira's forehead, where the child was already marked, she twisted her hand in the manner prescribed by Geea—reciting the numbers . . . "zero-six-four . . ."

Ali did not know it, but she had closed her eyes. A loud popping noise made them open. It scared her—it sounded as if Nira's skull had cracked. Yet when she looked at the child, she was astonished.

Nira's eyes glowed with a clear violet light!

The child was smiling at her. A quiet smile of hidden joy.

"Ali," Nira whispered.

Ali felt a river of tears coming. "You know my name?"

"I have always known your name."

Ali put her scarred hand on the child's shoulder.

"You just couldn't say it? You were locked up inside?"

"Inside I was always free." Nira lowered her head and stroked the Yanti as it began to cool. "I always am," she added.

Ali reached out and hugged her. "I love you so much! You're the one . . . the one who's really my big sister!"

Nira hugged her in return, and when they parted, she held the Yanti up for Ali to take. "It was yours to begin with," she said.

But Ali shook her head. "Keep it. And the name I use to open it is—"

"Alosha . . . Alosha . . . Alosha."

"You know?"

"Of course." Nira cocked her head to the side, and, it was uncanny, but there was ancient wisdom in her expression. "You might need it. For protection."

"When it's with you, you're with me. It belongs with you." Ali gestured to her face. "See these scars? I got them because I misused the Yanti. I'm not worthy of it. Please keep it, Nira. Before this war's over, I have faith you'll know what to do with it."

Ali then told her Geea was awake on the other side.

Nira nodded. She already seemed to know.

Ali tried to pump the child as to what she planned to do next. But Nira just smiled and shook her head. "You follow your own path," she said, meaning, Ali assumed, "*I will take care of my own business.*"

Although it hurt to do so, Ali had no choice but to let her go.

The others were ecstatic when Ali let Nira out of the room. Ali took the occasion to try to sneak off. But her father caught up with her in the parking lot. "Where are you going now?" he asked.

"Home."

"Let me come with you."

"Sorry, Dad. For now, you guys have to stay hidden. Tell Hector that." Ali added, "Nira is now much more important than I am."

Her father took her arm. "There's no one more important than you, Ali. Take care of yourself, at least for my sake." He reached up to touch her scars, then sighed as his hand fell back down. "You know, if anything else happens to you . . ."

Ali squeezed his arm. "I'll be careful," she promised.

Ali sat in her room in front of her computer and typed in Nemi.com.

Immediately the blue background of the webpage and the word NEMI—printed in large gold letters—glowed atop a picture of her Yanti. No, she had to remind herself, it was Nira's now . . .

Ali went directly to the live chat room and was pleased to find a member online. He had changed his user name to Devil-in-the-Machine, but she knew he was just teasing her. She typed in *hi*. He responded in an instant.

"How do you know I'm not one of the bad guys?"

"Because you're too cute. And you keep saving my butt."

"Close call on the Isle of Greesh. Almost lost your butt."

"They were blocking you from coming?"

"They never saw me coming until it was too late. But they will not make the same mistake again."

"You said they are ancient but not very bright."

"I was trying to be insulting. There are different types of intelligence. Ever meet someone who gets A's on all his tests, has a fantastic memory, is nominated valedictorian of his school—yet he doesn't have a single original idea in his head?"

"Sounds like me."

"Not true. To accomplish as much as you have takes creativity. The Entity is *huge*. In a sense it has infinite intelligence. Yet it lacks fresh ideas. That is one of the reasons it needs to continually conquer new races."

"Then we should be able to outwit it."

"*We?* Didn't Queen Geea tell you that saving one world was enough? You have to focus on Sheri Smith."

Ali sulked. "Fighting the Entity seems so much more important than that witch."

"That witch is your sister. Right now, she's the Entity's main agent on Earth."

"Is she its only agent?"

"It would never put all its eggs in one basket. But for now focus on Sheri Smith. Or should I say Lucy Pillar?"

"May I ask a few questions about what the Entity said before we turn to her?"

"Sigh . . . Two."

"The Entity makes a great case for why the Earth needs help. Except for it taking over and running everything, I have to admit I was convinced by its argument that human beings are destroying this planet. True?"

"Yes."

"That's it? All I get is a yes?"

"Yes. And that is the answer to your second question. Now back to Sheri Smith and Lucy Pillar."

"Hold on. You tricked me into giving up my second question. I want it back."

"All right, whiner."

"Yeah, I'm a whiner. Half the skin on my body gets fried off and do you hear me complain?"

"Is that your second question?"

"No! I really need to know about the Earth. Are we doing the right thing by stopping the Entity? They're cold, they're cruel, but they probably do have the power to save the planet. Talk to me, Nemi, I'm torn on this issue."

"As well you should be. Everyone should be concerned about the direction the planet is headed. Few are. The reason is as the Entity stated. Love is not the dominant trait of this world. Most people think of themselves first, their family second, and, if they are bighearted, their friends and neighbors next. Few consider the global situation. For that reason, the

Entity makes a persuasive argument. Perhaps we should sit back and let it take over."

"Yet you fight the Entity?"

"You are now at question number three, I believe."

"Shh, stop that, Nemi. Why do you fight the Entity if it's probably our best chance at survival?"

"It all goes back to one question. Does the end justify the means? The Entity would answer yes. The need—to survive—is all that matters. But I know you feel as I do. No end justifies what the Entity is doing. It tortures people, it kills them, and it feels nothing. The odds of humanity surviving are not good, that is a fact, but I would rather take that slim chance, than buy into the future the Entity has planned for humanity. You understand, Ali, you always have. Love does not weigh odds. It only knows that it must keep loving."

Ali was moved by his words. "We can talk about Sheri Smith and Lucy Pillar now," she said.

"You talk to me about them."

"The connection between the two is key. She was a good girl and then she became a monster."

"Why?"

"She got burned and was in terrible pain. Someone must have approached her and offered her a deal. Beauty in exchange for . . . what? Her soul?"

"Close enough," Nemi replied.

"Wait. She was given beauty. But was her pain taken away?"

"The Entity cannot heal."

"How sad. Still, the deal parallels the deal Doren made with the Entity."

"Yes. The same drama had to be reenacted on Earth. How does this help you?"

Ali sighed. "I haven't a clue."

"There are many clues here. Be creative. Use them."

"But before I do, I need to ask a question. Do you talk to Sheri Smith online?"

"No."

"Then Mike Havor was lying to me."

"Maybe. Maybe not."

"I have to know. I have to know if everything he told me was just garbage."

"Let's discuss what he told you, then maybe we'll be able to decide."

"Well, he said Sheri regularly talks to a General Kabrosh—the man in charge of dismantling America's nuclear arsenal. From researching online, I know he's for real."

"Good. He is a real person. Mike Havor was not lying about that."

Ali nodded. "From the outside, it seems she feeds him tons of money. Which makes me wonder if she has purchased a bomb from him."

"What would she do with a *single* bomb?"

"How do we know it's one bomb? He might have sold her a dozen."

"Think creatively, Ali, and practically."

"One missing bomb might be possible to hide. A dozen would be hard?"

"Very good. I ask again, what would she do with a single bomb?"

Ali frowned. "It doesn't seem it would alter the invasion much, unless the invasion were localized, to say, Breakwater. But that bothers me. I can't see the elementals using a hick town like this as their base of operations, before taking over the whole world. I keep thinking of the six caves—like the one I took to Kilimanjaro, the one that led me to Ra. If I were Vak, I would try to use them all, come at humanity from several directions at once."

"Smart girl. I ask again, what would Sheri Smith do with a single bomb?"

"I don't know, tell me."

"That's against the rules."

"What rules? Do you know what kind of day I've had? Police trying to bust me. Dragons chasing and burning me. Entities scheming to possess my soul. Talking myself into leaving myself scarred and ugly."

"Nice touch, Ali, that last point."

"Thank you. But what I'm saying is, I deserve a break. Please, just answer the question. No more riddles."

"I don't know."

"What?"

"I don't know."

"Then why do you keep posing the question?"

"Because it's obviously important. Go find the answer to it. While you're at it, since I'm super plugged into the Internet, I can tell you that Lucy Pillar's mother lives at 1246 Fairview Avenue in Costa Mesa. That's in Orange County, Southern California. Her name is Nancy Pillar. General Kabrosh is in his Washington, D.C. home at 1618 Florence Street, apartment number 902—on the south side of town not far from the Pentagon." Nemi paused. "Will you remember all this?"

"Yes. Do I need to talk to these people?"

"You really need to talk to Lucy Pillar, and ask her to quit being a bad girl. But since that's unlikely to happen, you might want to try these others."

"At least tell me what I'm looking for."

"Information. You never know what piece completes the puzzle until you hold it in your hand."

Ali took one of the plugs she had swiped from the Entity's chamber from her pocket, the ones with the crystals at the ends. "What are these for?"

"They plug into your cell phone."

She took out Hector's cell, tried it. "So?"

"They provide amazing reception."

"In case I need to call you from a weird place?"

"Yes. You have been in some strange places already today."

Ali heard a knock at her front door. She typed quickly. "Who's that?"

"Go see. But whoever it is, don't kill him."

The person knocked again. Hard. It was probably Garten.

"Gotta go. I love you, Nemi."

"Nemi knows. Your love grows."

Ali exited the Internet and turned off her computer. By that time the guy on the porch—and it was Officer Garten—was pounding the door and shouting her name. Ali threw open the door.

"What do you want?" she demanded.

He had his fist raised to strike the door again. But his expression crumpled when he saw her scarred face. "What happened to you?" he asked.

"I was heating a burrito and stood too close to the microwave. What can I do for you?"

"Ali. Those burns look serious. Shouldn't you go to the hospital?"

"Don't believe in medical doctors. What do you want?"

His pity did not last long. He took out a piece of paper and thrust it in her face. "A warrant for your arrest. New evidence has been uncovered in the disappearance of Karl Tanner. I have to take you in."

"What kind of new evidence?"

He pulled out his handcuffs, and there was a gleam in his eyes. "I'm not at liberty to discuss it, but it looks like you're in serious trouble."

Ali crossed her arms over her chest. "I'm not going with you."

"You have to come with me. I told you, that's a warrant."

"Listen! I'm not coming with you. Now what are you going to do? Shoot me?"

Angry, he stuffed the warrant in his back pocket and drew his revolver and pointed it at her. "You'll do what I say, girl, or else . . ."

Ali went into hyper-mode, for an instant, plucked the weapon from his hands. Checking out its long barrel, and the six bullets in its chamber, she suddenly pointed it at him. "All right, I confess," she said.

It was fair to say he went into shock. She couldn't blame him. She had just short-circuited his brain. He must be thinking: *How did she steal my gun?*

"What do you confess to?" he mumbled, scared.

"That I killed Karl Tanner. Murdered him right here in the house. Shot him in the head with a gun just like this one. Blew his brains all over the wall and the carpet. It was so gross! Cindy and I had to spend the whole night cleaning up the mess." Ali added, "Cindy's coming over in a few minutes, I think."

Garten was pasty white. "What did you do with Karl's body?"

"We ate it. Hacked it up and put it in the fridge and had barbecue five nights in a row. Steve had some, too, he liked it." She added, "That's why you could never find Karl's body. It was in our bellies."

"Then what happened to Steve?"

Ali spoke in a wicked tone. "We ate him next. Once you get

a taste for human flesh, nothing else satisfies. It's like a drug, you've got to have it." Waving the pistol, she motioned him inside. "Get your butt in here. Come on, don't start crying, you're going in the basement. That's where we put Karl and Steve before we ate them. Cindy and I—we like to tenderize our meat for a few days."

Garten was a ghost. "Ali, please . . ."

"It's too late, Garten, you were right about everything. We're a cult of cannibals and you caught us fair and square. Now you've got to die." She cocked the revolver. "You don't get in that basement this instant, I'll blow your brains out where you stand." She licked her lips. "Might even eat them raw."

Garten fairly ran for the basement. Once there she used his cuffs to chain him to a pipe not far from an extra toilet. She even brought him down some food and water, and an extra blanket and pillow. But she warned him not to shout for help, not that anyone would be able to hear him. Their house was relatively isolated, and the basement had no windows.

All she had to worry about was his patrol car in the driveway.

"Give me your car keys," she demanded when she saw him on his knees begging for mercy. With shaking hands, he pulled them out.

"What are you going to do with my car?" he asked pathetically.

"Going to run it off the Clemson Pass, into the ocean. It'll take forever to get a crane to lift it out, and by then they'll assume your body floated out to sea."

"They'll think I committed suicide!"

"That's better than getting skinned alive," she said, kneeling by his trembling side. He stared at her with eyes that bulged so big they looked like they might explode.

"You aren't really going to eat me, are you?" he wept.

Ali smiled and ran a hand through his buzz cut. Without answering, she turned to leave.

"When will you be back?" he pleaded.

She called over her shoulder. "When I get hungry!"

The disposal of his vehicle was a piece of cake. It exploded as it hit the rocks where the cold waves pounded. The cliff was high and sheer. The way things moved in Breakwater, she wouldn't be surprised if it took them three days to get the patrol car out of there. Well, at least it would give the cops something to keep them occupied.

Running toward the trees, Ali then soared into the sky, and on the spur of the moment decided to head south. Orange County, here I come.

Nancy Pillar—her body had been placed beside the rest of them on that greatest kloudar of all. The woman was a high fairy—she could not be underestimated. Perhaps she would enjoy hearing that her only child was still alive. Of course, Ali would have to be careful when they talked about her evil daughter. No reason to upset the woman in her old age.

CHAPTER

14

After Ali left for Earth, Geea moved fast. Ra was soon to see that was her way. She made a decision, acted on it, did not waste any time.

Drash flew them to Yom, where Geea was happily welcomed by the remainder of the high fairies. Before, they had been relieved to see Ali, but now they were overjoyed at Geea's return. The arrival of their *real* queen—Ra could not blame them for feeling that way. Geea's presence obviously gave them a better chance of survival. Yet they were considerate enough to ask if Ali was all right. It was indeed a miracle for the fairies to see *two* aspects of the same person within a matter of days.

Geea told them Ali was fine and busy fighting the Shaktra on Earth.

Geea healed Amma. Although Ra was not permitted in the room for the actual operation, it did not take her long to get rid of the Shaktra's mark. In minutes, Amma was back to speaking in a normal voice. But when Geea went to leave with Drash and Ra, Amma tried to come. Geea forbade it.

"The Shaktra's scar is gone but it will take you time to recover your strength," Geea told her mother. "Best you rest. But have the others pack and prepare to return to Uleestar."

"Isn't it guarded with dragons?" Amma asked.

"They'll be gone soon."

"Why do we return there?" Amma asked.

Geea stood to leave. "You'll see."

When they were airborne again, with Drash flying high, in the direction of Anglar itself, Geea erected a field around the dragon that kept the three of them supplied with warm air. Again, Ra found it best not to look down. He felt like a hang glider that had caught an updraft off Mt. Everest and never escaped it.

Ra and Drash both had to prod Geea to reveal her plans.

"We're heading toward a kloudar called Denzy," Geea said, the blue light of the moon equally as bright on her face as the green light of the setting sun. Directly overhead, although it was not yet night, a few brave stars were visible. "Heard the name, Drash?"

"Drash has heard about it but only in whispers."

"I bet they were forbidden whispers," Geea replied, before explaining to both of them. "Denzy is a kloudar that orbits *extremely* close to Anglar. For that reason, its revolution around the moon is brief. It's only out of the atmosphere six hours. That's what attracted Doren to it, besides the fact that it's hollow."

"I'm not sure I'm following you," Ra said.

"Long before she launched her war on the elementals, Doren knew she'd need the dragons as allies. They were simply too powerful to ignore. Whoever had them on their side would probably win the battle. That became painfully clear when Doren ordered the dragons to melt off portions of the kloudar and drop chunks of ice on anyone who stood in her way."

"We saw the results of such attacks," Ra said. "When we first entered this land—in the area where the leprechauns used to live—the whole place was empty. But in spots, there were acres of crushed trees and bushes."

Geea nodded. "That turned out to be the single worst weapon Vak and his army had to face. It turned the tide of the war. But few knew then that Doren's alliance with the dragons was related to Denzy. She worked on that kloudar for months, preparing it, with the sole purpose of seducing the dragons to her side."

"Did the Shaktra allow the dragons to ride that kloudar to the far side of Anglar and bathe in the blue light?" Drash asked. "Drash heard that was the promise that led to Kashar's betrayal of the other elementals."

"Yes and no."

"Drash is not sure what yes or no means."

Geea smiled. "In a short time you'll see the truth."

That was all they could get out of her, for the time being. But after an hour more of flight, she pointed into the distance, to what at first Ra mistook to be a star, but which was in reality an icy kloudar. Geea confirmed his guess. It was Denzy.

As they came near, it looked like any other kloudar they had passed along the way. However, as Drash took them around the far side, they were met with a remarkable sight. A gigantic door—composed of two swinging portions, that were unmistakably made of metal—stood almost hidden at the base of a snowy gorge. At the foot of the door were dragons—three on each side.

They leapt into the air at Drash's approach.

"Keep going, I'm strengthening our field," Geea said. "They can't harm us."

"Drash believes Geea," the dragon replied, his voice hopeful.

Ra saw the luminous green field that had surrounded them since they had left Yom grow more dense. But he did not know how that related to dragon fire. Personally, he hoped Geea could talk their way inside.

That appeared to be her intent, at least for the moment. When it looked as if the dragons would attack, she ordered Drash to halt. Drawing her silver sword, Geea held it high for all the dragons to see.

"I'm here to speak to Chashar, and his spouse, Tashi. I've no desire for battle."

"Your desires are unimportant, you will not be let inside," a dragon spoke. He was old and wrinkled; the flame in his nostrils was weak. He was having trouble staying in the air, but he managed to add, "One of your kind killed many dragons today. There are rumors that Kashar himself is dead. His brother has gone so far as to take command, and the last thing Chashar will welcome is a visit from a fairy."

"Have you grown blind as well as dense, Laspar?" she asked. "I'm Queen Geea. I'm no ordinary fairy, and it's not just a rumor that Kashar is dead. A child of mine killed him, and I'll kill all who stand guard here if I'm not let inside. Now!"

The dragons conferred amongst themselves, and Ra thought that Geea must have carried one heck of a reputation. There were six of them and they didn't even bother to try to blast her with their fire.

Ra did notice one of them scurry inside the steel doors. He was not gone long, and when he returned he spoke to Laspar. Then the old dragon came near to where Drash hovered.

"Chashar will see Geea, but Geea alone," Laspar said.

"My friends must accompany me. It is not open to negotiation. Now get out of my way, all of you, before you feel the sting of my sword! This is my last warning!"

After a weary look at his partners, the old dragon backed down, and Drash flew forward, through the wide open door. Ra continued to marvel at its height. It must have been two hundred meters tall. Yet it was nothing compared to the sights inside. There was a wide stone tunnel beyond the door, that ran for perhaps three kilometers, before it opened into a cavern so vast it could have swallowed Mt. Kilimanjaro whole.

Here there were neither floors nor ceilings nor walls. Thousands of dragons either drifted lazily through the open space—their wings set on glide-motion, not truly beating—or else the dragons held fast to a seemingly endless number of stone crevices fitted about the hollow kloudar.

Red light shone from the dragon's own smoldering snouts, but the vast majority of fire and light burned off the top of gigantic stone jars that were set like ceramic pots in an earthly home. They sat in clever corners, or else stood along stone walls. The scent of the burning oil was pleasing. It reminded Ra of a mixture of sandalwood and camphor.

Yet there was a spot that puzzled Ra. Its center was dome-shaped and smoothly polished, but something that resembled an inverted purple umbrella hung from it. Clearly artificial, it appeared designed as a *spraying* tool. There were thousands of sinister holes all over it. Ra did not know why he felt as if the holes were evil, he just did.

Oddly enough, the dragons did not overreact to their arrival. More than a few looked over, and got out of Geea's way as she prodded Drash toward the far side of the hollow kloudar, but none made a threatening move. Ra found the reaction strange. After all, a fairy—well, a fairy/human—had killed their king earlier in the day. But maybe Kashar had been unpopular.

They reached Chashar's and Tashi's thrones. The furniture

resembled lengthy beds of gold and silver, rather than upright chairs. Still, the thrones were raised with slabs of gray granite that were laced with quartz crystal, and which shimmered in the red light of many burning jars.

Neither Chashar nor Tashi wore ornaments to distinguish their royal standing. Ra figured Tashi was the female because her snout was longer and thinner, more attractive actually. Perhaps it was an old memory from his life as Jira, but he found the dragons did not scare him.

Not like the Isle of Greesh had . . . God, no.

Drash landed on the stone floor before the thrones, and Geea gracefully slid off the young dragon's back. Ra did likewise and stood nearby.

Chashar and Drash exchanged looks. Clearly they recognized each other, but Chashar seemed somewhat surprised to see his nephew alive.

Geea bowed to the dragons. "Queen Geea of the high fairies offers her greetings to the new rulers of the dragons, oh King Chashar and Queen Tashi."

Chashar snorted by way of hello. Two bands of flame extending three feet shot from his nostrils. "Geea comes to pay her respects on the day Chashar's brother dies, and at the hands of a fairy? Such hypocrisy surprises me—even coming from you, Geea."

"Hypocrisy?" Geea asked. "I've come here to offer my help in what are troubled times. Although it is true a fairy did slay your brother, he was the one who attacked first. What else was she to do but defend herself?"

"It was not an ordinary fairy!" Tashi spoke suddenly, her voice high and shrill. "The dragons know this fairy to be Geea's *direct* offspring—to be the human mirror of Geea. That is why Chashar speaks of hypocrisy. The great and moral Geea—who goes about the land lecturing other races on behaving in strict accordance with the natural order—has decided to commit the greatest sin of all! One life isn't enough for Geea! She must have two at the same time!"

"Only to counter the threat of the Shaktra—a creature you well know inhabits both an elemental body and a human body," Geea replied.

"If Geea is worried about the Shaktra, why is Geea here?" Chashar said. "It is in the south, near Vak's army. Why don't you go meet it, settle your differences directly?"

"You know the answer to that question," Geea replied. "Vak's army is being herded by a thousand dragons toward Tutor—as a prelude to the invasion of Earth. Don't you see what is happening? The Shaktra is emptying the green world. When it is done with the other elementals, it will complete the job by getting rid of the dragons."

"Nonsense!" Tashi swore. "The dragons have no intention of entering the yellow world!"

Geea nodded. "I understand. The Shaktra has no intention of letting you go there. But it's not going to let you stay here, either. You see, all the dragons, very soon, will be dead."

They had begun to attract an audience behind them—and *above* them, Ra noted. With Geea's last words, they snorted huge streams of fire—apparently a dragon's version of laughter. Chashar also acted amused.

"How is it that the dragons are all supposed to die?" he asked.

Geea turned and studied the throng of dragons that filled the cavern. Ra would not have been surprised if she recognized each and every one of them, for her green eyes glowed, and the light in them was as subtle as it was powerful. Finally her eyes came back to rest on Chashar.

"I see less than two-thirds of your flock," she said. "And

since there is only a thousand in the south, near Tutor, and a few about Uleestar, then I have to conclude that you've lost many thousands in the last few months."

Chashar shrugged. "The war with Lord Vak was tough. And Lord Balar, of the dwarves, and your own General Tapor, are worthy opponents. Many were slain, that is the nature of battle. No one hears a dragon complain."

Geea nodded. "It is said dragons are slow to complain, but quick to lie. You lie now, Chashar. Few of your dragons died in battle. Most died after coming here. In fact, this is probably where the remainder of you will die—when the Shaktra stops feeding you the *dust*."

A murmur went through the crowd that grew into an uproar. Chashar had to leap up and signal for silence. Yet he glared at Geea, and Ra could feel the heat of the dragon's snout on his face.

"You dare to come here, before Chashar's throne, and talk of that!" he shouted. "Chashar is of a mind to slay you here and now! Best you beg for my mercy and leave immediately!"

Geea met his gaze. "You're upset because your dirty little se-cret has escaped these supposedly secret walls. When the Shaktra—*my* sister, Doren—came to bargain with you for help in the war, she offered you the blue light beyond Anglar. She said you would ride the kloudar, like an ice maiden, out into the galaxy, and bathe in the blue light of the next universe. But I look around this kloudar and see no windows where blue light might shine through. I see only doors designed to keep the air trapped inside. Air that every day is filled with dust, which you turn to smoke with your flame, and inhale. A smoke that flows straight to your befuddled brains, and lets you pretend you're something you're never going to be."

"Silence!" Tashi screamed. "Geea has no right to judge us!"

"I've every right to judge!" Geea said. "You and your dust have cost millions of elemental lives. Doren came nowhere near to fulfilling her end of the bargain, and still you fall for her lies—even to this day. So you ride a kloudar beyond Anglar? So what? You're locked inside. With drug-saturated dust that sprays from the ceiling. You're dragons. You're the most powerful of all elementals. But you traded it all for what? On Earth they have a term for it—*addicts*. You've become addicts, which are seen as the lowest of the low. Because every one of them is a coward. When Doren came here, you tried to get something for nothing. You wanted the blue light beyond Anglar, and all you got in return was a drug that's slowly killing you. Now wait until she takes it away. Make no mistake, that will be her next step. Then we'll see how slowly you die, and how painfully." Geea paused. "Is this what you want, Tashi? Chashar?"

Tashi went to snap at Geea but her king bade her to remain silent. For the first time Ra noted the yellow around Chashar's eyes, the cracks in his wings. Also, for once, he appeared to be listening. Geea had said something that had hit home.

"Some of what you say is true," Chashar said. "The dust does exact a toll. Some dragons can take it, others cannot. But for those of us who have the strength to absorb it, we no longer care about the blue light beyond Anglar. If given a choice, dragons would not even try to carve a window in this place, and look out on the stars. Geea knows it all comes down to choice. Geea knows that the Shaktra gave us that choice. The dragons like the dust. They like it more than they like the rest of the elementals, who never cared much for us anyway. To the fairies and elves and dwarves, we were just powerful brutes that had to be controlled. But now we have taken control of our own destiny, and we are content."

"Have you not listened to me?" Geea asked. "Doren answers to a force above her. That force wants the green world for its own. I admit, I don't know what it plans to do with it. But I do know that when all the others have been forced from this world, the dragons will be expendable. The dust will stop flowing from your ceiling, and the pain of its stopping will kill you all."

Tashi snorted. "You bluff!"

Chashar was curious. "How do you know Doren will take away the dust?"

"She was once my sister. I know her better than anyone. She never cared for dragons, even before she was transformed into the Shaktra. Once you're no longer of service to her, she'll only be too happy to see you die."

Chashar considered. "Speculation on Geea's part."

"Lies!" Tashi spat.

Geea gestured to the rest of the cavern. "The deaths of thousands of dragons is not speculation! If two thousand have already died from this dust, then isn't it easy to envision that ten times that number will perish when she cuts off your supply?"

"Get her out of here!" Tashi snapped at her husband.

Yet Chashar continued to show interest. "What is your offer, Geea?"

"Have the dragons join my side in the war that is about to erupt in *this* world, not in the yellow world. Help me protect Lord Vak and his army, along with Uleestar. In return I promise to seize control of this kloudar and the mechanism it uses to dispense the dust. You think I've been sleeping for the last thirteen years, but my mind has traveled far beyond my body. I've discovered the secret of the dust. When the war is finished, I'll continue to supply you with it—but in smaller and smaller amounts, until you no longer need it."

Chashar growled. "Dragons don't want that! Dragons want more each week. Geea can't give dragons less."

"Take less each week, and you won't need it at all. That I promise."

Chashar spoke to Tashi, who shook her head vehemently. He turned toward the assemblage. By this time there was not a dragon in the cavern who was not listening. He addressed them in a thundering voice.

"Chashar is your new king, but Chashar has always been one to listen to fellow dragons. All have heard what Queen Geea has come to offer. How do the dragons respond to her? Yea or nay?"

The chorus of "nays" was loud, some might have said overwhelming. Yet Ra did hear many "yeas" as well, and apparently, so did Chashar, for he did not immediately pass judgment. For a long time he sat in thought. Then he shook his head.

"Geea can see the dragons have made their choice. As their king, Chashar can only support their wish. So be it. But out of respect to our old alliance, Chashar will allow . . ."

A loud pounding echo filled the chamber.

Ra suspected what it meant. The outer doors had closed!

Chashar confirmed his fear. "Chashar was about to set Geea and her companions free. Now it is too late. The kloudar moves into space, where Anglar shines bright. Soon the dust will begin to fall from above. With our flames, it will be transformed into smoke, and it will be your choice to join us in this secret sacrament. If Geea so wishes."

Geea gave Ra and Drash a quick glance. She gestured.

"Come close to me, immediately," she said, as her green field expanded.

CHAPTER

15

Nancy Pillar, of 1246 Fairview Avenue, Costa Mesa, California. White house at the end of a cul-de-sac in a boring section of town. Ali landed on its front lawn. It was now nighttime. None of the streetlights were on. But she saw a bright lamp on inside the house, and sensed a single person in the living room.

However, she did not sense a high fairy—they shimmered brightly in her subtle vision. She wondered if Nemi had gotten his facts mixed up. One way to find out. Ali walked up to the door and knocked.

The woman who answered had gray-streaked red hair and lovely green eyes. Thirty pounds overweight, and at least sixty years of age, she wore a simple green dress but had an expensive emerald ring on her right hand—on the long finger. She did not wear a wedding band, though; and Ali recalled that Lucy Pillar's father had died in the blast that had rocked Toule thirteen years ago—the same year Ali had been born.

The color of the ring matched the woman's eyes. Both were of rare quality, and hinted, to Ali, of a fairy bloodline. Yet the woman's eyes were powerless, and Ali could not imagine any high fairy being born on Earth and not possessing at least a token of her magical ancestry inside her.

Through the screen, Ali peered at the woman's face, searching for a sign of the Shaktra's mark. In her subtle vision, she felt a darkness present, but could not be sure. The truth be known, not many human beings looked very bright on the subtle. Sadly, Nemi—and the Entity for that matter—were right. Love was not a dominant human quality, although love was the one thing that made a person glow the most.

"Hello. May I help you?" the woman asked in a pleasant voice. In her own dull way, she appeared to be studying Ali—particularly by staring at the burnt half of her face. Ali realized it was something she was going to have to get used to.

"My name is Ali Warner and I'm from up north, from a town called Breakwater. It's not far from Toule, and I have a friend there, Hector Wells. Do you know him?"

The woman strained a moment, then brightened. "Why yes, Hector! He used . . . I used to know him."

"So you're Nancy Pillar?"

"Yes. What did you say your name was?"

"Ali Warner."

The woman glowed at the memory of Hector—yet, that was all. She did not invite Ali in nor ask other questions. To Ali, she seemed slow. But she wondered if that was all there was to it.

"May I come in?" Ali asked. "I've come a long way and I'm tired."

"But of course, please," the woman said, holding the door open. "May I get you a glass of water? Or would you like milk? Something to eat?"

"Do you have a Coke?"

"Yes. I try not to drink it too much because my doctor says

it makes me fat. But I'm already fat, so I don't know if it matters. What do you think? Ah, excuse me, I've forgotten your name already."

"Ali. I think it depends on how many bottles you drink a day. I love Coke, but I try to have just one bottle a day."

"Gosh darn! That might be my problem. I drink three a day."

"Three's not so bad."

The woman looked guilty. "I drink three of the large ones. The liter bottles."

Ali smiled. "That's probably not such a great idea."

The woman headed for the kitchen. "Would you like ice with your Coke? A sandwich?"

"Sure." Ali scanned the living room. There was a couch, a chair, a TV, a coffee table, a single lamp. That was it—talk about plain living. However, on the walls were two paintings of mountains, both exquisite. Ali recognized Mt. Blanc in France. The other was vaguely familiar, but she couldn't place it.

The woman called from the kitchen. "What kind of sandwiches do you like?"

Ali yelled back. "What do you have?"

"I don't know!" the woman shouted. "They sell them at the store! I don't know what's in them!"

"Just bring me whatever you have!" Ali said, studying the paintings closer. They had been done in oil, and they did not *feel* old, less than five years. Neither was signed, which struck her as odd, but both were nicely framed. Indeed, whoever had framed them had spent considerable money. They were covered with nonreflective glass. Plus the wooden borders were finely carved, gold-leafed, worthy of masterpieces. The artistic quality was indeed very high.

Ali lifted the one of Mt. Blanc off the wall, held it to her chest.

She almost dropped the blasted thing!

"Yuck!" she muttered. The painting was gorgeous but carried with it a montage of foul feelings. Ali knew in an instant why. Sheri had painted it. And her mood, her bitterness, whatever, had been imprinted on the work. Even though it was beautiful to the eye, it was a pain to the heart.

So Sheri Smith had been in the house.

How old were the paintings? Why had she painted these particular scenes?

The woman returned with a liter bottle of Coke, two glasses, containing ice, and a basketful of plastic-wrapped store-made sandwiches. Acting like a nervous hostess, she set them on the lone coffee table. All the furniture was appallingly cheap. It must have come from a Goodwill store. Not that Ali was judgmental about such places. Since her mother had died, and money was tight, she had bought clothes at the Goodwill in Breakwater.

"Look through the sandwiches. If you find one you like, just eat it," the woman said, unscrewing the cap off the Coke bottle. "I'm so glad you wanted Coke instead of milk. I don't actually have any milk. My doctor says dairy can make you fat."

Ali sat across from the woman and studied the food, found a turkey sandwich with cheese, lettuce, and tomato on it. She was no fan of mayonnaise. Ali let her hostess pour her a drink. The woman filled the large glass to the rim. It seemed to make her happy.

"You must be hungry and tired after coming such a long way," the woman said, sort of repeating Ali's earlier remark.

Ali nodded, took a sip of her drink, opened her sandwich and dug in. When had she eaten last? She was getting as bad as the woman, she could not remember . . .

"How is it?" Nancy Pillar asked anxiously.

"Great." Ali casually nodded to the paintings. "Did Lucy paint those?"

"Why, yes. How did you know? Oh do you know my Lucy? I thought maybe you just knew Hector. They used to date, you know, before . . ." The woman didn't finish.

"Before what?" Ali asked.

The woman's fingers shook as she tried to open her own sandwich. The question had disturbed her. Lines wrinkled her face.

"Before they stopped dating," she said.

Ali acted nonchalant. "I know Lucy. Saw her just the other day."

The woman suddenly smiled. "How nice for you! How is she doing?"

"Fine. Hector's fine, too. I saw him today."

"Lucky you. Such a lovely boy."

Boy, Ali thought. The woman had not seen him in ages.

Then Nancy Pillar got distressed or confused—it was no doubt a combination of the two. Much of her emotional states seemed to swing between the two moods. Ali was not sure what she had done wrong, but the woman's next remark was revealing.

"She did not *hurt* you with her secret?" the woman asked softly.

Ali knew she had to move carefully. "No. She let me know her secret. The secret that she was still alive. You and I—we share that same secret." Ali added in a soothing tone, allowing her internal power to strengthen the effect of her tone, "It's all right."

The woman relaxed, nodded to herself. "It's all right."

Ali tried to move gently forward. "When was the last time you saw Lucy?"

Unfortunately, the woman stopped again and frowned.

"It's been some time," she said.

Ali smiled. "But she must stop by at holidays?"

The woman mimicked her smile. "Lucy loves Christmas! Sometimes she stops by then!"

"Did she stop by last Christmas?" Ali asked.

Nancy nodded, then shook her head. "I don't remember. Last year, I didn't buy a tree, so I wasn't sure when Christmas was. Without a tree and presents, it's hard to tell."

"I know what you mean," Ali said, her mouth full of food. Boy, was she hungry! It would be interesting to compute how many calories flying burned per minute. She pointed to Nancy Pillar's ring, added, "Did Lucy give you that emerald?"

"Yes!" Setting down her sandwich, she held it out for Ali to admire. "Do you like it?"

"It's beautiful," Ali said, although it had an awful vibe. "May I see it, please?"

The woman drew back her hand, frowned. "What do you mean?"

"Can I hold it?"

Nancy Pillar suddenly stood, angry. "You may certainly not! What are you trying to do, steal my ring? Is that why you came here?"

Ali looked up in surprise. The transformation in the woman was shocking. Yet Ali tried to keep her voice and expression friendly. "I'm sorry, it was wrong of me to ask that. I just liked it so much. It's so pretty. But of course you should be careful with it."

The woman continued warily, "Why did you come here?"

"I told you. I know Lucy and Hector, and I was in the area. I just wanted to meet you."

Slowly, the woman sat down, nodding to herself. "I'm sorry."

"There's no reason to be sorry," Ali said.

"I shouldn't have yelled at you. You're a nice person, I can tell. Your ugly scars are not your fault."

Ali had never before been called ugly.

She nodded. "I got them not too long ago."

Nancy Pillar put a hand to her mouth. "Poor dear. What happened?"

"Oh, it was my fault. I was making some tea, and I tripped and pulled the boiling pot down, and it spilled on my face."

"I'm so sorry. That must have been terrible for you. Did it happen at Christmas?"

"Closer to Easter." Ali nodded to the paintings. "Did Lucy just paint those? Or was it a long time ago?"

"It was some time ago. They're beautiful, aren't they?"

"I love them. Are there any other paintings of hers in the house?"

"Yes. There are other mountains. Do you like mountains . . . Alice?"

"Yes. Very much. May I see them, please?"

"Of course." The woman stood, but not before she took several swallows of her glass of Coke. "The others are in her bedroom."

Ali followed her down the hall. "You keep a room for Lucy here?"

"You know Lucy. Never know when she's going to stop by."

"Does she call much?"

"She calls."

"Does Hector ever call?"

"No! I wish he would. Such a lovely boy."

Nancy Pillar turned on the light in the last room on the right. Again, the furniture was sparse, cheap. A bed, carefully made up, and a desk with a chair that looked as if it might have been used by a teenager, not a grown woman.

However, there were five paintings on the walls. Each of a different mountain. Ali recognized Pete's Peak, along with Mt. Fuji, from Japan; Mt. Kilimanjaro, from Tanzania; and Mt. Shasta, from California.

The fifth and last painting—like the one in the living room—she did not know, but she made a point to commit both to memory. Later she would find them on the Internet. The mountains might be significant.

Besides the seven doors inside Pete's Peak, there were six tunnels. Ali had only explored one, which had led to Kilimanjaro and Ra, in Africa. She would have laid odds that these other mountains were where the other five tunnels led. If she had time, Ali told herself, she would try to confirm her theory. The mountains might be the spots through which the elementals planned to invade the Earth.

Lucy had painted each mountain with extraordinary care and detail.

Mt. Shasta, which in Ali's humble opinion was one of the most beautiful mountains on Earth, was directly above the bed. The other four hung opposite the bed. Each had been handsomely framed, and left unsigned.

Were these places Lucy still regularly visited? Or had she lost her attachment to them long ago? The latter was probably the case, for why had she left them here, with a woman who hardly knew her own name?

Standing in the center of Lucy's bedroom, Ali turned and stared deeply at the mother. Catching the woman's eye, she let her field expand and placed the woman in a deep hypnotic trance. Ordinarily she did not like to use such power on people.

It felt like an infringement of free will, something the Entity might do. Yet Ali was certain a spell had been placed on the woman and hated to leave her in her present condition.

Nancy Pillar stared at her without blinking.

"Can you hear me, Nancy?" Ali asked.

"Yes."

"Do you understand I'm a good person and I'm here to help you?"

"Yes."

"How do you understand that? How do you know that I'm good?"

"Because you are a high fairy."

"You know about high fairies?"

"I used to know about them."

"You used to know about them and then you forgot?"

"Yes."

"Why did you forget about them?"

"She made me forget."

"Lucy made you forget?"

"Yes."

"Why did she make you forget?"

Nancy hesitated. "I don't know."

"Why do you think? If you had to guess?"

Nancy winced. "She did not die in the fire. I thought she died in the fire. That is what they told me."

"Who told you that?"

"The police. They said . . . Lucy is dead."

"But they were uncertain at first, right?"

"Yes."

"Why were they uncertain?"

"Because they could not find her body."

"Because she was still alive."

"I don't know . . . Yes."

"You know she is still alive because she visits you sometimes?"

"Yes."

"When was the last time she visited you?"

"Years ago."

"How many years?"

"Four . . . Five. She came to show me her baby."

"She had a baby?"

"Yes."

"Was the baby named Nira?"

"Yes."

"Was she happy to show you the baby?"

The woman hesitated. "I don't know. The baby . . . made me happy."

"How long after the fire did Lucy first visit you?"

"Years."

"Do you remember how many years?"

"Two . . . Three . . ."

"Were you shocked when you saw her?"

"Yes."

"Were you happy?"

"Yes."

"Was Lucy happy, too?"

Nancy hesitated. "I think so."

"Did she tell you to keep her visit secret?"

"Yes."

"Was she burnt? Did she have scars?"

"No."

"Did that surprise you?"

"Yes . . . At first."

"But then you accepted that her scars were gone?"

"Yes."

"Why? What did she do that made you accept that her scars were gone?"

Nancy hesitated. "I don't know."

"What did she do that made you keep secret the fact that she was still alive?"

"I don't know . . . She asked to me to keep it secret."

"Did she do anything else to you?"

"I don't know."

"When she visited you—the first time after the fire—did you feel different after she left?"

Nancy winced. "I don't . . . think . . . I don't . . . know."

The woman had begun to wobble on her feet. Ali told her to sit on the edge of the bed. When the woman was comfortable, Ali knelt before her, maintaining eye contact. She was in a hurry to get on with her many tasks, but knew it was dangerous to rush what was nothing less than psychic surgery.

"Think back to that first visit after the fire. Did Lucy just show up at the door here?"

"Yes."

"Did she drive a car here? Did you see her car?"

"I saw . . . no car."

"Did she say why she had come to see you?"

"She came . . . She said . . . she missed me."

"Did she act like she had missed you?"

"I don't know."

"Was it hard to keep her secret? The secret that she was really alive?"

This time the woman did more than wince. She shook in pain. Yet she continued to stare at Ali, although Ali had to exert more power to maintain control over her.

"I wanted to tell . . ." Nancy began.

"Who did you want to tell?"

"People."

"You wanted to tell other people that your daughter was alive?"

"Yes."

"Did you want to tell Hector?"

"Yes."

"But Lucy said you must keep it a secret that she was alive?"

"Yes."

Ali moved near. "When she told you this, did she come close to you?"

"Yes."

"Did she stare in your eyes?"

"Yes."

"Did she order you to keep her secret?"

"Yes."

"Did you try to fight this order? This command?"

"Yes."

"Did you fight it because you knew you were a high fairy?"

"Yes."

"Did you know she was putting a spell on you?"

"I didn't know . . . no."

"But still, you fought her."

"Yes."

"Was it then she slipped the ring on your finger?"

The woman did an odd thing then. She shut her eyes. Beads of sweat formed on her forehead, and she panted. Ali could feel she was losing control, but feared to force her to open her eyes and stare at her again. God, how she hated using this ability! But not so much as she hated what the witch had done to her own mother.

Nancy Pillar began to weep.

"I can't take it off! She told me not to take it off!"

"I'm a high fairy, Nancy. You know I've come here to help you. Will you let me help you? Will you let me take the ring off you?"

Nancy shook her head. "No! She won't let . . . No!"

"Keep your eyes shut and lie back on the bed. That's right, lie back and put your head on the pillow and go to sleep." Nancy did as she was told, even pulled a blanket over her body. Ali tucked her in as best she could and continued in a soft voice.

"As you sleep, you're going to have a dream that your queen, Geea, came and visited you in the night. And when she visited you, she took away that horrible ring your daughter forced you to wear. That ring that's made your mind so dull and confused. Do you understand?"

The woman spoke in a faint whisper. "But I can't . . ."

"You can't take it off, I understand. But Queen Geea can. You know Geea, don't you?"

"Yes."

Ali put her hands on the woman's heart and forehead, and felt the warmth, even without the Yanti. "Go to sleep now and don't worry. In the middle of the night Queen Geea will take away the ring and destroy it. After it's been destroyed, your mind will be clear. In the morning, when you awaken, you'll feel better than you have in years. And you'll call Queen Geea on this number I'll tell you right now." Ali gave her Hector's cell number. "Can you remember that number?"

"Yes."

"There's no reason to fear. Geea will care for you now."

The warmth grew to a powerful wave of heat. Nancy smiled quietly.

"No fear . . ."

"Sleep now, Nancy. Sleep."

In seconds the woman was deeply asleep, snoring. Gently, Ali reached over to remove the ring. Nancy must have gained weight since Lucy had put it on her finger. The fit was *extremely* tight—Ali would practically have to break her finger to get it off. At least, a normal human being would have to do such a thing.

But Ali had a better idea. Since she had control of the fire element, she allowed a tiny but steady stream of heat to flow from her fingertips into the band. Naturally, the ring swelled in size, and with a sudden yank, Ali was able to pull it off.

Nancy stirred but did not awaken. Ali put the ring in her pocket.

Outside, once again high in the starlit sky, Ali took a detour over the black sea. There she crushed the ring until the emerald cracked and the gold melted beneath her fingers, before she threw it into the water. General Kabrosh of Washington, D.C. was next on her list, but she decided her friends and father deserved a brief visit.

The only problem was, when she got to the hotel, they were gone.

The guy at the desk said they had checked out two hours ago.

"Were the four of them alone?" Ali asked the guy at the counter. He had blond hair and looked like he surfed most of his free hours.

"Yeah. There was the two men, the blond chick, and the kid." The guy added, "You know the girl? She was kind of cute."

Ali was used to guys asking about her, not Cindy. Just another thing she was going to have to get used to, she thought sadly. The guy was at least eighteen, but Ali knew Cindy was often mistaken for someone older.

"She's too young for you." Ali was annoyed they had left.

Didn't they understand how difficult it was to protect them?

"Did they leave a message?"

He checked a row of mail slots. "You Ali Warner?"

"That's me."

The guy handed her a plain white envelope. Ali tore it open and read the paper inside. It was not in Cindy's or her father's handwriting. It did not look like grown-up handwriting at all. Simply holding it, Ali could tell Nira had touched the page.

The message was short.

Dad's gone home. The rest of us have gone on an adventure!

It made Ali wonder. Was Nira already in charge?

CHAPTER

16

For Ra, it was either a night to remember or else one that would be impossible to forget. Sitting beside Geea and Drash, and shielded by the queen's powerful field from the smoke of the dust and the wild flames of the intoxicated dragons, Ra felt as if he had been the one who had inhaled a powerful drug. The hollow interior of the kloudar known as Denzy supposedly spent only six hours on the far side of the moon, Anglar.

For Ra, it felt like an eternity.

However, he had Geea and Drash for company, and that was never a bad thing. The fairy queen gave them many insightful observations about power, and its corrupting influence, as they watched the dust spray from the gigantic inverted umbrella on the ceiling of the kloudar. The dust emerged brown, but as the dragons set it aflame, the smoke turned purple, and the dragons sucked it up as if it was heaven's very nectar.

Perhaps to them it was, for after reveling in the smoky cavern for only a few minutes, the dragons' behavior underwent a distinct change. They flew wildly through the enclosed space, smashing into each other, but laughing all the while. Well, Ra

273

thought they were laughing—it was hard for him to say exactly what a dragon sounded like when it was happy.

Yet Geea cautioned that they were not happy at all, only satiated.

Ra asked what was the difference.

"Joy does not come from pleasure," Geea said. "That is a lesson the dragons—as well as your world—have yet to learn. Joy is an internal state separate from all sensation. Joy is the nature of the soul, and is only found in silence. Not that there is anything wrong with pleasure. It has its place in life, as much as pain does."

"Drash prefers pleasure to pain," the young dragon said.

Geea laughed. "Of course you do. But as we grow, and come closer to the blue light, we learn that intense pleasure is inevitably followed by a sense of disappointment—even loss. Few on Earth would agree with me, but it is true. At this time, on Earth, the majority of humans have a bit of dragon in them. They want power and pleasure, and they want it now."

"Aren't you being a little harsh in your judgment?" Ra asked.

Geea shook her head. "I do not judge. I merely observe. Look at these dragons. They live longer than any other elemental. They consider that a blessing, but because of that fact, they end up living fewer lives on Earth. And when they are born on Earth, they crave positions of power and authority. The majority of your politicians are descendants of dragons, which is a pity."

"Why?" Ra asked.

"Because the last person who should be nominated to a position of power is the person who craves power."

Ra had to laugh when he thought of Earth's leaders. "That's so true! There should be a law that says that if you really want to be president, you're immediately disqualified."

274

"Drash does not want to be king of the dragons," Drash said.

Geea patted the young dragon. "That's why you'll make a great king."

"Is this desire for power the reason Doren went after the dragons as allies in the first place?" Ra asked.

Geea nodded. "Doren knew they would be susceptible to her offer. But right now, Chashar thinks—with the other elementals gone—he'll rule the green world."

"Despite Doren?" Ra asked.

"He thinks he can take her."

"Can he?"

"With the Entity at her back, he doesn't stand a chance."

Drash stared at the purple smoke. "Would it be wrong to try the smoke for a moment?" he asked.

"It would be a mistake," Geea said. "You would enjoy it tonight and miss it tomorrow. Each day, thereafter, the dust would give you less pleasure, and yet you would miss it more. That's a bad deal, Drash. As the new king of the dragons, it's important you set a good example."

"Drash is not king yet."

"Drash is going to be king before we leave here," Geea promised.

By the time the kloudar reentered the green world's atmosphere and the steel doors opened, the smoke had been flushed from the interior of Denzy. By then the vast majority of the dragons seemed asleep. But Ra worried as he studied them. From his experience, most dragons slept with one triangular eye open—yet a quarter of them had both eyes shut. Worse, they did not appear to be breathing. Ra mentioned this to Geea and she nodded solemnly but said nothing.

Geea allowed her shimmering green field to decrease, and

came near Chashar's throne. She went so far as to wake him up with a gentle kick to his right wing.

"King Chashar, we have a serious problem," Geea said.

The dragon raised his head from his stupor. "What now, Geea?"

"The Shaktra gave you a parting gift that contained an extra powerful dose of the dust. It was too much for many of your dragons." Geea paused. "A lot of them are not sleeping. A lot of them are dead."

Chashar stared at the cavern with uncertain eyes. "Is this true?" he asked.

"Check on your spouse, and you'll see what kind of ally the Shaktra has turned out to be. I'm sad to say, Tashi was one of those who inhaled too much dust."

Chashar prodded his spouse with his snout, but there was no response. Tashi was not breathing, and her flame had gone out.

Then seeing that Geea's words were true, Chashar rose suddenly into the air, and let out a loud roar, and a mighty flame, that woke all the other dragons—at least the ones still left alive. Then Chashar bitterly cursed the Shaktra. He swore that the dragons were no longer her allies, but her deadly enemies.

Geea pounced on his announcement.

"Then you must throw your power behind us!" she shouted.

Chashar was too upset to be reasoned with. "You? Who are you? Your army and Lord Vak's army have already been defeated."

"Nonsense. We've only begun to fight. And with you on our side, our chances of victory are excellent."

Chashar continued to beat his wings above his throne.

"Chashar has just lost his queen. Chashar does not want to talk of battle."

Geea came closer. "I grieve with you over your loss. But we

have to talk now, if we're to avenge what's been done to Tashi and the others. We don't have much time."

Chashar considered a long time. "What does Geea want the dragons to do?"

"Come with me and help me intercept Vak's army. We need to steer it toward Uleestar. The Shaktra will send scabs and scaliis and marked elementals to stop us, but with the help of the dragons, and a fleet of ships that lies docked on the west shore not far north of Elnar, we can gather our forces in the fairy capital. There, I believe, we can make a decisive stand."

Chashar considered, then asked a most unexpected question. "How did Geea's human child defeat Chashar's brother?"

"She used the Yanti as a weapon," Geea said.

"How come Geea never used it as a weapon against her sister?"

"The Yanti was not made to destroy but to heal."

Chashar glanced at his dead spouse, and sighed. "Can it be used to bring Tashi back to Chashar?" he asked.

"No."

"Could it be used to heal dragons of the sickness caused by the dust?"

Geea nodded. "Yes. That much I can promise you."

That appeared to seal the deal. He went to shout out to the thousands of dragons that they were switching sides in the war. But Geea had the nerve to interrupt him once more.

"The dragons are to join the side of the fairies and all other elementals who fight the Shaktra," Geea said. "But you are no longer to lead them."

Chashar was insulted. "Who would dare take Chashar's place?"

"The son of your last king. The only dragon untouched by the dust. Drash."

Chashar stared at his nephew in amazement. "Didn't Chashar almost kill Drash a couple of days ago?" he asked.

Drash spoke with pride. "But Drash recovered."

A shocking wave of belches and fiery snorts swept through the hollow kloudar—what Ra now knew to be dragon laughter. Apparently Chashar was not popular with his constituency. There was no vote, but it was clear they wanted the big guy out and the little guy in. Ra would not have believed it possible.

The dragons had a new king, and the Shaktra had a new enemy.

When they were once again high in the sky, flying toward Tutor, Geea began to prepare Ra for what appeared to be a critical task.

"You didn't agree with everything I said in the kloudar," she said. "That is fine. On Earth, each of your religions teaches that their holy books are the final word of God. In their minds, the truth is set in stone, and that makes most of your people comfortable. They can point to a source of inspiration and say to themselves, there, in that book, is the supreme truth."

"I prefer a set truth," Ra admitted.

"Well, you're an elf," Geea said. "Fairies prefer to see truth as fluid—more like a river that flows along twisting bends. We see truth as too sacred to define. It's one way today, different tomorrow."

"You wouldn't last long on Earth," Ra said.

Geea smiled. "But fairies are the least dogmatic of all the elementals. Our favorite tenet is to say, 'We know that we don't know.' Does that make us so radical?"

"No. I can see the wisdom in that. But . . ."

"But you don't see what this has to do with saving the Earth?"

"I trust you'll get to your point when it suits you."

Geea nodded. "As queen of the fairies, I was something of a renegade for having an elfish companion, Jira. You've heard his name?"

Ra squirmed on Drash's back. "I was led to believe I used to be him."

"Did Ali tell you that you were him?"

"No. It was more . . . when I heard the name, I knew it belonged to me."

"Trust me, you're him. We're going to encounter Lord Vak and his army in a short time. Your old name still carries deep meaning to the elven king. Jira was his only child. He loved him very much, some said too much. When Jira died, Lord Vak changed. He lost all joy of life and became bitter toward the Earth. He blamed it for the problems the green world was facing. In that regard he had a point, but he was confused as well. When humans hurt the Earth, it hurts us too. Do you understand?"

"Yes. I was told we're like two sides of the same coin."

"The analogy is useful but limited. Let me explain. The high fairies understand that humans and elementals pass back and forth, from one realm to the next. The elves strongly deny this belief. They see themselves as far beyond humanity. They would not even want to be touched by a human being lest they be contaminated."

"They sound prejudiced."

"They take the word prejudice to a new extreme. Yet they are not an evil race. They have been tortured by the Shaktra to give up their homes and create new ones on the Earth. But they wouldn't do this—even under the threat of death—if they truly believed that our souls are one and the same. Elves are honorable. They have high principles. They just happen to be wrong when it come to the highest principle of all."

"Which is?" Ra asked.

"Recognition."

"I don't understand. Recognition of what?"

"The soul."

Again, Ra felt uncomfortable. "The dragons have joined us. That's all Lord Vak will care about."

Geea shook her head. "This is the second time Lord Vak has tried to conquer Earth. Ali drove him back the first time. Out of sheer pride, he will not allow himself to be driven back a second time. You're the only one who can conquer his pride. I can't do it."

"You just need to talk to him. Explain . . ."

"I talked to him for years!" Geea interrupted. "Lord Vak needs to *see* you, he needs to *know* you. Then he'll recognize the truth of the relationship between humans and elementals. It's the only way."

Ra swallowed heavily. "What am I to do?"

"I don't know. Follow your instincts. If he recognizes you, we stand a chance. If he doesn't, he'll probably run you through with his spear."

"Can you protect me?"

"Death stands behind every wrong decision we make. Even the right choice can get us killed. This is no time for the faint-hearted." Geea paused. "That means no, I cannot assure your safety. Do you want me to let you off at the next interdimensional doorway?"

"No."

"Good."

"Speaking of which, do you know how Ali is doing on Earth?"

"She struggles."

"With what?"

"Nira has the Yanti and Nira has plans. Sooner than she wants, Ali's going to have to accept that we're all just pieces playing a small part on the gigantic board of life."

"When this is all over with, will you heal the rest of her face?"

"When this is over with, I doubt both of us will still be alive."

They found Lord Vak—king of the elves—and Lord Balar—king of the dwarves—and General Tapor—head of the fairy armed forces—in an odd place. The three were standing on a huge black boulder, and staring out at a vast army of every type of elemental imaginable. An army which was bogged down by a foot of running water.

One foot did not sound threatening, but Ra knew better from flash floods back home. Just twelve inches of fast-moving water was enough to lift a car and float it away. Particularly if there was mud or debris in the water.

This particular flood came from Elnar, which was moving west toward Tutor, and the sea, but which had burst its seams due to Ali's destruction of Tiena. Ra saw that Ali had gained Earth precious time with the explosion of the underground dam. The elemental army was clearly stuck.

Vak, Balar, and Tapor looked as if they had climbed onto the boulder just to get out of the water. Vak and Balar were not pleased to see Geea, but Tapor was obviously relieved his queen was alive. High overhead circled a fleet of dragons. Ra doubted the dragons had been informed yet that they were now working against the Shaktra, and that there were going to be a lot fewer "dust" parties in the near future.

As Ra and Geea dismounted from Drash, Ra finally came

face-to-face with the leaders of the elves and dwarves. Ra felt an odd stirring of emotions as he studied the elven king, but was not sure if it was the *recognition* Geea had spoken of.

Lord Vak was an imposing figure. Taller than most men, he had broad shoulders and carried a black spear in his hand that tapered to a silver blade. His gold crown was unique. Lined on all sides with jewels, it rose to a sharp point.

Yet his face was more human than any other elemental Ra had met. He was classically handsome, looked youthful, and had curly blond hair. Only his blue eyes set him apart from humanity. They were so bright, so clear—they could have lit a dark room.

Lord Balar was old. His long beard was snow white and his dark eyes burned like dying red suns. He clearly had many scars, both physical and emotional, and Geea had told Ra the dwarf was no one to beg mercy from. He was never without his golden ax.

Ali had never talked to Ra about General Tapor, and he did not think she had met him in her "Ali Warner" incarnation—as a human. Tapor was practically as tall as Vak and wore silver battle armor over a green robe. His sword was also silver, but the hilt was gold. Geea had told Ra he was stronger than any fairy in the land. Ra noted his serious green eyes, yet there was mirth in them as well. Tapor carried less bitterness than the other two.

Ra found it hardest to look at Lord Vak. For his part, the elven king acted like he didn't exist. As he strode toward Geea, he carried his black spear. Balar, also, held his ax ready. Tapor stayed back, his hand on the hilt of his sword, but he remained alert. In an instant, Ra knew, he would give his life for his queen.

Geea sought to disarm Vak and Balar with a smile and a joke.

"So we meet again Lord Vak and Lord Balar," she said. "Surely you two could have picked a better spot to camp out?"

"We'll not set up camp until we're on Earth, Queen Geea," Lord Vak replied. "We're merely resting here awhile."

Geea gestured to the flowing water. "What's happened to Elnar?"

Lord Vak gave her a look. "Yesterday morning, in the distance, we saw someone fighting dragons. Know anything about that?"

"I was asleep yesterday morning."

"But you're awake now," Lord Vak said sharply.

Ra understood. The elven king was pointing out the fact she was *alive* now. However, Ra knew Vak had met Ali and recognized her as Geea. Yet that face-to-face encounter had not forced Vak to accept the connection between humans and elementals. Ra could only rationalize that the elves saw Queen Geea as unique—someone who was able to take on such a low birth at will.

Lord Vak impatiently shook his spear. "You know we've already surrendered to the Shaktra. That war is finished. Now we invade the Earth. If you're here to help us, fine, we can use your help. But if you're here to try to stop us . . . Geea, you'll remember that I warned you about interfering in matters that don't concern you."

"Your warning no longer applies." Geea gestured to the sky. "The dragons are no longer allies of the Shaktra. It can still be defeated, here, in this world."

"Since when have the dragons come over to our side?" Lord Balar demanded.

"In the last hour." Geea pointed to Drash. "This is Kashar's son, Drash. Presently, he's king of the dragons. Kashar perished yesterday."

"Chashar rules the dragons, not this child!" Lord Balar growled.

"Not so," Geea said, and once more she pointed to the sky. "If you'll look up, you'll see Chashar going from dragon to dragon, telling them that they're to assist your army in reaching Uleestar."

Lord Vak showed his temper. Ra felt the heat of it in the pit of his stomach. So familiar . . . "We're not going to Uleestar! We're going to Earth! Now you join us—as General Tapor has done—or else you die! There's no other choice for you, Geea!"

"I go where my queen goes!" General Tapor called out.

Geea drew her sword and took a step near Lord Vak. She didn't point it directly at him, nor did she point it away. A murmur swept the army. She snapped at the elven king. "You kill me now and a quarter of your army will turn on you!" she said.

Lord Vak nodded grimly. "Let that be the quarter that we don't need to defeat humanity!"

Geea shook her head. "You and your hatred for humanity! You blame them for everything that's gone wrong in your life. Admit it, in your own perverted way, you even blame them for the death of Jira!"

Lord Vak swiftly lowered his spear, as if to run her through. Just as fast, Geea put the tip of her sword to the tip of his weapon. To Ra, it all happened in the blink of an eye. They locked eyes; he would not have been surprised if flames ignited in the narrow space between them.

"No. I blame you," Lord Vak whispered.

"Me?" she cried.

"You should have caught him!"

"I didn't know he was going to jump!"

The army continued to stir restlessly. But Queen Geea and Lord Vak were locked like two statues—two pieces of painful history that could not be altered by words. Lord Vak sucked in a breath and appeared to return to the topic at hand.

"I warned you not to go against me again," he told her.

"And I warned you, even before Jira died," Geea said, clearly wanting to keep his mind on the larger picture. "Humans are as much a part of us as our arms and legs. But if neither of you stubborn old kings will accept that—after all the proof I've given you in the past—then I've brought a human being with me for you to slaughter. He's for you, Lord Vak, to kill. He can be the first victim of your historic battle. Trust me, he's not afraid of you. He came into this world for this purpose. To look you straight in the eye and see if you're a murderer."

Geea motioned Ra to come closer, and Ra obeyed. In an instant he grasped her strategy, and didn't like it, but decided to risk it anyway. Because listening to them argue, Ra finally did hear the sound of his former father. Geea had said it was all about recognition, and Ra *recognized* him. Not totally, but enough to know Geea's philosophy was more fact than faith. And it gave Ra the faith that if he—a mere human—could see an elven lord as a relative, then surely the powerful king with his magical abilities must be able to see their connection.

Ra walked until he stood between the two.

Each of their blades almost touched his neck.

"You have to look him in the eye before you kill him," Geea said.

"Why . . ." Lord Vak began, after a hasty glance at Ra.

"In the eyes! Then you can thrust your spear through his heart!" Geea swore. "If you can do that—now, before this assembly of elementals—then I'll promise to join your army and help destroy humanity. You want to kill a world? Just kill this boy and we'll kill Earth together!"

Sounded like a bargain to Lord Vak. Pulling his black spear off Geea's sword, he turned toward Ra and raised his weapon. In that last second Ra almost closed his eyes, to block the horror that was sure to follow. But somehow he managed to keep them open, and stare up at the fury-driven creature. It was then he felt an unexpected sensation. A warmth in his chest, exactly where he was about to be stabbed.

Ra felt love, yes, and then, *total* recognition. Memories washed over him. This *was* his father; who had loved him so much; who had almost died the night Jira had died.

Lord Vak paused with his spear held high.

He frowned. "What's your name, boy?" he demanded.

"Ra Omlee. I'm from the country you might know as Tanzania. My people, the Kutus, live beside Mt. Kilimanjaro."

Lord Vak nodded. "I know this mountain. How did you come to enter the green world?"

"Geea's alter ego, Ali Warner, brought me here."

Lord Vak sniffed the air. "There is something about you . . ."

"I have been told that before, my Lord."

"Who told you?"

"Different creatures I've met in this world. Drash for one."

"Ra is a bit elfish," Drash muttered.

"How dare you!" Lord Vak snapped at the young dragon.

"Drash dares nothing. Drash merely states what is," Drash replied.

Lord Vak turned back to Ra. "Has Geea tricked you into this?"

"Into what, my Lord?"

"Why are you willing to sacrifice yourself this way?"

"I suppose you might see it as a sacrifice, my Lord. But I don't believe you're the type that will strike down an unarmed person."

Lord Vak shook his spear. "You're not unarmed. You have a sword. Draw it. Fight me fairly!"

Ra shook his head. "I'm not here to fight you, my Lord."

"Then why are you here? Answer my question."

"I asked Geea that question just before Drash brought us here. Her answer made no sense to me then, but it does now. She said I was here for recognition."

Lord Vak was impatient. "I don't know what you mean."

Lord Balar raised his ax. "If you want me to chop off the boy's head, I would be happy . . ."

"Stay where you are!" Lord Vak snapped, without taking his gaze off Ra. It seemed as if the elven king was unable to turn from him. Ra felt the same way. The warmth he felt changed into a painful ache, a profound longing. Suddenly he wanted to run to the man and embrace him. The spear was in the way. Lord Vak had lowered it somewhat, but the tip was still aimed at him. Ra tried hard not to imagine what it would feel like to have it pierce his chest.

Suddenly Lord Vak shook his head, as if awakening from a dream.

He turned to Geea. "I'll not play this game with you. Take this boy and leave. I have more important things to concern myself with."

Geea stared at Lord Vak. "You won't kill him?"

"No."

"Why not?"

"He's a child!"

"So what? When you reach Earth, you'll kill millions of children."

"Enough, Geea. I have spoken! No more of this game!"

Geea turned her sword toward Ra. "Coward. Then I'll kill him for you. I'll cut off his head and you can wear it on the tip of your spear as you ride victorious into Earth."

Quickly, Geea raised her sword to slice his neck. This time Ra was forced to close his eyes. The nerve of Geea! She was really going to kill him!

There came a loud clang of metal.

"No!" Lord Vak shouted.

Ra opened his eyes. Queen Geea's blow had been halted by Lord Vak's spear. The two weapons were only a fraction of an inch from Ra's neck.

Geea panted. Lord Vak sweated. Ra felt close to fainting. There was love here, he thought, in the middle of all this hate and violence. There was a deeper meaning. All of them, they just had to find it.

"Why did you stop me?" Geea shouted at Lord Vak.

Lord Vak did not answer.

Geea went to snap at the elven king again, but then she looked down at Ra, and her sword fell from her hand. Tears burned her eyes—Ra would not have thought it possible.

"Why do you weep?" Lord Vak demanded.

"Because he's your son," she whispered.

"Geea . . ." Lord Vak began, but his voice was unsteady.

"How can you be so blind?" she asked.

Lord Vak backed up a step, shaking his head. Now he would not even look at Ra. "No. It can't be true. It is not true."

Geea went after him, grabbed him by the shoulders. "He's Jira!"

Lord Vak made a feeble attempt to push her away. "Jira's gone! He was here and now he's gone and that's it! He is no more!"

"Then kill the boy!" Geea cried.

"No!" Lord Vak snapped.

"He's only a human! You hate humans!"

"No! I don't hate . . ." Lord Vak did not finish his sentence.

On the vast field, there was a long moment of silence. Ra saw that Geea knew how to use it. She let Lord Vak be with his doubts. She let them grow.

Finally the elven king said, "I will question the boy further."

Lord Vak's approach was not threatening. Indeed, when he reached Ra, the elven king went down on his knee and handed Ra his black spear.

"What did we call this?" he asked, referring to the weapon.

"Starshaft," Ra said, the name coming to him out of nowhere.

"Why did we call it that?"

"I remember something . . ." Ra strained.

Lord Vak nodded, and there was a hint of desperation in the gesture, and in his next words. "No one knew why except my son and me."

Ra had it; the answer made him smile. "This spear—the ore we made it from came from a falling star."

Lord Vak nodded, and perhaps his eyes burned as well.

"Why did we use it?" he whispered.

"Because the ore was so strong."

"What did I used to . . ." Lord Vak began.

"You used to say it could cleave metal as if it were a loaf of bread."

Lord Vak stared deep into his eyes. "Is it you, Jira? Is it really you?"

"Yes, Father," Ra said, and he hugged him.

Lord Vak hugged him in return, and they wept in each other's arms.

CHAPTER

17

After checking on Officer Garten to make sure he was comfortable and not crying too loudly—she brought him a sandwich and swore to him she was just teasing about the cannibal stuff, but she still couldn't let him go—Ali flew to Washington, D.C. Landing on the south side of town, not far from the Pentagon, it did not take her long to locate 1618 Florence Street, apartment number 902.

It was after midnight, but Ali would have knocked on General Kabrosh's door right then and there had she not heard a party going on inside. She was tired of major confrontations, and besides, she was physically exhausted. Best to rest and speak to him in the morning, she decided.

By chance, there was a five-star hotel across the street from the general's place.

Ali did not try checking in. She flew around the top floor—where there were the most expensive suites—and found one unoccupied but with a window open. Picking up the phone inside, she was delighted to discover she could order room service by simply giving her room number. She asked for a small steak, well-done, a baked potato; plus, of course, chocolate cake, and a bottle of Coke.

While waiting for the food, she took a quick shower and called her father's cell. She got no answer. That worried her—he never turned it off. She called Hector Wells's home in Toule next. He answered on the first ring.

"I knew it would be you," he said. "I was about to call you."

"So you guys just decided to throw all caution to the wind and run off with Nira?" she asked. "Was that smart?"

"I did not run off with Nira, obviously. I was told to wait here until you called."

"By Nira?"

"Yes."

Ali scratched her head. "After I left, did she just sort of announce to the gang that she was taking over?"

"She didn't have to. We could all tell she was."

"Hector, she's your daughter. And she's only six years old."

"Yeah. You're thirteen years old and you're flying from one world to the next and slaying dragons and God knows what else. If we have to listen to you, then we have to listen to Nira even more."

"Why even more?"

Hector hesitated. "That girl . . . she's got power. No offense, Ali, but when she said she thought we should do such and such, we couldn't argue. And she told us to leave that hotel immediately, and she said I would be safe here. She said the last thing Lucy wants is to hurt me."

"I wouldn't count on that," Ali said.

"I do count on that. I trust her, and not just because she's my daughter. You didn't have a chance to talk to her much. But she *knows*."

"What does she know?"

292

"She just knows what's going on, you can feel it."

"Did she leave any instructions for me?"

"She said you would come for me at some point."

"When? Why?"

"She didn't say. Don't you know?"

"I'm afraid not."

"Where are you calling from? You're using an East Coast line."

Ali had used the hotel phone. "I'm in Washington, D.C."

"What are you doing there?"

"Trying to figure out how the world's going to end. Where are the others now?"

"I have no idea. Did you try calling your dad?"

"Yes."

"So did I. All I know is, they're not at your home. Nira did say it was not safe to go there. Not yet anyway."

Ali thought of Garten tied up in the basement. "Yeah. That's not a safe place. If you had to guess, where do you think they went?"

"I really have no idea. But Nira had a confidence about her."

"Cindy's parents must be freaking out."

"Yeah. The cops have called me about her."

"What did you say?"

"I played dumb. Which is what I am at this moment. You still think this invasion is going to happen?"

"Unless something major is done to stop it." Ali paused. "Nira's probably right that Lucy or Sheri or whoever won't harm you. Get a good night's sleep and I'll call you tomorrow. By then, I'll know what I need you for."

"You rest, too. You're still a human being."

Ali yawned. "I'm sure feeling that side of me right now."

Her food came not long after. She just signed the bill as

Sheri Smith and gave the guy a big tip and dug in. After she had finished saving the world, she would settle up the bill more honestly. In the meantime, she just hoped the kitchen didn't realize the room was supposed to be empty. She didn't want to give up her dinner. She was famished! She had not finished her sandwich at Nancy Pillar's home. Plus she was convinced flying burned up more calories than any treadmill.

A pity. She had a feeling she would be doing a lot of flying come tomorrow.

Ten minutes after she finished eating, she laid down to sleep, and blacked out in seconds. She dreamed, though, about dragons and purple smoke.

Ali did not need more than five hours of rest to make a complete recovery. She was at General Kabrosh's door at dawn. Before she stormed the place, she paused to listen, heard just one person, a male snoring in the far bedroom, She opened the door by turning the knob firmly. The inner lock mechanism cracked in her hand, but she did not hear any alarm go off.

But there must have been an alarm of some kind, for she heard Kabrosh stop snoring and swiftly sit up in bed. Ali heard a drawer open—no doubt he was reaching for a gun. That was fine with her. Stepping inside, she softly closed the door behind her, and walked into the kitchen and purposely broke a glass. She did not have long to wait. He came after her in a gray robe, holding a cocked semiautomatic. As he turned the corner that led into the kitchen, she surprised him from behind.

A smack on the side of the head and a blinding chop to his gun arm, and he was down. Picking up the pistol, helping him up off the floor, she tossed him in a chair in the living room and sat on a sofa across from him. As he emerged from his daze, she leveled the gun in his face.

"General Kabrosh, I presume?" she asked.

He was sixty and gray, but lithe and wiry. He worked out. His eyes were cold and dark, his skin grizzled from too much sun. He looked like a soldier, a hard man, but there was a discipline in him, courage as well. He did not panic when he saw the gun. Nor did he act surprised that she was thirteen years old. A bird must have whispered in his ear . . .

"Answer me. I know of your connection to Sheri Smith," Ali said. "In fact, she told you I might stop by, didn't she? But you did not really believe it. But I'm here, and she's not, and you've got no one to protect you."

He squinted at her. She might have hit him too hard. His voice came out gravely. "What do I need protection from?" he asked.

"Me." She gestured to her scars with the tip of the gun. "The person who did this to me, he looks pretty next to me."

Kabrosh drew in a ragged breath. "Who are you?" he asked.

"Just someone who worries that all the nuclear bombs in this country aren't where they're supposed to be." Ali paused.

Kabrosh grew quickly alert. "Why?"

"You just bought two expensive homes. One in Switzerland, the other on an island in the Fijis. And you supposedly live on a soldier's pay."

"Who told you that lie?"

"Someone familiar with the money Sheri Smith gives you."

"I don't know any Sheri Smith."

"You talk to her regularly."

He snorted. "You can't prove that."

"Because you use a secure line?" Ali paused. "Do you know a

character in your partner's bestselling computer game is named after you? Don't you think that was rather sloppy of her? To point such a huge finger in your direction? I bet that annoyed you. But you couldn't complain, could you? You wanted the money and she wanted to give it to you—in exchange for a bomb."

He paled slightly, but kept his voice even. "You still haven't told me who you are. FBI? CIA? Homeland Security?"

"Do I look old enough to belong to such organizations?"

"No. You don't." He sat up and nodded to the gun. "You don't even look old enough to know how to fire one of those. I bet you never have. I'm right, right?"

Ali aimed at his knee. "Want me to blow off your kneecap to show you what a great shot I am?"

"Fire that gun and every cop in the area will be here in a minute." He stood. "I suggest you take your conspiracy theories and get out of my house before I call the police and . . ."

Ali was on him in an instant. He did not see her coming. Leaping over the space that separated them, she grabbed him from behind, broke his right arm in three places, and gagged him with her free hand. Then she pulled him lower, so that she could whisper in his ear.

"General Kabrosh, you've got to take me seriously. Your arm is hurting, I can feel your pain, honestly, but it's a mere fraction of the agony you'll suffer if you don't answer my questions. Understand?"

He nodded weakly. Ali released him, let him fall back into the chair. Again, she took her place on the sofa. She pointed out the window at the hotel across the street. "Do you know they serve the best chocolate cake in the world over there?" she asked.

He coughed to clear his throat, shaking. He really was in pain.

"How can you be so strong?" he gasped.

"Like Sheri, I'm special. In all your dealings with her, you must have noticed a few unusual things around her." Ali paused. "Please don't tell me you don't know her. Not again."

Kabrosh nodded weakly. "I noticed she was unique."

"Did she explain to you why she wanted the bomb?"

He did not answer. Merely stared down at his broken arm. The kinks in it were grotesque; it was already turning purple. She could tell he wanted to reply to her question but was afraid—of her and Sheri. Yet she felt not a shred of pity for him. A man who would sell the agony of millions for money? Such a person did not deserve to live.

"She did not say," he finally admitted.

Ali sensed truth in his words. "Was it a powerful bomb?"

"Yes."

"Was it a single bomb?"

"Yes."

"How much did she give you for it?"

"Five hundred million dollars."

"In cash?"

He nodded. "Cash, diamonds, negotiable bonds."

"What was the specific designation of the bomb you sold her?"

"It was a very old bomb. One we retired in 1957, named MK-41. Back then, it could only be delivered by a B-36 jet plane or larger."

"Why would she want such an old bomb?"

"It was the most powerful bomb the U.S. ever constructed. It gave off a potential blast of twenty-five megatons."

"That's the equivalent of twenty-five million tons of dynamite?"

"Yes. It was never actually tested. But there's no reason to think it won't work. In the fifties, we tested bombs with yields close to fifteen megatons."

"Did Sheri worry—because of its age—that it wouldn't work?"

"Part of our deal was that I would have the detonator replaced with a modern mechanism. It's the plastic explosives in the detonator portion that degrade with age. The nuclear components can sit for decades and not be affected."

"So you primed her bomb with a brand new detonator and sold it to her. Didn't you worry what she was going to do with it?"

"She assured me it was going to be used against an Arab nation that's hated inside the Pentagon, and everywhere else in the world for that matter. She also assured me that the blast would not be traced back to the U.S."

"How could she make that last promise?"

"The age of the bomb helps. I doubt anyone would recognize what it was—after it detonated. Except an internal Pentagon expert."

"But to deliver such a weapon . . . How much does it weigh?"

"Nine thousand pounds."

Ali shook her head. "It all sounds so neat and clean. You get half a billion dollars, and this woman who just walks into your office gets to buy a bomb that I assume can level practically any city on Earth."

"It could do that, yes."

"May I ask you a question, General?"

He squirmed in pain. "Go ahead."

"I'm sure you must have considered it."

His arm was killing him. "Just ask your question!"

"What if she decides to blow the sucker off in downtown L.A.?"

"She won't do that. She's an American citizen and she loves this country. She's also a devout Christian. She hates Islam.

Her goal in life, she confided in me, was to wipe that heretic religion off the face of the Earth."

"A devout Christian? Boy, I wonder what the Jesus I read about in the Bible would have to say about someone like her."

"She won't use it here."

"It's so heavy . . . How will she get it out of the country?"

He didn't answer her question, just tried to readjust his aching arm.

"You're not telling me everything you know," Ali said.

"That's not true."

"Right. Sure. When and where did you give her the bomb?"

"Two days ago. Not far from Edwards Air Force base."

Ali was surprised she'd only had the bomb such a short time.

"At that time, did she arrange to rent an Air Force bomber?"

"No."

"Then how is she supposed to get these twenty-five mega-tons over to this evil Arab nation?"

"That was never my concern."

"How convenient." Ali paused. "Did she ever talk to you about the explosive force—how it radiates—if the bomb is detonated underground?"

Kabrosh swallowed thickly. "No."

Ali sighed. "You're lying."

He looked up. "I'm not, I swear it."

She leaned forward. "I can do a lot worse to your other arm. This is your last chance. Did Sheri Smith want detailed information about how the power of the bomb would radiate when placed deep inside a cave?"

He hesitated. "She wanted our secret data on all our underground nuclear tests for the last twenty years."

"Were you able to get it for her?"

"I was able to get her some of it."

"Did it satisfy her?"

"I don't know. She kept asking for more. Look, I've answered . . ."

Ali interrupted. "Could a bomb of this power—carefully placed deep inside a potentially active volcano—help trigger an eruption?"

Kabrosh was a long time answering. "She asked me that."

"What did you tell her?"

"That there was no way to know for sure."

"General Kabrosh. What are you going to do after I leave here?"

"Probably go to the hospital and have my arm treated."

"But at some point you're going to call Sheri Smith, right?"

"I've no reason to call her. Our business is finished."

"Ours isn't. I need to know where that bomb is."

"The last I saw it, the bomb was on a truck twenty miles outside of Edwards."

"Two days ago?"

"Yes."

"What direction was the truck headed?"

"North." He added, "Not that that means anything."

Ali sat a long time in thought. The general looked worried.

"What are you thinking?" he asked finally.

"You're a dangerous man to leave walking around."

He got *very* anxious. "I've been cooperative. I've told you everything I know."

"When she calls, or you call her, you'll be cooperative all over again. You'll tell her I was here, and everything you told me. That might cause her to alter her plan."

"But you don't know her plan!"

Ali played with the gun. "This might surprise you, but normally I'm not a cruel person. Unfortunately, lately, situations have demanded the worst of me." She paused. "You sold a bomb knowing it would be used to kill millions of people. You did it for money. That was your only motivation."

Kabrosh stared at her with pleading eyes. "I have a wife. I have twin daughters. They're good people. I took the money for their sakes. My daughters have children and . . ."

Ali had raised her hand. "Quiet."

He fell to his knees, pleading. "I swear, I won't tell Sheri Smith I even met . . ."

"Shut up! I'm thinking!" He fell silent. Ali added, "Are any of your family or friends going to come by in the next two days?"

"No." He was speaking the truth.

"Do you have rope and duct tape in this apartment?"

He looked uneasy. "Yes."

"Okay. I'm going to tie you up—very tight—and return later, when I get the chance. Then, depending on the status of the world at that time, I'm either going to kill you or let you go. But whatever happens, the money you took from Sheri Smith, you're to give it to the poor in Africa. You're to sell both your new homes and not keep a penny for yourself. Deal?"

"But I have to go to the hospital. The bones of my arm have to be set."

"No. I want you to live with the pain, and reflect on the pain your evil deeds would have caused millions of people if I hadn't shown up this morning." Ali paused. "Deal?"

He sounded beaten. "Deal."

Ali stood and tucked the gun in her belt. "If you attempt to escape while I'm tying you up, I'll break every bone in your neck. Two days ago I did that to a school buddy of mine, and that was a guy I used to have a crush on."

General Kabrosh proved very cooperative as she tied him up.

CHAPTER

18

The relocation of the elemental army to Uleestar did not go easily. In fact, it soon became apparent to Ra—and Geea and Drash for that matter—that the bulk of the army could not be gathered onto the fairy island—at least not in a day's time. For that matter, it was going to be difficult to simply transport the elementals to Karolee—the wooded lands surrounding the fairy capital.

The obstacles were enormous. First there was the sheer size of the army. Flying around on Drash's back, trying to organize the situation, Ra and Geea could see millions of elves, fairies, dwarves, and trolls. There just as well could have been *hundreds* of millions. Geea admitted a portion of the army was still backed up against the Morray Mountains—in the far east.

Yet, studying Geea, Ra began to get the impression that the fairy queen was not determined to get everyone to Uleestar. He began to see she merely wanted to create a focal point where the Shaktra's wrath would fall. A place where Doren would attack with what strength was left her.

But Geea warned that—even with the dragons on their side—her sister's power was great. Over the years, Doren had marked millions of elementals. They were mindless thralls, that would quickly spring into fierce warriors at an instant's notice. Even worse were the elementals that had been attacked by scabs, had their brains eaten, and were now the walking monsters known as scaliis. Both the marked thralls and the hideous scaliis had backed off Vak's army since his surrender, and since the dragons had been shepherding the army toward Mt. Tutor.

Now all that had changed. The Shaktra knew it had been tricked.

"Doren must be furious at the dragons' shift to our side," Ra said as they flew toward the fleet of ships anchored in a bay on the coast of the green sea. To save time, the dragons were ferrying as many elementals to the boats as possible, rather than all the way to Uleestar, which was much farther north. But Geea said she might change their transportation technique if the Shaktra attacked soon.

To Ra's surprise, Geea shook her head.

"Doren probably anticipated this," Geea said. "She's clever—she knew there was a chance she'd lose the dragons. They're hot-tempered—no pun intended. They're hard to control period. Remember, Doren's immediate goal is to invade the Earth. That would be easier with more elementals on her side. She will definitely hit Uleestar hard, try to kill the heads of the different armies—myself, Vak, Drash, Balar. She'll figure that if all us leaders fall, then the elementals will turn back to her as their leader."

"Will they?" Ra asked.

"Probably."

"But they hate the Shaktra!" Ra protested.

"It doesn't matter as much as you'd think. Doren will have the power. Enough elementals dislike humanity anyway. It's an old prejudice. If Vak, Balar, Drash, and myself are gone, the majority will feel compelled to follow her. At the same time, if the fight goes against Doren, she can still unleash millions of scabs and scaliis on the Earth. That'll cause global panic."

"Will her creatures enter the Earth using different mountains?" Ra asked, remembering how Kilimanjaro and Pete's Peak were linked.

"Yes."

"Then why don't we concentrate on securing Tutor?"

"It's too late. The interior of the mountain is filled with scaliis and scabs."

"How do you know?"

"When I rested on the high kloudar, I was able to leave my body and study what was going on throughout the land. Doren has planned well for this day. There are layers and layers to her plans."

Ra was worried. "I hope you've made some plans of your own."

She smiled. "But of course." She added, "At least we have Nira now, awake and holding the Yanti."

"She's just a child!"

"I admit she's a wild card. I've no idea what she has planned, I just know she'll do the unexpected."

"How come she's so powerful?"

"She's a goddess. She's of the violet ray."

"She's your younger sister?"

"Yes."

"Why wasn't she made queen of the fairies?"

"The position was offered her but she turned it down. She was not here long, in this world, before she desired to rest in the kloudar and be born on Earth."

"She purposely chose Sheri Smith to be her mother?"

"Ironic, isn't it?"

Ra shook his head. "You have to know, on the Isle of Greesh, I did nothing but stand outside the forbidden door. I don't understand this Entity you and Ali spoke of."

"Nor do I, really."

Ra was surprised to hear that. "You couldn't examine their chamber while out of the body?" he asked.

"I couldn't get near it. It was totally blocked off." Geea added, "Until Ali went inside. Then I could see."

"But what if they jump into this war on Doren's side?"

"They can't. They're constrained to use agents they've already corrupted to their cause."

"The marked thralls and the scaliis were never brought over to their side. They just had their lives stolen from them."

"Because Doren acted as their agent and created the monsters."

"Where do you think your sister is now?"

Geea pointed to Tutor. "She's in there, busy unleashing her plans."

"Can you see what they are?"

Geea hesitated. "I have my guesses."

Ra studied the dragons that flew alongside, ferrying the elementals to the boats. "The dragons joined us so quickly. I fear they could turn on us just as quick."

Geea nodded. "They'll all be craving their dust soon. But I've taken steps to secure Denzy. They can go there for brief treatments."

Ra had to laugh. "They don't want treatments! They want parties!"

Geea nodded. "Sad but true."

"May I ask a blunt question?"

"Why, Ra, darling, all your questions are blunt! Just as Jira's were!"

305

Ra felt embarrassed being called "darling" by the queen of the fairies.

"Your goal is to lure Doren to Uleestar so you can fight her, right? One-on-one? You're going to try to kill her, aren't you?"

Geea nodded. "Ali's going to try to do the same on Earth."

At the same time Ali was in Washington, D.C. with General Kabrosh—and Ra and Geea were in the green world preparing to do battle with the Shaktra—Cindy was exiting a cave high on the slopes of Pete's Peak.

With Cindy was a host of unusual characters: Ali's father; Nira; Mike Havor; and the blind man's personal guide, a teenage boy named Terry. While Mike couldn't use his eyes, Terry was mute. He did not speak, simply held out his bent elbow so Mr. Havor could hold onto it.

There was something about Terry that gave Cindy the willies, but Mr. Havor was always so kind and gentle, she felt she did not have the right to question his guide. Plus Nira did not seem to mind the guy. Indeed, Nira had welcomed both of them on their *adventure*.

It had all started when Ali had removed the mark from Nira's forehead, then flown away to only God knew where. Immediately, in a kind and yet powerful voice, Nira had told them they had to leave the hotel. She had pointed to Hector first.

"You have to return home and wait for Ali to come get you."

"How do you know she'll come for me?" Hector asked.

"She will." Next Nira pointed to Mr. Warner. "What do you want?"

He stared at the child. "I think you know what I want."

Nira nodded. "You want to see Amma."

"That's the name you use for my wife, right?"

"Yes. The soul is the same, the body is not."

"Can you take me to her? Ali said it wasn't possible. But . . ." He didn't finish.

"We shall see." Finally, Nira turned to Cindy. "You miss Steve."

It was not a question, just a statement of fact. Cindy nodded.

"His body is at my house. He should be returned to his parents," Nira said.

Cindy shook her head. "Ali checked out that place from top to bottom. She said he was not there."

"He has always been there," Nira replied confidently.

They drove back to Toule, dropped Hector off to await Ali's call, and went over to Sheri Smith's mansion. Cindy felt ill entering the place, but Nira held her hand and that helped. At first there was no sight of Steve, or the trapdoor that led to the caves where the witch had held her and Steve hostage.

Then Nira showed her power, or at least, her secret knowledge. All around the house were computer monitors that gave off a dull purple light. They had no keyboards in front, nor did they appear attached to any visible computers. But each had a black cable that ran from the rear of the monitors and into a wall.

Moving fast, Nira tore the cables from the walls.

The monitors went blank. Suddenly Steve's body became visible, exactly where they had laid him on the living room sofa. The trapdoor also reappeared. At that point Cindy and Mr. Warner almost fainted. Nira took it all in stride. She told them to call the Toule police and have them pick up the body.

Before the police arrived, Mike Havor and Terry came to the door.

Cindy had heard nothing but good things about the blind

man from Ali. That made her comfortable with him—even though he worked for Sheri Smith. But his assistant, Terry, was a walking zombie. He wore a smelly hooded sweatshirt, torn blue jeans, and kept his head lowered—hiding his blond hair and blue eyes as much as possible. Like Mr. Havor, he was pale. In his defense, he was skilled at keeping Mr. Havor from bumping into stuff.

Quickly, Mr. Havor got to the point of his visit.

"My initial reason in coming here was to confront my boss about what she's been up to. But since she's not here, let me explain what I told Ali—plus a few things that I've just discovered. I'm blind, after all, there's a limit to what I can do to stop this madness. But I'm hoping, if you can listen to me with an open mind, you'll understand the danger we're all in, and help take up my cause."

"Our minds have been pretty blown open in the last two days," Mr. Warner said. "Please, tell us whatever is on your mind. And by the way, my name is Jason Warner."

"You are Ali's father?" Mr. Havor asked, interested.

"Yes."

Mr. Havor took a seat before beginning. "My employer, Ms. Sheri Smith, has purchased a nuclear bomb from a general in the Pentagon. I've shared this information with Ali, but so far, today, I've not heard back from her. But by hacking into Ms. Smith's computer files, I've discovered that she's having the bomb deposited on a spot high on the east side of Pete's Peak. I'm in a quandary with what to do with this information. I tried bringing it to the attention of the local police but they treat me like I'm a lunatic. Then I called the FBI and Homeland Security. They acted like they checked on the matter, and then called me back and reassured me no nuclear bombs were missing. The way they said it—each agency—it was as if they were trying to muffle a chuckle." He added, "For some strange reason that I don't understand, Ali seems to be the only one who has a clue what's going on here."

"My daughter is a pretty special girl," Mr. Warner said.

Mr. Havor nodded. "I knew that the moment I met her. I *felt* it, somehow. But I just wish she would answer her phone."

"Let's try calling her on Hector's cell right now," Cindy said. "She'll want to know what you just told us."

Unfortunately, when they tried, Ali's phone just rang and rang.

"I wonder why she's not answering," Ali's father said, worried.

"Maybe she's gone, you know, to another place," Cindy stammered.

"She is not in the green world at this time," Nira said confidently.

Hearing the child's voice, Mike Havor did a double take.

"Who is that?" he demanded.

Nira did not respond. Cindy replied for her. "It's Nira. She can talk now."

Mike Havor shook his head. "Is this some kind of prank? Nira is autistic."

"You're hearing her voice," Mr. Warner said. "It's no prank."

"But . . . it's impossible!" Mr. Havor exclaimed. "At best, she can mumble."

"Listen to her again. You'll hear it's the same voice, just clearer." Cindy added, "Nira, say hello to Mr. Havor."

"Hello, Mr. Havor. You know me, I know you," Nira said.

Mr. Havor appeared unconvinced—who wouldn't be? He had Cindy's sympathy. It was hard—with no eyes—for him to argue his case. He asked if he could feel her face. Nira was happy to oblige. Studying her features with his fingertips reassured him a bit, but he was far from a believer. Yet he let it

go, for now. He was clearly more worried about nuclear holocaust.

"I hope you people don't think I'm joking about this
bomb," he said, removing some papers from his coat pocket.
"I printed out much of the information in Ms. Smith's private
files. You can study it if you like. My documentation is thor-
ough."

Mr. Warner took the papers, glanced at them. "How were
you able—"

"I have voice-boxes on my own computers," Mr. Havor interrupted. "But I kept my headphones on the whole time I
worked on her files."

"Did you fax these papers to the FBI or Homeland Security?" Mr. Warner asked.

"Yes. I don't think they even read them."

"Why not?" Mr. Warner asked, holding up the papers.
"Your documentation looks genuine to me."

Mr. Havor sighed. "One man, at Homeland Security,
warned me that they get sixty crank calls a day about stolen
nuclear bombs. They just have it so locked in their brains that
no one can sneak onto an Air Force base and steal a bomb,
they won't consider the idea. And when I said no, my boss
bought the bomb from a general at the Pentagon, then I lost
the man altogether." He paused, growing impatient. "Listen,
that's two hours of reading I just handed you. I can summarize
the information if you like."

"Please," Mr. Warner said.

Briefly, Mr. Havor related his talk with Ali, explaining how a
General Kabrosh at the Pentagon was receiving huge sums of
money from Sheri Smith, and that this same man was in charge
of the disposal of old nuclear weapons. When he was finished,

Mr. Warner insisted they had to give Homeland Security another try. Mr. Havor shook his head.

"We'll get nowhere because all our accusations are based on General Kabrosh. And to these people, the man is a hero. In fact, he is a war hero. For combat bravery in Vietnam, he won the Congressional Medal of Honor. That's the highest award possible for a soldier. They see the man as almost a god and we're saying he's a criminal."

"Then what can we do?" Mr. Warner asked him.

"Mr. Warner . . ." Mr. Havor began.

"Call me Jason."

Mr. Havor shook his head "Jason, I know from the outside I look useless. Without Terry's help, I couldn't walk a hundred yards into the woods. But I've let too much go on in that office that I should have spoken up about years ago. I'm going to hike up that mountain and find out what that woman's up to—even if Terry's the only one I've got with me."

"I admire your courage," Mr. Warner said. "But how far up the mountain was she planning to deposit the weapon?"

"From her files, it looks as if it was to be dropped near some kind of cave."

"Which is located where?" Mr. Warner persisted.

"Near the top of the peak, I'm afraid to say."

A light went off in Cindy's head. "I wonder if it's that same cave we took?"

"What cave is that?" Mr. Warner asked.

"You remember, Ali told you about it," Cindy said.

Mr. Warner's face changed. Of course, they were talking about the cave that led to the seven doors. And on the other side of one of those doors was his wife. The tension in the room jumped noticeably. Especially when Nira spoke up.

"I've explored all the caves that lead from beneath this house. One comes out near the central cave Ali and my mother are familiar with—high on the mountain." Nira turned in Mr. Havor's direction. "You'll find the tunnel I'm talking about tall and wide. An easy hike."

Mr. Havor shook his head. "You sound like Nira, but . . ."

"I am Nira," the child replied.

"But Nira can't talk!" he almost shouted.

"It's Nira, please, just trust us," Cindy pleaded.

Ali's father knelt in front of the child. "Are you saying we should all go up the mountain? Is this the adventure you were talking about when you left Ali that note at the hotel?"

Nira nodded. "We have to leave soon."

Mr. Warner went to ask, "Will I have a chance—"

Nira put a finger to his lips. "We will see. No promises."

It was decided then. They were going up the mountain to find a nuclear bomb.

And Cindy had been worried it was going to be a slow day.

They gathered together a handful of water bottles, several daypacks—which they stuffed with snacks—and three flashlights, with extra batteries. At Nira's insistence, they sneaked out the mansion via the trapdoor. The little girl wanted to make sure they were long gone before the police arrived for Steve.

The hike through the tunnel was long and uneventful.

Mr. Havor, however, kept trying to quiz Nira. He did not get far. The child did not mind his company, but did not want to share her secrets with him. Again, Cindy felt sympathy for the blind man. He acted like someone whose whole world had just been turned upside down—and for him, it was doubly worse, because he could not see the world.

When they finally exited the cave, into the woods, Cindy

realized they were not far from one of the spots she and her friends had camped at during their first expedition to the top of Pete's Peak. Karl Tanner—that traitorous jerk—had called it "Overhang."

The name was appropriate. With its large but narrow slice of rock jutting from the mountainside, it created a natural shelter from wind or rain. That was a concern, because in their rush to leave the mansion before the police arrived, they had packed no camping gear. Plus, even though it was well past dawn, the sky was cloudy and the air chilly.

They were all exhausted. Cindy led them straight to Overhang and asked if anyone else wanted to sleep for ten hours. It was agreed they should rest before continuing on.

"We can make a fire," Mr. Warner suggested. "I brought a lighter, and there's plenty of dry wood in the area. We can rest near the flames, recover our strength." He glanced at Nira. "Unless you think that's a bad idea?"

The child closed her eyes and stood motionless a moment.

Then she opened them and nodded. "There's time," she said.

Nira's confidence and seemingly omniscient insight should have reassured Cindy. Yet it did not—not in a normal way. Cindy thought she understood why. For a while, she'd imagined she'd been taking care of the girl, when in reality Nira had probably been taking care of her.

Yet Steve had died on Nira's watch.

Cindy saw that Nira was so far above them, that the everyday fears human beings felt did not touch her. In other words, she would probably accomplish what she set out to do, but she was not going to get upset if one—or even all of them—died in the process.

The child was from a dimension where death was an illusion.

However, standing on the side of the mountain, with her bizarre traveling troop nearby, Cindy felt death was more concrete and more close at hand than ever before.

What was Sheri Smith doing with a nuclear bomb?

Why wasn't Ali answering her phone?

The answer to the second question was simple. Ali's cell phone, the one she had borrowed from Hector, was not ringing. Maybe it had something to do with the crystal plug Nemi had told her to attach to it. Maybe there was another reason.

After Ali tied up General Kabrosh, she flew home to the West Coast, fed Officer Garten in the basement, and got back online in order to talk to Nemi. He hurt her feelings by telling her that he was kind of busy.

"Busy? The world might end today! How can you be busy?"

"Is it possible that's the reason I'm busy?"

"I'm sorry, I know you're working on the situation from your side."

"True. What did Nancy Pillar and General Kabrosh have to say?"

"Nancy had a spell on her, but I removed it. I expect to hear from her today. But she was able to tell me that Lucy had visited a few times over the years. More important, I think, I found a number of paintings Lucy had done of seven mountains. They were each exquisite, created with great care. I recognized five: Pete's Peak, Kilimanjaro, Fuji, Shasta, and Blanc in France. The other two . . ."

"Are Mt. Popocatepeptl in Mexico and Mt. Ararat in Turkey."

"Thanks. I assume these are the places the caves inside the mountain lead to?"

"Yes."

"What's special about them?"

"You tell me."

"Each one is potentially volcanic. Or at least, each one has erupted in the last few hundred years."

"Correct," Nemi said.

"The nuclear bomb General Kabrosh sold Sheri Smith was an MK-41. It's an old bomb, made in the fifties, when America and Russia were racing to see who could create the bigger bang. Most modern weapons are smaller. But this one generates twenty-five megatons. Is that enough to start a chain reaction that could lead to a volcanic eruption?"

"Now you're thinking. What are the last few pieces of the puzzle?"

"I was thinking she might need billions of tons of volcanic ash to help shelter her elemental invasion. Trolls can't tolerate sunlight, and since dragons can't fit into the caves to come here, the trolls are probably her strongest allies—from a purely physical point of view. Am I right?"

"Yes. Continue."

"The scaliis have a single huge eye, where their faces should be. I suspect they're also sensitive to bright sunlight. When they attacked the first time, they came at us after sunset. Is that important?"

"The scaliis dislike the green sun, but can move around in it. A few of them tried to nibble on you yesterday, by Lake Mira. But they would have trouble with Earth's yellow sun. So your reasoning is solid. Continue."

"If volcanoes erupt all over the world, gigantic clouds of ash will darken the skies. It will create a global phenomenon. Not only are the elementals protected by the darkness, the whole world is thrown into confusion and fear."

"Yes. When your opponent is scared, the battle is already half over. Now give me the final piece of the puzzle."

"If Sheri detonates the MK-41 at the place where the tunnels all meet in their different caves, then she only needs one bomb to start a reaction that will trigger all the other mountains—all over the Earth. That's why you kept asking me what she would do with just one bomb. In *that* one place, one bomb is equal to seven bombs exploding in seven separate places."

"Bravo, Ali."

"So all I have to do is go up to the cave and kill her!"

"It won't be that easy."

"Why not?"

"She's smart. She's powerful. She might kill you."

"I'm smart and powerful. I defeated Kashar."

"Look what that fight did to you."

"So what are you saying?"

"You discovered Sheri Smith's plan in the last few hours. She's been meticulously planning it for years. Also, Sheri is a master when it comes to creating backup scenarios. If one fails, you can be sure she'll have another handy."

"I can't just sit here and do nothing!"

"I suggest you do exactly that. You need to stop and consider your options. Furthermore, Geea is not yet in position to challenge the Shaktra."

"So?"

"Ali Warner is Geea. Sheri Smith is Doren. To have any chance of success, all your forces against the enemy must converge—at the same time. Give Geea a chance to catch up with you."

"If I can take out Sheri in this world, I might be able to help Geea in her world."

"Didn't Geea herself warn you about taking care of your own world?"

"Yes. But . . ."

"Respect her wishes. Furthermore, don't try to compete with her. You'll fail."

"That's silly, Nemi! I'm not in competition with her!"

"When she awoke, she took over, and started giving you orders. Your pride was wounded. Now, worse, you have three bosses above you telling you what to do: myself, Geea, and Nira. You're no longer in charge, and you like being in charge."

Ali sighed. "It was fun while it lasted."

Nemi replied, "And you're no longer the green-eyed beauty queen."

Ali found her hands shaking. "Ouch," she typed.

"It's all right, Ali. I know how you feel."

She *felt* like crying. "Then why rub it in?"

"So you will admit that it bothers you."

Ali wiped her face and typed. She would *not* talk about her looks.

"I just felt Geea sent me here to accomplish a goal. Now it's within my grasp. I understand Sheri's strategy now. I can defeat her."

"*When* you defeat her and *how* you defeat her will determine if you *do* defeat her. Each point is connected. Likewise, ponder your connection to Geea. You are one and the same, and yet you have cut yourself off from her."

"I have not. I am here. She is there. She sent me here."

"Still, if you will sit quietly, let your mind settle, you might discover that you can communicate with her. Trust me, she waits for you to do so. She knows much that you need to know, especially the time you should attack." Nemi paused. "You understand?"

Ali sniffled, nodded. "I just wish . . . I could talk to her."

"You've been given the key. Use it. Now I must go. Goodbye, Ali."

"Goodbye, Nemi."

Her heart heavy, Ali turned off the computer. Going downstairs, she released Garten and gave him back his gun. She warned him to keep his mouth shut about the whole affair.

"If you try to explain where you've been, and what's happened to you, no one will believe you. They'll just laugh in your face. It would be better if you just went home and called in sick and rested up for a few days."

He nodded vigorously. He was pretty scared of her.

"You promise to leave me alone?" he pleaded.

"Let's promise to leave each other alone." To both their surprise, she leaned over and hugged him. "You're not a bad man. You're just too anxious to be the boss. But don't worry. I have the same problem."

He shook in her arms. "So you didn't kill anyone?" he asked anxiously.

She let him go and stared him in the eye. "I'm not a murderer, Officer Garten."

When he was gone, Ali sat to meditate. To feel Geea.

But all she saw were vast armies moving beneath dark skies.

CHAPTER

19

The black smoke came all of a sudden, seemingly out of nowhere.

At the time, Ra was with Geea, Amma, and Trae—sitting in Geea's bedroom, in the Crystal Palace. Already the boats were fully loaded and sailing north toward Karolee at a brisk clip, a strong wind at their backs.

Presently, the dragons were bringing as many elementals as possible directly to Uleestar. Geea had given the dragons a massive incentive to work fast. Ra had to tip his head to her, she was always a step ahead of everyone else. Earlier, she had sent Trae and other high fairies—who could fly—to Denzy to break apart the umbrella on the ceiling of the kloudar.

The umbrella that held the brown dust.

Trae had returned with literally tons of it.

Every time a dragon brought in a load of elementals to Uleestar, it was given a "snort" of the dust—not enough to intoxicate the dragon, but enough to keep it happy. Ra knew the method of inspiration disgusted Geea.

War was war, she said, and they had to win at any cost.

"You wouldn't have said that years ago," Amma gently chided Geea.

"That was before I understood to what extreme the Entity would go to achieve its purpose," Geea replied.

"You saw through Ali's eyes when she was on the Isle of Greesh?" Ra asked.

Geea stood and went to the balcony that opened onto the north side of Uleestar, near the rapidly flowing Lestre. Far off could be seen the Youli Mountains, Anglar, and hundreds of floating kloudar, twinkling like large sapphires beneath the enchanting rays of the stationary moon.

Yet something in the view troubled Geea. Frowning, she answered as if distracted. "I saw much more than Ali saw in that chamber," she said quietly.

"What did you see that Ali did not?" Amma asked.

"The Entity has never failed to conquer a world it has gone after." Geea added, "Except those worlds that decided to commit mass suicide."

"Whole planets did that?" Ra gasped.

Geea nodded sadly. "To avoid enslavement."

"The ice maidens will not allow that to happen here," Amma said.

Geea looked at her. No, it was more like she studied her.

"You have been thinking about the ice maidens a lot today," Geea said.

Amma lowered her head. "I pray to them."

"Be careful what you pray for," Geea warned. Then her gaze was distracted. She strode across her room, opened a curtain on a south-facing window, pointed with her arm. There was black smoke coming out of the south. "I should have guessed," she muttered.

The others stood. Yet no one seemed to understand what

the smoke meant. "Has the Shaktra begun its attack?" Ra asked.

"Yes," Geea said, as she turned toward the door, the rest of them on her heels. "That smoke—the red tinge to it—it comes from beyond the red door."

"The dark fairies!" Amma cried.

Geea nodded. "Somehow Doren has managed to break the lock Ali put on the red door. And she has reopened the green door. Even with Radrine dead, the dark fairies are coming to Doren's aid."

"They are cowards at heart. They must feel she can't lose," Trae said.

Geea nodded as she strode through the palace halls, and they hastened to keep up. "They'll have brought their fire stones, and they'll head for the ships. Try to set as many as possible on fire."

"Surely the dragons can take care of them," Ra said.

"Yes and no. The dark fairies outnumber them ten to one," Geea replied.

Amma tried to come with them, to fight.

But Geea refused to let her leave the palace. Ra found it odd how she repeated the order twice to her mother. Speaking to Amma, her tone was almost hostile. "You are not to leave the palace. You are to go nowhere without my permission."

Fifteen minutes later Ra was flying with Geea on Drash's back not far from the rear of the main fleet, as it tread up the green coast toward Karolee. Yet Drash was high up, above the clouds of the choking fumes. Thousands of dark fairies were hidden in the smoke, and had begun to attack the ships with their fire stones. Naturally, the dragons fought back, but Ra had already seen what happened when a dozen of Radrine's offspring concentrated their firepower on a single dragon.

The huge reptile's armor swiftly began to peel off.

Once more, Ra watched in horror as it began to happen to one directly beneath them. The dragon's flame was much more fierce than the red bolts of the fire stones, but the dark fairies were more maneuverable. They were like swarms of bees, with lasers for stingers. Six literally evaporated as the injured dragon swept the immediate vicinity with flames, but another six took their place. The screams of the dragon rent their ears.

Ra wanted to close his eyes, but could not. He could only watch as the back of the dragon showed glimpses of raw flesh. After a concentrated blast from the fire stones, pieces of its heavy armor fell off like chunks of overcooked meat. One wing began to wither, to lose strength, to burn. Finally it was torn off, and the dragon began to fall toward the sea, like a flaming meteor. It hit the shoreline with a thundering crash.

"Drash must help! Drash must fight!" Drash appealed to Geea.

"Drash must listen!" Geea snapped. She pointed to a dozen boats that were already burning. The elementals leapt off the sides and into the water. Some were trolls . . .

"Can they swim?" Ra asked, vaguely remembering that they couldn't.

Geea sadly shook her head. "They're doomed."

"Does it cost Doren a great deal of energy to keep the red door and the green door open at the same time?" Ra asked.

Geea nodded. "You begin to read my mind. Yes, Doren must

remain at the junction of the doors to keep them both open simultaneously. For that reason, we're going to take a risk. Drash! I'm going to expand my field to protect all three of us. I want you to fly directly toward Tutor. We're going to try to shut the cave!"

Their descent—into the bloody smoke, the swarms of dark fairies, and the flaming dragons—was something Ra was never to forget. It was as if they had literally fallen into hell. The inferno raged all around, particularly when the dark fairies realized what they were up to. It was then they began to concentrate *thousands* of fire stones in their direction. Beneath the onslaught, Geea's green field changed to red, to orange, finally to a searing blue. Instinctively, Ra knew Ali could not have withstood the attack for a minute. Geea herself sweated as the temperature of the field began to mount.

"Drash is hot!" the young dragon called out.

"A minute more!" Geea called back. "They'll withdraw their attack once we reach the cave entrance! Or else they'll risk burning their own!"

Her guess proved correct. As they reached Tutor, and the side where the cave opened onto the green world, the dark fairies let up. They had to because Geea forced Drash to fly directly into the swarm of exiting beasts, who seemed to ride a black wave of filthy exhaust out of the heart of the mountain. Remembering how beautiful the spot had seemed to him when he had first entered the green world, Ra felt bitter about the sheer mess the Shaktra was making. He shuddered to think what it would do if it reached the Earth.

Geea urged Drash to move into the doorway of the cave. There she employed something she and Ali called voom. Blowing on her palms, she clapped them together, shouted out words—they may have been simply sounds—Ra did not expect. A sonic boom exploded all around. A large crack appeared in the rim of the cave. Geea used voom six times in a row before the top of the cave collapsed.

They barely escaped the fall. Geea liked to play close to the edge.

For now, at least, the smoke and the dark fairies were sealed inside.

"Were we in time?" Ra asked as Drash flew above the top of Tutor, still shielded by Geea's magnetic field, but feeling the effects of the laser bolts. Yet, for some reason, the dark fairies had ceased to attack them.

"The dark fairies have a hive-like mentality," Geea told them. "When they get separated from each other, or a portion of their clan gets killed, they have a tendency to panic in unison. Doren knows that. She's just used them to throw us off balance. The ones trapped outside here—their attacks on the dragons will fall apart. The dragons will have no trouble killing them. But the damage is done. Smoke covers the land. The scaliis will now have cover to attack."

"Surely we can take care of them," Ra said.

Studying Mt. Tutor, the fairy queen did not appear so certain.

Beneath the yellow sand, it seemed as if the bedrock shifted.

Or else it was the sign of a million monsters crawling. Scabs.

Geea sighed and bid Drash to return home. Finally she answered Ra.

"One way or the other, Doren's going to hit Uleestar with a hammer."

"Any idea how to stop her?"

Geea's answer made no sense. "Maybe by helping her," she said.

When Cindy awoke, the sun was bright and high in the sky. She felt a moment of embarrassment; that while she had been peacefully snoring, the others had gathered their things together and gone off without her.

But when she crawled out of her spot, beneath the shade of Overhang, she saw Mr. Havor and Terry having breakfast, and Mr. Warner heating a pot of coffee. Nira was also nearby—refilling their bottles from a stream that flowed over the smooth stone. Odd, but Cindy did not recall the stream from their last visit.

What was even stranger was Terry was not eating breakfast. He stared down at the protein bars Ali's father had given him with an expression so blank, he could have been the one who was autistic. At least he had let the hood of his sweatshirt fall back.

During the night, while hiking through the tunnel, she had not seen him drink once. Now, in the light of day, he looked familiar to Cindy.

She had seen the guy before, she could have sworn it.

Where? When? She did not know. But Ali would know.

Cindy tried to call her friend again. The phone just rang.

Nira looked over at her. "Ali is fine," she said.

"You're sure?" Cindy asked.

Nira faintly smiled. "Are you sure you love her?"

"Yes. But what does that have to do with how she is?"

"When you love someone, you feel them, even when they are not there. A new mother does not have to hear her baby cry in the night to know it needs attention. She is up to take care of it in a moment. You hear wise people say we are all connected, but that is only true when the love is complete. Then the connection cannot be broken." Nira added, "I am sure Ali is fine."

"Was it hard for you to watch Steve die?" she asked.

Nira hesitated. "I never saw him die."

"But you were there . . ."

"I do not see death," Nira interrupted. "There is no death."

The lesson was too abstract for Cindy. They were chasing after a crazy woman with a nuclear bomb. Death was all around them. She did not need to see it to feel it.

Not long after, they continued their hike toward the cave. She turned out to be their main guide. It was not far away, Cindy remembered. Soon they would be back underground, and searching for a nuclear bomb. God.

Whenever Cindy felt tired, or that the air was too thin to breathe, she would hold Nira's hand and a few seconds later she would feel fine. Cindy noticed Mr. Warner doing likewise. Nira did not seem to mind sharing her energy.

Yet Mr. Havor and Terry seemed to get by without help, although the blind man did occasionally call for a break. Cindy could not help worrying about him. He acted so guilty—as if he should have stopped Sheri Smith years ago. At the same time, Cindy found him a difficult read. He never took off his dark glasses.

Ali tried following Nemi's advice, by sitting quietly and feeling for what Geea was doing. The task was perhaps the most difficult he had ever assigned—to simply be still. What was she seeing anyway? Visions of reality? Or her own projected fears? Ali could not be certain, but she did sense Geea was already at war with a number of creatures: dark fairies, scaliis, dragons maybe . . . At the same time, an even more dominant image began to form in her mind.

Ali sensed that her friends were up on the mountain.

326

She was about to fly up and have a look when she received a call on Hector's cell. Nancy Pillar. The woman sounded sane.

"You told me to call you," she said, and she sounded close to tears, happy ones. "I wanted to thank you so much for what you did for me."

"I didn't do much," Ali said.

"You gave me back my life! I remember now what happened to me." Hesitating, her voice dropped to a whisper. "I just don't know *why*. Why my own daughter placed a compulsion on me."

"In the same way she put you under a spell, she was placed under a much more powerful one after she got burned in the accident with Hector."

The words seemed to make sense to Nancy. "There was this time at the hospital, after she had an operation—she was having one every month—when a man came to visit. I don't recall his name, but he came several days in a row. Lucy enjoyed his company, but he gave me the creeps. When I asked what he did for a living, he was vague. He hinted that he could help Lucy with her scarring. That made me think he was some kind of doctor. But then . . ." The woman didn't finish.

"Then what?" Ali prodded.

"Then I'm not sure what happened. It's one of the reasons I didn't call you earlier in the day. I've been sitting here trying to remember the sequence of events. It's a blur. The man kept showing up. After Lucy was discharged from the hospital, he began to stop by our house. It was then I felt as if I sometimes lost track of time. Does that make any sense?"

"Yes."

"I'd be talking with Lucy and the man and then, it would be later in the day, or even the next morning. Then I remembered coming home from work one evening, and I saw Lucy studying herself in the mirror. She didn't know I was there, at first, because I came up from behind her. But then I saw her reflection in the glass and it was . . . well, this is hard to explain."

"She was no longer scarred."

"Yes! She looked perfectly normal!"

"Then what happened?"

"I think I must have made a noise. She turned around, and suddenly her face was as bad as ever. She got angry at me, very angry, like I had never seen her before. It was like she wanted to hurt me for discovering her dirty little secret. Only I hadn't a clue what was going on."

"Then?" Ali said.

"That's it. That's the last *clear* memory I have . . . until I woke up this morning. Of course I remember Lucy visiting occasionally, and I can recall the last few years of my life. But all these memories I've had since that day I saw my daughter's reflection in the mirror—they're not mine. It's as if they happened to someone else. Do you know what I mean?"

"Yes."

"You worked a miracle on me. You gave me back my mind."

"But you know who you are. *What* you are. It was no miracle."

There was gratitude in the woman's voice. "Yes it was, Geea. And yes, I know who you really are now. I even know my own Doren. You say she was put under a spell, but I still don't understand why."

"It wasn't her fault. She didn't want to hurt you, or her father. Or anyone for that matter. But after she was burned in that accident, an evil power entered this world. We don't know how many people it pursued, but because Lucy was a powerful soul—in a weakened condition—it went after her. And I'm sorry to say it got a hold on her, a hold she hasn't been able to break off." Ali paused. "That's why I'm here. I'm here to stop that power from doing any more damage."

Nancy Pillar hesitated. "You mean, you have to stop Lucy?"

Ali closed her eyes, had to take a breath. The woman was no longer a fool. She deserved the truth. "Yes," she said.

"*How* are you going to stop her?"

"I'm going to do whatever it takes."

The bluntness of Ali's answer shocked the woman. A note of strength entered her voice—a note that would not have been possible yesterday. Ali had to remind herself she was now talking to a high fairy. She had her own strength.

"She's my daughter. She's your sister. How can you . . . ?"

"What's inside her . . . she's not Lucy or Doren anymore. She's something else, and the horror she's preparing to inflict on Earth, there's no way to imagine it. She could very well plunge this entire world into a living hell."

"But there's good in her. Why else would she have bothered to come to see me? And I know how much she loves Nira."

"Perhaps she loved her, but she put a spell on her as well. If there's any way I can stop Lucy without hurting her, I'll do it. At the same time, I don't want to lie to you."

There was a long pause. "Do you know where she is now?"

"I have an idea."

"Is there any way I could talk to her?"

"No."

The woman considered. "I hear it in your voice. I caught you just before you were going to leave. You're going to kill her now, aren't you?"

"I'm going to do what I have to do." Ali added, "I'm sorry."

Nancy was not exactly bitter. There was more pain in her

voice than anything else. Yet she was not going to roll over and let her only child die.

"There must be some way to save her," she said firmly.

"Tell me what it is and I'll do it."

"Geea was a healer, not a killer."

"Geea—I—have always been a warrior—when the situation demanded it. I am sorry, truly, to have to speak to you this way. But, short of killing her, I can see no other way to stop her."

A long silence passed between them.

"I wish you had never visited me last night," Nancy said finally.

"Pardon?"

"I could have just floated along, you know. Thinking about my Lucy. Thinking about . . . nothing. Now that I have my mind back, that's all I'm going to have. I'll be back where I started from. My husband's gone thirteen years now, and soon my only child will be dead." Nancy added quietly, "I'll have nothing."

Ali sat in silence with her for a few minutes. Finally she spoke.

"As you say, I am your queen. If there is anything else I can do for you?"

"Save her soul," the woman said. "Don't let her die like this. Not . . . in darkness."

"I understand," Ali said.

There was nothing else to be said. Setting down the phone, Ali had to wipe away a wealth of tears. In all this time, how seldom had she thought of her enemy as her sister. How little she had considered Doren's suffering at the hands of the Entity, and the pain she had endured inside Hector's burning car.

Ali had just wanted to kill the witch. It had taken Doren's own mother to remind her that her sister deserved at least pity, if not love.

"How can I let myself love her?" Ali whispered aloud. How? When she had to ready herself to kill her.

Ali flew over the mountain in the bright sunlight, keeping her elevation high, not wishing to be seen by any hikers or campers. Not for the first time, she wondered if she showed up on the armed forces' radar screens. Or even local airport radar. There would probably be reports of UFOs in tomorrow's papers. She had been zipping back and forth across the country so often and so fast, *somebody* had to notice something.

Ali searched for her friends but did not see them. Unknown to her, had she started her search ten minutes earlier, she would have seen her father, Mr. Havor, Terry, Cindy, and Nira just before they entered the lower portion of the cave.

Yet that entrance held little interest to Ali. It was too far from the six tunnels and the seven colored doors, not to mention the other three doors—which she still did not understand. The top of the cave, where she'd killed Radrine, was where she put her focus. She was hoping to see either a helicopter—that might have lifted the nuclear bomb to the cave—or else signs that the helicopter had come and gone. Such a vehicle would have left tracks in the earth, or in the small pools of snow that continued to linger in the vicinity of the peak.

Unfortunately, Ali saw nothing from the sky. Even when she landed beside the cave entrance, she found no extra set of footprints on the ground. It was possible Sheri had yet to bring up her weapon, or else she might have used the lower entrance, although that would have complicated her task. Taking the lower entrance, it was over eight times farther to the doors.

Nevertheless, Ali was on the verge of flying down to check it out when she heard a noise in the cave. Stepping inside, she put an ear to the stone wall and listened intensely. There it was again! An echo. Metal hitting metal. Sheri must be inside. She must have the bomb with her.

Ali shuddered with excitement. She did not know if it was a good day to die, she just knew one of them must. Her fear was matched only by her desire to attack. Yes, to kill the witch, and end the war . . .

However, Nemi had told her . . . what? She had to somehow coordinate her attack with Geea's attack on Doren? Sounded good in theory, but how was she supposed to do it? Geea might be able to read her mind, but the reverse was not true. For all Ali knew, Geea could be eating lunch right now.

No, Sheri was in the cave with the bomb and it was time.

Time the witch paid for her mother and Steve.

Drawing in a deep breath, letting her field swell to maximum potency, Ali allowed her shimmering green bubble to lift her off the ground and carry her down the length of the black cave. She did not need a flashlight to see. Her powerful green eyes generated their own soft glimmer. And she did not care that Sheri would see her coming. It was good her sister should know that her queen had stopped by to say hello.

Again, they were in Geea's bedroom, and again Ra, Trae, and Amma sat on the floor at the feet of their queen, as Geea rested on a corner of the bed, her gaze somehow near, somehow far off as well. To Ra, when he was with Geea, he felt he was with Ali as well. Geea's next words only confirmed that fact.

"She moves too soon," Geea whispered.

Ra sat up with a start. "Ali?"

"Yes."

"Is she going after Sheri Smith?"

Geea nodded. "Too soon, and she is not well-armed . . ." Her voice trailed off as her eyes went to Amma. "I remember what you did for me."

Amma nodded. "The question is, does she?"

"Nemi has warned her. She does not listen. She acts without thinking."

"Is Sheri Smith capable of killing her?" Ra asked, anxious.

Geea nodded. "Just as Doren is capable of killing me."

Ra stood, frustrated with how calm they were all acting. "We have to help her!"

Geea spoke patiently. "All her life I've tried to help her, whispering inside her heart. It's the same for all humans. In each there's a voice that resides in the silence of their innermost being—a voice they can choose to listen to whenever they wish. The trouble is, most never stop to do so."

"But Ali . . ." Ra began.

"Is very human," Geea said. "That's her strength and her weakness. On the Isle of Greesh, she dared what I was afraid to try. She is bold and fierce. Yet she is reckless and not always wise. Right now, as we speak, I tell her to back off, to let events unfold further, but she does not listen."

"Because she cannot hear you," Ra protested.

"Because she is *human*. The Entity is accurate when it says you are reckless when it comes to your own world. The majority seldom pause to look around and let the Earth tell them what it needs to survive. In the same way, Ali needs . . ."

"Send her a stronger message!" Ra shouted. He could not believe he had just interrupted Geea. Yet she smiled down at him, and brushed a lock of dark hair from his eyes.

"Nira and Nemi have given her enough messages to guide her. If she survives this encounter with her sister, then she'll have more time to reflect upon them." Geea stood and walked to the south-facing window. "The truth is, we have to help ourselves."

Amma stood and came up behind her. "What do you see?"

Ra could see only black smoke and flying dragons out the window. The dragons' whips of flame steadily destroyed what were left of the dark fairies—the unfortunate ones who had not been trapped inside Mt. Tutor.

The shift of the elemental army to Uleestar went smoothly. Already the boats had docked at a harbor not far from the fairy capital. With Lord Vak, Lord Balar, and General Tapor guiding the elementals through the exotic woods of Karolee, it would not be long before Uleestar was a place of concentrated power. Surely, Doren would not dare attack the Earth with such a threat at her back, Ra thought.

Yet Geea was troubled. "I see something on the back of a dragon."

"Is it a scab?" Ra asked.

"Yes."

"That should not worry a dragon," Trae remarked, also coming to the window. Geea glanced his way, then back out the window.

"This one is big," Geea said.

"How big?" Ra asked, standing behind her.

"The scab on the back of the dragon is as big as a house," Geea replied.

Sheri Smith did not seem surprised to see her. Sitting on what looked like the tail-end of the bomb, she glanced up as Ali came near. At the same time, she lifted a beautifully polished silver sword—the golden hilt studded with a dozen different jewels—and pointed it in her direction.

"Stop," she called out.

Ali stopped. *Near* was a relative term. There was still a hundred yards between them. But the gap felt smaller, because Ali could fly, and cover it in less than a blink of an eye. Plus the sheer size of the bomb made it—and its owner—appear much closer than the length of a football field. But no matter how you looked at it, the distance remained, and it was important to Sheri that Ali did not cross a certain line.

The bomb was an ugly contraption. The basic design was of a grossly overweight torpedo, but it was way too thick and bulky to fit in a submarine. The dull gray paint and the wide rear fins made it look very fifties. But why should it look pretty anyway? It had been designed to kill as many people as possible.

Ali studied her surroundings. In numerous spots in the walls, it looked as if holes had been drilled, then covered over with cement—which had now hardened. There were many such "buried holes" on Ali's side of the bomb, and on the far side of Sheri and the weapon. These holes had been carefully drilled on *either* side of the six tunnels, but far from them as well.

Ali understood. Whatever her sister had placed in the holes—it was probably dynamite—she didn't want it *damaging* the six tunnels. The holes and the tunnels had to be far enough apart to keep the tunnels safe.

On the other hand, the bomb had to be in the precise *center* of the tunnels, which was where Sheri now sat. The logic behind her plan was simple. Sheri needed the power of the blast to flow equally through the tunnels. It was her intention to blow off the tops of seven mountains, and create seven fresh volcanoes.

Yes, there would be *seven,* not six.

Because Pete's Peak would explode with the others.

It all got a little confusing in Ali's head. The reason was the queer nature of the mountain's interior. It not only possessed doorways into other dimensions; the tunnels somehow *folded space* over the surface of the Earth. That meant a straight line was not necessarily the shortest distance between two points. Somehow, the tunnels superseded that basic law of physics.

Ali could never forget the shock she had felt—when she had raced down one of the tunnels to escape the dark fairies— and she had ended up in Tanzania! And just a minute before she'd been in Breakwater . . .

Ali cautioned herself to focus on the problem at hand.

She could not let her sister detonate the bomb.

"Looks like you've been busy," Ali called. The truth was, with their supernatural hearing, neither of them needed to shout. It was old human habit, Ali supposed.

Sheri wore a fine red gown, as befit a fairy princess, and her sword-belt was studded with rubies. The latter matched the ruby necklace she wore around her neck.

Unfortunately, Ali could stare at neither her sister's gown nor her jewels without seeing Sheri's scars. The veil of beauty was simply too transparent for her now that she had been to the Isle of Greesh and back. Not all the "gifts" the Entity had bestowed on her sister were potent.

Sheri studied Ali's own scars.

"The violet ray proved too much for you?" she asked.

Ali nodded. "You tricked me. Clever."

"I heard my trick saved your life. Old Kashar couldn't swallow the Yanti."

"True. But he tried."

Sheri shook her head. "Stupid old dragon."

336

"His was not an easy death."

"Burning is no fun. You must know that by now. But I'm confused, why the scars? Was Queen Geea stingy when it came to her healing touch?"

Ali drew her long red hair back from the right side of her face.

"I kept a few out of respect for you," she said.

Sheri snorted. "Please! You break my heart!"

"Your heart doesn't break so easily. But like you said, at least now I know what it feels like to burn."

"Ha! You didn't like me calling you a fool at the police station."

"Trust me, that was not my motivation," Ali said.

"Then explain yourself. We have time. Not a lot, but some."

Ali took a step forward. "Why not stop the clock on the bomb? Then we can talk as long as we want."

"Sorry, sister. You never were my favorite company."

Ali took another step forward. Sheri interrupted her in midstride.

"Stop! You're keen-eyed, and you're not stupid. You must have noticed the holes in the walls. You must have guessed what's inside them."

Ali nodded. "Explosives."

"Very good. So stand back. There's no reason for you to lose your head, is there, little sister?"

Ali stopped. "I visited the Isle of Greesh. Had a chat with the Entity."

Sheri studied her forehead, and Ali knew she searched for a purple crystal that she would not find. "You lie," she said.

"You can hear what is true and what is a lie. While trying to inspire me to sign up for its unholy cause, the Entity showed me a short film of you and Tulas. I saw how the Entity manipulated you into accepting the implant. It helped me understand why you kept going to Hector, to see him, even after Lucy Pillar was supposed to be dead."

"Don't talk to me about Tulas or Hector!"

"Why not?"

"Neither of them means a thing to me now."

"Doren . . ."

"And don't call me by that name!"

Ali nodded. "Should we add Nira to your list of unmentionables? When I was with the Entity, Father came and helped. He saved me from their grip, and at the same time provided me with the key to unlock those you've marked. Nira speaks now. You should hear her. The first words out of her mouth were orders. You would have loved it. She contradicted everything I'd told the others!"

Sheri showed interest. "I'm happy to hear she's not your stooge."

"She's no one's stooge. Certainly not the Entity's." Ali paused. "I gave her the Yanti. She knows how to use it in ways neither of us imagined possible. With it, she could remove that implant in your forehead."

Sheri sneered. "That was placed inside Doren, not Lucy!"

"Don't lie to me. It's in both of you. Even from here, I can see it." Ali paused. "What was the name of the man who came to visit you at the hospital?"

Sheri chewed on that one. Did not answer.

"Your mother told me about him," Ali offered.

"I suppose she talks now, too?"

"In a sense, she talks less."

Sheri was amused. "Mom never knew when to shut up."

"She showed me your paintings. You're quite the artist."

"General Kabrosh showed me his arm. You would have made a lousy doctor."

"How is the good general?"

Sheri shrugged. "I hated to see him suffer."

"So he's dead. And Tulas . . ."

She raised the sword angrily. "I told you to leave him out of this!"

"You cannot pretend you were not manipulated! You cannot act like this is what you wanted! You've become a thrall, nothing more. When you were young, and still had dreams, was this one of them? I don't think so! Admit it, it's all become a nightmare."

Sheri stood away from the bomb. "You surprise me, Geea. With everything you've seen and experienced the last few days, you still act the fool. You say you've spoken with the Entity. It must have explained to you why it's here. Without help, this planet is doomed."

"With their kind of help, humanity would be better off dead!"

"So you just decide that for everyone on Earth? Sorry, but I think if it was put to a vote, the vast majority would choose life rather than extinction."

"You are not talking about life. You are talking about slavery."

"Slavery is better than death!"

"Humanity *abhors* slavery!" Ali snapped. "They'll fight to the last one of them to get out from beneath it."

"That's just your opinion. To me, most human beings are cowards."

"You just don't get it, Doren. You've decided the very destiny of the human race without asking another soul their opinion."

Sheri threw up her arms. "Who was there to ask? Tulas was gone. Father was gone."

"No. Father was there, inside the purple cubes . . ."

"Then why didn't he help me?" Sheri interrupted, and there was more anguish in her tone than hatred.

"You didn't reach out to him the way I did," Ali said in a gentle tone. "That's how I survived my encounter with the Entity. Not because I'm smarter than you. But because I asked for help, Doren, and help came."

"I told you not to call me that!"

"You're my sister. I can call you by your real name. And there's no reason we can't talk about Nira and Tulas and Hector. These are people you still love."

"Didn't the Entity give you its lecture on the uselessness of love?"

"I chose not to listen to it. Why don't you stop listening to them?"

"No."

"You have the choice. It still exists. Doren . . ."

"No!" Sheri shouted, shaking her sword in the air, causing waves of purple light to convulse the air. Or did they come from her head? Ali could not be sure, only that it felt as if something evil had suddenly entered the cave. Dizziness swept over Ali, as her sister ranted on.

"The time to choose has passed. It passed for Doren when Tulas caught fire. It passed for Lucy when she caught fire. After that kind of pain, nothing matters. There's survival and that's it. In the coming days, the world's going to learn that lesson." Sheri paused to catch her breath. "Now go, Geea, just leave. Or I'll kill you where you stand. I swear it."

Ali took a step forward. "I cannot allow you to detonate that bomb."

Her sister caught her eye. "You cannot stop me."

Sheri pressed a switch on a black instrument attached to her sword-belt. There was a deafening noise. Behind Sheri and the bomb, Ali saw a rapid sequence of bright explosions. The fire-balls erupted on both sides of the cave wall—simultaneously—and tore apart the tunnel. A geyser of dust blasted Ali's face. It must have been harder on Sheri, since she was closer to the blasts. Yet her sister stood firm—in the center of the cave—as well as in the depths of her madness.

The cave had been blocked from the south side. And if Sheri pushed the next button, Ali realized, it would be blocked from the north side. Then Sheri would be all alone with her bomb, and no one would be able to stop her.

Energizing her field, Ali tried to fly forward.

Sheri countered with a slice of her sword.

The shiny weapon never left her hand. It touched only dust-choked air. But it sent forth an invisible *blade* of pure pain. Ali caught the phantom blow in her abdomen. It felt exactly as if she had been stabbed there. The agony was immense. Her sweatshirt was torn and a line of liquid red appeared. It was blood—she was bleeding from a wound inflicted by a weapon that had not touched her!

Only then did Ali recognize the fairy sword. It had belonged to her father.

Sheri reached for the next button on the black instrument. Reversing her field, Ali tried desperately to fly backward, away from her sister. Before she could move ten feet, the second sequence of bombs went off. The noise was deafening, the debris choking. It was only the magic left in her depleted field that kept her from being crushed beneath the stones. It humbled Ali to realize that just one swipe of Sheri's sword had been enough to drain her entire reserve of power.

For a while, holding onto her bloody shirt, and the torn flesh beneath it, Ali let herself drift on autopilot. It was not long before she saw the light of the sun shining outside.

Finally, free of the confines of the cave, she was able to stop and rest on a rock that stood beside a pile of snow. The latter reddened as the blood from her cut flowed over the white ice. Physically exhausted, mentally devastated, Ali doubted she had the strength to heal herself.

CHAPTER

20

Once more, Geea and Ra rode Drash back into battle, but this time, with less hope. Geea had been right about the new element of attack. In the sands south of Mt. Tutor, the tiny scabs emerging from the desert were somehow fusing together—first in pairs, then in quadruplets, and so on, until they formed one gigantic monster—that was made up of thousands of the brain-sucking creatures. How they were able to do this, no one knew, but Geea said it must have been part of Sheri's long-term strategy.

"I told you she would never trust the dragons to remain loyal."

"How can we stop them?" Ra asked.

Geea shrugged. "There must be a way."

Presently, they were flying high above the woods south of Karolee, where the bulk of the dragons were meeting the on-slaught of the new threat. What was remarkable to Ra was that even though the new scabs were a thousand times larger than the old ones, they behaved the same way as the originals.

To get airborne, they had to inflate themselves with air, and then whirl a mass of hanging tentacles to give themselves both direction and speed. Yet the spinning tentacles acted as their main weapons, too—along with being the central part of their propulsion system.

Periodically, a tentacle would stop spinning and reach out a sticky claw—from beneath an inflated gelatin bulb—and grab whatever was in the vicinity. These tentacles were fast and hungry. From his vantage point in the sky, Ra watched in horror as fleeing fairies and elves and dwarves had their heads torn right off the top of their bodies.

The scabs had changed in one respect. They were no longer trying to create scaliis. They just wanted to feed, and besides gobbling down elemental heads, they went after the dragons with a vengeance, possibly because they offered the most meat. Or more likely, Geea had said, because they'd been programmed by the Shaktra to take them down.

"Doren knows she cannot strike Uleestar with the dragons protecting it," Geea told Ra. "Even if she forces a million marked thralls or scaliis onto our capital, they'll be beaten back. But these new scabs—let's call them drones—could change all that."

Even as they spoke, two drones began to rush toward Drash. Geea commanded the dragon to turn about, fly back to Uleestar. But the drones—once they had locked in on them—dropped their tentacles and set them spinning. Their speed was amazing. One minute the drones were a mile below, the next they shot past Drash at over two hundred kilometers an hour.

That was their goal, Ra saw, to get above them. Because once they had the superior altitude, they could drop down their tentacles and use them as weapons. Ra could not help but panic as twin drones closed in over their heads.

But Geea remained unconcerned. Rubbing her hands fiercely together, she let loose six powerful vooms. One drone ruptured like a blimp that had been struck by a cruise missile. But the other showed no signs of damage.

A two-foot-wide tentacle swung by their heads.

"Duck!" Geea ordered. Ra did not need the order. He practically glued himself onto the dragon's back, as Drash dove toward the ground. The drone proved stubborn. Again, it positioned itself directly above them, but this time it went into simple free-fall—aimed directly at Drash's back!

Geea took out her sword and stabbed up at the creature. The blade, of course, was no longer than a yard, but it did not seem to matter. A slice of blue light shot off the tip of it. In an instant the drone was sliced in two. What a noise! What a stink! The foul gases—as they left the drone behind—were nearly poisonous. Ra choked on them as he complained to Geea.

"You could have told me your sword could do that!" he said.

"I like to show off," Geea said, patting Drash on the back. "Let's get some more of these monsters. Before they get to your friends."

Drash was fearless. He flew directly into the smoky fray.

Cindy and her traveling companions were resting in the seemingly endless cave when she *felt* rather than heard a roar. It came in two waves. Mr. Warner noticed it as well. "What was that?" he asked.

Mr. Havor sat up with a start, almost lost his dark glasses, quickly replaced them on the tip of his nose. "Could it have been an earthquake?"

"It sounded more like explosions," Cindy said. "Could Sheri Smith's bomb have already gone off?"

Mr. Warner and Mr. Havor looked sadly amused.

"If a nuclear bomb went off anywhere in this mountain," Ali's father explained, "We would definitely know about it."

"Or rather, we wouldn't know anything at all," Mr. Havor said.

Cindy grimaced. "We'd just be dead?"

Mr. Warner nodded. "But it takes expertise to detonate such devices. She's a genius at software development, but she's not a physicist. It's not going to be that easy for her to set it off."

Mr. Havor was less encouraging. "She wouldn't have bought it if she didn't know how to set it off. Trust me, she's a master at everything she touches."

"How did you get involved with her?" Mr. Warner asked.

Mr. Havor shrugged. "I had ideas for computer games and she had money. She understood my vision. Or at least I thought she did."

"You were just wanting to play *end of the world*," Cindy said. "She wanted the real thing?"

"Exactly," he replied with a sigh.

Cindy had a bottle of water in her hand that was almost empty. But Terry hadn't brought anything to drink. She couldn't stand to see him hiking all this time uphill without taking a sip. She offered him her bottle. "Please take a little," she said.

He stared at her with unblinking eyes. In the harsh shadows cast by their flashlights, they seemed to have lost their color. For the first time she noticed what looked like a birthmark on his forehead—a dark smudge between his eyebrows.

Terry did not answer Cindy.

Mr. Havor spoke up. "He can't talk. It's not his fault."

"But he can hear, can't he? He has to eat. He has to drink," Cindy said.

"I've seen him go days without doing either," Mr. Havor said.

Of course, the blind man was speaking figuratively when he spoke of "seeing." Cindy understood that much. But what she didn't understand—and it filled her with dread—was that she'd finally figured out where she'd seen Terry before.

The first day they visited Toule, Ali had left her and Steve to check out Omega Overtures on her own. The two of them were resting in the park with Rose and Nira, when a blond teenage boy was suddenly struck by an SUV—not twenty yards from where they were sitting. At the time Rose said the guy's name was Freddy Degear, and got all upset. Leaving Nira in their custody, she rushed off to tell Freddy's mother what had happened to her son.

Only later they learned it was all a lie. There was no Rose—it was Sheri Smith in disguise. Plus there was no Freddy Degear, either, or at least, no one in town had heard of the name. Yet *someone* had died that afternoon, and had subsequently been taken to the local hospital. Indeed, Ali had gone to the morgue to check on the guy's body, and even she had said he was beyond hope.

Yet here he was, sitting two feet away from Cindy.

"How long have you known Terry?" she asked Mr. Havor, trying to keep her voice steady.

"Just a couple of weeks. I know he acts kind of strange but . . ."

"How did you meet him?" Cindy interrupted.

Mr. Havor hesitated. "Sheri Smith introduced me to him. As a favor, she said, to help me get around. Why do you ask?"

Cindy waved the flashlight over the guy's face.

No blinking. No pupil response. No nothing.

"Just wondering," she whispered.

Somehow, after resting near the cold mountain peak for an hour, Ali managed to gather enough strength to expand her field so that she was able to fly home. Once inside, she showered and then collapsed on her bed. For a long time she just lay there with her palms placed over her wound. The bleeding had stopped but the pain remained. Just as bad, her blood loss had drained away much of her magical powers.

Yet she was Ali Warner. Queen Geea. She had only begun to fight.

She tried reaching Nemi online, and was not surprised when he did not respond. She had ignored several of his earlier instructions; and he was not one to repeat himself. His silence probably meant, *Stop whining and think about what I told you.* Somehow, she had to coordinate her attack on Sheri with Geea's attack on Doren. Nira—as well as Nemi—might have provided her with a clue as to when these events might coincide.

"Did she leave any instructions for me?"

"She said you would come for me at some point."

"When? Why?"

"She didn't say. Don't you know?"

"I'm afraid not."

Both Geea and Nemi had agreed her sister's Achilles' heel was Hector. But in her hurry to get Sheri, Ali had ignored the importance of Sheri's obsession with Hector. Now Ali was willing to take any help she could get. However, she did not want to bring Hector into the picture until he could be useful. Also, she did not want to get him killed.

Plus, Sheri had sealed herself in tight with the bomb . . .

Or so it seemed on the surface. There were six other mountains on Earth—besides Pete's Peak—that had caves that contained tunnels that led to Sheri and her bomb. Her sister must know she would figure that out.

So Sheri would still be waiting for another attack . . .

"Which mountain should I approach from?" Ali asked herself. In her weakened condition, the closest one sounded best. That would be Mt. Shasta, in California. Now that Ali thought about it, Sheri had probably had the bomb delivered there—rather than risk crossing state lines with her "slightly suspicious" cargo.

There was something else about Mt. Shasta that rang a bell with Ali. She couldn't quite place the reason why, only that her mother had taken her there when she was young. Four or five—no older. What had they done on that trip? Ali couldn't remember.

Ali gave Hector a call. "Are you almost ready?" she said.

"Have you figured out what I'm getting ready for?" he asked.

"It involves Mt. Shasta. But before I bring you there, I want to first check out the scene."

"Then what? You'll fly me there?"

"That's a problem. I can't hold anyone living while I'm flying."

"Why not?"

"It has to do with fairy magic . . . it's complicated. But I was wondering if I could tie you into some kind of harness . . . with a long rope attached. One that reaches outside my field."

"I'm not following you."

"I'm asking if you would let me drag you there."

"Through the air?"

"Sure. You don't want me to drag you on the ground."

Hector paused. "I don't like the sound of this."

"Why not?"

"I've seen the way you fly. You're as fast as a jet."

"I could slow down for your sake."

"When do we have to be at Shasta?"

"The sooner the better."

"Why?"

"Your ex has a nuclear bomb and she's itching to set it off."

"God."

"I said the same thing."

"You've seen this bomb?"

"Oh yeah."

"Then you have to take me there now. You can't make two trips."

He was right, Ali thought.

"What can I put you in that would make you feel safe?"

Hector considered. "A deep-sea diving bell. They're usually attached to long thick cables. They can withstand incredible pressure. But you'd still have to be careful not to rock me around too much." He added, "They weigh a ton. Can you handle that?"

"Don't worry about the weight. Where can I get one?"

"They don't exactly sell them in stores."

"Where can I *steal* one?"

Hector paused. "There's a ship designed for deep-sea exploration in Seattle's main harbor. It has two high-pressure bells aboard. But the place will be swarming with security."

"Where should I bring the bell?"

"You know the park outside of Toule? Just before you enter town?"

Ali nodded. "Hansons Park. Are you sure it will be empty?"

"Yeah. Contractors I'm working with have just torn it all apart. There should be no one there." He paused. "When should I be there?"

"In forty minutes."

"What if you run into trouble?"

"Listen, after what I've been through today, I'm not worried about harbor security." She added, "Hector?"

"What?"

"Lucy is not the Lucy you used to know."

"In the car, driving back to town, Nira said the same thing."

"What did she say exactly?"

"She said, 'Father, if you see her, she might kill you.'" Hector added, "She meant if I went after her."

"But Nira's right. Are you sure you want to do this?"

"Yes. I need to confront her. And ask her why. Just that."

"You might not like the answer you get," she warned.

Ali met with only a slight delay in Seattle. As she was ripping apart the cable that attached to the deep-sea diving bell, she was approached by two armed guards. Since she was doing all this with her bare hands, they drew their guns on her before asking any questions.

"I need to borrow this bell," she said. "But I'll bring it back later."

One guard shook his gun nervously. "Stop what you're doing! Put your hands on top of your head!"

Ali smiled at him, stared him in the eye, expanded her magical field. "Stop. Lie down and close your eyes. Go to sleep." She glanced at the other guard. "You, too. Lie down and rest. Don't wake up for two hours. And forget I was ever here."

The guards lay down and went immediately to sleep.

Ali was a bit disconcerted to discover how heavy the diving bell was. It was more like *two* tons. It took her longer than she planned to reach Hansons Park. As she set the bell down in the trees, out of sight from the road, Hector stared at it with more than mild trepidation.

"Is there any chance you might drop me?" he asked.

Ali groaned as she rubbed her shoulder. "I am kind of beat."

Hector saw she was not kidding. "You already saw her today?"

"Yes."

"How did it go?"

"Badly."

"What makes you think you're going to do better this time around?"

Ali grew serious. "I honestly don't know. But we're out of time. And for the first time, I can feel the same is true in the other world. Doren's about to attack Geea. We're going to have to go after Lucy, and we're going to have to do it now."

"Is there anything—anything at all—that can improve our odds?"

"Maybe you could kiss her or something."

"Ali . . ."

She suddenly held up her hand. "Wait a second! Mt. Shasta! I was thinking about this earlier. My mother took me there as a child."

"So?"

"She took me there without my father!"

"So?"

"We never went on vacation without my dad. Plus I was real small at the time, she had to carry me a long way up the side of the mountain. And she had a package in her arms."

"What was in it?"

Ali was thinking. "I remember she buried it on the mountain near a cave . . . Yeah! The cave intrigued me, and I told her I wanted to go inside, but she said I would have to wait until I was older. But when the time was right, I would dig up the package and go inside that cave!"

"Was your mother psychic or something?"

Ali nodded. "She has special gifts no one else has."

"What do you think is in the package?" Hector asked.

Ali smiled. "I have a pretty good idea."

Geea killed at least two hundred drones before finally admitting they were not going to stop the monsters with ordinary fairy magic—even with an army of dragons at their backs. There were simply too many drones, and the dragons were dying at too fast a rate. Some were simply fleeing, even though Drash tried his best to set a good example by leading the way in the fight. But Geea herself told Drash it was unfair that so many of the dragons should die for the sake of the others. It was a quandary.

Plus, there was trouble on the ground. The majority of the elementals had reached Uleestar, but there were still plenty trapped in the surrounding woods of Karolee. With the drones gaining the upper hand in the air, Doren had unleashed her armies of marked thralls and ravenous scaliis. She had also blasted the cave on Tutor back open. Dark fairies were pouring out on massive clouds of black smoke, their fire stones sending red stabs through the already burning heavens.

Ironically, the drones often attacked and devoured the dark fairies—they were not exactly discriminating eaters—but such mishaps did nothing to deter Doren's forces. Geea ordered Drash to signal the dragons to retreat to Denzy.

"They're to lock themselves inside until the threat of the drones has passed," Geea said. Drash nodded that he understood. He dropped them off at Uleestar before flying away to spread the message.

"Is that wise?" Ra asked as they walked toward the palace. "The drones will just attack Uleestar."

"I want them to attack Uleestar."

Ra was stunned. "Why?"

"You'll see."

"I would rather be told than to be kept in suspense."

Geea smiled. "Just like Jira."

"Don't say that."

"Why not?"

"Next you'll be wanting another kiss."

Geea laughed as if there were no war. "You wish! Human!"

"So you are prejudiced, after all!"

"Only when it comes to skinny African boys who insist on calling my dear Ali a fat American."

"She told you I said that?"

Geea gave him a knowing look. "I *heard* what you said."

The dragons were only too happy to obey Geea's order to retreat. Yet their sudden disappearance appeared to confuse Doren. Perhaps anticipating a trick, she did not immediately order a strike on Uleestar. Geea was pleased for the delay. It gave her a chance to address the heads of the other elemental forces: Lord Vak, Lord Balar, General Tapor, and even the trolls' leader, who called himself Lord Loaf.

"We're going to retreat to beneath the palace. To where Tiena used to be. The cavern's mostly dry by now. It can hold us all comfortably. We will fight as we retreat, as if we're being pushed back against our will. But we'll bring supplies—water and food. Then, when we're safely in the cave, I'll seal the known entrances to the underground harbor. The enemy will rejoice at having taken our city. They'll think they've won."

"If Uleestar falls, they will have won," Lord Vak said.

"Not at all. I have a plan. Trust me," Geea said.

"Don't ask," Ra warned his father. "It'll be a waste of time."

As the last dragon vanished, Doren apparently changed her mind, and the attack intensified. The dark fairies, the scabs, the drones, the scaliis, and the marked thralls were now all concentrated on Uleestar. The rushing waters of Lestre, pouring around all sides of the fairy capital, slowed them down but it did not stop them. Soon it was no longer a question of it being Geea's strategy. The elementals were simply forced back.

Ra oversaw the bulk of the retreat. He did not want to go underground until he was sure that most were safe. Lord Vak noticed his reluctance to flee and complimented him on the fact.

"You must have a brave Earth father, to have taught you so well," Lord Vak said.

"My father died when I was young. I was raised by an uncle. But he was a powerful *chimvi*—what you would call a sorcerer. He raised me to face my fears."

Lord Vak nodded. "Perhaps, all these years, I've been wrong to judge humans so harshly. Even if you were not my son, I see you as someone I could consider a friend."

"Thank you," Ra said.

Lord Vak frowned. "It is just that humans cause the Earth so much pain—pain we feel here as well. Your people seem so determined to destroy their world. It is hard for an elf to understand."

"There's much they could learn from you. Perhaps one day, you could come as a leader, instead of as a conqueror, and they would listen to you."

Lord Vak stared at the swarms of approaching drones and dark fairies. Finally he nodded. "I hope we're given a chance to see that day."

As the drones fell on Uleestar, the first thing they did was behead many of the dark fairies, who—like gluttonous invaders—were anxious to ransack the ancient home of the fairies. It gave Ra some satisfaction to see how the enemy's troops cared nothing for each other. But then the massive drones began to force their way toward the palace. Geea had to grab Ra and Vak by the arms and pull them underground to Tiena's harbor.

"Are you sure this was a good idea?" Ra asked, as they rushed down a spiral stairway he was unfamiliar with.

"There are many layers to my plan."

"Be so kind as to share a few of them with us," Lord Vak said gruffly.

"Fine. I'm about to set off some takor," she said.

Lord Vak's eyes widened. "I have heard of those. But . . ."

"It's what Ali used to seal Tiena with," Geea interrupted. "Now it will help us in different ways. First, it will help destroy Doren's army. Exactly how it will do that—I want to save that surprise for you both. You will enjoy it! At the same time, it will bring Doren here."

"How can you be sure?" Lord Vak demanded. "Her base is inside Tutor. She is safe there. She has no need to show her face."

"I don't just plan to wipe out her army. I'm going to wreck the palace as well, and you have no idea how much it means to Doren. She always assumed she would inherit it, but when I was crowned queen, and it was handed over to me, it ate at her night and day. That's why—throughout this war—you've noticed she's never had the dragons melt any kloudar directly over Uleestar."

"That's right!" Ra realized with a shock. "She's been preserving this spot!"

Geea nodded. "She wants to rule from here. But if she hears I've done something to harm the palace, no matter where she is in the green world, she'll come running."

"But the drones *will* smash the palace," Lord Vak said.

"On the contrary. Did you not see them lining up to protect it? Did you not see them killing the dark fairies that were trying to burn down the gardens? Doren does not want the building seriously damaged. And she knows I'll never damage it." Geea added with a note of sorrow in her voice, "She thinks she knows me."

Ra understood. "It's hard for you to sacrifice this place."

Geea shook her head bravely. "Lives are worth more than palaces."

With Geea, Ra and Vak finally reached the cavern. The retreat of the elementals into the black dry riverbed of Tiena had created quite a sight. There had to be at least a million creatures—of all sizes and shapes—gathered in the gorge that had once held the famous river.

The crowd grew tense when Geea briefly left them and went partway upstairs. There she detonated a series of takor, cutting off the palace from the underground harbor. In the mass of jammed elementals, Ra saw that Lord Vak had found Lord Balar and General Tapor. The three leaders appeared displeased with the explosions.

"We'll be penned in, with nowhere to flee," Lord Balar growled.

"They'll come at us from Lake Mira," Lord Vak agreed.

"Lake Mira," General Tapor muttered with a frown. "I think I know what she's trying to do, but timing is critical."

"She knows what she's doing," Ra said flatly.

The three leaders appeared unimpressed with his confidence. Especially when clouds of smoke and dust from takor blasts filtered down to the subterranean cavern. It was not a pleasant sound to hear a million elementals start to cough at once. Ra tore off a portion of his sleeve, put it over his mouth, using it as a mask. He had nothing to shield his eyes from the dust. For the most part, he tried to keep them shut.

But he had them open when Geea suddenly reappeared and

floated over the elemental mass, glowing with the full majesty of her shimmering green field. Pulling out her sword, she pointed toward the invisible palace above them, and when she spoke, somehow her rich voice carried to every living creature in the cave.

"The enemy thinks they have us trapped down here. Right now they're totally focused on breaking through the temporary barrier I've erected. As of yet, they haven't given any thought to the waters high in the Youli Mountains. And by the time they think of them, they will be as good as dead."

With that, Geea suddenly turned and disappeared up the long dark cave.

North, Ra saw. She was definitely heading for the lake.

They could only sit and wait. Ra stayed near his father. Lord Vak appeared unusually interested in hearing about the Kutus tribe that lived around Mt. Kilimanjaro.

"You say you make a living helping Americans climb to the top of the peak?"

"It is one of the many things the Kutus do in order to survive," Ra replied.

"Your father, how did he die? Was it in battle?"

"It was during a hunt. A lion killed him." Ra added, "To graduate as a *chimvi*, my uncle required that I slay a lion."

"Did you?"

"Yes. At night. I used only one arrow."

Lord Vak nodded with pleasure. "You are more elf than human."

Less than half an hour after Geea departed, they heard a terrible explosion. Red and orange fire lit up the north end of the cavern. The ground shook violently, and they got another downpouring of smoke and dust from the ceiling.

Yet it was nothing compared to the noise that followed.

Fifteen minutes after the explosions, a dull roar started to vibrate the roof of the chamber. It did not sound like a wave of water—more like the steady concussion of relentless artillery fire—but that was precisely what it was. Only this wave was a tsunami on a scale neither human nor elemental history had any record of. It sounded as if the actual atmosphere of the world above them was being ripped away by cosmic forces. Lord Vak and General Tapor understood what had happened. The fairy general spoke proudly.

"Geea rigged the mountains around Lake Mira with takor, causing the walls sheltering the watery valley to collapse. As we speak, water—as deep as the ocean—is flooding Uleestar."

"Will it wash the palace away?" Ra asked.

General Tapor shook his head. "Doubtful. This building was carved out of a single giant crystal. It is heavy."

"But everything inside it will be flushed away," Lord Vak added grimly.

Lord Balar sighed. "All those riches . . . so much gold and jewels. What a waste."

Lord Vak nodded. "Geea's wiser than I gave her credit for. She used Doren's lust for the beauty and riches of this capital against her." He added, "Geea will drown her sister's army."

There was soon lots of evidence to support Lord Vak's claim.

A hundred cracks in the ceiling spouted narrow sprays of water, but the basic integrity of the cavern remained. The pulse of the miniature ocean, as it raked overhead, was like a beating heart. In a sense, Geea had used an old trick on her enemy—merely repackaged it in a new form. She had invited her enemy into a supposedly safe sanctuary, and then abruptly changed it into a place of cold death.

Ra could not help noticing that the water sprinkling down

on them was well below freezing. Then he recalled how Amma had explained that the magnetism of the levitating kloudar—floating so near Lake Mira—kept it from freezing. The cold was just another way Geea was going to wipe out Doren's monstrous army.

For a time, Ra feared Geea had done all this at the expense of her own life, but then she came blazing out of the long darkness of the now empty tunnel. As she arrived, everyone cheered, celebrating the fact that the war was over. But Geea shook her head and told them that the battle was not finished. The majority of the drones, the scaliis, the marked thralls, and the dark fairies, were dead or fleeing. Yet the Shaktra still lived.

"The Shaktra is on its way here now!" she shouted.

Lord Vak leapt up with his black spear. "We'll stand together and meet it as one!"

"Aye!" Lord Balar cried. "My ax craves the witch's blood!"

Geea flew near them and took out her sword. Smoothing her hand over the sharp blade, she shook her head. "I think it's best if I met her alone," she said.

"Why?" Ra asked.

"Because she'll possess powers that only she and the Entity know of."

"More the reason we fight with you," Lord Vak insisted.

"We all have a score we'd like to settle with that creature," General Tapor said, perhaps for the first time in his life questioning his queen's orders.

Geea went to respond, but suddenly halted in midair. Scanning the vast crowd, she frowned. "Where is Amma?" she demanded in a voice that was heard far off.

No one knew for sure, but there were two elementals present who had an idea. It was Paddy and Farble who finally wiggled their way to the front of the crowd.

"Amma went with Drash to Denzy," Paddy said.

Geea was shocked. "Why?"

Farble growled. "Love Geea's Amma."

"Tell me where Amma is," Geea demanded.

The leprechaun was uncertain. "Paddy heard them talking. Something about Ali's father. Amma told the dragon that the good man would not be able to bear the loneliness if all of you ladies should be gone. Or else if you be killed." Paddy scratched his green head. "She said something like that, Paddy thinks."

Geea flew near the leprechaun and troll, who stared up at her fearfully.

"You're friends of Amma. Why didn't you stop her?" Geea demanded.

Paddy trembled. "Excuse me, Missy, I mean, Queen Geea. But no high fairy would listen to a leprechaun or a troll."

"What does Denzy have to do with Ali's father?" Geea muttered to herself.

Paddy nervously added, "Queen Geea, Paddy does not think she was interested in the kloudar. Only in where it was going."

Geea's face darkened. "And where might that be?"

Paddy blinked anxiously. "She spoke of it going beyond Anglar."

"What did she say exactly? Tell me!" Geea demanded.

"Paddy don't know! Amma just said she needed to go that way!"

CHAPTER

21

Cindy and her gang finally reached the place in the cave where the three metal doors were arranged, set one beside the other, in a modest semicircle. To make room for the doors, the cave had been forced to swell in size. The doors were plain rectangles, devoid of markings, although each had a dome-like curve at the top.

Cindy knew Ali still considered the three doors a mystery, although she hinted that they might be connected to time travel. Ali was never given a chance to test her theory because the only door that she could open was the central one—and that definitely led to the present.

Their gang met with the same failure. Mr. Warner and Mr. Havor tried yanking on the other two doors without success. It was as if the knobs had frozen in place ages ago. There was certainly no place to insert a key.

"Let's continue to the seven doors," Cindy said. "Those are the ones Ali said lead to the other dimensions."

They pushed on the central door. It swung open soundlessly—all two feet thick of it. Cindy wondered why the door had to be so thick. What did it keep in? What did it keep out?

From her last trip, Cindy knew it took two hours to hike from the three doors to the seven. What she had conveniently forgotten was that—after the three doors—the cave inclined sharply, and the air got much thinner. They had to stop for frequent water and rest breaks. Even with Nira helping Mr. Warner and Cindy with her magical energy boosts, the two of them struggled.

Mr. Havor, in particular, suffered. His white skin took on a blue tinge. But he didn't complain—it was not his nature—nor did his seeing-eye dog, Terry. Then again, Cindy thought, since Terry was dead, he had no right to complain.

It made her sick just to be near him. She struggled to bring up the topic with Nira. Isolating her at the rear of the slow-moving caravan, Cindy tried to explain the accident at Toule, pointing out the fact that Nira herself had been there.

The child was not in the mood to talk.

"We need to reach the seven doors," Nira said.

"Then what?" Cindy asked.

"Then everything will be fine."

"But this guy, Terry . . ." *He was a corpse,* she wanted to scream!

Nira put a finger to her lips, as if to "shh" her.

The child's lack of interest did nothing to calm Cindy's nerves.

All she could do was stay as far away from Terry as possible.

Finally, they reached the cavern that held the seven doors, which were arranged in a semicircle. Like the other three, they were made of metal, but they had handles instead of frozen knobs. Each door was a different color. Starting on the far left they proceeded in the order of the spectrum . . .

Red. Orange. Yellow. Green. Blue. Violet. White.

Well, the last actually covered the *whole* visible spectrum.

Nira did an odd thing when they reached the cavern. Moving to the white door, she knelt before it and closed her eyes and folded her palms. Then she stood and placed both hands on the door, finally pressing her forehead against the white portal. She stayed in that position for several minutes. No one spoke to her or interrupted her. No one had the nerve, Cindy thought.

Finally, Nira turned and stared at each of them individually.

"So here we are," she asked. "What shall we do? What do you want?"

Mr. Warner spoke in halting tones. "I'd like—if possible—to see my wife again. To at least say goodbye to her. I never got to do that." He added, "But most of all I'm worried about Ali. I want to see her. I'm afraid she's alone up here, fighting that Sheri Smith woman." He paused. "Do you know anything about that?"

Nira nodded and turned to Cindy. "What do you want?"

"I just want to get out of here!" Cindy blurted out.

Nira continued to stare at her. Apparently the answer was not good enough.

Cindy composed her thoughts. "Well, what I'd like to do is help end this war as soon as possible. So the least number of people have to die."

Nira turned to Mr. Havor. "What's on your mind?"

"I'm here to stop Sheri Smith from detonating the nuclear warhead."

Cindy had to ask herself how he knew Nira was talking to him.

The answer did not impress Nira. She stared at him hard.

"Don't you want your eyes back? You keep your glasses on because they're gone, aren't they? Someone burned them out of your head."

Mr. Havor frowned. "I don't know what you're talking about."

"Are you sure?"

"This is crazy!" he said, annoyed.

"You did it yourself. You burned out your own eyes."

The blind man shook his head angrily. "Where is this conversation headed? I'm not here because of myself."

Nira nodded. "A puppet does not worry much when its strings are pulled. Do you know why?"

"Nira. If you're even her. I . . ." Mr. Havor began.

"Because it's only a puppet," Nira interrupted.

"You're talking nonsense," Mr. Havor said, sharpening his tone. "I don't even know who you are. The Nira I've known all these years could not talk. There's no way you can be her. I don't know where you came from or what you want. But somehow you've fooled these decent people into thinking you have some kind of special knowledge or power. You sound like a little devil to me."

"You don't trust me, that's fine," Nira said. "I don't trust you." Nira pointed to Terry. "I don't trust him, either, although it's not his fault that he's here. As Cindy has pointed out, I was at the morgue when we examined his body. You, Mr. Havor, believe it was your *kind* that gave him the energy so that he might walk again, and behave as your puppet. But it was I who touched him with the Yanti." Nira drew out the Yanti and held it out for all to see. She stared at Mr. Havor. "Isn't this what you really came here for?" she asked.

"I don't know what you're talking about," he replied.

"Do you, Cindy?" Nira asked.

"I saw this Terry guy get hit with an SUV. He had his skull cracked wide open. That was just a few days ago," Cindy said. "And now he's here, climbing mountains."

"Are you serious?" Mr. Warner asked, startled. "Why didn't you say something?"

"Like what? We have a dead-zombie-dude as a hiking buddy?" Cindy asked.

Nira continued to focus on Mr. Havor, the Yanti in her right hand. It was almost as if she were offering it to him. She spoke in a soft voice. "Yesterday, I listened as we escaped Breakwater and went into hiding. In the car, as we drove south along the coast, I heard Ali talk about what happened at the meeting at the police station. You see, I can know many things, but even though I'm of the violet ray, there are still things in this world that are hidden from me. As we left town, I wasn't sure who was the Entity's agent on Earth. On the surface it appeared to be my mother, but that was unlikely. She had too much desire to be in control. Even after all these years, she still didn't understand that the Entity allowed no one else to be in charge. Mother did not know she would be killed the instant they were finished with her."

"Nira, I'm not sure . . ." Mr. Warner began.

"Let her finish!" Cindy said.

Nira's eyes never left Mr. Havor. "When Ali spoke of how time stood still in the police station, I knew immediately she was dealing with a powerful radiation—beyond the green or blue vibrations. My mother does not have the power to stop time. Plus you gave yourself away in another way—that was really kind of dumb."

Mr. Havor acted bored. "What was this *dumb* thing I did?"

"My mother put a sleeping spell on the people at the police station. You took it one step further and stopped time. You wanted to give Ali the impression she was facing an enemy that couldn't be defeated. But you made a mistake. While time was frozen for all of you—you took a nap."

"So?" Mr. Havor asked.

"You snored. Ali told the others that but missed its significance. If time was truly stopped, then how could you be snoring? It takes time to snore. The only answer that made sense was . . . you were unaffected by the spell because you were the one who caused it. Also, you are the one who has kept us from being able to call Ali." Nira held the Yanti higher. "Isn't this what you want? Isn't this why you're here?"

There was a long pause. Finally Mr. Havor smiled.

He reached up and removed his dark sunglasses.

He had no eyes. Just burnt black holes.

However, between his eyebrows, Cindy saw what she thought was the tip of a purple crystal. It looked like an amethyst—a sharp shard embedded in his forehead. He shook his head in answer to Nira's question.

"You are mistaken," he replied in a voice much deeper and colder than anything they were accustomed to. He sounded more machine than human. "The Yanti might be of benefit to us, that remains to be seen. Certainly we will leave here with it. But when you ask what it is *we* want most . . ." He glanced at Terry, then back to Nira. "It is your head."

Terry had removed a rusty machete from the folds of his smelly sweatshirt. Mr. Warner went to rush him. "Stop!" Nira commanded.

Everyone in the cavern stopped, not just Ali's father.

"Who's the puppet here?" Nira asked Mr. Havor.

Mr. Havor shook his head. "Your mother is still under our control. But you are right, soon she will have to be eliminated for the reasons you've stated. But the body you see here—it's more than an agent for the Entity. Long ago, the personality that inhabited this form made a deal with us. It was made directly online. He found us, we found him. His name was Peter

Traver. He was what you would've called the consummate hacker. He desired nothing more than to immerse himself in the most advanced technologies of his time. He was obsessed with computers and software, and as you might know, obsession is really only a step away from possession. When he contacted us, he found a source of information and knowledge far richer than anything he had dreamed possible. Peter was enthralled."

"And so he became your thrall?" Nira asked.

"Naturally. He was happy at first."

"Then you made him burn out his eyes," Nira said.

"We always demand a sacrifice of those who join us."

"Was he happy then?"

The blind man merely shrugged. Nira nodded to herself and continued. Cindy knew her next words were for their benefit.

"So the Entity does not mind revealing a quality it usually prefers to keep hidden. You do not merely desire control. You are not here just to save planet Earth. You feed off of pain and fear. That's your ulterior as well as your ultimate motivation."

"To us they are inseparable." Mr. Havor shrugged again. "A deal requires an exchange of goods. Peter Traver gave us his eyes. Lucy Pillar offered us hundreds of burnt bodies."

"But she did not give you the body of my father," Nira said.

Cindy understood she was talking about Hector Wells.

Lucy Pillar had helped him survive the power plant explosion.

"That showed her lack of commitment," Mr. Havor said. "A weakness."

"A weakness to you, maybe. But to me it showed a hidden strength."

Mr. Havor mocked her. "You say that because she's your mother."

Nira was not flustered. "It showed the flaw in your design."

"How so?"

"Is it not obvious? You let me be born. You let me come here, right now, into this place." Nira added, "Even now you do not understand what a mistake that was."

Mr. Havor smiled and gestured to the yellow door. "Beyond that door there is a bomb and your mother. Both are well protected. But even if your mother turns on us now, or is overcome by Ali, she cannot prevent the bomb from exploding."

"Because you adjusted it?" Nira said.

"We adjusted it after we helped Sheri Smith purchase it."

"You made the initial contact with General Kabrosh?"

"He was flattered to be made the star of a bestselling game."

Nira nodded. "And now he is dead."

"Yes, now he is dead. Just as soon, all of you will be dead." Mr. Havor turned to Terry. "Take the head of the child now, and the Yanti. The others won't interfere. They cannot move."

With the mere utterance of his words, Cindy discovered she couldn't move.

Mr. Warner stared at her in desperation. He couldn't move, either.

Cindy tried to scream for help. Her lips would not move.

"When you have her head, then you may kill the others," Mr. Havor said.

Terry lifted up his rusty machete, preparing to strike Nira. The child didn't flinch, merely stared into his blank eyes. Oddly enough, a spark appeared in the depths of his eyes. The guy hesitated as Nira spoke to him.

"I only touched you with the Yanti in the morgue so that you would not leave this world marked. This man came for you later, and reactivated your flesh for his own selfish purposes. To strike me or my friends down is to further his purposes. Your body—even though it is technically dead—remembers certain morals that you used to live by. For that reason, I'm not here to give you orders. I won't try to take control of you. All I'm going to do is remove the controls that have been placed on you. Then you can choose what you want to do. Honestly, it is all up to you. You can chop off my head, or you can take his."

Terry stopped, lowered the machete. He may have been a mere corpse, yet his flesh strove with serious emotions. He turned toward Mr. Havor, then back to Nira. He was clearly confused.

"If you wish to go on living, you have to do what I say," Mr. Havor said.

"He lies," Nira said. "The life he promises you is no life at all, just a continuation of this hellish existence you find yourself trapped in. Do what you know to be right, and I promise you'll be free of this rotting body and this dark place. You will return to the light, where you belong."

Terry came to a decision. He turned toward Mr. Havor, slowly began to approach him. The man looked shocked, but he was still physically blind. It was not easy for him to try to escape.

"The power to override our compulsions doesn't exist at this level," he stammered.

Nira smiled a little girl's smile. "You had your chance, Uncle Havor, when I used to sit on your lap. You should've fed me poison, instead of all of that wonderful ice cream."

"But . . ."

Terry swung his machete. Cindy caught a glimpse of a flying head, a fountain of dark blood, heard the sound of a corpse striking the ground. No, there were two thuds. Briefly, she shut her eyes to block out the gruesome attack, but then reopened them to see what had become of Terry.

370

The boy lay on his back beside Mr. Havor's headless torso. In a mysterious way, his face looked peaceful. The opposite was true for Mr. Havor. There was only horror in the empty eye sockets of the dead man's skull.

Casually, Nira turned back to the colored doors.

"Now the fun begins," she said.

The secret inside the package was, of course, a fairy sword. But not just any fairy sword. It was Geea's! The weapon Geea had worn while she slept in the kloudar the last thirteen years had been Amma's sword. How did that come to be, Ali asked herself.

Long ago, her mother and Geea must have arranged for her to have this weapon—probably because it was the most powerful in the entire elemental kingdom. But exactly how they had managed the feat, Ali was not sure.

Clearly, Amma possessed the gift of prescience—the ability to see into the future. How far and accurate the gift extended, Ali did not know. But somehow Amma had seen that her daughter would one day arrive at Mt. Shasta and need a weapon. For now, Ali was just happy to have it, and was not in the mood to figure out exactly how it came to be there. What mattered most was that she was returning to fight her sister with two distinct advantages—the sword and Hector.

With the diving bell lying outside the cave, they cautiously crept into the interior of Mt. Shasta. Hector asked if he could use a flashlight.

"It will signal our approach," Ali warned.

"Won't she know we're coming anyway?"

"Probably. Use the light."

He turned it on. "How do you see in the dark?"

"I don't know," Ali said honestly.

"I assume you know how to use that sword?"

Ali made a slashing cut. "I feel like I was born with it in my hand."

Because they had to walk, it took them time to reach Sheri. They came out of the tunnel on her left, behind her. Casually munching on a sandwich, Sheri didn't even turn to acknowledge their arrival. Not until she'd washed down her meal with a bottle of water did she address them.

"Why did you come, Hector?" Sheri asked without turning.

"Ali told me you were in trouble," Hector said.

Sheri finally looked over. "I doubt she put it that way."

"Does it matter? You *are* in trouble, and I'm here to help."

The bomb was even more ugly up close. Its gray hide was stenciled with black code numbers, and Ali noticed the paint was rusted and chipped in several places. Yet there was a shiny stainless steel plate on the side, with fresh screws in it. Ali guessed that was where the new detonator had been installed. She could actually smell the new plastic explosives. From what she had read online, this was a three-stage bomb. It had a fission trigger—made of plutonium; a fusion core—made of hydrogen and helium isotopes; and an outer shell—constructed of uranium 238. The bomb was called "dirty," because when it detonated, it left behind a massive amount of radioactive fallout.

It gave Ali an odd feeling to stare up and down the cave, and see how they were walled in. She just wished there was a deserted mountain at the end of one of the tunnels that they could push the bomb through—and let it explode harmlessly. She suspected the weapon had been rigged to detonate no matter what they did to it.

Sheri seemed to read Ali's mind.

"If you try to move it, the thing will go off," she said.

"But you must know a way to turn it off," Ali said.

Sheri shrugged. "You're welcome to try your hand at it. Or else you can try shoving it down the tunnel that leads to your boyfriend's home. Where's he from by the way? Oh yeah, Tanzania. That must make dating difficult. Then again, you know how to fly."

"How come you haven't flown away?" Ali asked.

"I've been waiting for your gutsy return." Sheri nodded toward Ali's abdomen. "You heal quickly."

Ali raised her sword. "Probably quicker than you, I think."

Sheri smiled. "But I know that *you* know that killing me won't help your cause." She scooted off the bomb and walked toward them. Ali quickly moved to the right, to give herself room to maneuver, forming what had to be one of the most unstable triangles in all of history.

Yet Sheri made no threatening move. Hector held her attention.

"Why did you come?" she asked again.

He spread his hands. "A couple of mornings ago I get a call to come watch my daughter. A daughter I don't even know I have. A daughter from a woman who I didn't even know was still alive." He stopped. "Isn't that reason enough for me to be here?"

Sheri nodded. "I could say I am sorry, but at this point I suppose that would sound a little trite."

"You can still say it," Hector replied.

Sheri forced a smile. Ali noticed she never took her hand off the hilt of her sword. For that reason, Ali magnified the strength of her shield. Sheri was most dangerous when she appeared most vulnerable.

"I'm sorry," Sheri said.

Hector was annoyed. "For what exactly? That you faked

your death and left me grieving for years? Or are you sorry that you would come to me in the middle of the night—and then in the morning make me forget you had ever been there?"

"I thought it would be better—for your sake—that I made you forget."

"You didn't think to ask my opinion, did you?" Hector snapped, bitterness in his voice.

Sheri looked truly hurt. "What did I have to offer you anyway? If you knew who I was, then you could only pity me. Pretending to look beautiful wouldn't work with you. At least as long as I remained dead . . ." She didn't finish.

Hector glared at her. "Go on. At least as long as you remained dead, you could seduce me in the middle of the night when you were in the mood. That's the truth, Lucy, isn't it?"

"Hector . . ." Sheri began.

"Oh. And you did all this with me while you were in the middle of preparing to destroy the Earth. Let's not forget that. That's sort of important, don't you think?"

Sheri shrugged. "You've only heard Ali's side of the story when it comes to this invasion. There's a purpose behind it. A noble purpose. It's called survival."

"This noble purpose calls for the death of how many billions?" he asked.

Sheri spoke with passion. "The Earth is desperately overcrowded. It cannot continue to exist without major changes. Yes, billions might die, it's possible. I admit these changes will be painful. But all significant change—whether on a personal or on a social level—is always painful." Sheri added, "It's where the phrase 'tough love' comes from."

Hector sighed. "Love has nothing to do with what you're planning."

"How would you know?" she snapped back.

"Because you can't even look me in the eye. In fact, you won't even let me see how your eyes really look." Hector reached out his hand to steer her chin so that she had to look him in the eye. But she slapped the hand away with her gloved hands. He nodded when he saw the gloves. "The scars are still there, for both of us. Why do you bother to cover them up?"

Sheri snorted. "You have the nerve to compare your scars to mine?"

"I never said that."

"Then what are you saying? After the accident, you went to jail for a few months. Big deal. Then, after I was gone, there was never any shortage of women in your life."

"Sure. There was a parade of women going in and out of my house. Since you died—since I thought you died—I've had just one serious relationship." Hector paused. "And I never loved Patricia the way I loved you."

"I couldn't tell from the way you behaved around her."

Hector's face darkened. "Is that why you killed her?"

Sheri looked as if she had been struck. "Who told you that?"

Ali spoke. "Steve did. My friend. Before you had him killed."

"Is that also true?" Hector asked quietly. "Did you kill that boy?"

Sheri looked away. "No."

"She had someone else kill him. But she gave the order," Ali said.

Sheri gave her a look to kill. "What do you know? You weren't even there."

Ali nodded. "No. I wasn't there. That's why he died. I was a couple of minutes late. But the guy who stabbed Steve's heart—he worked for you. I'm surprised you're afraid to admit

375

it. That's a change. You usually love to boast about your cruelties. But I suppose that technique doesn't work so well in front of the one man you still love."

Sheri glared at her. "Who says I love anyone?"

"If that's true, why did you have Nira?" Hector asked.

Sheri whirled on him, to scream, to shout, whatever. But then she stopped, and it was as if all the hate in her expression fell to the floor. "Nira," she whispered. "Nira was an accident."

Hector didn't believe her, nor did Ali. "If she had been an accident, you wouldn't have kept her," he said.

There was a long pause. The clock ticked. The one inside the bomb. Ali had no idea how much time they had left. She assumed they were safe, for now, because Sheri did not act in a hurry to leave. But maybe that was a dangerous assumption. It was clear the woman was not operating with a full deck of cards. Sheri shook her head, spoke in a mocking tone.

"This is crazy—talking about these things right now. Our personal problems pale when compared to what's going to happen to the world in the coming days. A new order is taking over, and it's simple—you're either for it or you're against it. If you're against it, you're going to die."

"Then I'll die. I'm against it," Hector said.

Sheri stared at him like he was a fool. "You don't even know what you're rejecting! Listen to me, Hector, the things . . ."

"I'm rejecting you!" he interrupted. "What you've become. Ali told me you were a murderer, and you know what? I didn't believe it, not until this moment. Pretty stupid, huh? You're sitting on top of a nuclear bomb and I'm still thinking, but you're Lucy Pillar—the kind-hearted girl I used to love. Lucy wouldn't hurt a soul. Well, I was wrong and Ali was right. The way I feel right now, I wish you had died the night of the power plant explosion."

Sheri forced a vicious smile. "I love how you stand there and judge me for the sins you think I've committed. Let me tell you something. Ever since you ran your truck into that tree and I burned, I've had to make a thousand hard choices. Not one of them has been easy!"

"Lucy . . ." Hector began. But she cut him off.

"Or have you forgotten about that day? How many beers you had that afternoon?"

"That was an accident," Hector said.

Ali interrupted. "It was no accident. When I saw the Entity, it admitted that it programmed Hector to smash his truck into that tree in that precise manner. It used the Internet to program him. So that you would burn, Doren. So that it would have that lever over you."

Sheri went to snap at her, then stopped. "Is that true?"

Ali nodded. "You can hear the truth when it's spoken."

Hector was shocked. "That was not an accident?"

"Nothing that's led up to this moment has been an accident," Ali said. "Another thing, Doren. When I was with the Entity, they offered me your job. They're going to kill you the second they don't need you. Which will probably be ten seconds after this bomb goes off."

Sheri shook her head. "I'm to rule this world!"

"The Entity does not create rulers. You of all people should know that. It only creates thralls."

"You just want to take over! You'll use the Yanti to . . ."

"I gave the Yanti away," Ali interrupted. "Remember?"

Sheri froze. "You really gave it to Nira?"

"Yes."

"Why would you give up so much power?"

"It doesn't belong to me, or to you. It belongs in the hands of a goddess." Ali added, "At least that's one wonderful thing your love for Hector brought into the world."

Sadly, Sheri was too caught up in her thoughts of power and betrayal. Her sister couldn't hear her. She couldn't talk about Nira. Her mind was trapped in the pain of her past.

"I came out of the blue light," Doren muttered. "The Yanti should have been mine. Father should have given it to me, I was the oldest. The palace, too, it all should have been mine. And then, when I got burned, there was no one there to help me. No one there to heal me . . ."

Ali felt a profound anguish at what she had to tell her next. Because it went way beyond life and death, or who was to be king and queen. It dealt with her sister's soul.

"Doren. The Entity has lied to you about something that is more important than this bomb and this war and everything else we're talking about. This time, when you die—and I assure you they'll murder you soon—the ice maidens will not come for you. You'll not return to the love of the blue light. You'll go to the Entity. You'll become one of them, and you'll be trapped in that evil realm forever. No one knows better than you the horror they're capable of. Think, Doren, remember what they did to Tulas. Look at Hector, right now, and remember Tulas. Please! Remember what they did to him!"

The expression on Sheri's face altered. But it did not shift toward reason as Ali had hoped. In that moment, Ali saw she had gone too far. Pushed buttons so painful, and so deeply buried, that merely to draw near them was enough to precipitate an avalanche.

Sheri lost control of the illusion that held her beauty intact. As it broke, the shock of her endless scars leapt out. Instinctively, Hector took a step back. It was not his fault. The sudden horror of her ruined face would have shaken anyone. But it might have been the most fatal step backward the world had ever known.

Sheri suddenly raised her sword. Her voice came out crazed.

"You're saying I'm already damned for eternity? I know that! Just look at the way Tulas looks at me now. Look at the way Hector wants to embrace his dear Lucy. I'm better off going into the purple light. Who cares if the Entity knows no love? What difference does that make to me? When have I ever had love?"

Sheri swung her sword at Ali then. Ali saw it coming and ducked. Her sister's blade struck the ground, and there was an explosion of light and fire. Sheri pivoted and swung at Ali again. This time Ali met her squarely, blade against blade, and the noise of that metallic clash was strong enough to make any human being go deaf.

Maybe that was why Hector did what he did next. For even though Ali shouted at him to stand back, he did not appear to hear her. As Ali darted left and right, trying to slip under her sister's guard—and as Sheri made several countermoves—Hector held up his arms and stepped between them.

"Stop. Please," he said.

The timing could not have been worse. On the verge of fooling her sister, Ali presented to Sheri what appeared to be a major opening. Her sister went for it, with a powerful stroke Sheri surely believed would be fatal. And it was fatal—it was just that her blade pierced Hector's chest instead of Ali's. It struck him deep in the center. The amount of blood that gushed out said it all. The blade had gone through his heart. Even as Sheri pulled out her sword, Hector began to fall. Ali had to drop her own blade to catch him. It didn't matter. There could be no last-second healing. He was already dead.

Even though Geea had ordered Lord Vak, Lord Balar, General Tapor, and Ra to remain behind underground—they rushed with her to the surface. They were anxious to see what remained of the enemy's army, and what the unleashed fury of Lake Mira had done to the Crystal Palace. And, of course, they all wanted a piece of Doren.

Two facts caused them to drop their guard. *Every* single creature belonging to the Shaktra had been washed away. There wasn't a drone in sight, never mind a measly dark fairy or a scalii. Even their foul corpses had been vanquished. It was as if the gentle green sea—to the far west—had changed its shape and mood and opened up an angry maw and swallowed the evil creatures.

Also, as they returned to the surface, they went straight to Geea's quarters, the highest point in the palace; and the latter inevitably gave them a false sense of security. They all knew the position and structure of the bedroom made it practically inaccessible from the outside.

However, none of that mattered to the Shaktra. Riding a huge dragon that had clearly disobeyed Drash's final order to retreat, Doren had the audacity to crash through the bedroom's balcony window.

The boldness of the attack caught them all by surprise.

They were given no time to prepare a defense. A blast from the dragon incinerated General Tapor. The brave fairy turned to ash where he stood. Yet they were fortunate to have Lord Balar with them. Dwarves wore the heaviest armor, and were especially skilled at killing dragons—or so Ra had been told.

Certainly, Lord Balar had killed a few in his days. He was the first to move, and a bold move it was. He leapt directly onto the back of the beast and chopped off its head with his ax. He was an experienced warrior. He must have known that the move left his back exposed, but he took the risk anyway.

Doren thrust a spear through his spine, so deep, it came out his front.

Lord Balar died with the dragon.

Lord Vak countered by hurtling his famous black spear at Doren. It hit her shield and shattered it. Leaping off the back of the dead beast, Doren dropped her ruined shield and threw a black knife at Lord Vak's leg. Her aim was sharp—the cruel blade impaled his hamstring, and the elven king stumbled against a wall. Ra went to pull it out, but Lord Vak stopped him.

"It will only bleed worse! Take my sword! Protect Geea!"

Ra did as he was told, but as he turned, he saw the fairies had already exited the room. They had gone out and over the balcony railing. Ra had to race down a flight of stairs to reach the soggy lawn and gardens where the final battle was to be waged.

Lestre continued to churn with foam and mud. Many large stones that normally sheltered the northern tip of Uleestar from the river had been overturned and thrown onto the lawn that stretched below Geea's private quarters. The shrubs, the trees, the hedges, the flowers—all were gone. Even the sweet aroma of the spot had been washed away. The place smelled like a swamp.

Not that it mattered. The water-encased battlefield was damp and muddy but the two warriors blazed with such fire that Ra would not have been surprised if the entire area dried before one of them fell. Geea wore green; Doren's robe was red. Geea also had on her emeralds—bracelets and anklets. Doren displayed a single ruby necklace. The latter was more than enough. As the light of the green sun caught the red jewels, Ra was almost blinded. The crimson light pierced deep into his eyes, and made him wonder how many foes Doren had hypnotized and then defeated with her necklace alone.

Geea's sword was silver, with a gold hilt. Doren's was a shiny black metal that tapered into burning gold. Doren also wore armor, a breastplate, but Geea had none. As Ra watched, they cautiously circled each other.

"Ra. Listen and do not argue," Geea said. "You cannot help me now. You can only hurt me. Stay back."

He held up Lord Vak's sword. "My father says I am to protect you!"

"Not another word. You can only distract me from what I must do."

Doren grinned as she nodded toward Ra. He was stunned by her beauty, and he had thought he had seen the limit of the word when he had met Geea. Doren was taller, her eyes larger, her nose sharper, but she moved with a slithering motion that reminded him of a reptile. Besides the green in her eyes, there were also shades of red and purple. These same colors vibrated through the magical field that surrounded her, and Ra saw it was brighter than Geea's, more powerful, and that worried him.

"Who is that one?" Doren asked Geea.

"A toy, nothing more. Who was that dragon Lord Balar decapitated?"

"A pet. Did you like the way I took care of Lord Balar?"

"He was getting old. He died bravely, and in battle, the kind of death he would have wanted."

Doren laughed. "What about Lord Vak? Has he lost his nerve? One knife in his leg and he decides to sit out the final round?"

"Doren?" Geea said.

"What?"

"Shut up and fight."

Doren chuckled. "But maybe I want to savor our time together, sister. I know how short it's going to be. Maybe I just want to catch up on old times. You know, we haven't seen each other in ages. How was your long sleep?"

"Fine. Occasionally, I would leave my body and spy on you. Your daily activities would amuse me more than any comedy. But I suppose any stooge working for the Entity would have made me laugh."

Doren glared. "Liar! Inside or outside of the body, you never came near me."

Geea made a face. "Oh my, you're right. You're so scary. I mean, you got that scary name. What does *Shaktra* mean, anyway? Where did you get it?"

The remark annoyed Doren. "You will never know."

"Such a pity. That I might die so ignorant."

Doren made a slash with her sword. Even though they were a good ten meters apart, Ra saw that Geea had to counter the swing. The air between them crackled with sparks. There was a loud bang. Doren continued to circle, to talk.

"You know what our two counterparts are doing right now? They're talking, same as we are. Stalking each other as well. Like us, they have a witness to the final fight. That guy your Ali has brought along is trying to pass himself off as Tulas. Imagine that?"

"Sister. If you would close your mouth for once and take a look inside, you'd see that he is Tulas."

"Tulas would never take birth as a human!"

"Are you sure?" Geea asked.

"He finished with that species ages ago!"

"Yet your dear Entity promised you two would be born together."

A hideous wave of purple light pulsed through Doren's massive field. Ra got only a hint of it, but still wanted to vomit. Also, Geea's last remark had so angered Doren that the evil sister had made another slashing motion with her sword. Again, even though the blade came nowhere near Geea, she had to quickly counter. This time the air between them briefly erupted in flames. The fire was dark, the smoke it left behind pure black.

"He's not Tulas!" Doren screamed. "I would know if it was him!"

"Then why are you getting emotional if he's just an impostor?"

Another touchy question the hotheaded Doren did not like.

Doren leapt toward Geea. This time the Shaktra brought her blade straight toward Geea's neck. Geea barely had time to duck, and lost a chunk of red hair in the process. It floated away on a breeze the flood had stirred up. Geea countered with a blow of her own—a stab at Doren's breastplate. Sparks flew and the armor cracked. Doren groaned in pain, backed off quickly.

"I always thought you looked better with shorter hair," Doren said, as she returned to stalking; moving right to left, left to right. Yet now Doren was panting. The blow had hurt. Ra suspected it had cracked a few ribs.

"You don't have much strength left to attack the Earth," Geea said. "Don't think the elementals you've been killing for the last few years are going to sign up for another bloody campaign. You've worn out everyone's desire for battle. Even the dragons just want to lie around and get high."

"They were on my side two days ago. With you dead, they'll come back. Besides, they hate humans. Everyone hates humans, except fairies. And soon I'll be the only fairy left of note."

"What about Amma? She loves humans," Geea said.

"Amma's marked! Amma's mine!"

"Have you tried seeing through her eyes lately?"

Doren paused. "What are you talking about?"

"Ali Warner dared what I feared to dare. She went to the Isle of Greesh. She confronted the Entity. Now we know how to unmark your thralls. We also know how the Entity tricked you into joining their side by using Tulas."

Doren's eyes blazed red. "Stop saying his name!"

"We both know the deal you made with the Entity! You were tricked! Plain and simple! But it wasn't your fault, Doren." Geea added, "There's still time to stop."

Doren sneered. "Stop what?"

"This war! Your mistake! It's all been just one big mistake! The Entity cannot do anything unless we let them! And *you're* the one helping them. All because of what they did to Tulas!"

"I warned you . . ." Doren began.

"They incinerated him in front of you! But there's no reason . . ."

Geea did not get to finish. Once more Doren attacked, but this was no ordinary charge. Her leap carried her high above Geea. At first she seemed to move in a single direction. Yet as Geea strove to follow her leap, Doren suddenly spun in midair. Then, for a split second, the course of her path was impossible to determine. Her actual body appeared to blur, to go out of focus.

It was a weird combination of a spin and a flip. It violated every law of motion. The end result was that Doren was able to come straight down on Geea, with her sword stretched out in front of her.

Geea was unable to block the thrust with her own sword. The best she could do was to try to dodge it. That was not good enough. Doren was too close, and her blade tore through the left side of Geea's back. In an instant, Geea's gown was soaked in blood.

Still holding onto her sword, Geea rolled on the muddy ground and tried to stand. Doren casually stepped forward and kicked her in the mouth. She kicked the teeth from her sister's gums. Nevertheless, on her knees in the dirt, her mouth dripping blood, Geea swung at her with her sword. But Doren had taken control. She hopped up, briefly, then came down on the sword, pinning Geea's blade to the ground.

Doren howled with laughter.

She thrust her blade under Geea's throat.

"Where's the Yanti? Give it to me and maybe I'll let you live!"

Geea choked on her own blood as she stared up at her sister.

"You stopped living the day you made your deal with the Entity!"

Spitting in her sister's face, Doren drew back her sword to cut off Geea's head.

Cindy and Mr. Warner had asked Nira what she was doing. Nira had answered, "Switching the doors around."

That had been the extent of her explanation.

As they sat in the dim light of the cave—they were using only one light, trying to save their batteries—they began to understand that Nira was employing the Yanti as a welding gun of sorts. A narrow violet beam shone from the talisman, as Nira ran it over the hinges of the yellow door. This took time, but when she finished, she did not try to remove the door. She simply moved on to the green door, and worked on its hinges.

"She's going to switch the green and yellow doors?" Cindy guessed aloud. Mr. Warner shook his head.

"What effect could that possibly have? They're just doors."

"Doors that happen to lead into other worlds."

Mr. Warner was depressed. "I'm worried about Ali. My guts are in knots."

Cindy patted his arm. "Think of all the weird monsters she's killed in the green world. Then think of who her big enemy is here. That Sheri Smith—she's just a software executive. The last time, when Steve and I were alone with that witch—and she heard Ali was coming—man did she run. Trust me, Mr. Warner, Ali can take care of herself. I'm not worried about her at all."

Mr. Warner sighed as he glanced at the doors. "Somehow it's hard to imagine I'll ever see my wife again. I feel guilty for just having the desire."

"No reason to feel guilty. She was the greatest woman in the world. You've gotta miss her. But if you do meet her, call her Amma. That's her name now." Cindy added, "At least that's what Ali told me."

"I'll call her whatever she wants. Just as long as it's her."

They removed Hector's body from the cave with the bomb, and placed it in a tunnel Sheri seemed familiar with. She said it led to Fuji, and it probably did. But before they had a chance to look outside at Japan, they came to a cavern where there were seven colored doors on one wall, and three plain doors on the other.

It was here they laid Hector down, between them.

Sheri explained that the Mt. Fuji setup was identical to Pete's Peak, except the doors were all in the same spot. When she was growing up in Toule, she said, it was her favorite spot to visit. Fuji had been the first mountain she had tried to paint.

"How old were you when you discovered you were a fairy?" Ali asked.

Sheri answered in a lifeless voice. It was possible she was in shock. Clearly she was in a place where her pain was so great, no human word had been invented that could contain it all. At last, she had dropped her illusion of beauty. Yet even her external scars seemed unable to equal her internal wounds. And now she had a fresh one. She was bleeding. But she didn't want that to show, not Sheri Smith . . .

"It came in stages," Sheri said. "I was nine when I knew I was different than other girls my age. But I was eleven when I found this cavern."

"I was slower to catch on," Ali said.

"That which comes late, comes strong," Sheri muttered.

"Where did that come from?"

"Father. He used to have such great one-liners." Sheri reached up and wiped away a tear. It was from her right eye, the only one that actually opened. Ali had her own tears to wipe away. Sheri added, "I wish he was here now."

"I'm sure he would tell you that it wasn't your fault."

"But I did sort of stick the sword in Hector's chest, you know."

Ali shook her head. "Who was the fool who brought him up here?"

Sheri reached down and picked up Hector's right hand. She used it to wipe away her tears. The simple act seemed to comfort her. "Why did you bring him along?"

"I thought maybe he would have more luck talking to you than I did."

"What did you expect us to talk about?"

"War. Pain. Morality. Nira, maybe, I don't know. He wanted to see you." Ali added, "He still missed you, you know. After all these years."

Sheri sighed. "It's hard to believe."

"You don't have to believe. You know."

"How? How do I know?"

"Because I warned him that he might die if he came, and it didn't matter to him."

"As long as he got to see me?" she asked, a pathetic note in her voice.

Ali nodded and patted her on the back. "You were his only love."

Sheri pressed his hand to her heart. "He was mine."

A long silence fell between them. But after a while, Sheri checked her watch and told her that she had to go. The bomb was going to detonate in five minutes. Ali said that was fine, but she had to come with her. But Sheri shook her head and took hold of both Hector's hands. She wasn't going to leave him.

Sheri began to get a dark mark between her eyebrows.

"I understand. I'll stay with you," Ali said.

Sheri gave her a look. "This is not like that stupid scar trick of yours," she said, getting impatient. "You have nothing to prove to me by staying."

"I know."

"Then why are you staying?"

"I don't know. Maybe because I love you," Ali said.

"I don't love you."

"That's fine, I don't care. But why are you anxious for me to leave?"

"You bug me. Just get out of here."

Ali nodded. "You just wanted to be with Tulas?"

Sheri went to snap at her, then sighed. "When the Entity took him away, I felt I had to fill the void with something bigger than myself. A noble purpose. The Entity said I could save the Earth, and I believed it."

"And have Tulas back as well."

Sheri smiled sadly. "Yeah. What a bargain. Look how little I got to love him in this world. We were happy together for what, a year? Then came the accident and it was all taken away."

"Hector still wanted to be with you."

"I couldn't even hug him. How could I be with him?"

"What about Nira? Was she an accident?"

Sheri shook her head sadly. "No. She was a gift. I just wish . . ."

"Mike Havor hadn't forced you to mark her?"

"Yeah." Sheri paused. "So you knew about him?"

"Only figured it out recently. What did he promise you when you met?"

"What else? The world. He had his eyes then. He was a real smooth talker."

"He confused me. When I was around him, I always felt his warmth."

"So did I at first. It was because he was so empty. He could become whoever you wanted him to be. He's the ultimate manipulator. You saw him one way. Others at the company saw him in a completely different way."

"Were you trying to get ahold of the Yanti to gain the upper hand with him?"

Sheri nodded. Probably without knowing why, she reached up and scratched at the dark mark between her eyebrows. It was growing. "I knew the Entity might decide to get rid of me. The Yanti was going to be my insurance," she said.

"They don't understand what it is, do they?"

"I don't think so. But who does?"

"I think Nira does."

"Nira, yeah." She reached over and squeezed Ali's hand.

"Thanks for fixing her. It means a lot to me, you know, that she'll live a normal life now."

Ali had to smile. "I think it might end up being a little supernormal."

Sheri was stroking Hector's hair now. Probably like she used to in high school.

"Yeah," she muttered.

"Was that you in the barber shop that day? Dressed as a wizard?"

Sheri blinked. "What? When?"

"The same day I went to your firm in Toule. I ran into a wizard in the local barber shop. I thought it was you because he wore long white gloves."

"It wasn't me. What did he do?"

"Demanded to see the Yanti. When I refused to show it to him, he vanished in a flash of bright light."

Sheri looked genuinely puzzled. "I've never met anyone like that before."

"But you told Steve and Cindy you had met me before?"

Sheri smiled faintly. "Yeah. Just once. But you were only ten."

"What did you think of me?" Ali asked.

"That you were going to be trouble."

Ali continued to struggle with the wizard issue, but then figured it didn't really matter. Not now, not with a nuclear warhead sitting fifty yards away. Ali glanced in the direction of the bomb. "There's no way to stop it from exploding?" she asked.

"No way. It came with an internal timer. If need be, I could have set it off earlier. But as it is . . ." Sheri checked her watch. "You have three minutes left."

"That's time."

"Time for what?"

"For us to become sisters again."

Sheri chuckled. "Geea, you still drive me nuts, you know that?"

"Same here. Could I ask a favor?"

"What?"

"You may not have noticed this, but while we've been talking, a dark spot has grown between your eyebrows. It keeps getting bigger."

Sheri reached her hand up and felt around. "There's a lump."

"I know what it is."

"What?"

"It's the implant the Entity placed inside you. It's coming out."

"Why now?"

"Because it cannot stand love."

Sheri snorted. "I cannot stand love! If there was no love in my life, my heart wouldn't be broken right now. To hell with your love. It doesn't fix anything. Hector—Tulas—he's still dead!"

"'To hell with your love.' That's an interesting quote. Since we're both about to die, I want you to come with me into the blue light. I don't want you to go to the Entity." Ali paused. "Let me remove the implant from your head. It's coming out anyway."

"I don't deserve your help."

"Do it as a favor to me. Please?"

Sheri shrugged. "If you don't mind getting your hands messy."

Ali leaned over and, using the nail on her right thumb, she poked a hole in the space between her sister's eyebrows. The crystal shard was about to pop through the surface, anyway, so it was easy for Ali to pluck it out. Using a handkerchief from her pocket, she wiped away the blood. She tossed the implant down the tunnel, toward the bomb.

"How do you feel?" Ali asked.

"I have a headache."

"Doren . . ."

Her sister reached over and hugged her. "I feel free. And I feel . . . I feel your love." She let go of her, and Ali was surprised to see her sobbing now. She added, "That's why you have to leave. All the damage that's going to happen . . . The world will need you to help pick up the pieces."

Ali stood and stretched out her hand. "I'll leave if you come with me."

Sheri put a hand to her head. "Seriously, I do have a headache. A bad one. I don't think I can fly. When you took that thing off me . . ." Sheri didn't finish.

"What?" Ali asked.

"I don't think I can live without it."

Ali shook her head. "We just have to get out of here is all."

Wincing in pain, Sheri checked the time again. Since Ali had taken the implant out, her sister had turned white as a bedsheet. Holding a hand to her head, Sheri lay down and curled up. Her voice came out weakly.

"Go. Honestly, my strength is gone. I just want to lie here beside Hector."

"But . . ."

Sheri was fading, but she had enough strength left for tears. "You've only two minutes left. Please go, at least for Nira's sake. I need you there to take care of her. I need to know . . . she has a mother."

Ali plopped back down beside her sister and stroked her back.

"It's all right. Everything's going to be all right now," Ali said.

Sheri had closed her eyes. Her voice came out very faint.

"I do love you, you know," she whispered.

Ali sniffled. "I've always known it."

Another minute passed. Another thirty seconds.

A half-minute to go. Now there was no possibility of escape.

Her cell phone rang. Hector's cell. It was incredible that she could get reception inside the cave. It must have been that weird attachment Nemi had insisted she plug into the phone.

Ali flipped open the cell. "Hello?"

"Hello, Ali. It's me."

"Who? Wait! Nemi?"

"Of course. Do you have a minute?"

"I have twenty-five seconds."

"Hmm. I'm not sure if that's enough time."

As Doren lifted her sword to cut off Geea's head, her stance wavered. It was as if the last drop of energy had just left her body. Staggering around her sister, the sword fell from her hand and she dropped to the ground and rolled on her back. Still bleeding badly, Geea crawled to her side.

Ra ran over as fast as he could.

"What's the matter?" Geea asked her sister. A bulge had appeared in Doren's forehead. Sharp and purple, it looked like a small chip of amethyst. As Doren began to gasp for breath, Geea used her nails and pinched it from her sister's head, throwing it into the flowing river. Even though she was bleeding from serious wounds, Geea managed to cradle Doren in her lap. "Tell me what's happening!" she pleaded.

Doren smiled. "You know our human halves. They're really our better halves."

"Why do you say that?"

"Because their lives are so frail, their love has to be real." Doren reached up and brushed her sister's red hair. "I was just teasing when I said you looked better with short hair. Don't ever cut it. I love it . . . this way."

Geea had tears in her eyes. "The spell is broken?"

Doren nodded. "The purple light is gone. Now . . . I must go."

Geea hugged her. "Wait! I can heal you! Don't leave!"

It was too late, Ra saw. She could not live without the implant.

Doren had returned to the home she had come from.

When Nira was finished working with the Yanti, she stood back from the two doors, stared at them a moment, then suddenly reached out and grabbed the green door and took it off and set it aside. Then she seized the yellow door and put it in place of the green door. Finally, she picked up the green door and tucked it where the yellow door had been.

The switch had taken her all of five seconds.

Holding forth the Yanti, she closed her eyes and shone a broad violet beam over the doors. It was not very bright, but it seemed to help seal the doors shut. Now they appeared the same as before—except they had swapped places.

Nira studied her handiwork. "Now comes the tricky part," she said.

Cindy shuddered. If Nira thought it was tricky, then that meant it probably could destroy the Earth. Nira cracked open the yellow door, and then, placing a foot against it, she stretched out as far as she could and grabbed the green door-knob. Tight.

"What are you doing?" Cindy asked.

"You really don't want to know," Nira whispered.

"I do," Mr. Warner insisted.

Nira spoke without looking over. "The bomb's in this world—it has to detonate in this world. But because I've switched the doors, if I open one and close the other at the right moment, the energy from the blast will exit the yellow world and enter the green world."

Cindy gasped. "What will that do to the elemental kingdom?"

"Nothing too serious. Clean out Tutor of a lot of unpleasant creatures."

"How can you time your trick to a millionth of a second?" Mr. Warner asked.

"It would be a lot easier if I didn't have to keep answering your questions."

Mr. Warner came close to Nira. "Wait a second! What if Ali's with that Sheri Smith woman? And she's got the bomb with her?"

"I cannot worry about that right now."

"But Ali . . ."

Cindy grabbed Mr. Warner from behind and tried to calm him down, all the while pulling him away from Nira and the doors. "Ali will find a way to escape. She always does. No one equals her when it comes to surviving. Let Nira do her job."

Mr. Warner hung his head. "It's just that I can't lose them both."

Cindy led him to the far side of the cavern. "Let's sit over here and keep quiet."

They were sitting only a minute when a bright glare formed

around the yellow door. Nira closed it—and the glare started to form around the green door. Then the child kicked that door shut as well, and leaned on it, hard, as the glare flew off the scale.

It didn't matter that Cindy shut her eyes. The light swelled inside the center of her brain, and she thought her skull would explode. For sure, she knew she was going to end up like Mr. Havor, blind as a bat, with two black holes for eyes.

Then, in the space of seconds, all went completely dark.

And the three of them were alone.

Except for the two dead bodies on the ground.

In a silence filled with more shock than peace, they prepared to leave the cavern. A palpable grief hung in the air. The bomb had exploded and it appeared the Earth had escaped unharmed. That was good. Yet there was a feeling in the air that other good things had departed the planet as well.

There came an unexpected knock on the blue door.

Nira hastily strode over and opened it. For a second Cindy was flooded with a light and joy so wonderful, she almost forgot her name. Then it vanished, and she had to blink her eyes just to be able to see.

What she saw was Mr. Warner hugging a beautiful woman in a green gown. They were both weeping for joy. Both calling each other names that seemed to make sense to them, but to no one else.

When they finally parted, Nira stared up at the tall red-haired woman with the soft green eyes. "Amma. Did the ice maidens bring you here?" Nira asked.

Amma hesitated. "I think so. I rode Denzy—the dragon's kloudar—behind Anglar. Then I found a way out of their den, and sucked in a breath and then flew into space, into the blue light beyond the moon. I prayed they would bring me here."

Nira nodded. "You were fortunate. They usually don't help that way."

The woman knelt beside Nira. "Do you know where Ali is?"

Nira closed her eyes, and it seemed as if she searched behind every door in front of them. In fact, Cindy was sure that was exactly what she was doing. Unfortunately, when she was done, she shook her head.

"Ali is gone," she said.

Mr. Warner spoke. "What do you mean, she's gone?"

"Is she dead?" Amma whispered.

"Wherever she is, I can't find her," Nira said.

Ali's Story Will Continue
in the Next Book in the Series,
Nemi